The Bladesman of Darcliff

EDGEWHEN® ADVENTURES:

The Dragonslayer of Edgewhen
The Artificer of Dupho
The Klindrel Invasion
The Burglar of Sliceharbor
The Bladesman of Darcliff

Edgewhen®: Fantasy adventure stories of heroism and friendship.
Learn more at edgewhen.com.

The Bladesman of Darcliff

JASON A. HOLT

Edgewhen® is a registered trademark of Jason A. Holt.

Published by the author.
JasonAHolt.com

print ISBN: 978-0-9860717-9-9
epub ISBN: 978-0-9860717-8-2

For the woman with the sword.

The 27th of Bluemonth,
Four Nights before the Autumnal Equinox

A DROP OF WATER fell from the stalactite overhead and splashed onto the chisel-roughened floor of the passageway. That was drop eighteen. Vinnagon was halfway through his watch.

Vinnagon was a bladesman, sworn to guard the Temple of Darcliff. His post in the temple caverns was not very comfortable—even now, in the middle of a summer's-end drought, the torchlit passage was chilly and damp—but the post did carry some prestige. The only other people allowed in the caverns at this time of night were the three women of the Holy Council. It was a position of trust, and Vinnagon had it because Captain Brekko was his uncle.

Of course, all bladesmen were trustworthy. Though some of the locals said the temple guards were "mercenaries", Brekko's bladesmen could not be bought. They were Arvethidrel—red-skinned men created by Kashram, the god of battle. A bladesman was bound by his word as strongly as he was bound to Kashram. Perhaps that was a thing the striped-skinned, luck-worshipping, womanish men of Darcliff could not understand.

Vinnagon had sworn to guard this temple against enemies. He had never seen any enemies—so great was the temple's authority that no one dared to oppose it—but Vinnagon had sworn an oath, and so he remained alert. And that was why, deep in the night, shortly after the eighteenth drip from the longest stalactite, Vinnagon heard the scuffing.

It was not a bat. Bats avoided the main passage because of the smoky torches.

It was not the wind—although Vinnagon could hear that too, whispering through the caverns.

It was a soft leather sole scuffing against the rough stone floor somewhere near the door to the council chamber. Vinnagon could recognize the women of the Holy Council by sound. This footfall was not theirs.

It could be Kennadarl, the bladesman posted at the passage's back exit. But Kennadarl normally had a trudging tread. This was either an intruder or Kennadarl sneaking around. Either way, Vinnagon had to investigate.

Vinnagon's own boots were hard-soled. His uncle praised men who purchased durable equipment. They were good boots for a temple guard, but Vinnagon now wished he were outfitted like a scout. His steps were audible, though he tried to stay on the balls of his feet as he followed the curving passage toward the council chamber.

A sharp intake of breath told him he had been heard. Vinnagon froze. The soft-soled intruder scuffed the floor once, then began padding away.

Vinnagon quickened his pace, but remained on the balls of his feet, using a glide step to keep his footfalls as quiet as possible. Let the other man strain to hear. Let him wonder which sounds were his own echoes and which belonged to his pursuer. Perhaps the other man would stop to listen. Or perhaps he would panic and run.

But the other man did neither. He kept calm and kept padding away.

At first, Vinnagon thought the intruder was heading for Kennadarl's guard post at the back exit, but a foot scuff told him that the intruder had taken an unlit side passage.

The side passage was an enlargement of a natural fissure. It led through a small storage chamber and then into deeper caverns that had never known torchlight or chisel. Vinnagon reached for a torch, then thought better of it.

The intruder wanted to hide in the dark? Let him try! Vinnagon could feel the shape of the limestone in his bones. Darkness was to his advantage.

Vinnagon passed through the storage chamber. In the darkness on the other side, the smooth floor became a narrow ledge around the perimeter of the first dark cavern. The drop was three feet—not enough to kill a man, but certainly enough to frighten the intruder if he fell off the ledge. Vinnagon had heard no cry. He had heard no body striking stone. The intruder knew about the ledge. Either that or he was lucky, and no enemy of the temple could be lucky.

Vinnagon held his breath to listen. The intruder's footsteps echoed strangely, but Vinnagon felt confident that the intruder had gone to the right. He followed.

It was all darkness now. He felt the boundaries of the ledge with the soles of his boots. He heard the size of the cavern by listening to the echoes of his breath. And deep in his bones, an unnamed sense revealed to him the shape of the rock, the locations of fissures. It distinguished the true passages from the narrow squeezes that became too tight. The stone was all around him, and Vinnagon knew his way.

He found the first side passage, heard a pebble fall. This was the way the intruder had gone. No carved floor here. This was wild stone, a gap twisting upward. Either the intruder knew these caverns well, or he was very bold.

Vinnagon followed, his scabbard scraping against the stone as he climbed. He had never explored this fissure far. It seemed like a chimney.

Vinnagon's hand flailed about in empty space. The way branched here. Vinnagon sucked in a deep breath and held it.

Above the thumping of his heart, he could hear the intruder scrambling down the side branch. The intruder had given up on being quiet. This was a race now.

Vinnagon could not refuse the challenge. He clambered head first into the side branch. Knees and elbows scraping against the sides of the fissure, he pursued the intruder, determined to catch up. The rock brushed against his back, but he was not afraid. Being surrounded by stone was a comfort.

Vinnagon did not know how to fight in a space so tight that he could not even turn around, but that did not matter. He was beginning to suspect that this chase would not end in a fight, for the timbre of the puffs and grunts suggested the intruder was actually a woman—a woman brave enough to trespass against the most powerful institution in Darcliff, but still just a woman.

The intruder made a scrabbling, tumbling sound and suddenly the craggy walls of the fissure were visible. Vinnagon crawled toward a torchlit opening and found himself looking down through a hole in the ceiling of the main passage. He grabbed a stalactite and swung to the flat stone floor.

The intruder was out of sight. She ran quietly, but Vinnagon could hear where she was heading. She was trying to reach the unrestricted part of the temple. He broke into a sprint.

She had guessed wrong. Had she run for the back exit, she would have faced only Kennadarl. To escape through the front doors of the temple, she would have to contend with the bulk of the night watch.

Unless Vinnagon caught her first. He smiled to himself—he was gaining.

At the next twist of the passage, he glimpsed her shoe. It was more like a moccasin, actually.

He rounded the corner and saw the black streaks in her white hair, saw the black stripes on her bone-white hands. She was running for the steps that led up to the main part of temple, but she would not reach them.

His legs found a burst of speed. He closed the distance and leapt, catching her by her striped ankle.

Her leg tried to shoot forward, but he held on, scraping his leather cuirass against the rough stone floor. His prey lost her balance and slapped onto the stone. Before she could rise, he was on her, pinning her pelvis to the floor by kneeling on the small of her back. With a foot, he pinned her right wrist.

He had caught her! His triumph was undeniable, but it was not enough to suppress the dread that was rising in his belly, for this was not an ordinary woman. The colorful branching zigzags embroidered on her blue, knee-length tunic marked her as a taishrefi—a holywoman of the Darcliff Temple. She had been running to the part of the temple where she was allowed to be. Vinnagon was fairly certain she did not belong in the caverns, but if he were wrong, he would be in serious trouble.

"Good evening, Taishrefi," he said. "Please forgive my roughness, but you did not seem inclined to stop."

Gasping for breath, the taishrefi made no reply. Her body trembled—from exertion or fear, perhaps both.

"You are not among those permitted in the caverns at night," Vinnagon said. He could not recognize her by the back of her head—many taishrefis had long white hair with only thin streaks of black—but, as far as he knew, only three women were allowed to move through the caverns freely, and they were all in the council chamber.

The woman found her voice. "Will you kill me, Bladesman?"

"Of course not," he said. He was strong enough to restrain her without causing permanent injury.

"May I get up?" she inquired.

Vinnagon considered. "Very well," he decided. He sprang to his feet, instantly relieving the woman of his weight and putting himself just out of reach in case she decided to do something very, very foolish. "But if you try to escape again," he added, "I shall have to tackle you again."

"I shall not give you the pleasure." She was attempting to be haughty, but the effect was spoiled by the way she dabbed her sleeve against her bleeding lip.

Vinnagon decided he liked her.

He recognized her now—Taishrefi Crystal. Standing at her full height, she was a little taller than Vinnagon. Her white face had three black stripes. One curled away under her ear to disappear into her hair. The other two stripes came down

vertically across her eyelids, followed the curve of her face to
the corners of her mouth, and thinned as they continued down
her throat into her tunic. Distinctive markings.

Her hair was mostly white, but among her kind that was
not a sign of age. Her face said she was about the same age as
Vinnagon—somewhere in her twenties, though he was not
certain whether she were younger or older than he. Regardless,
she was too old to be breaking the curfew rules just for fun.

He wanted some answers. If they were good answers,
perhaps neither of them would have to get into trouble. But
just then she glimpsed something behind him, and her eyes
went wide with fear.

Vinnagon's hand shot out and seized her wrist before she
could turn and bolt. It was a reflex, faster than the realization
that she *was* turning to bolt.

He glanced over his shoulder to see what had frightened
her. It was the Holy Advisor: slender, gray-skinned, barely five
feet tall, green eyes glowing in the dimness of the passage.
Eerie she was. She made Vinnagon want to bolt, too. They said
she was an emissary from the Woshites—the people who had
been created by Woshi, goddess of the moon. Vinnagon did
not know why she was the Holy Advisor at a temple sup-
posedly dedicated to Lashrefi, goddess of luck. That was one
of the many questions that Brekko's bladesmen did not ask.

Vinnagon felt Taishrefi Crystal's movement through his
grip on her wrist. She had drawn her knife.

With a curse, Vinnagon sidestepped behind her and shoved
her body against the wall.

"Drop the knife," he ordered.

She dropped it. That was good. Vinnagon knew only one
armlock and he wasn't sure how to apply it from his current
position.

Sounds from the passage told him that the other two
women were approaching. Under the gaze of the Holy
Advisor, Vinnagon was no longer free to negotiate with his
prisoner. Their fates would be decided by the bashrefi.

The bashrefi came around the curve of the passage with her seneschal just behind her shoulder. Bashrefi Wintersmoke was short, though still taller than the tiny Holy Advisor, who stepped aside without making the gesture seem deferential.

The bashrefi's gentle bulges jiggled as she strode down the passage. Her age-ripened cheeks were plump, but her striped face was far from jolly.

"What is this?" she asked.

Vinnagon released the prisoner's arm and stepped toward the stairs. He stood between the prisoner and her escape—and she stood between him and the power that overshadowed the land of Darcliff.

"I found this woman outside the door to Your Fortuitousness's meeting chamber," Vinnagon said.

"Then what is she doing *here*?" asked the Holy Seneschal.

"We had a chase through the caverns," Vinnagon said. The abrasions on his bare elbows, the rip in the knee of his trousers, and the scuffs on his leather cuirass would have been obvious in better light. But he was, by intent, standing a good distance away from the three women, so perhaps the seneschal could not see this evidence of his travails.

The seneschal grunted dismissively.

The bashrefi cocked her head like a vulture looking for meat on a week-old carcass. "So, little Crystal, curious about our meetings, are you? Well, come join us, then. I would like your perspective on what the temple should do with spies."

The seneschal advanced.

The taishrefi looked over her shoulder at Vinnagon. What did she expect *him* to do? She was the one who'd been caught spying.

The seneschal grabbed the young taishrefi by the arm. A quick twist, and the seneschal was behind the prisoner.

Taishrefi Crystal gasped.

"Let's go," the seneschal said. "Don't keep us waiting."

As the women disappeared around the curve of the passage, Vinnagon tried to puzzle out how the seneschal had applied that armlock.

* * *

Crys had been a taishrefi for nearly two years, but now she felt like a temple initiate again. The seneschal guided her into the council chamber with gentle pain—and the promise of excruciating pain if she attempted to escape the armlock.

Though the council chamber was small, the walls were lined by thirty-nine candelabra. A wooden wheel decked with twenty-six candles hung from the ceiling to function as a chandelier. The smell of rancid tallow thickened the air, and the heat from the tiny flames kept the room noticeably warmer than the passage outside.

Curtains of blue and black linen adorned the walls. A horse-hair rug covered the floor. Only the stone ceiling arching into shadowy darkness overhead reminded Crys that she was still in the caverns.

As an initiate, Crys had visited this room frequently. Initiates were treated as servants, and one of Crys's duties had been to keep the candles lit. But taishrefis did not enter the council chamber, not even the taishrefis of the First Choir.

Or rather, taishrefis did not enter the council chamber unless they were about to disappear. Crys suspected she was not the first to be invited in this way.

Bashrefi Wintersmoke and Rathi, the eerie Holy Advisor, went ahead and took their seats at the triangular meeting table.

The Holy Seneschal stopped in the doorway. The sene-schal's name was Evensky, but the taishrefis always referred to her by title. She released Crys's arm and shoved her forward.

Crys flexed her wrist and elbow, trying to massage away the pain from the armlock. The heels of her hands were still numb from her fall on the rough stone floor, and her leather riding trousers had not protected her knees as well as she had hoped. But Crystal Farrider was not a fragile figurine. She was a farm girl and half nomad. She had once been kicked by a bucking horse. She was not going to cry over a few scrapes and bruises.

Besides, she thought as her knees began to shake, the scrapes did not matter when she was about to die.

"Tell us who sent you," the bashrefi said, "and this will go easier for you."

"No one sent me," Crys said. "It was my own idea."

The bashrefi looked to Rathi. Rathi nodded.

Are you reading my thoughts? Crys asked. *Then read this, viper.*

She tried to imagine the dainty Woshite tied hand and foot, gutted like fresh-killed venison. Rathi's gray face did not change. Crys simply received the image of a wall.

So it was true. The little leech had power over minds. Oh how Crys hated her for what she had done to the temple! Oh how Crys wished she had learned to shield her thoughts.

"If no one sent you," the bashrefi said, "then no one will miss you when you are gone."

"There are women in this very temple who will miss me," Crys said. "You have not corrupted everyone. Not yet."

"I have corrupted no one," the bashrefi said.

"You serve Shakredo," Crys accused.

"I serve the goddess who smites our enemies," said the bashrefi. "And those who serve with me do so willingly. Those who oppose me, little Crystal, are enemies of the temple."

"So you admit that you do not serve Lashrefi," Crys said.

"Lashrefi. Shakredo. Are they not two sides of the same coin? Lashrefi offers luck to help us win. Shakredo offers luck to help our enemies lose. The only difference, little Crystal, is that one side wins and the other loses. And your side is not the winning side, or you would not be here now."

Lashrefi, I know you have not deserted me, Crys prayed. *I will not listen to her. I know there is still a chance for me to escape.*

But if there was such a chance, it was not one she could see.

"Can you kill her in the hall?" the bashrefi asked. "I don't want more bloodstains on the rug."

Behind Crys, the seneschal stepped forward.

Rathi said, in her strange accent, "I think that idea is not so good."

The seneschal halted.

The bashrefi waited for an explanation.

"While listening through the door, she may have heard our plan."

Crys hadn't. At least, not enough of it. *How will people know they are Flamebringer clothings?* Rathi had asked. And then Crys had heard the guard approaching, forcing her to flee without hearing the reply. A pity, as the answer might have helped her make sense of the question.

"If she has heard our plan," the bashrefi said, "that is a good reason to kill her."

"Yes," Rathi said. "But not here. If she greets her death in this place, her ghost may haunt this place."

"Ghosts cannot harm us," the bashrefi said.

"Ghosts can talk," Rathi said. "I am not the only woman in the temple who can hear them. Even if dead, she may reveal that which should be hidden."

"So what should we do?" asked the seneschal. "Give her a funeral to ensure she goes to Heaven? Somehow, I don't think Lashrefi will be eager to cooperate."

Rathi ignored the seneschal's sarcasm. "Ghosts cannot move far," she said. "Let her ghost haunt somewhere else."

"Where?" the seneschal asked.

"Ask the mans to drown her in the river."

The bashrefi nodded thoughtfully.

"They won't like it," the seneschal said. Her tone had changed from challenging to uneasy. "They have funny ideas about killing women."

"Let us then make it easy," said Rathi. "Let us put her for them in a box."

A box in the river. Crys realized this was her chance. A slim chance, to be sure. She was not a strong swimmer. But with Lashrefi on her side—

Rathi's magic seized Crys's mind and slammed it into the side of her skull. The room disappeared in a flash of white. As Crys's vision faded to black, she heard a distant thump, but she was already too deep in sleep to realize it was the sound of her head bouncing off the horse-hair rug.

* * *

A body inside a crate does not lie still like a sack of flour. It does not slide and grind like a heap of stones. No, a body flops. Its weight shifts abruptly. An arm thumps into the side when the crate is tilted. The head and heels bounce against the bottom. The hips roll if the crate is tipped too far.

Vinnagon knew what he and Kennadarl were carrying, but he could pretend he didn't. In the morning, everyone would learn that Taishrefi Crystal had transferred to another temple, or that she had been asked to serve a distant village, or that she had left on a holy pilgrimage.

It was important to believe these stories. Believing the stories was part of the job.

So Vinnagon and Kennadarl were just carrying out some trash—trash that had to be carried out the back way on a moonless night and tossed into the river at a point where the cliffs would shield their actions from view of the sleeping town of Darcliff.

"I wish we could have taken this out the front way," Kennadarl said. "Then we could have used a cart."

The trail from the caverns' hidden clifftop exit down to the Dothedarl River was better suited for goats than for men carrying heavy crates. And Vinnagon was making the descent backwards.

"Just pay attention to what you're doing," he said.

"Don't get grumpy with *me*," Kennadarl said. "This wasn't my idea of how to spend the night's watch."

Nor was it Vinnagon's. But if he hadn't caught the woman spying … well, then he would have failed in his duty to protect the temple.

The woman *had* been spying. Spying was wrong. It did not matter what the bashrefi was up to. That was her business.

Vinnagon had sworn to serve the temple. It did not matter

what he thought of their methods. Thinking was not his job. If any thinking needed to be done, it would be done by Captain Brekko. He knew as much about what was going on here as Vinnagon did.

More, actually, since he shared a bed with the seneschal.

Vinnagon put that out of his mind. It was another thing that he must pretend to not know.

The rocky slopes were warm here. The night air held none of autumn's crispness, though the equinox was only four nights away. The grass along the trail rasped against Vinnagon's trousers. The scent of warm pine trees filled the air.

Or perhaps that was the scent of the crate. Cheap wood. Recently split.

The air cooled as they neared the river. It took on scents of cottonwood, marsh grass, and the rank mustiness of once-wet earth now crumbling into dust.

Hungry insects bit into Vinnagon's bare arms, and he could not swat them. So they became one more thing to ignore—one more thing to ignore so that he could do his job.

"Let's set it down here," Kennadarl said. "We need to scout the bank."

They eased the heavy crate to the ground. Vinnagon tried to work the knots out of his back.

"The water's so low," Kennadarl said. "When was the last time it rained?"

Vinnagon didn't know. He spent a lot of time indoors. Deep indoors.

Someone groaned.

Startled, Vinnagon reached for his sword. Then he realized the sound had come from the crate.

"Damn!" said Kennadarl. "I hate it when they do that."

A hand thumped against the crate and suddenly went still.

"Death twitches," said Kennadarl. "Quick. Let's dump it."

Vinnagon put his ear to the crate. He heard a pounding heart, though it was probably his own.

"I think she's still alive," he said.

"Not our problem," said Kennadarl.

"But—"

"Our orders were to dump the crate in the river. We dump it in the river."

Had that been a groan of pain? Did Vinnagon have an obligation to put the prisoner out of her misery? He did not want to run her through, but that would be swifter than drowning.

Kennadarl lifted his end of the crate. "Vinnagon," he said. "Let's go."

"Wait," said a clear voice from inside.

"Ah!" shouted Kennadarl, dropping the crate again.

Vinnagon waited.

"Your orders were to dump the *crate*," said the taishrefi in the box. She didn't sound like she was in mortal pain. "Did anyone say I have to be *in* the crate when you dump it?"

"Damn it!" said Kennadarl. "I wondered why this thing wasn't leaking blood."

"Let me out, and I'll disappear," the taishrefi said. "No one ever needs to know."

It was tempting. But it was dishonest. Vinnagon would know.

"I don't hear anything," Kennadarl said. "Let's get this done."

Vinnagon leaned against the rough pine box. So that was the answer, was it? Just pretend he hadn't heard her.

Pretend he hadn't heard her. Pretend he didn't know she was in the box. Pretend he believed she had left to serve elsewhere. Pretend that everything was normal. Pretend that evil was good. Pretend that all his actions were honorable as long he was following orders.

So many lies. And yet he balked when one helpless woman asked him to let her go and pretend she hadn't escaped.

Vinnagon was Arvethidrel. Arvethidrel were loyal. But they were also Kashramites—red-skinned men whom Kashram, the god of battle, had created to defend the weaker peoples of the world. Would Kashram be pleased when Vinnagon drowned this woman? Would Kashram think it honorable to obey such a command?

It was a dilemma … and yet, it wasn't. Killing this helpless woman was wrong. Vinnagon could not do it.

"Very well," he said. "We'll let you go."

"Truly?" she asked.

"What?" asked Kennadarl.

Vinnagon pulled at the top of the crate. "Hurry up before I change my mind."

With a squeak of nails, the lid popped free. It had not been on very tight.

The woman's white face was plainly visible in the starlight, although the black stripes made it difficult to read her expression.

"Thank you," she said.

"Can you walk?" Vinnagon asked.

"This is *not* wise," Kennadarl said.

"Yes, I can walk."

"What about run?" Vinnagon asked. "Can you run? Because you'll need to be far from Darcliff by daybreak."

"Yes, I can run," she said. "You will not regret this."

She touched three fingers to his forehead and blew gently into his hair. "May the blessing of Lashrefi be upon you."

She slipped away among the trees, moving silently on her moccasins.

Kennadarl exhaled in disbelief. "Friend, you just made a big mistake."

Vinnagon slugged him in the jaw. Kennadarl staggered and fell against the empty crate.

"What was that for?" he asked, more surprised than angry.

"Now you can pretend I overpowered you," Vinnagon said. "You can pretend you had no way to prevent her escape."

Vinnagon set out toward the temple.

"What?" Kennadarl called behind him. "Who will know she escaped?"

Without breaking stride, Vinnagon called over his shoulder, "Captain Brekko."

"You aren't going to tell him, are you?" Kennadarl's voice was already distant. "Vinnagon?"

Vinnagon *was* going to tell Uncle Brekko. Vinnagon was done pretending.

* * *

The flame of the room's single torch flickered in Uncle Brekko's eyes. His frown deepened as Vinnagon related the evening's events.

"Captain, for four years we have guarded this temple against enemies. But except for a few skirmishes with bandits on the Shankito Road, we have never needed to fight. The temple's enemies always seem to come from within.

"When I heard the taishrefi's voice, when I realized that *I* was the one expected to kill her ... Captain, she was helpless! Drowning helpless women is not an honorable task for Kashram-created men."

Brekko ran his scarred hand through his coarse black hair. He was shirtless in the late summer heat. He had donned only sword belt and trousers when Vinnagon had awakened him.

"Vinnagon," he said, "when I assigned you night duty in the caverns, I knew it might come to this. Sooner or later, every soldier faces an order that knots his guts. It's part of being a bladesman."

His uncle laid a kindly hand on his shoulder. "Tonight the task fell to you. And why? Why were you assigned to guard the caverns? Because I knew I could depend on you. You swore an oath—to this temple and to me. And although right now you may feel that your act was dishonorable, it was not. It was the bravest, most honorable thing you have ever done. You did the thing you least wanted to do. And that has proven your loyalty. You are true Arvethidrel."

Vinnagon shook his head in disbelief. "Uncle, I didn't kill her."

"What?"

"I couldn't."

Brekko's grip on his shoulder grew stiff with apprehension. "What did you do?"

"I let her go."

"You let her go?"

"She's a taishrefi of the temple."

"No." Brekko's hand went limp and slid off Vinnagon's shoulder. "No she's not, Vinnagon. She's a dead woman. And you're a dead man."

These last words were spoken without heat, almost without strength, as though Brekko needed all his strength to wrestle with the fact that Vinnagon had disobeyed the bashrefi's orders.

"Captain, you know that what happens here is not right—"

"Right and wrong are not our concern, Vinnagon. Bladesmen obey orders. That is who we are."

"Then perhaps I am no bladesman," Vinnagon said as a hollow pit opened in his stomach.

Brekko was now breathing shallowly, rapidly, as though he, too, felt this horror. He licked his lips. "I can give you a head start," he said. "If you walk out the front door, the men won't stop you, not until I give the alarm. But once you are out, run hard. Run far. I don't want to be the one who catches you."

Vinnagon knew his uncle was a good man. Surely he could be convinced to follow his heart. "Captain—"

"Go!" Brekko put his hand on his sword. "If you love me, go before I have to draw!"

And at last Vinnagon understood. He had followed his own heart too far.

Vinnagon left the captain's chamber and headed for the temple's main entrance, as ordered. Malk and Shangrel made no move to stop him.

"Trouble?" Shangrel called at Vinnagon's back.

Vinnagon went down the steps without answering. He was on the road before the captain's voice rang out through the temple's stone interior: "Stop him! Don't let him get away!"

Vinnagon broke into a lope—not a sprint, because the road from the cliff-side temple down into the town of Darcliff was too steep for sprinting. He clutched his flopping scabbard with one hand and tried not to stumble, reaching with stride after stride into open air and striking the bedrock road with his leather-soled heels.

Behind him, scabbards clattered and boots pounded the temple's limestone steps. Malk and Shangrel were coming after him, obeying their orders.

Vinnagon had a good lead. He looked over the edge of the road, wondering if it would be smarter to shortcut the switchback. That would be risky in the dark.

Vinnagon's heel caught in a crack and he went tumbling. His iron helmet scraped against rock as his legs somersaulted over. His helmet was knocked askew, obscuring his vision.

Vinnagon yanked the helmet straight again and rose to his feet.

"Hold," Malk said. The two men were barely distinct forms in the starlight. Mostly, Vinnagon could see their shiny helmets. "Yield, Vinnagon. The captain wishes to speak to you."

No. Vinnagon and Brekko had already said what they had to say to each other. Vinnagon bolted.

His legs had not been injured by the fall, but the heel of his boot had been knocked off, lost somewhere in the darkness. The bootheel was not all that he was leaving behind.

Malk and Shangrel were once more in pursuit. They did not waste their breath shouting.

Vinnagon rounded the switchback, hoping the other men would not attempt to shortcut it in the dark. But Malk was fearless. The burly man leapt from above as Vinnagon passed by, even though the drop of the shortcut was over six feet.

Vinnagon dodged toward the rock wall and bounced off. The bulk of Malk's body passed overhead, clipping Vinnagon's shoulder with a foot or perhaps an elbow. Vinnagon reached out to steady himself and planted his hand in a cliff cactus. He yelped and kept running.

"Malk?" Shangrel called, concern in his voice.

"Catch him," Malk said.

From the temple above, Vinnagon heard more orders. The captain was marshalling men on the steps.

Vinnagon glanced back. The two shiny helmets were still near the switchback. Shangrel was helping Malk to his feet. He stayed with Malk not because he feared Vinnagon's blade— though Vinnagon *was* the better swordsman—but rather because he was not the sort of man who could leave a comrade.

Vinnagon hoped that Malk was not badly injured by that rash leap, but truth be told, he needed Malk to be at least a little injured, at least enough to slow everyone down.

Vinnagon did not check on the two men again until he turned the corner of the next switchback. Malk was once more on his feet and running, but they were far enough behind that not even Malk would attempt to leap the distance when Vinnagon passed below them.

Vinnagon glanced up to see how the main force was progressing and something landed in his eye—a pebble, he discovered as he wiped the thing loose. One of the men in the main force had knocked a pebble off the road, and somehow it had chanced to bounce into Vinnagon's eye!

Holding his uninjured hand to his weeping eye, Vinnagon loped into the town of Darcliff with only one bootheel.

The men descending from the temple might be able to see him running along the broad streets that ran parallel to the river, but there were plenty of narrow alleys he could cut through if he wanted to go downhill. Did he? He didn't have money for the ferry. And anyway, they would be expecting him to cross the river. He had a wife on the other side.

No, he should head upriver. But to where? He needed advice—guidance. And now that he had made an enemy of his uncle, the only man he could talk to was Harl, a holyman of

Kashram. But Harl's smithy was not far from the shack where Vinnagon kept his wife. The bladesmen would probably look for him in both places.

The bladesmen. He wasn't one of them anymore, was he?

He tossed his helmet over a fence into a pumpkin patch. It was the only thing on him that would show up in starlight. And it wasn't his, anyway.

His leather cuirass also belonged to the temple. Vinnagon decided he could shed it later. He could no longer hear the footsteps of his pursuers, but this was not the time to fumble with the buckles. Vinnagon worked his way through the streets and alleys of Darcliff, running from the oaths that bound him to the Darcliff Temple.

A Few Months Earlier:
Sandpiper

SANDPIPER HAD A LITTLE FARM on the sunaway bank of the Dothedarl. In her lifetime, she had seen two floods, one grasshopper plague, and even a near-miss tornado, but she believed that none of these was as great a disaster as the new leadership in the Temple of Darcliff.

After the last big flood, the temple had levied a special tax to help the victims. Grateful that Lashrefi had spared her from the flood, Sandpiper had paid the tax.

The next year saw no flood victims, but the temple still levied the flood tax—"to build up a reserve against misfortune," the Holy Seneschal had said.

The next year the tax was higher, and Sandpiper had little left beyond what she needed to feed her family and her husband's livestock. They considered trading Dancy, her husband's faithful mare, to obtain the extras they needed, but her husband loved Dancy so, and they decided they could make do without extras for a year.

Now the Holy Seneschal was assessing her farm again. Sandpiper hoped for good news this time, but everyone suspected that the temple would raise taxes a tiny bit more, just to see how much meat they could gnaw off the bone.

"Tell her you won't pay," her husband advised her.

"Well, perhaps I *could* ask for a little more leeway this year," Sandpiper said. "You need new oxen, and—"

"Just tell her you won't pay," he said. "That's what my brother's village has decided to do."

That was easy for his brother to say. As mayor of a village, he had sixty families who would stand behind him. Sandpiper's family had only a few neighbors nearby.

"Everyone has to pay *some* tax," Sandpiper said.

"Yes, but it is time to take a hard line. That's what my brother said. Take a hard line and force them to offer something reasonable."

Sandpiper glanced at the Holy Seneschal, who was overseeing the inspection of the cornfield. Even without the heavily armed, red-skinned Kashramite guards, the Holy Seneschal was not the sort of woman with whom one could take a hard line.

The taishrefi-assessor wrote something down in her ledger. The seneschal smiled in satisfaction. She led her retinue back to Sandpiper.

"Congratulations on your excellent corn crop," the seneschal said.

"Thank you, Seneschal." Sandpiper struggled to keep the dread from her voice.

"We expect quite the harvest this year," the seneschal said. "The Goddess has indeed favored you."

"We are blessed," Sandpiper said, fearing what would come next.

She felt her husband's eyes boring into her back. She could almost hear him thinking it: *Tell her we won't pay.*

The Holy Seneschal said, "And so the assessor believes we can raise your corn tax to ten bushels and still leave you enough for any obligations you might feel toward the family of your brother-in-law."

Ten bushels? Sandpiper stared at the cornfield. Most of their labor would be going to the temple. And what was left would be eaten long before spring.

"What obligations?" her husband asked.

"Ah," said the Holy Seneschal. "You have not yet heard about your brother."

"Heard what?" asked Sandpiper.

"I fear your husband's brother had an unfortunate accident yesterday afternoon. Vultures startled his team of oxen as he was unhitching them. Somehow, he was caught in the harness and dragged to death."

The 28th of Bluemonth,
Morning

IT WAS THE PINCHING THAT WOKE CRYS UP. And the sunlight streaming through the loose strands of her white hair. But mostly the pinching.

She sat up, rummaged around in her riding trousers until she found the earwig, squashed it, and then took stock of her situation.

She was in a cottonwood grove close enough to the Dothedarl to hear the river's liquid murmurs. The grass was nearly four feet high and still green, even though the grass on the uplands had been yellow for a month.

Thoughts of the tall-grass prairie reminded her of her grandmother, who was a taishrefi, too. But her grandmother was not affiliated with the flock of vultures that had come to roost at Darcliff Temple. Her grandmother was a Flame-bringer, a leader among the nomads who roamed the sunaway prairies on horseback.

Rathi had been speaking of the Flamebringers when Crys had been startled by the approaching bladesman. And then, when Crys was captured, Rathi had revealed that the Holy Council was working on a plan.

If the plan involved Flamebringers, Crys needed to warn her grandmother. And she also needed her grandmother's advice on what to do next. Sometimes, even a taishrefi needed help from a taishrefi, and her grandmother was the only one Crys could trust.

Staying in the cover of the tall grass, Crys crept to the riverbank. The river Dothedarl was broad, but the cottonwood grove held plenty of logs big enough to keep her afloat. It was time for a swim.

No one saw her cross—she hoped. Her striped skin dried swiftly in the morning air. As soon as she was dressed, she asked Lashrefi for a blessing and set off in search of a horse.

Her grandmother's band would probably be following a bison herd at this time of year. Wherever they were, Crys would need a horse to find them.

She followed a road leading generally upstream. A short time later, she came to a farm.

It was not so different from her parents' farm, and for an instant, Crys had the urge to run home.

A younger woman sat in the shade of the farmhouse, nursing a baby. A husband and wife were busy loading squash into a basket. They were about the age of Crys's parents.

They eyed her warily as she approached the squash patch. Though Crys was wearing her buckskin moccasins and riding trousers, she was still recognizable as a taishrefi, for she wore the blue tunic of the Darcliff Temple. She stood close to a fence post, hoping they would not notice she was dressed like a nomad from the waist down.

The wife put her hand on her husband's shoulder, her expression fearful. He muttered something and pushed her hand aside. He rose and stalked to the fence.

"I bid you good morning," Crys said.

"What do you want?" he asked. His sun-wrinkled face was not friendly. His eyes were hard.

Crys was not certain how to respond. She *did* want something, but she had hoped to come to the topic less directly. Ah, but there was no sense in dissembling. That would only make the farmer more suspicious and apprehensive.

"In truth, good man, I am in need of a horse."

"A horse," he said.

He looked along the road in the direction from which she had come. Crys followed his gaze. She was quite alone on the road today.

"We paid the wheat tax," the farmer said.

"I am certain you did," she said.

"And we shall pay the corn tax," he growled. Clearly, he was not pleased by this.

"Yes, the corn tax is quite high," Crys agreed. As a child, she had been told the taxes went to poor children who lived in town and had nothing to eat. Perhaps that had even been true, then. Now it was used to feed Wintersmoke's army of red-skinned bladesmen.

"Is there now to be a horse tax, Taishrefi?"

"No," she said. "I asked not for a tax, but for a favor."

"A favor," he said. Again he glanced down the road, and Crys was certain he was assuring himself that she was alone, that she had no armed men with her who could punish his insolence.

In a voice full of hatred, he asked, "And how would you propose to repay this favor?"

His wife's eyes widened at his tone. She hastened toward the fence, clearly hoping to stop him, but she was too late now.

"Will you offer to curse us less than you curse our neighbors?" he asked. "Or will you simply threaten my family if I do not obey?"

"Have you received many such threats?" Crys asked. "Have you borne many such curses?"

"You know what happened to my brother."

"Forgive me," Crys said. "I do not."

His wife was beside him now, her hand on his back. "His brother was killed by ... an accident."

"Oh, how ..." Crys was about to say *unfortunate*, but the word was too mild. She knew what sorts of accidents befell people who lived near Darcliff.

"I am sorry for the evil that has been done to you," she said. "You spoke truly. I have no right to ask you for a horse."

She pressed three fingers to his forehead and blew into his wispy hair.

"May the blessing of Lashrefi be upon you, and may she

shield you from this evil as well as she is able."

Crys left them standing at the fence, staring.

This family's story was just one more reason to seek help from her grandmother. Lashrefi would provide a horse somehow. And if the Goddess chose not to, then a horse was not what Crys truly needed. Regardless, it was far too early to give up the idea. The player who quits after the first loss never wins again.

Crys was already contemplating the next farm along the road when she heard a call behind her:

"Wait," said the husband.

Crys stopped.

He came out through a gate and caught up to her.

"You seem to be on a journey," he said—a polite way of noting that her clothes were filthy. "Can we ... offer you some bread before you go?"

"Thank you," Crys said. "That would be very kind."

"Please forgive me," the farmer said. "I saw your tunic and ... well, I did not know the Darcliff Temple still offered blessings."

"The temple's blessings have ceased," Crys agreed. "And I need guidance to bring them back. I hope to find my grand-mother. She is wiser than I."

"Does she live far from here?" the farmer asked.

Crys smiled. "She is a Flamebringer."

"Ah."

The man contemplated Crys's moccasins, thinking. "If I let you borrow a horse, will that help you end the curses?"

"Such miracles are not in my power," Crys said. "But I shall do the best I can and leave the rest to Lashrefi."

"Then you may borrow my Dancy."

"You are most generous," Crys said.

"Is there anything else we can do to help?" the man asked.

Crys looked down at her Darcliff Temple uniform. "Might I ask your wife or daughter for a tunic? This one no longer suits me."

* * *

Gwenshi squatted in her neighbor's garden, shelling vine-dried peas. The sun was already hot on her red skin and it was not even noon yet. Another dusty day in Camptown.

At noon, she and the neighbor would share a meal and then go to Gwenshi's garden for more squatting and shelling. Gwenshi knew exactly how her day would go. And the next. And the next.

The day after that, Vinnagon would come home. He'd bring her his wages, and she would wife for a day. Then he'd be gone and she'd be grubby Gwenshi again, squatting in the garden.

"I think harvest is the best time of year," said Plesi, the neighbor. She rose to empty her bowl of peas into the storage crock.

"The sad thing is, Plesi, I think you're right."

"You're in a mood today," Plesi said. "When is Vinnagon coming home?"

"In three days. If he comes home this time."

"He always comes home."

"Last time he slept the whole morning and then left early to run an errand for his uncle."

"But he did come home."

"Aye." Gwenshi knew she should shut up. Plesi's husband was part of a river patrol garrison and would not be home until winter.

"At least you've got the kids to keep you company," Gwenshi said. She wasn't very good at shutting up.

"Yes," said Plesi. "They are plenty of company." The two-year-old was underneath her skirt, clinging to her leg. The one-year-old was gnawing on the wooden bowl that the two-year-old had abandoned after shelling one pod and a half. The infant was sleeping in the shack.

"You could have company, too," Plesi said, "if you stopped visiting the herbalist."

"I haven't visited the herbalist for months," Gwenshi said. "At least not for that."

"Really? Why didn't you tell me?"

"There's nothing to tell."

"Well, sometimes those herbs take a while to stop working."

"I noticed," Gwenshi said. In truth, it had been over a year since she had last taken herbs. Vinnagon didn't seem to care one way or the other.

"Well, if he's coming home three times a month," Plesi said, "you don't have anything to worry about. Just be patient and try to relax."

" 'Relax'? What are you talking about?"

Plesi raised her eyebrows sagely. "Have you ever noticed that women who want kids the most have to wait the longest? They're trying too hard."

That was easy for Plesi to say, since she got bred once a year like a milk cow. But this time Gwenshi did know when to shut up.

A thin wail from the shack announced the awakening of the newborn. Plesi stood up, scooped up the two-year-old in one arm since that was the only way to make it let go of her leg, and went inside.

The one-year-old was still trying to fit the wooden bowl into its mouth. The bowl was bigger than the kid's head, but Gwenshi thought the kid might have a chance, anyway. It had a big mouth.

Gwenshi rose from her squat and dumped her bowl of peas into the crock. It was a good crock, but Gwenshi preferred to keep peas in a sack. Sacks of peas attracted mice, and sometimes she needed something to throw her knife at.

Just then, a movement on the other side of the fence caught her eye. Someone was opening the back door of her shack.

A few peas escaped to dribble onto her bare toes. Her back door stayed open, but only by a handswidth, as though someone was scanning her garden before daring to venture outside.

After a few heartbeats, the door opened wider and out poked a face the color of a recent bloodstain topped by a brushlike tuft of hair.

"Vingo!" she called.

Vinnagon looked in her direction. He didn't look happy to see her. In fact, he reminded her of a dismayed steer. But usually he just looked tired when he came home, so a little variety was nice.

Gwenshi put a hand on the wooden fence and vaulted over into her own garden.

"You're home early," she said. "What news?"

"Have they been here yet?" His hair was damp. On a day like this, it could have been sweat, but he smelled like the river.

"Did you swim the Dothedarl?" she asked.

"Yes," he said. "Gwenshi, have the bladesmen been here?"

"What? No. I mean—which bladesmen?" There were always a few men in Camptown. They all had leave on different days.

"Temple guards," Vinnagon said. "They're looking for me. If they haven't been here yet, they will be soon."

"Vinnagon? Did you run away?" He looked like he was on the run, but that didn't make any sense. Vinnagon would never run from duty.

He shook his head. "It's more complicated than that."

"Why are they looking for you?"

"It's bladesmen's business. I don't have time to explain it right now. Gwenshi, have you been saving any of the money I've brought home?"

"Aye. Some." Whether she saved it or spent it was her business, but she was too bewildered to stick up for herself right now.

"How long can it last you?"

"What?"

"Can it last you through the winter?"

"The winter? Vingo, where are you going?"

"I don't know. And if I did know, you'd be safer if I didn't tell you. Look, I want you to claim succor from Harl."

"Claim succor? Do you aim to widow me?"

"I don't know what will happen. I want you under the protection of a man who can take care of you."

Harl the blacksmith was one of the few men who actually lived day in, day out in Camptown. His household was well off, but that did not mean Gwenshi wanted to join them.

"Vingo, what happened?"

"I should go." He stepped over what was left of summer's onion crop and kissed her on the forehead. As he stepped away, she caught his wrist.

Vinnagon was a full head taller than she was, and he outweighed her by a good bit. But after two years of marriage, Gwenshi had mastered the wifely glare. She fixed him with the glare now, and that was enough to keep him from breaking the hold she had on his wrist.

"You are not going to disappear for six months and send me off to live with the blacksmith. He's a fine, pious man, but both his wives snore. You are going to take the time to give me a decent explanation or else ..." Or else what? If he was leaving, she did not have anything she could withhold. "I'll get even," she finished.

That was good. Better to leave his punishment to his imagination anyway.

Vinnagon shook his head in disbelief. "Woman, you'll never understand."

A pounding of fist on wood made Gwenshi jump. Someone was knocking on her shack.

Vinnagon stepped past her and dashed for the garden's back gate.

"Temple business," said a man's authoritative voice. "Open up."

Gwenshi glanced into the darkness of her shack. All her

belongings were in there. She looked at Vinnagon unlatching the garden gate.

Gwenshi shut the door and turned her back on her home. Halfway through her garden, she remembered an implicit responsibility. She leaned over the fence and called, "Plesi! I'm leaving for a bit!" She glanced at the child she was supposed to be watching and added, "And your kid's eating dirt!"

Then she left to follow her man.

* * *

Vinnagon dashed down the lane. A flock of chickens clucked at him and burst into flight.

"Vingo!" his wife called after him. "Vingo, we aren't done talking yet!"

The forge was at the end of the lane. Harl might help him. If Vinnagon explained swiftly enough, Harl might even talk the bladesmen into letting him go. As a blacksmith and a holyman, he commanded as much respect as any of the captains.

But the temple guards had sworn loyalty to Uncle Brekko, not to Harl.

It didn't matter anyway, because three bladesmen had just stepped around the corner of the forge. Vinnagon skidded to a halt, his heel-less boot slipping in the dust.

He turned and ran the other way. Gwenshi stood in the lane, wild-eyed. She turned and ran ahead of him.

"Go home, woman! They don't want you!" Why was she making him waste breath?

Four men stepped into view at the other end of the lane. Counting the three coming out his shack's back door, that made ten. Apparently, his uncle thought highly of his skills.

With bladesmen closing in from both ends of the lane, Gwenshi vaulted a fence and ran through a patch of sunflowers. "Vingo, come this way!"

Silly woman. As though he couldn't tell it was the only way left. He clambered over the fence, caught his foot, and fell on a rake that had been left tines up among the squash.

He rolled to his feet cursing whoever worked the garden he was trampling. Why did women never put their tools away?

Gwenshi was waiting for him, standing on the garden fence, peering into the street.

"This way looks good," she reported. She reached out a hand to help him up onto the fence.

Vinnagon ignored her and unlatched the gate.

"Go home!" he said.

He ran out into Camptown's main street.

Some of the men in the lane began shouting, "Thief! Thief!"—a smart tactic in the streets of Darcliff, perhaps, but in Camptown, most of the denizens were women and children.

"This way!" Gwenshi called, sprinting off in a random direction.

Vinnagon ran after her shouting, "Woman, go home!"

"Thief!" called the bladesmen as they spilled out of the gardens and onto the street, cutting off Gwenshi's proposed escape route.

"This way!" Vinnagon called, taking a side street.

Doors were opening and women were poking their heads out. A boy of about ten emerged from a garden carrying a hoe.

"Stop, thief!" he yelled and swung the hoe at Vinnagon's legs. Vinnagon jumped over it and landed cleanly. Apparently, he was getting used to his missing bootheel.

He accelerated away and glanced over his shoulder to see how Gwenshi would fare. The boy held up the hoe to block her path, but she just went around him. The bladesmen were close behind.

Vinnagon didn't think they would do anything to Gwenshi. Although a man could be punished if one of his wives committed a crime, it did not work the other way around. Not unless she had somehow aided the crime ... for example, by helping her husband escape justice.

Damn it, Gwenshi, why could you not stay home?

Vinnagon stopped and turned. They were going to catch her.

He drew his sword and charged at Gwenshi's pursuers.

The bladesmen stopped and drew their weapons. One against four, with more men coming. Vinnagon had trained against two of these men, and neither was a man he was certain to defeat.

Gwenshi grabbed his arm as she ran past. "Don't be stupid," she said.

Vinnagon slammed his sword back into its sheath and started running again.

"I was trying to save your life, woman!"

"Run now," she gasped. "Save me later."

"You should have stayed home."

"Cornfield," Gwenshi suggested.

The corn grew on a wedge of land between Camptown and Clifford. Patches of six-foot-tall corn stood drying in the sun. Vinnagon and Gwenshi jumped a dry irrigation ditch and ran in among the rustling stalks.

Gwenshi was fast for a woman, but Vinnagon knew she was too weak to outrun the bladesmen forever. It was time to be smart.

He grabbed her arm and made her change direction—a sharp turn, one he hoped the men would not be expecting. Then he dove into the thickest patch of corn and crouched low. Gwenshi joined him, and he slapped a hand over her mouth.

She glared and brushed his hand away, but at least she kept quiet.

Men passed in a susurration of dry corn leaves. Vinnagon thought he counted eight or nine.

"Spread out," one called, "and draw swords."

Blades slid from scabbards. Only one bladesman was nearby—a straggler, taking his time through the cornfield. He moved carefully, not disturbing the corn. Vinnagon could locate him only by his breathing.

The man stopped. To rest? No, he seemed to be stopped where Vinnagon and Gwenshi had made their hard cut away from the obvious path. That was not a coincidence.

Leaves began to rustle—a quiet noise, but getting closer.

Vinnagon looked at Gwenshi and pointed out of the cornfield.

She nodded.

He helped her up and gave her a slap on the rump to get her moving.

"This way!" called the straggler. "He's back here!"

Vinnagon chased after Gwenshi's flapping skirt. He didn't look back until they emerged from the corn stalks.

Judging from the wiggling of the tassels, he and Gwenshi had a good lead. Now if he could just convince her to go home, he could escape.

"Horses!" said Gwenshi, pointing toward a meadow on the outskirts of Clifford. "We need horses."

"Woman, you can't ride!"

"I can ride. Can you?"

One of the horses snorted, and they all raised their heads.

Vinnagon did not know much about horses, but he did know that they were skittish creatures and a dead run was not the best way to approach them. They danced nervously as he and Gwenshi drew near, but fortunately, their halters were tethered to wooden stakes in the ground.

Gwenshi chased one down to the end of its rope and vaulted onto its back.

Vinnagon did not want to be outdone. He grabbed the nearest one by the halter. The beast reared, and Vinnagon moved with it. He kept his grip firm but let his arm move freely enough that the horse's antics could not pull him off balance.

The horse gave four bucks, dancing a circle around its tether stake. Vinnagon danced with it, and when it paused to contemplate its next course of action, he pushed himself up onto its back. Now he was astride a huge beast, with muscles rippling beneath his loins.

Gwenshi already had her horse loose. She must have cut the halter. She was sliding her meat-cutting knife back into its sheath.

Vinnagon reached for his own knife, wondering how he would cut the halter without accidentally stabbing the point into the beast's wildly tossing head. No, that was too chancy. Vinnagon drew his sword instead.

With an underhand swing, he nicked the taut tether with the tip of his blade. The rope parted, and suddenly his steed was racing after Gwenshi.

Horses are fast, he thought. And then he did not bother thinking anymore because he had to concentrate on staying on.

Gwenshi seemed to be headed for the ferry dock. Vinnagon believed the river would provide poor terrain for horses, but the fool woman wouldn't turn her mount, and Vinnagon's mount was going wherever Gwenshi's went.

As the broad expanse of water drew uncomfortably near, Gwenshi finally showed some sense and turned aside, but she turned toward town instead of away. A moment later, they were galloping through the Clifford market.

Vinnagon could feel his horse's hooves slip as they hit the paving stones. Wide-eyed Lashrefites jumped out of the way.

Ahead, Gwenshi's horse clipped a melon stand with a back hoof. Ripe, round melons rolled into the street.

Vinnagon's horse skittered through the rolling fruit, dodged the girl with yoked waterbuckets at the well, and accelerated after Gwenshi.

Gwenshi's horse found a gap between a duck vendor and a squash farmer's stall. The squash farmer, a scraggly man with a tunic like a loose sack, stepped into the gap and waved a long, bony arm at Gwenshi's back.

He didn't see Vinnagon.

The horse was now faced with a stack of duck crates on the left, a hill of squash on the right, and an oblivious angry man standing in the middle.

The horse picked the ducks.

Muscles bunched, and then Vinnagon was floating. No more clatter of hooves against the cobble stones. No more jiggling of the bones. Vinnagon and the horse were soaring over a wall of ducks, four crates high, with the cringing duck vendor looking up at them in fear.

Then hooves hit stone.

The horse's head dropped between its knees. Vinnagon went sliding forward along its neck. With a clattering scramble, the horse rose again, tossing its head to shake Vinnagon loose.

Vinnagon retreated to the horse's back, and they galloped out of Clifford.

As the winded horses slowed, Vinnagon looked back over his shoulder. There was no sign of pursuit.

* * *

Crys was not certain why the old mare was named "Dancy". Perhaps she had engaged in some coltish antics long ago. Now, a better name would have been "Trudger" or "Stonefoot". The horse knew how to trot, but she needed a reminder every eight steps or so. It was only noon, and Crys's legs were already tired from nudging the mare's ribs.

At least the mare's trot was gentle.

* * *

Gwenshi's mare stopped to sniff the pile of horse dung in the road.

Gwenshi asked, "Anyone you know, love?"

The mare snuffled and flicked her ears. She turned her head back toward Clifford.

Gwenshi tugged to indicate that the mare should not turn around. Her belt made a functional rein when looped around the mare's nose.

"Keep going, love. Vingo's in a hurry, remember?"

Vinnagon said, "Woman, I wish you had brought your boots."

"Why?" she asked.

"Because then we could walk."

"We can walk now, if you want. I just thought riding would be more comfortable—at least until we can get your boot fixed."

"It is not a question of comfort," Vinnagon said, almost as though he were disgusted by the idea. "It is a question of logistics. You can only walk so far before your feet become sore. And then I shall have to abandon you or carry you."

"I reckon your knees and ankles will get sore before my feet do. Your boots are uneven."

"I can take the other heel off."

"Vingo, you love those boots. You're too proud to take off the heel."

"Bah! Watch me, woman!"

He dismounted and began wrestling with his intact boot. This was not a man who was having a good day.

"We'll walk, then," Gwenshi said, dismounting. "My feet won't get too sore if I stay in the grass along the edge."

"We can't follow the road forever," Vinnagon said. He had the boot off now and was working his knife between the sole and the layers of leather that made the raised heel.

"Even better," said Gwenshi. "Meadows and fields are softer."

"What about the sharp stubble in the wheat fields? What about woods full of sharp sticks?"

"I'll be fine."

"You'll be a burden, one way or the other. Damn it!" Somehow he had managed to nick his thumb as he slid the knife through the bootheel.

Gwenshi slipped her belt off the mare's nose. "Run with Kashram, love."

She began removing the gelding's halter so that it would not get caught on anything. The gelding snorted.

"Yes, you're a fierce boy, aren't you?"

"Don't talk to my stallion like he's a baby," Vinnagon said.

"Stallion? It's a gelding."

Vinnagon scowled. "Whatever."

Gwenshi slipped the halter loose and the two horses turned for home.

Sure, love, now you trot.

Gwenshi smiled. She hadn't gotten to ride since her father had brought her to Vinnagon.

Metal snapped.

Vinnagon stared forlornly at the hilt of his knife. The blade was broken. Most of it was still embedded in the bootheel.

He shook his head. "Nothing is going right for me."

"Want me to try?" she asked.

"No." He began wiggling his broken blade into his bootheel.

She gave him a pat between his shoulder blades. He just grunted.

That wasn't their only knife. Vinnagon had Gwenshi's knives, too. He had, somewhat grudgingly, agreed to keep them jammed between his belt and the small of his back when she had removed her own belt for use as a bridle. She hastened to reclaim them now, before he decided to do something that would break them, too.

Once her knives and belt were secure about her waist, Gwenshi felt better. One for throwing, one for dueling, one for food—she was ready for anything.

Her stomach rumbled.

Especially, she was ready for food.

Vinnagon popped the heel loose. He contemplated the broken knife blade.

"My uncle gave me this knife," he said. "I've had it since I was a boy."

"So it was pretty old, then."

Vingo was only six years older than she was, but he thought that made him twenty years wiser.

He scowled at her. "Woman, it is time you started taking this seriously."

"I suppose," Gwenshi agreed. "But so far, being a fugitive is more fun than squatting in the garden shelling peas."

"This is not a game!"

"I know," Gwenshi said. But it kind of was. Kind of like a really wild game of tag. Kind of like hide-and-seek with an entire world of hiding places. It *was* a game; it was just a game with very high stakes.

"What will they do if they catch you?" she asked.

Vinnagon shrugged. "They'll kill me in battle if I fight them. If they capture me, my uncle will have to execute me. I'm a deserter."

"I thought you said it was more complicated than that."

"It is."

"Well, now you've got time to explain it."

Vinnagon sighed. "Very well," he said. "But let us get moving."

* * *

Crys and Dancy reached a fork in the road a little after noon. The fork under the rising moon led to Shalbroon, a market town on the frontier. Lashrefi willing, Crys would meet a trader who could tell her where to look for her grandmother's band.

The other fork led to the village where Crys's sisters and parents lived. She had no reason to go that way, except to seek comfort from her family. That would be not only irresponsible and foolish, but also dangerous, given that the temple was certainly hunting for her. Crys would not have even considered going that way had it not been for the lith, the multi-faceted heavenly body sparkling in the sunlight. It was at its highest point, due lithward, and it seemed to hang directly above the fork that led to her mother's farm. Was this a sign from Lashrefi?

There was only one way to be certain—well, she was dealing with the goddess of luck, so there was no way to be *certain*, but there was a way to be less uncertain—she could cast her die-of-the-heavens.

Crys dismounted. Relieved, Dancy drifted to the edge of the road and began nosing through the dry grass, looking for the greener bits.

Crys reached into her sacred pouch and withdrew an iron cube plated on each side with deer antler. The smith in her grandmother's band had made it for her.

Each face was marked with a symbol representing one of the six directions. When the die was new, the symbols had been difficult to read—they were carved into the polished antler, not painted. But the dust of travel had filled the carvings with a black grime that strengthened the connection between Crys, the die, and the Goddess. At least, that was what her grandmother claimed.

Crys smoothed a patch of the road with the sole of her moccasin, asking Lashrefi for guidance. Lithward toward her parents or moonward toward the traders? She tossed the die.

Sunward, it said.

She looked back the way she had come. Only a quarter-lithic after noon, the sun was still more-or-less at true sunward.

"I want to find my grandmother," Crys said. "Should I go lithward to my family, or moonward to Shalbroon?" She tossed the die again.

Sunward, it said.

She picked up the heavy die and pressed it to her forehead. She closed her eyes and let her mind grow calm, open to guidance from the Goddess. She took a deep breath and blew across its surface.

"Lithward or moonward?" she asked, letting the die roll from her fingers.

The die struck a rock, bounced away, and skittered toward the side of the road. Before it could stop rolling, Dancy took a step forward and clopped her heavy hoof on top of it.

Crys scowled up at the heavens. "Very funny," she said.

But she deserved to be laughed at. The Goddess had already told her twice.

Crys pushed against Dancy's shoulder and moved her off the die. It still said sunward, of course. Neither the die nor Dancy's hoof seemed to be hurt. Good. That meant Lashrefi wasn't angry.

Crys put her die-of-the-heavens back in her sacred pouch. She mounted up and turned her horse sunward.

Dancy seemed pleased to be going back the way they had come.

* * *

It had been some time since Vinnagon had last seen the countryside. Oh, he had surveyed it from the temple steps, on the cliff high above town, but it was different to be walking along the road, past the fences and meadows and fields. He could smell the grazing cattle, see the stubble on the wheat fields, hear the rustling leaves of the drying corn.

The countryside was mostly open, but here and there were woods carefully maintained for timber. They were passing through one of these when Gwenshi said, "We should stop at a farmhouse and see if we can steal some eggs."

" 'Steal'?" Vinnagon asked.

"Why not?" Gwenshi asked. "We're criminals now, aren't we?"

Vinnagon wasn't a criminal. Well, perhaps he was, but he was not a thief. "I'm a fugitive," he said. "That doesn't mean I steal eggs."

"Just horses, then?"

"That was an emergency," Vinnagon said. "Besides, woman, we gave them back."

"We let them go," Gwenshi said. "That's not quite the same as giving them back."

Vinnagon didn't like the idea of stealing. He had not even kept his temple-issued helmet and cuirass. But he *did* need to provide food for his woman.

"I'll try to get you to Shalbroon," he said. "Our people have a few households there. Someone may be willing to take you in."

"Shalbroon?"

"Unless you'll agree to go back to Camptown and stay with Harl."

Gwenshi clutched his elbow. "I'm staying with you."

"You're slowing me down."

"You don't even know where you're going," she said. "So how can I slow you down?"

She was right. Vinnagon was going "away". But every place was away from Darcliff.

Was he going to look for work in a different province? Perhaps he should leave Yardwen altogether.

In truth, he was directionless. He'd made his decision. He'd reported to his captain. And his captain had ordered him to run away.

Vinnagon supposed he could have stayed and demanded a fair execution. But he preferred to live. In fact, he wanted to live as a bladesman. But there was much that was wrong in that temple, and he was no longer able to ignore it.

He heard a distant sound like clopping hooves. Vinnagon stopped, trying to discern the direction. The trees around him broke up the sound, making it difficult to tell whether the rider was ahead or behind them.

Gwenshi stopped, too, and looked up at him. Her stomach rumbled.

"Quiet your stomach, woman, and listen."

Gwenshi cocked her head. "It's a horse."

Vinnagon gestured for her to follow.

He led her into the trees. They dropped over the crest of a hill and hid behind a hackberry bush.

The *clop clop* of hooves grew louder. It sounded like only one horse, heading sunward, toward Clifford. Still, one horse and one rider were all it would take to confirm that Vinnagon and Gwenshi were traveling along the road.

Whereas now, the rider could attest that Vinnagon and Gwenshi were nowhere to be seen. *That* would mislead potential pursuers.

Vinnagon smiled. It was about time that he had a bit of luck.

* * *

Crys was somewhat nervous about riding through the oaks. The trees surrounded her, limiting her choices for escape. She couldn't trust Dancy to dodge trees and jump fallen logs. She needed to stay in the open.

So she breathed a sigh of relief when she finally emerged from the wood. The road before her was flanked by meadows and fields—plenty of room to run.

Crys urged Dancy forward, then saw a cloud of dust behind the next hill. Horses were coming—most likely a cavalry unit, unless the local farmers had all decided to drive their carts home from market at the same time.

Her first instinct was to turn Dancy and gallop across the pastureland, but then she realized how easily she would be seen, even at a distance. This could be a Clifford Militia patrol. It might not be Kashramite bladesmen looking for runaway taishrefis.

And Crys was no longer dressed as a taishrefi. Should she keep riding, try to fool them? Lashrefi had instructed her to seek her fortune back at Darcliff.

Well, to be precise, Lashrefi had told her to ride *sunward*. That could mean a number of things, and situations could arise that Lashrefi had not foreseen. That cloud of dust would turn into riders coming around the hill any moment now.

Crys fished her die-of-the-heavens out of her sacred pouch, clenched it tightly in her fist, then opened her hand so that the die rested on her palm.

Sunaway.

Good enough. Crys dropped the die into her pouch and cinched it tight. Then she turned Dancy around and galloped for the cover of the trees.

* * *

"Vingo! Mushrooms!"

Vinnagon looked at the shriveled brown things.

"Not very fresh mushrooms," he observed.

"Then you can eat acorns like a squirrel," Gwenshi said. "I'm eating mushrooms."

Vinnagon knelt and picked one. He lifted it to a splotch of sunlight filtering through the oak leaves.

"Are you certain these are edible?"

"They're fine," Gwenshi said. "I cook with these all the time."

"They look wrinkled," he said.

Gwenshi popped one into her mouth and chewed it deliberately. She stuck out her tongue to show him the masticated contents. Then she swallowed.

Insufferable woman.

Vinnagon nibbled at his mushroom. It tasted like a dry mushroom.

Well, it was the only food they were likely to have today, unless they were willing to become beggars or thieves. After two or three of the chewy things, the flavor began to appeal to him, and he realized just how hungry he was. Maybe he could kill something with meat on it. Had Gwenshi brought her flint? Did she know how to start a fire without flint?

He was about to ask, but then he noticed she was staring at him wide-eyed. No, not just wide-eyed. Her eyes were bulging.

Gwenshi clutched at her stomach. Her cheeks puffed out. Her lips parted in a horrific rictus ...

... and then she burst out laughing.

She pointed at Vinnagon. "You should have seen the look on your face! You really thought I had poisoned us, didn't you?"

Vinnagon stared at her in disbelief. She had put them both in grave danger by choosing to come along. He was trying to get her to safety. And instead of being quiet and contrite, she was mocking him!

Vinnagon stood up in disgust. "Woman," he said—and in his pause for breath, he heard the sound of galloping hooves.

"Get low," he said, dropping to the ground and flattening himself.

They were not far from the road. Undergrowth was sparse. But perhaps there was just enough vegetation to hide their figures from a galloping horseman.

Vinnagon met Gwenshi's eyes. She was no longer laughing. She was alert, listening as the hooves came closer and closer.

But he saw no fear in her.

Vinnagon's own heart was pounding. Perhaps that was only excitement. Perhaps he had no fear at all. But for a moment he wondered if Gwenshi might not be braver than he.

He frowned, but she did not notice.

The horseman passed by without slowing.

* * *

As they emerged from the wood, Crys let Dancy ease into a canter. She had heard no sounds of pursuit. She doubted she had been seen. With luck, the riders had not even seen her dust.

But now which way to go? Speed would keep her ahead of them, but Dancy was not particularly speedy. Crys felt she should set off cross-country, but she was not certain she could get out of sight before the riders emerged from the wood.

She fished out her die-of-the-heavens and shook it in her hand. If it showed sunaway, she would know she should stay on the road. She let the die rest on her hand and opened her palm: *Sunward.*

Back into the wood? Crys looked up at the heavens and asked, "Are you mocking me?"

* * *

When the hoofbeats had died away, Vinnagon led Gwenshi back to the road.

"Good thing I found those mushrooms, huh? Otherwise we would have been on the road when that rider turned around."

She was trying to make him forget her cruel jest. Vinnagon would not. But he had more important concerns.

"He must have seen our signs," Vinnagon said.

"What signs?"

"When we relieved ourselves on the edge of the wood."

Two spots of fresh urine on opposite sides of the road implied one man and one woman. The scout probably even knew how long it had been since their passage.

"He saw our pee from horseback and immediately knew it was us?"

"Among the bladesmen are many good scouts," Vinnagon said. "We are just fortunate that we were not found in our hiding place."

"So someone knows we peed in the woods," Gwenshi said. "Now what?"

Vinnagon thought about it. "Now we go back the way we came," he decided.

"What? Why?"

Vinnagon put his plan into action. His wife followed.

"Vingo, why are we going back?"

"Just a short way," he explained. "We'll take that cut-across to Clayhill Road."

"So we aren't going to Shalbroon?"

"Not immediately. The scout knows we reached the edge of this wood. He'll report that. If we go back a quarter-lithic and leave the road there, we will be leaving at a point that everyone is certain we walked past."

Gwenshi thought it over. "Sure, Vingo. That makes sense."

Of course it made sense. Vinnagon knew what he was doing. But he said nothing because he did not need to belabor the point.

"Only one thing," Gwenshi said. "That rider passed us twice. That means he started someplace we haven't been to yet. How did he know to look for us?"

"Someone must have given him a message."

"How could he get a message? Any messenger would have passed us."

"Not so. We have been following a horse for some time."

"Oh, right."

The messenger had a good head start on them. Vinnagon was no scout, but he could make rough guesses about the age of horse dung.

"So that messenger wouldn't know about me, would he?" Gwenshi asked. "He would have already been on the road when we left Clifford."

Vinnagon thought about that. She was right. The messenger would have had to somehow recognize Vinnagon alone. Gwenshi's sign, had it been observed, would have told a story other than "runaway bladesman".

Well, they were coming to the edge of the woods. Vinnagon could study the horse tracks and figure out what had caused the rider to turn around.

"Now what?" Gwenshi asked.

Vinnagon opened his mouth to explain his plan, but then he saw what Gwenshi was staring at. Two columns of riders were coming toward the woods.

* * *

Gwenshi could tell the riders were not bladesmen. They were not even Redfolk. They were Stripedfolk, mounted, lightly armored, armed with swords and bows. Women rode among them, armed as well as the men.

The lead rider hailed Vinnagon with a raised hand.

"Do we run?" Gwenshi asked.

"We can't outrun horses," Vinnagon said.

"In the woods we might lose them," Gwenshi suggested.

Vinnagon frowned. "Let us see what they want."

The lead rider was now close enough that Gwenshi could see the stripes on his face, despite the shade of his iron helmet. His expression seemed stern.

He spread the fingers of his upraised hand. Gwenshi realized it was not a hail; it was a signal. He gave a brisk wave and the riders behind him began to fan out.

"Vingo, I think they want to surround us."

Vinnagon nodded and took a cautious step back.

The riders quickened their pace.

"This is a militia patrol," Vinnagon said. "They usually stay out of temple business."

The lead rider slowed to give his riders time to arc around Gwenshi and Vinnagon.

"What do you want?" Gwenshi called. "We're just travelers on our way to Shalbroon."

The lead rider halted and cocked his head at her. "Shalbroon is behind you," he said.

Damn it! "Uh, we decided to walk the long way."

"Woman, be silent," Vinnagon muttered.

"Where are you from?" the striped soldier asked.

Gwenshi shrugged and looked up at Vinnagon.

Vinnagon didn't have any quick answers, so Gwenshi gave it another try. "Shalbroon?" she suggested.

Vinnagon gave a tiny grunt of pain.

"We're looking for two horse thieves," the soldier said. "Kashramites. A man and a woman."

Oh! So that was why they were being surrounded. Of course. That made sense.

"Someone on a horse just rode by here," Gwenshi said. "We didn't get a good look at him. He might have been a Kashramite."

On either side of them, horses were picking their way through the trees. Gwenshi was beginning to feel trapped. She hoped Vinnagon could hack a way free with his blade. Perhaps he was just waiting for them to spread themselves thin.

"I would like you to drop your weapons," the soldier said.

Gwenshi looked up at Vinnagon.

"I do not feel inclined to do so," Vinnagon said.

His hand was resting on the pommel of his sword now, loose, relaxed. Gwenshi could sense tension in his stance. She adjusted her own feet, ready to spring in whichever direction he decided they should go.

"I need to take you back to Clifford," the soldier said.

"Your needs are not mine," said Vinnagon.

"You will force a fight?" the soldier asked.

Vinnagon did not answer.

The soldier studied them a moment longer. Then he raised

his hand, slowly, deliberately. This time the signal was a fist with the thumb and smallest finger extended in opposite directions.

Wood scraped against leather as the soldiers in the surrounding circle took up their bows. Iron arrowheads clinked softly as shafts slid from quivers.

"Your odds do not look good," the lead soldier observed.

He was the only one who had not yet drawn a bow. Gwenshi judged the distance between them. His helmet left enough of his face exposed that Gwenshi reckoned she could stick him with a good throw of her knife. Then the other nineteen would loose arrows and she would be as bristly as a porcupine. It was not really the way she wanted to die.

She looked up to Vinnagon to see if he had any ideas.

Behind them, a woman-soldier cried out, "Halt! Who goes there?"

"I might ask you the same question," replied another woman. "You may address me as 'Taishrefi'."

Gwenshi looked over her shoulder, but the speaker was obscured by horses and trees.

"Let her pass onto the road," the lead soldier called. He pumped his fist twice and the soldiers around the circle lowered their bows.

A Stripedwoman stepped onto the road. She was tall, with long, unkempt, white hair. She wore a plain tunic and long buckskin trousers horseback-polished along the inner calves and thighs. She carried herself like a leader. Her face was smooth, beautiful, and strong.

Vinnagon's eyes grew wide, and he murmured something under his breath. Gwenshi glanced up at her husband's face, then checked the Stripedwoman again. She was attractive, yes, but under the circumstances, it was surprising that Vinnagon would be so awestruck. Maybe it was the riding pants. Gwenshi decided to get a pair—if she and Vinnagon managed to get out of this somehow.

"You lead these soldiers?" the woman asked.

"I do," acknowledged the one who had been giving the commands. "Captain Eversun of the Clifford Militia. And you are ... ?"

"Taishrefi Sweetgrass," the woman said.

"Forgive me," said the captain, "but you do not look like a taishrefi."

Annoyed, the woman reached inside her bodice and withdrew a pouch. From the pouch, she took a small object and displayed it on her striped palm. "This die was given to me by my grandmother, taishrefi of Blackstorm's band. We Flamebringers have no need for the ostentatious trappings of the Darcliff Temple."

"Very well," said the captain.

"And now that you have required me to prove my authority, I should like to know the authority by which you detain these people."

"They are suspected horse thieves, Taishrefi."

"Horse thieves?" she asked. "But Captain, they have no horses."

"Nevertheless, they are a Kashramite couple on the road far from any Kashramite settlement. This morning, a Kashramite couple stole two horses from the mayor of Clifford and set off on the road to Shalbroon."

Those were the *mayor's* horses? Gwenshi was in more trouble than she'd thought.

The woman asked, "Do you know any more about these horse thieves, other than that they were Kashramites?"

"Darcliff Temple said the man was a runaway guard named Vinnagon and the accomplice was his wife." The captain looked hard at them as he said these words. Gwenshi tried not to look guilty.

The woman came closer to get a better view of Vinnagon. She scrutinized his face. Then she turned to the captain.

"I have carried messages from the Flamebringers to the Darcliff Temple many times," she said. "I know this man. He is, in fact, a temple guard, but his name is Malk. Vinnagon is shorter, with a scar on his right cheek." She demonstrated by drawing a finger along Vinnagon's face. "You have the wrong Kashramites."

The captain frowned down at the three of them, considering. "Are you certain?" he asked.

The holywoman looked to Vinnagon and asked, "Are you Vinnagon or Malk?"

"Malk," he said. Gwenshi could tell that the lie did not come easily to his lips.

"You see?" said the woman. "It is the will of Lashrefi that I should arrive in time to prevent you from arresting an innocent man. You should be grateful to the Goddess."

The captain stared down at her. "Very well," he decided.

The captain turned his attention to Gwenshi. "Enjoy your walk," he said. "But Shalbroon is that way."

He nudged his horse into motion and rode past. As he entered the wood, his soldiers fell into columns behind him.

"Disciplined men," Vinnagon observed.

"And women," Gwenshi said. "They have women-soldiers, too."

Vinnagon grunted.

* * *

As the soldiers disappeared into the wood, Crys raised a hand to the small, muscular, red-skinned woman and said, "Taishrefi Crystal."

The woman looked puzzled. "Crystal Sweetgrass?"

Crys shook her head. "Crystal Farrider. I'm no more Sweetgrass than he is Malk."

The small woman looked from Crys to Vinnagon. "Oh," she said. "Is she the one who ...?"

The bladesman nodded.

"Well, that explains it," the woman said.

"Explains what?" Crys asked.

"He recognized you," the woman said, her eyes flicking unconsciously to Crys's legs.

"Well, he did save my life," Crys said.

The red-skinned woman raised her hand. "Gwenshi," she said. "Vinnagon's wife."

"It is a pleasure to meet you, Gwenshi. And to see you again, Vinnagon."

"Mutual," Vinnagon said, but he was frowning into the wood. The horses were whinnying.

"Ah," said Crys, recognizing a whinny. "It seems they have found Dancy. I was hoping she would stay quiet."

Gwenshi looked up at Vinnagon. "Should we go?"

"Let us not be hasty," Crys suggested. "Unless you stole a sorrel mare."

Gwenshi shook her head. "Black," she said.

"Then remain calm," Crys said, though her own stomach fluttered. "With luck, the militia captain will have a description of the missing horses, and he will realize that Dancy belongs with me."

"He will think it suspicious that you left your horse behind," Vinnagon said.

"Ah, he was already suspicious," Crys said. "But he knows enough to leave a taishrefi to her business."

Please let him decide to continue on, she prayed. Her air of self-assurance was a gamble, but if her words proved true, she would gain much credibility with these Kashramites. And she needed their confidence, for she now understood what the die-of-the-heavens had been telling her.

"Lashrefi led me to you," she said.

"Aye, we were lucky you came when you did," Gwenshi said.

Vinnagon snorted. "First luck I've had all day."

Gwenshi said, "We heard a lone rider pass through these woods twice. Was that you?"

"It was."

"We were hiding from you," Gwenshi said. "Vingo thought you were a scout."

Trying not to smile at Gwenshi's adorable nickname for the

stern-faced bladesman, Crys said, "I was following the will of Lashrefi."

"Well, we're right glad you found us," Gwenshi said. "We thought we were alone."

So did I. But now I am beginning to understand. "You are not alone. Lashrefi has brought us together for a purpose."

Gwenshi frowned. "Are you sure?"

"I am," Crys said. "I need your help to bring down the temple."

Vinnagon looked as though he thought she was crazy.

Gwenshi's eyes widened. "What do you mean?"

"A great evil has taken the Temple of Darcliff," Crys said. "Bashrefi Wintersmoke makes secret plans with her seneschal and a foreign confidant. She has elevated one group of taishrefis above the others, giving them the authority to suppress dissent. Some dissenters have disappeared, never to be seen again."

Crys shuddered. The bashrefi was powerful, but it was the women of the First Choir who ensured that she kept that power.

"When people come to us," she continued, "they no longer seek blessings. They ask for curses, and many of these curses are effective. I do not believe the Darcliff Temple is still the home of Lashrefi. I believe most of the so-called taishrefis are actually serving Shakredo."

Crys let the vile name hang in the air like smoke from charred feathers.

Gwenshi looked confused. "What's Shakredo?" she asked.

"Shakredo is Lashrefi's bane," Crys answered. "The demon of misfortune."

"Demon worshippers?" Gwenshi asked. "In Darcliff?"

"I fear it is so."

"And you want *us* to help you fight them?" she asked.

Crys nodded. "I do."

Gwenshi seized her husband's hand. "Vingo, isn't that amazing?"

Vinnagon's dark red face wrinkled into a scowl. "It's preposterous."

Gwenshi's eyebrows folded into a worried frown. "What do you mean?"

Vinnagon said, "Captain Brekko has fourteen men on duty at all times, with another fourteen awake and dressed for combat. The bashrefi and the First Choir have powers beyond our ken. Lashrefite men—even the warriors—cringe beneath the gaze of any woman who names herself taishrefi, as you just now saw. The three of us are not going to bring down that temple."

"But Vingo—"

"Woman, this is not a thing for discussion. You and I will head lithward for Mazibo. Taishrefi Crystal, if you need the protection of my blade, you may travel with us for as long as you wish. I intend to take my wife as far from Darcliff as I can."

"But Vingo, if they really are serving this Shakredo demon—"

"Then they are insane, and the only wise course of action is to leave them to their insanity."

There was some measure of truth in his words. But Crys could not run from Lashrefi's calling. And she could not afford to let her allies run away, either.

"Vinnagon," Crys said, "will you answer one question?"

"What?" he growled.

"Why did you let me go?"

"Because drowning you in the river would have been wrong."

The reply came without hesitation. Clearly, this was a man with confidence in his righteousness. She could use that.

She asked, "And now you think fighting the temple is wrong?"

"Not wrong," Vinnagon said. "But foolish."

"More foolish than throwing away your entire career just because you got a little squeamish about following one order?"

"But that was—" He shook his head. "I thought the captain would understand. I thought he would see things my way, perhaps stand up to those women, make them start dealing honorably. But ..."

"But he didn't," Crys said.

"No," Vinnagon said, voice shaking.

"Instead he called you a traitor," Crys said, pushing her advantage.

Vinnagon shook his head. "No. No, he just said there was nothing he could do, and he gave me a head start."

"A head start?"

Vinnagon nodded. "He told me to run. To get as far from Darcliff as I could."

Ah, so that was it. Vinnagon was still following orders.

Crys put a hand on his hairy red arm. "Do you think that's the right thing to do?" she asked. "Do you think the deities want you to run from the demon worshippers?"

Vinnagon looked at the ground and shook his head. "No," he said. "Kashram created men to fight."

Crys said no more. Vinnagon now saw his duty clearly. She was certain he would not turn away from it.

Four Years Earlier:
Marshwind

THE BASHREFI WAS DEAD. Her corpse lay open to the sky on the ledge at the base of the temple steps. Under the gaze of the temple's taishrefis, sacred crows landed, pecked at her flesh, then flew away toward Heaven.

Marshwind, who had just become the oldest taishrefi at Darcliff Temple, led the taishrefis in singing the funeral song. She sang with joy and confidence, knowing that Lashrefi was listening. Of course, Lashrefi was always listening, but in this moment, Marshwind could feel the Goddess's presence blowing through her soul.

As the singers reached another chorus, a gust of wind struck the cliff and startled the remaining crows into flight. They took off into the wind, circled back overhead, and climbed into the bright, blue sky. As Marshwind finished the chorus, she knew that the bashrefi's soul had risen to Heaven.

The gust of wind relented. A black feather drifted down. On an impulse, Marshwind opened her hand, and the dancing plume landed on her palm.

The taishrefis standing beside her gazed at it in wonder. Even Marshwind was amazed. She knew that Lashrefi favored her, but she had not expected the Goddess to show her favor so blatantly.

That funeral was the first ritual over which Marshwind had to preside. The second ritual was the dice game that would determine the new bashrefi.

After seeing the sacred feather land in Marshwind's hand, some taishrefis laughed and said that the dice game was now pointless, but they were only jesting. Ceremonies were important, even when everyone knew who would win.

Marshwind's seniority gave her the responsibility of choosing the game, and she chose whither-go-I. The next day, all the women of the temple assembled in the grand worship hall. Those who wished to play sat on the floor around the gilded game board.

Once everyone was ready, Marshwind collected each woman's die-of-the-heavens and dropped them all into a deep wooden cup. She resumed her seat and asked Lashrefi to bless their ceremony.

Then she turned to the woman on her left and asked "Whither blows the wind?"

Taishrefi Sunlark, who was too young to be a good bashrefi and not yet wise enough to realize it, answered, "Sunward."

Marshwind smiled and shook the dice. "The wind blows sunward. Whither go I? May Lashrefi guide us."

She spilled the dice onto the board. Sunlark's die showed sunaway, which meant she was out of the game. Marshwind spread out the other dice to the other points of the compass, according to the symbols rolled. Marshwind's own die was the only one that showed sunward—a fact irrelevant to the rules but full of portent. Lashrefi wanted Marshwind to win.

The others took turns choosing the direction. Marshwind rolled the dice for them. Any woman whose die showed the opposite direction picked up her die and left the circle.

After a few rounds, the women began to notice that Marshwind's die always matched the chosen direction. No one was surprised. Marshwind remained serene as the other taishrefis' dice removed them from the game.

When there were only five players left, the choice of direction fell to Wintersmoke, the taishrefi from the hard-luck town of Clayhill. Wintersmoke was old enough to be bashrefi, but Marshwind thought she lacked compassion. Wintersmoke laughed at others' faults and misfortunes. Her smile held a twist of cruelty. It was surprising that she was still in the game.

"Whither blows the wind?" Marshwind asked.

"Lithward," suggested Wintersmoke.

"The wind blows lithward. Whither go I? May Lashrefi guide us."

Marshwind tossed the dice. Her own die landed lithward atop Wintersmoke's. Marshwind picked hers up expecting to see Wintersmoke's showing lithaway, but it showed moonward, which meant that Wintersmoke was still in the game.

In fact, all five of them were still in the game, for no die showed the forbidden direction.

As Marshwind moved the dice to their places on the game board, Sunlark said, "That one showed lithaway."

"Which one?" Marshwind asked.

"The first one you picked up. It did not land showing lithward. It showed lithaway."

The die in question was Marshwind's own.

"It most certainly did not show lithaway," Marshwind said. Sunlark was just trying to cause trouble. Probably she resented being the first one removed from the game.

The seneschal—a stern woman who took her ceremonial sword much too seriously—said, "I also thought it showed lithaway when it landed."

Then everyone began talking at once. Some insisted it had shown lithward, others could remember only that it had landed atop another die. While they argued, Marshwind found her composure and gestured for them to quiet themselves.

"The easy way to settle this is to roll the die again," she said.

Before anyone could object, she picked up her die, dropped it into the cup, and rolled it onto the table, certain that it would show lithward again and convince them all that she still had the favor of Lashrefi.

Her die showed lithaway.

"That doesn't count," someone said. "She forgot to ask for Lashrefi's blessing."

"The asking is just a formality," said another. "The roll must count."

Voices rose around her. Women started side-arguments over the original roll.

Marshwind stared numbly at the *lithaway* symbol. She had rolled it. And a worthy taishrefi would not have forgotten to ask for Lashrefi's blessing.

Marshwind picked her die off the board and rose to her feet. Voices quieted as she went to stand outside the circle.

The remaining women finished the game. Wintersmoke won.

Wintersmoke became the new bashrefi.

Two months passed before Marshwind realized that Lashrefi was not the only supernatural being who could affect dice games. She began to suspect that Wintersmoke's victory had not been the will of Lashrefi.

She went to confront Bashrefi Wintersmoke, but on the way, she met the Holy Seneschal. Marshwind suspected that the seneschal served Shakredo as well. She said as much, hoping to startle the woman into admitting her guilt.

The seneschal was a woman of action. She admitted her guilt by pushing Marshwind down the stairs.

Lashrefi took Marshwind's soul immediately to Heaven.

The 28th of Bluemonth,
Evening

AT NIGHTFALL, they left the wood and traveled cross country. Vinnagon expected Gwenshi to complain about her bare feet, but she remained cheerful—possibly just to spite him.

The moon was low, and Taishrefi Crystal knew the terrain well enough to keep them in shadow. As they drew near the river, the moon went down, which suited Vinnagon just fine. In starlight, they were much less likely to be seen.

Taishrefi Crystal left her horse at a farm some distance upstream from Darcliff and Clifford, and that was where they decided to attempt a crossing.

Vinnagon expected this maneuver to be simple: He could use his clothing to bundle his boots and forearm guards, tie the bundle to his scabbard, and keep everything on top of a log as he kicked his way across the river. He had already accomplished this once, and presumably the taishrefi had, too.

It would be inappropriate for them to cross together, even in darkness, but this problem was easily solved by letting the taishrefi cross first.

"All right, she's in," Gwenshi said. She slipped her dress off over her head.

Vinnagon began unlacing his trousers. "We need a frost to kill off the damn gnats," he said.

"We're a long way from a frost," Gwenshi said as she wrapped her knives up in her dress. In the starlight, her skin was as dark as the vegetation, and Vinnagon could barely discern her silhouette. Still, it was a good silhouette. He wished he could take her back to the shack.

Vinnagon made his own bundle and set it atop his log. They pushed out into the water, Vinnagon following Gwenshi's bobbing head. The taishrefi should be somewhere out in the middle by now.

The Dothedarl was still warm from the day's heat. It was far nicer than being eaten by gnats. Vinnagon propelled his log with steady kicks, and after a time, it seemed that the opposite bank might be drawing nearer.

Gwenshi was swimming well, easily staying ahead of him—which was good, because he wanted to watch out for her. They were in the middle of the river, and the current seemed swifter.

Gwenshi turned her head and called, "Vingo, beware the tree."

Tree? What tree? Vinnagon was far from either bank.

And then he saw the dark shadow drifting gently into his field of vision. A massive, leafless, branching chunk of dead wood was floating down toward them.

Vinnagon stopped kicking, trying to keep himself out of the swiftest part of the current while the tree passed by, but an eddy spun his log. The current grabbed his legs, drawing him in.

The underside of the tree caught on something, and the tree began to roll. Branches like giant talons descended on Vinnagon's back. They struck and pulled him under.

* * *

Gwenshi watched the rolling tree pass between her and her husband.

"Vingo?" she called. "Are you all right?"

The liquid ripples and eddies were louder in the current, but not so loud as to drown out a man's voice. Why didn't he answer?

Gwenshi couldn't see Crystal anywhere. Perhaps the Stripedwoman was already out of the water. Regardless, she was too far away to help.

Gwenshi spun her log around and kicked back toward the

swift current. A rippling wake indicated that the tree was moving slower than the rest of the river. Perhaps its long, scrabbling branches were dragging along the riverbed.

"Vingo?"

Still no reply.

The tree had him. That was all Gwenshi could think of. It must be the tree.

Unless he was playing a joke, to get even with her for the mushrooms. Oh, she wished it were so! But Vinnagon did not joke.

As Gwenshi kicked nearer, an underwater branch got snagged on the river bottom and the great trunk swung around. She glimpsed a hollow darkness inside.

Gwenshi reached out and grabbed the splintered end. The current bounced her log against it, scraping her bare chest. Well, she didn't need the log anymore. She had this huge tree to keep her afloat. Gwenshi stuffed her bundle into the hollow of the tree and clambered onto it.

"Vingo?"

In the darkness, the water was as opaque as a winter cloak. Her husband could be a thumbwidth below the surface and she wouldn't see him. Gwenshi crawled along the trunk, peering at the water, looking for any bump or ripple that might be Vinnagon's body breaking the surface.

Kashram, give him strength, she prayed. How long had he been under?

From somewhere among the branches came a tiny, wet cough—a sound so weak that Gwenshi could scarcely believe it might come from her powerful, muscular man.

But it had to be him. And Gwenshi had to find him before those pitiful coughs ceased.

She rose to her feet and stepped swiftly toward the sound. The tree was still spinning its slow spin. The bark felt loose under her bare toes, but beneath that was solid wood that bobbed only a little as she glided along its length.

No clothes meant no skirt to get tangled in the branches.

Gwenshi twined her way between them, her gaze fixed on the place the coughs had come from … but that "place" was now a couple hundred feet upstream. Her man could be anywhere now.

No. Not anywhere. He was right there. That was his nose—his nose and the curve of a cheek barely above the surface of the river.

"Hang on, Vingo!"

Gwenshi stepped out onto a branch and the tree began to roll. Vinnagon's nose submerged.

Gwenshi grasped another branch for balance. Her ankles dipped into the water. She lifted her legs and swung herself out to where she had last seen her husband.

Her rump smacked the water. A wet branch jiggled along her spine. Then she was chest-deep in the river surrounded by branches reaching out into the darkness.

To stay afloat, she kicked her legs, and her toes pushed into pliant skin, firm muscle. All around her, the branches were moving, rolling back to where they had been before she had put her weight on them, and as they did so, Vinnagon's body rose, his face once more breaking the surface.

This time there was no wet cough. He rose, then dipped under again as the branches bobbed.

Gwenshi grasped him under the arms and ran her feet down his naked legs. One leg floated free. The other was caught.

Gwenshi's head went under as her toes worked their way down—down to the ankle, where they encountered one of the tree's numerous branches. Vinnagon's ankle was caught in a fork, the buoyancy of his body wedging his anklebones into the branch's grasp.

She pulled herself farther under the water's surface. Vinnagon's chest convulsed against her face—another cough. So he wasn't dead yet.

She hooked her instep underneath the fork that held his ankle. She put her other foot on his shin. Then, praying that he could survive one more dunking, she grasped his shoulders and pulled him downward.

With one foot, she pushed on Vinnagon's leg. With the other, she pulled the clinging branch upward. Vinnagon's anklebone popped free of the fork.

With Vinnagon's leg freed, Gwenshi kicked to push them back to the surface. As her face met air, she automatically tilted her head back and drew in a breath.

That damn tree had tried to kill her husband! Well, now it would help her save him. She reached up and grabbed a branch. Holding Vinnagon with her legs so he would not get away, she adjusted her position to slip her other arm under his. Then she pulled until both their heads were above the surface.

Her sinuses burned from the water that had been forced into her nose during her struggles. Only one ear cleared; the other remained muffled.

But at least she was breathing. Her husband wasn't moving.

"Vingo. Breathe!"

His head flopped limply against her shoulder. Water dribbled from his nose and mouth.

"Damn it, I just saved your life! Don't you *dare* die now."

Vinnagon's throat emitted a feeble little gurgle.

Then he gave a cough that was more like a heave. Water trickled from his mouth onto her shoulder. And then he was choking and coughing and gasping and making all the other satisfying sounds that are made by a man who has just been saved from drowning.

Gwenshi felt proud—and relieved. And she wondered how long she would have to hold him here like this because her arms were beginning to ache.

Vinnagon gave a little moan, and his grip tightened on her in a way that made her arms ache more. His eyes opened, bright in the darkness of his twilit face.

"I told you to beware the tree," she said.

Vinnagon coughed and shook his head.

* * *

Vinnagon sat shivering in the grass, rubbing his skin to discourage the bugs that were trying to suck him dry. As distraction from his misery, he was trying to tell his wife his story:

"I was thinking, *My father's sword; I can't lose the sword.* And then I remember little else, except that it was quiet and peaceful."

Gwenshi shook her head, wet locks plastered to her cheeks. "When I finally got you loose, you were *too* peaceful."

"Hm," Vinnagon acknowledged.

"Oh, Vingo, I thought I'd lost you!"

"But you did not," he said. He was strong enough to deal with a little water in his lungs. He had just been confused, that was all. Who expected trees to come floating down the river? Especially in autumn!

"Well, I'm glad you're all right," she said, and she put an arm around him.

Had they been at home, this would have been quite pleasant. But he was sitting on itchy grass being eaten by bugs, and Gwenshi was wearing a cold, wet dress. It had gotten soaked when she'd retrieved it from the hollow of the tree.

"I've got to get some clothes," he said. *And boots, and forearm guards,* he added to himself. Actually, what he really wanted was his father's sword back. He would go naked for the rest of his life if he could just get that sword.

Well, perhaps not. He would look rather silly. But still ...

"What are you doing?" he asked.

"Nothing," Gwenshi said. "Just ... got a bug in my eye."

She wiped the back of her hand across her face.

"Oh, tell me you aren't crying," he said.

"I'm not," she lied. "I just— Oh, Vingo, I didn't realize I could lose you."

I didn't realize you cared, he thought.

He said, "You were fine with me risking my life on that neck-breaking horse this morning. You were fine with me drawing my blade against four bladesmen in the streets of Camptown."

Gwenshi shrugged. "That was fun," she said. "This was serious."

Fun? She thought being a fugitive was fun?

"So have you changed your mind about helping Taishrefi Crystal?" he asked.

"No," she said. "I understand it's something you have to do."

"But it is not something *you* have to do," he said. "I can find someone to take you in."

"I don't *want* to be taken in." She pushed away from him and stood up. "I want to help Crystal defeat those evil women."

"They are the Holy Council and First Choir of the Darcliff Temple," Vinnagon said. "These aren't women you can just challenge to a knife fight."

"So how will *you* defeat them?" Gwenshi asked. "You don't even have a knife."

"I do not know what I can do," Vinnagon said. "Perhaps nothing. Perhaps they will capture me and execute me. That is why I asked you to claim succor from Harl."

"And that's why I won't leave you. You might need my help."

"I do not need your help."

"Vinnagon, I think we have just proven that sometimes you *do* need my help."

"That was a freak accident."

"What if you have another?"

Vinnagon didn't answer. The way his luck had been going lately, that was entirely possible.

"Vinnagon, there's no shame in needing help."

"I did not say there was."

"No, but you can't bring yourself to say, 'Thank you.'"

"What?"

"I saved your life, Vingo. And because I'm a woman, you're ashamed to admit it."

"Ashamed?" She knew nothing! "Let me tell you about shame, woman. I'm ashamed I lost my sword. I'm ashamed I couldn't get my wife to obey one simple order that would have kept her safe at home. I'm ashamed I quit my captain."

"Are you ashamed you didn't drown me?" Taishrefi Crystal's voice came from the trees, calm and quiet. Vinnagon had not heard her approach.

"No," he said, his voice sounding smaller than he would have liked. "I am not ashamed of that."

"But he is a little embarrassed by you seeing him naked," Gwenshi added.

"Ah," said the taishrefi. "I apologize. I thought you would be dressed by now. I assure you I have seen nothing."

"Good," said Gwenshi. Her voice held no threat, but her tone made clear what she thought of other women peeping at her man.

"I shall turn my back," the taishrefi offered. "Please tell me when you are ready to travel."

"Vingo lost his clothes in the river," Gwenshi said.

"Ah," said the taishrefi. "That could make it difficult for us to walk into Darcliff unnoticed."

* * *

Crys found a sleeping place a discreet distance away from the Kashramite couple. The gnats were annoying this close to the river, but the Kashramites would have to find a way to deal with that themselves.

They were a strange couple. She did not know any Kashramite women, but she had expected them to be timid. She had heard they were treated as property of the men, that fathers would arrange marriages as though trading horses. Gwenshi seemed too bold to have ever allowed herself to be some man's property.

Crys did not understand why Gwenshi tolerated Vinnagon's

rudeness. Why, he hardly even called her by name! She was just "woman" to him. Any man who spoke to Crys that way would find his possessions on the doorstep, that was certain.

But Beetle would never speak to her that way. The Kashramites were just strange.

They were strange, but they were hers. Lashrefi had brought them to her, and as she fell asleep, Crys prayed that Lashrefi would show her how to put them to good use.

* * *

It was still dark when Crys awoke. The stars were still out and the many facets of the lith sparkled in the sky beyond the canopy of trees.

The lith was sparkly, but not bright. That was not what had awakened her. No, she had been awakened by wagon wheels rumbling on the road.

Farmers sometimes rose early to get their goods to market on time, but this wagon would reach Darcliff well before sunrise. It was suspicious.

It was suspicious, and it was providential. The wagon could be something that no one was supposed to see. Crys had a feeling that she needed to discover what that was.

Trusting the noise of the wagon wheels on the gravel road to mask her footsteps, she moved through the trees. By the time she reached the edge of the road, the wagon had moved past, but she saw it had a two-horse team, a driver, and four guards.

It couldn't go very fast. She followed its sound, staying out of sight among the trees.

Her steps slowed as she neared the place where Vinnagon had let her out of the crate. The wagon stopped.

What were they doing? Was it bodies they carried? Was it helpless young women, bound and stacked like logs, prepared for disposal in the Dothedarl?

If so, what could she do for them? By herself—even with the aid of Lashrefi—she was no match for four armed guards.

They spoke in the accents of Kashramites—male voices giving terse orders. No one seemed to be coming toward the river. Trusting in her Flamebringer moccasins to keep her steps quiet, Crys approached the unseen wagon.

The wagon started up again. The rumble of the wheels masked her steps as she hurried to the road.

She caught sight of the wagon before it disappeared around the corner. It had only a driver now.

A clatter of rocks told her where the other four had gone. They were climbing the hidden trail up to the back entrance to the caverns, carrying bundles of something.

Crys made sure she had counted four of them before she approached the foot of the trail. Stashed behind a tree was a heap that had been left for the second trip. She reached down to test by feel what her eyes could scarcely discern in the starlight. It was buckskin clothing—the type worn by her grandmother's people.

How will people know they are Flamebringer clothings? The question Crys had overheard now made sense. This was the clothing Rathi had been speaking of—buckskin trousers, tunics, and moccasins—clothing worn by nomadic Lashrefites.

Crys still did not know why the clothing was being smuggled into the temple, nor what sort of plan would require it. But she did know that Lashrefi had given her a great boon by waking her as the wagon passed.

Praying to Lashrefi that they would not be missed, Crys took a pair of trousers, a tunic, and two sets of moccasins. Then she hurried away.

Three Years Earlier:
Butterfly

THE TEMPLE OF DARCLIFF had not been built. Rather, it had been carved from the limestone cliff. Its roof and triangular pediment jutted proudly from the rock, supported by pillars that were true monoliths. The temple's two wings receded into the embrace of the cliff, giving the impression that the building was still in the process of emerging.

The architects had designed the temple with no facade. People entered the grand worship hall without passing through any doors. When the moon was up, its light would pour into the hall, unobstructed by any walls.

Of course, in winter, the grand worship hall could be quite cold. When the air was frosty, the taishrefis and initiates remained in the wings, which were protected by walls of rock and thus easier to heat.

Bashrefi Wintersmoke said this was impractical. She proposed to wall off the front of the temple, leaving only a small entrance. She assured the taishrefis that the temple would remain doorless. The grand hall would always be open to the townspeople—even more so, she said, for the new wall would make it comfortable to use the grand hall all winter long.

The taishrefis were divided on the issue. Some argued that the wall would block out the light. Others argued that they had to use candles in the wings already, so why was it a problem in the grand hall?

In the end, the bashrefi got her way and the wall went up.

"It's not right," said Taishrefi Butterfly one morning in the temple dining hall. "The wall shuts out Lashrefi's clean wind, and the grand hall is always full of torch smoke now."

No one agreed with her. Her fellow diners became very interested in their porridge. And that was when Taishrefi Butterfly realized that the women who had opposed the wall had all been reassigned to villages on the periphery of the province.

The next morning, Taishrefi Butterfly herself was sent away. She never reached her new assignment.

The bashrefi told the temple that Butterfly had been killed by bandits. The temple would need to hire more bladesmen to adequately patrol the province's roads.

By tradition, road patrol was a task for the mayors' militias, but no one disagreed with the bashrefi. They had learned that she always got her way.

The 29th of Bluemonth,
Morning

LIMESTONE CLIFFS topped with oak and evergreens pressed the town of Darcliff against the brown river. Unlike the wooden shacks of Camptown, the buildings of Darcliff were whitewashed daub-and-wattle, decorated with eye-bending stripes. Traditional shops used jagged black zigzags. On newer buildings, black stripes branched and curved. Wealthier householders allowed themselves colors—rust, ocher, even blue.

Lashrefites enjoyed frivolous ornamentation. Vinnagon did not.

Especially not on his clothing. The trousers the taishrefi had given him had leather fringes along the outer seam. He wished more of that leather had been used to make the legs and seat. The trousers were tight.

Behind him, Gwenshi murmured, "You need to loosen your stride, walk more naturally."

Taishrefi Crystal glanced at him, but said nothing.

"I'm staying alert for danger," Vinnagon said over his shoulder. "Bladesmen always walk this way."

"But you aren't supposed to be a bladesman," Gwenshi said. "You're supposed to be from out of town, looking for work."

It was not a very good story. Travelers on this road were unusual, except for local farmers and temple tax collectors. Any Kashramite from out of town would arrive by boat.

"I need to loosen up your clothes a bit," Gwenshi said. "I reckon I'll have some time while we're visiting Crystal's slyman."

"I beg your pardon?" said Taishrefi Crystal. "My what?"

"Your slyman," Gwenshi said. "The man you visit on the sly."

"I don't visit Beetle 'on the sly,'" the taishrefi protested. It was the first time Vinnagon had seen her flustered. "There's nothing wrong with having a ... friend."

"Hm," Gwenshi said. "Man friend. Sounds like a slyman to me."

Vinnagon saw no need to delve into the exact nature of the relationship between this man and Taishrefi Crystal. He had a more important concern.

"How far is it to his house?" he asked.

"His shop is on the other end of town," the taishrefi said. "And legally, it is his mother's house."

"He lives with his mother?" Gwenshi asked.

"No. He lives alone, but she owns the house. Among our people, men do not own houses."

"Why not?" Gwenshi asked.

"Men own livestock," the taishrefi said. "Women own houses. It is just our way."

"Do you own a house?"

"No I live— I used to live up there." The taishrefi gazed up at the temple built into the cliff overlooking the town.

Vinnagon felt a prickling between his shoulder blades, and it wasn't just the tightness of his tunic. Being in sight of the temple made him uneasy, even though he knew that a man on the streets of town was unrecognizable from the temple steps. Usually. It depended on whether the man had a funny walk.

Vinnagon tried to loosen his stride, walk more naturally.

Gwenshi said, "Hey, there's someone I know."

Vinnagon turned, but Gwenshi wasn't looking at anyone. She was standing in front of the notice board at the intersection they had reached. Lashrefites were fond of painting letters on things and nailing them to boards. On this board, amid the scraps of wood and pieces of poorly tanned squirrel hide, a square of pale vellum depicted two faces. One had been stained red by what looked to be dried blood. The other depicted a white-haired woman with three black stripes, two of them coming down vertically across her eyelids.

"That's us!" said Taishrefi Crystal.

"Don't be silly," said Gwenshi. "That doesn't look anything like Vingo. But the other one ..." She surveyed the taishrefi appraisingly.

Taishrefi Crystal yanked the notice off the board. One of the tiny nails went flying into the street.

"This is most unfortunate," she said.

"What does it say?" Vinnagon asked. All taishrefis knew how to read letters.

"It says, ah ..." She gave Gwenshi a guilty glance.

Gwenshi raised her eyebrows.

"It says that we ran away from the temple to, ah, pursue a romantic relationship."

"With each other?" Vinnagon asked.

"Yes," the taishrefi said, with obvious distaste.

"Aw, why didn't you tell me?" Gwenshi asked.

"It is not true, woman."

"A little red striped baby would be cute," Gwenshi said. "I hope it's twins."

The taishrefi looked appalled.

"Woman, they are creations of a different god," Vinnagon said. "We can't breed with them."

Gwenshi shrugged. "You and I can't breed with each other, either, but we still enjoy trying."

Vinnagon stared at her. He couldn't believe she had just said that.

"Close your mouth," Gwenshi said. "The flies will get in."

"Gwenshi," the taishrefi said, "the thing of import here is that Vinnagon and I have been accused of a crime against Lashrefi. Anyone who recognizes us has an obligation to report us to the temple."

"Oh," said Gwenshi. "And the punishment is execution or something?"

"It would probably be forced labor if we were found guilty," the taishrefi said, "but we would not live to see trial. The temple wants us dead."

"So this doesn't really change anything," Gwenshi said. "We knew the job would be dangerous when we agreed to it."

Vinnagon opened his mouth to tell her that this was not her "job", that he was keeping her close so he could protect her until he found a safe place for her. But the words never came, for he caught sight of Malk and Shangrel coming up the street.

"Quickly," he said, giving the women a push to move them around the corner out of sight of the two guards.

The taishrefi looked to him for an explanation.

"Bladesmen," Vinnagon said. "I believe they are off duty, but that would not prevent them from trying to capture us."

"Very well," said the taishrefi. "Let us be moving, then."

"They will see us if we stay on this street," Vinnagon said. "We should cut through that alley."

The taishrefi agreed. Vinnagon led the way.

They came out of the alley one street closer to the cliff. "We do not want to get too close to the temple," the taishrefi warned. "Let us stay on this street and trust to Lashrefi that the bladesmen will not come this way."

"Very well," Vinnagon said.

They had not gone twenty steps when a wagon came around the corner one block ahead of them. It was flanked by four people on horseback. Vinnagon recognized the lead rider as the Holy Seneschal.

"The tax wagon!" he said.

"Unfortunate," said the taishrefi. "Let us take that side street. And pray they do not notice us."

From overhead came a flapping of great wings. Vinnagon looked up to see a pair of talons descending toward his eyes.

Vinnagon gave a shout and raised an arm to ward off the huge bird. Dark feathers filled his vision. A talon punctured his arm where his forearm guard should have been. With his other hand, he reached for his sword, but it was not there.

"Hey! Get away from him!" Gwenshi beat at the thing with her small, red fists.

Vinnagon glimpsed a malevolent eye in a grotesquely featherless head. Then the cruel beak struck at his nose.

"Ah!" he cried, flailing with his sword arm.

The bird rose. Wind from the wings buffeted his hair, and a claw like a blunt knife scored his scalp.

"What is that?" Gwenshi asked as the bird circled higher.

"A vulture," said the taishrefi in shock.

"It is now surely time to try a different street," Gwenshi said, nodding at the tax wagon.

The four-rider escort had abandoned the wagon and was trotting toward them.

Taishrefi Crystal bolted down the side street. Vinnagon and Gwenshi followed her.

"The fugitives!" cried the seneschal. "After them!"

Vinnagon had never much cared for the seneschal, but now he found her high, sweet voice particularly annoying.

At the intersection, Taishrefi Crystal turned away from the street where Malk and Shangrel had been. Good. She was wise, as taishrefis were supposed to be.

Vinnagon glanced the other way to see where the two bladesmen were, and he discovered that they were so close that he could see their eyes widen with recognition.

Vinnagon turned and ran after the women.

Malk shouted, "Stop him!"

The women were good runners. Even though Gwenshi was in a dress, Vinnagon had to sprint hard to catch her.

The sound of hooves galloping on gravel carried down the street. Vinnagon checked over his shoulder. Two riders had negotiated the corner and were gaining speed.

Vinnagon and the women in his protection could not be faster than horses. They needed to use the advantage of agility, make the horses go around more corners.

With a burst of speed, Vinnagon took the lead. "This way," he gasped. He turned hard and slammed his face into the end of a yoke of water buckets carried by a surprised Lashrefite girl.

Vinnagon staggered up the street, blinking tears from his eyes. Gwenshi's warm, familiar hand grabbed his and encouraged him to keep moving.

"In here!" the taishrefi called.

Gwenshi tugged Vinnagon into a house where they met a stunned family sitting on a bench with steaming bowls of porridge in their laps.

"Blessing of Lashrefi upon you!" the taishrefi called as she climbed out the back window.

Gwenshi dove through the window headfirst. Vinnagon clambered through after her. They were in a backyard garden.

The taishrefi climbed over a fence. Gwenshi took a run at it, stepped atop a pumpkin to gain height, and leapt over. Vinnagon took three strides and stepped on the tines of a rake. The handle popped up and smacked him on his vulture-bitten nose.

With a growl, Vinnagon took the rake in hand. Now he had a weapon!

He followed the women over another garden fence, through a squash patch, and into another stranger's house. This time they interrupted an elderly couple and their grandson in the middle of a dice game.

The taishrefi paused at the door. Outside, a rider galloped past.

Gesturing for quiet, the taishrefi opened the door and stepped outside. Gwenshi and Vinnagon followed.

The street was clear of enemies except for the rider, who was galloping away. The taishrefi pointed toward a side street.

Vinnagon shook his head. He didn't want to go toward the cliff; they could get pinned against it. He turned toward the rider, hoping to stay hidden behind the enemy's back. He gestured for the women to follow him.

At the intersection, Vinnagon crouched low beside the corner of a house and peeked around the corner. A few people were out in the street talking, but he saw no one from the temple.

As he rose from his crouch, a striped face appeared at the window—a young woman with loose hair. She looked from Vinnagon to the taishrefi. Then she turned and ran toward her back door, crying, "They're in the street! Go back to the street!"

Gwenshi and the taishrefi ducked into an alley—toward the cliff again, the foolish women!

Malk stepped out of a nearby house and drew his sword, advancing in a low glide-step. Vinnagon raised the rake. Perhaps he could stall Malk long enough for the women to escape.

Shangrel emerged from the house and drew his blade as well. Vinnagon couldn't win a two-on-one with blades, but the wooden rake gave him a reach advantage. Another advantage was that Malk and Shangrel had no idea what he could do with a rake. But perhaps this was not much of an advantage, because Vinnagon didn't know what he could do, either.

The two bladesmen glided apart—an intelligent tactic. If Vinnagon swung at one, he would expose himself to the other's attack.

Kashram, give me the power to do your will, he prayed.

Malk stepped in and raised his blade to ward off the rake. Vinnagon stepped in to meet Malk's challenge but swung the rake's head to ward off Shangrel. A quick thrust of the handle toward Malk's chin forced Malk to block and spin away.

Shangrel rushed into the gap opened by the thrust, but Vinnagon caught the arc of Shangrel's blade on the tines of the rake. With a quick twist, Vinnagon wrenched the blade from Shangrel's grasp. It fell to the graveled street with a dull clang.

Malk continued with the flow of his evasive spin and extended his blade in a swipe at Vinnagon's leg. Vinnagon lifted his foot, allowing the blade to swish past underneath. He came down hard, driving the butt of his rake handle into Malk's exposed kneecap.

With a shout, Malk collapsed.

Vinnagon dropped the rake and reached for Shangrel's blade where it lay in the street, but Shangrel stomped down on the hilt. In one smooth motion, Shangrel drew his knife and shifted in with a thrust at Vinnagon's abdomen.

Vinnagon blocked the strike, forearm-to-forearm, and stepped inside Shangrel's guard. He drove his forehead into the other man's nose, producing a gristly crunch. Wary of the knife hand, he spun around to the other side and put Shangrel in the only armlock he knew.

"Drop the knife," he said.

He must have done the armlock right, for Shangrel dropped the knife.

Galloping hooves alerted Vinnagon that the rider was coming back. Worse, the seneschal was riding in from the other direction. Vinnagon shoved Shangrel away and ran after the taishrefi and Gwenshi.

They were waiting at the next street. Foolish women! They had stayed to watch him, when they could have been far away by now.

Gwenshi called, "Well fought, Vingo!"

"Run!" he yelled.

They did so. Vinnagon followed them around the corner.

"Don't worry," Gwenshi said. "I can mend your trousers."

For a moment, Vinnagon did not know what she was talking about. Then he became aware of the breeze on his backside. His trousers had split at the seat.

With the seneschal about to come riding around the corner behind him!

"Run faster," he said.

"Go on ahead," Gwenshi said. "We'll be right behind you."

"Woman, if we survive this I will kill you!"

"Breathe now," the taishrefi said. "Argue later."

With a clatter of hooves, a rider cut off the street ahead of them. Behind them, the seneschal had rounded the corner.

Vinnagon slowed, looking for an escape path, but Gwenshi kept running at the rider ahead of them.

"It's nervous," Gwenshi said over her shoulder. "We can spook it."

The taishrefi nodded once and accelerated. Vinnagon had no choice but to follow.

The rider brandished his sword menacingly, but his mount was dancing and scuffing up dust. Even Vinnagon could see that the beast wanted to turn and run, but the rider was doing something with his feet or the reins to keep the horse's head pointed in their general direction.

Gwenshi reached the horse first. The rider tried to position the mount so he could take a swipe at her, but Gwenshi ducked under the horse's jaw and dodged past on the other side.

The horse's head jerked sharply—*Gwenshi must have hold of a rein,* Vinnagon realized—and the rest of the horse turned to follow the head. The taishrefi had to stop in her tracks to avoid the kicking rear legs. The rider lost his balance and managed to stay astride only by flattening himself against the horse's neck and grabbing at the saddle.

"Ki-ki-hai!" Gwenshi shrieked, and the horse bolted away.

"This way!" the taishrefi called, once again turning up a street that led toward the cliff. With the seneschal in pursuit, Vinnagon had no choice but to follow.

"Hide here," Taishrefi Crystal said, opening a garden gate. Vinnagon and Gwenshi ran in and the taishrefi shut the gate.

"Down!" she said, and they all lay flat on the ground at the base of the fence.

A horse galloped past. The seneschal called, "To me!" Her voice disappeared around a corner.

The taishrefi arose and led them over a series of fences until they came to an alley.

"Now we run for the brewer's house," the taishrefi said, "and trust to Lashrefi."

She led them to the corner of the alley. Across the street, striped-skinned Lashrefites sat in the shade of the cliff drinking beer and rolling dice. Hop vines sprawled along a garden fence and climbed trellises on the front of a small daub-and-wattle house set into the cliff.

They crossed the street swiftly.

"Crys!" exclaimed the proprietor.

Taishrefi Crystal raised a hand in greeting and furtively slipped inside. Gwenshi and Vinnagon followed.

The dim interior of the brewhouse was cluttered with crocks. Clearly, service was outside, manufacturing inside. The taishrefi passed a woman stooped over a washing bucket and told her, "Flicker, please tell them we went out through the garden."

Taishrefi Crystal pushed open a door to the outside, but she gestured for Vinnagon and Gwenshi to follow her deeper into the brewhouse.

"Crys, what's going on?" the woman asked.

"Please," the taishrefi said. "We need your help." Then to Vinnagon and Gwenshi: "Come."

They stepped into the next room. It was lit only by a faint glow of hearth coals.

"I ... can't see," Gwenshi said.

"Follow my voice," said Taishrefi Crystal. "But stay quiet."

The taishrefi gave a little grunt and something wooden thunked. A musty smell crept into the room.

"Down these steps," she said.

Vinnagon followed, Gwenshi behind him. He felt her fingers crawl frantically down his arm. He took her hand. The darkness was complete, but Vinnagon could feel that they were descending into a chamber of stone.

At the taishrefi's request, Vinnagon closed the trap door above them. Gwenshi gave a little whimper and squeezed his hand more tightly.

"Woman, it's just a cellar."

"It's dark."

"Gwenshi, Vinnagon, I can't light the candles right now because the seneschal might be able to smell them. I need you two to stay calm and follow me." Stone ground against stone.

"Vinnagon, there is a passage here."

"I know."

"Very well. You go first; we'll keep Gwenshi between us."

"Understood."

It was a hands-and-knees passage, comfortable enough if a man didn't mind not being able to stand up. Gwenshi was so close behind him that he could feel her breath—which reminded him that he needed the seat of his pants mended. The taishrefi entered last and slid a stone that closed off the entrance.

Gwenshi whimpered.

Vinnagon could feel that the passage was square. He could not tell where it ended, but from the echoes of his breath, he could tell that it was not open ahead.

"A door," he said, when he reached it. It felt wooden, and he knew there was a larger opening beyond it.

"The latch is on the top," the taishrefi said, her voice compressed by the stone walls and muffled by Gwenshi's body.

Vinnagon grasped the latch. It jangled like iron. The jangling wasn't a sound; it was just a feeling that vibrated through his arm, overriding his supernatural awareness of the stone around him. He drew the latch and let it go as the door swung away.

Different air here—wetter, mustier, and yet it smelled better, more alive.

Vinnagon crawled into a large room. It was round, though not perfectly circular. The ceiling was a low dome, barely high enough to stand under. A ledge of stone ran around the perimeter; it was the perfect height and width for a bench. All this Vinnagon saw without using his eyes. There was no light.

Gwenshi crawled out of the passage and pressed herself against him. Taishrefi Crystal came last. The echoes in the room changed as she shut the wooden door.

"Please stay quiet and still," she said. "The brewers will let us know when our enemies have gone."

The bolt slid back into place, sealing them in the chamber. Against Vinnagon's ribs, Gwenshi shuddered.

* * *

The strength of his muscular arm around her shoulders and the smell of his sweat were the only things that made the darkness bearable. All Gwenshi could hear were her own breaths and her heartbeat thudding in her ears.

She thought, *Now he'll think I'm a weak little girl.* But she wasn't. She would gladly have gone back out to the street to face those men who wanted to imprison her husband. She would gladly have matched knives with that Stripedwoman on the horse. Instead she had to sit here trapped in the dark like a mouse under a bowl, waiting to see what would happen.

That damn Crystal! It was all right for *her* to run and hide, but she should have let Gwenshi and Vinnagon fight it out. They could win. Vingo had defeated two armed men using only a rake!

Gwenshi let her anger and the smell of Vinnagon's sweat push down her panic. She laid her head on his shoulder. He was warm and comforting, though he probably didn't know it.

Poor Vingo. He didn't enjoy being a fugitive, did he? But he couldn't drown a woman in a box just because some other woman told him to. He was Arvethidrel. He had honor.

As Gwenshi calmed, she became aware of the third person in the room. Crystal sat not far away, taking short, tense breaths.

Gwenshi wanted to say something, but they were supposed to be hiding. She kept quiet, listening for whatever Crystal was listening for.

This chamber must be deep in the rock, she thought. Fifteen or twenty patrons were outside the brewhouse, men on horseback were riding up and down the streets, but Gwenshi could hear nothing except herself, Crystal, and Vinnagon.

In the darkness, Gwenshi had no way to tell time. Even

after she was certain that their pursuers had given up and gone about their business, Vinnagon and Crystal remained quiet and still.

Gwenshi was about to ask if it was safe to talk when they heard the grinding of stone on stone.

Vinnagon's body grew tense. Crystal sucked in a tiny gasp and stopped breathing. Gwenshi's ears buzzed in the silence.

Was someone coming through the passage? She could hear nothing. Gwenshi wanted to put her ear to the wooden door, but she knew she couldn't move without making noise.

That was probably what the Stripedwoman was doing— listening at the door.

Scritch, scritch, scritch. A fingernail against the wood. Then silence.

They waited. Nothing happened.

Then came that distant sound of stone grinding on stone, sliding into place with finality.

Crystal's clothing rustled. The door's bolt slid open with a gentle pop. Three sides of a square appeared in the darkness— just three yellow lines floating in air. Then the door opened and Gwenshi could see Crystal's face lit by the warm yellow glow of a tallow candle.

Crystal brought the precious light inside and placed it on a low table in the center of the room. Next, Crystal brought in a small linen bundle. Then she closed the door and latched it.

It was a relief to see that the bolt was accessible from either side. They could get out whenever they wanted.

Crystal unwrapped the bundle. It held bread and cheese.

"I believe this means we are safe for the moment," she said, breaking the loaf into three pieces.

Gwenshi and Vinnagon took their share.

"You are known to these people?" Vinnagon asked.

"Yes," Crystal said. "They are Beetle's parents. Thank Lashrefi that we arrived here. I knew they would be able to hide us."

"Is this a meeting room?" Vinnagon asked.

"It is. Or at least, it was, long ago, when the Bargainkeepers felt compelled to meet in secret."

"Who are the Bargainkeepers?" Gwenshi asked.

"A group of Yolimists." Crystal did not sound happy about that.

"Ah, that explains the height of the passage," Vinnagon said.

Crystal shook her head. "Not 'Yolimites'. Yolimists. Lashrefites who embrace philosophies of Yolim."

Gwenshi tried to puzzle this out. "You mean Stripedfolk who serve the god of wealth instead of the goddess of luck?"

"Yes," said Crystal. "And no. The Bargainkeepers honor Lashrefi and seek entry into her heaven, but they believe very strongly in the piety of keeping one's word. So we say that their philosophy is Yolimist."

"Does this have anything to do with those Stripedfolk traders who wear a dragon brooch?" Gwenshi asked. They showed up at the Darcliff market occasionally. They were reputed to be the most honest of merchants.

"Yes," said Crystal. "Most of those traders are Bargain-keepers. Although a few who wear the dragon brooch are actually charlatans abusing the Bargainkeepers' good rep-utation."

"So what do dragons have to do with oaths?" Gwenshi asked. She took a bite of the bread. It was good, but she wished the brewer had brought some mugs of beer to go with it.

"When the dragons came into the world," Crystal said, "there was one who sought to rule along the Dothedarl. She convinced a group of villages that they should serve her instead of Lashrefi. The taishrefis opposed this dragon, of course, but their hold over the people was weak, and terror of the dragon was strong.

"Even at that early time, Yardwen was far larger than just a few villages. The taishrefis called upon their sisters all along the Dothedarl, and those taishrefis gathered an army of warriors to drive the dragon from Lashrefite lands—and to punish the dragon's servants.

"At that time, the world held many dragons, and a second dragon came to the Dothedarl and visited villages on the edge of the evil dragon's territory. These villages did not know about the taishrefis' army, so they made a bargain with this new dragon that if she would slay the tyrant, they would allow her to live on the Dothedarl in peace."

Crystal pinched off a bit of the cheese, contemplative. "I do not know what happened next," she admitted. "The tyrannical dragon was defeated somehow. We taishrefis say it was our army that defeated the dragon. We say that this army created Yardwen, in fact, for it taught us to work together as one state.

"But the Bargainkeepers claim that the army's intervention was pointless. They say the evil dragon was defeated by this second dragon, who expected our people to keep their word."

"Only you didn't," Gwenshi said. Leastways, if there was a dragon living on the Dothedarl, she thought she would have noticed.

Crystal shook her head. "We didn't. The taishrefis refused to allow the helpful dragon to remain on the Dothedarl. So the dragon left. But a handful of people remembered their bargain, and they vowed to keep their word."

"By meeting in dark cellars?" Gwenshi asked.

The Stripedwoman shrugged. "The Temple of Darcliff has always been strong. Until about a hundred years ago, all other religions were illegal here."

"So they practiced their religion in secret," Gwenshi said.

"Just so," said Crystal.

Gwenshi chewed her bread thoughtfully. It was a pretty good story, she decided. "So what's this room used for now?" she asked.

"Hiding us," Crystal said. "Beetle showed it to me as a curiosity once. The Bargainkeepers don't meet here anymore … I think. I haven't asked."

"How long do we have to stay here?" Gwenshi asked.

"Not long," said Crystal.

Good, thought Gwenshi.

"At least," Crystal added, "I hope we will not be here long. I don't want Beetle's parents involved in this. We are fortunate to have escaped, and I would not like to see our good fortune become their bad fortune."

"The tax-collecting wagon was bad fortune," Vinnagon said. "It is not usually in Darcliff this late in the day."

Gwenshi said, "The stroke of bad luck was that giant bird flying at your head."

Crystal frowned at Vinnagon. "You have had a lot of bad luck, haven't you?"

Vinnagon shifted uncomfortably, and Gwenshi remembered the rip in the seam of his pants.

"I have," he said.

"When did it start?" Crystal asked.

"When we were crossing that river," Gwenshi said. She shuddered.

Vinnagon shook his head. "No, that whole day was bad."

"No, it wasn't," Gwenshi said. "It was fun. And we had a lot of good luck, too. Like, it was lucky we found those horses when we did."

"Those turned out to be the *mayor's* horses," Vinnagon said. "Now we have the Clifford Militia after us as well as the Darcliff Temple."

"Oh," said Gwenshi. "You're right." She thought a bit. "And when we found those mushrooms, I thought it was good luck, because it kept us from being seen by that rider. But the rider turned out to be your slywoman."

"She's not my slywoman!"

Crystal gave no reaction. Maybe she *was* a good match for Vinnagon. No sense of humor.

Calmly, Crystal asked, "Vinnagon, when did your bad luck start?"

Vinnagon looked down at his feet. "As soon as I left the temple," he said. "One of my boots lost a heel and I fell."

"Did you have any unusual incident while you were chasing me?" Crystal asked.

"You were chasing her?" Gwenshi asked. "You didn't tell me anything about that."

Shame-faced, Vinnagon glanced at Crystal. "I was the one who captured her so they could put her in the box."

Gwenshi felt a little jealous. Vinnagon had never chased *her*. He always expected her to stay put in that shack. Of course, if he *did* chase her, he would not be able to catch her unless she wanted him to. It sounded like fun.

"But to answer your question, Taishrefi, no. I did not start having bad luck until I left the temple."

Crystal rose with a grim expression on her face. She stood in front of Vinnagon and placed three fingers of each hand against his forehead. She closed her eyes and took three slow breaths.

She opened her eyes. "You do not have the blessing of Lashrefi," she said. "But neither am I able to sense a curse."

Gwenshi was concerned. "So it is just regular bad luck, then?"

"Perhaps," said Crystal, returning to her seat. "Or ..."

"Yes?" Gwenshi asked.

"You serve Kashram," Crystal said.

Gwenshi shrugged. "More or less."

Kashram was a pretty good god. All the others seemed a bit weak by comparison.

"Do you expect Kashram's holymen to be infallible?"

Gwenshi hadn't known many holymen. But they had just seemed like normal blacksmiths.

"Not really," she said.

Crystal said, "Taishrefis are expected to know more than other Lashrefites. The people expect us to be wise, but ..."

"Yes?" Gwenshi asked.

"I am just a woman," Crystal admitted. "There are some things I cannot do."

And that's a big confession for you, is it? "I see."

"One thing I cannot do is sense the influence of Shakredo," Crystal said.

"Oh," said Gwenshi. "So you think …"

"I do not know," Crystal said. "Vinnagon, did you swear an oath to Shakredo?"

Vinnagon shook his head. "I swore an oath to my captain," he said. "And he ordered us to swear an oath to the temple. But I thought that was to Lashrefi, not to … this demon you speak of."

"Did you say Lashrefi's name?" Gwenshi asked.

Vinnagon frowned. "I can't remember."

"You swore to serve your captain and the temple," Crystal said. "But they were both in service to Shakredo. I fear that this oath has allowed the demon to insinuate itself into your soul."

Vinnagon's face grew troubled. "I felt a burning in my lungs when I took the oath. But I thought that was from the smoke."

Crystal's mouth twisted with distaste. "Smoke and fire are in all the rituals, now. This is not what my grandmother taught me. Her people are called 'Flamebringers', but whenever she invokes Lashrefi, she uses the clean prairie wind."

Gwenshi tried to understand what Crystal was saying. "So you came to this temple and found that all the rituals were different, and you didn't tell anyone?"

"Wintersmoke's changes to the rituals were just beginning," Crystal said. "I was only an initiate, trying to learn the temple's ways. When Wintersmoke proposed a change, I followed the lead of my elders. They wanted to support their new bashrefi. Some women objected to the changes, but …"

Crystal shook her head. "Oh, I was naive. One by one, the grumblers disappeared. We were told they had chosen other assignments—which made sense! They were dissatisfied, so they chose to leave. That's what I believed. For a while. I suppose that sounds preposterous to you. But when one is on the inside, when everyone is pretending that all is well …"

Gwenshi looked at Vinnagon. How long had *he* known? And why had he never told her?

"Well," said Crystal, "after a time, I realized that my elders were not going to stand up to Wintersmoke. She had weeded out the brave ones, leaving only the evil and timid. The evil ones became the First Choir." She shrugged. "And I was among the timid."

"I don't think you're timid," said Gwenshi.

Crystal shook her head ruefully. "But I was. I wanted to expose the Holy Council to the people of Darcliff, but I was afraid to speak up without strong evidence. I thought that if I could listen in on their meetings, perhaps I could find a way to prove that they served evil."

"But I caught you listening," said Vinnagon. Pain tinged his voice.

"You were doing your job," she said.

"You couldn't know," Gwenshi said.

"I *did* know, woman! I knew that things were not right, but I had sworn an oath. I was serving wrong-doers, but I was serving them honorably. And now … I have neither righteousness nor honor."

"But, Vingo, didn't you agree to help Crystal?"

"I did."

"So you *do* have honor and righteousness."

"Were you not listening, woman? The taishrefi said my soul is linked to a demon!"

"So break the link!" Gwenshi said.

"You think that will be so easy?" Vinnagon demanded.

"Not easy," said Crystal. "But it *is* the next step. If we are to have any chance of revealing the evil in the temple, we must first remove the curse that gives that evil its power over you."

Two Years Earlier:
Bobwhite

BOBWHITE WAS A POTTER. He made durable, thick-walled crocks. A crock could store peas, flour, onions, corn mash—anything really. No matter how many crocks a household had, they could always find a use for one more.

And so Bobwhite had been very prosperous before the temple raised taxes. Now, however, the farmers complained that they had little excess crop to sell and little coin to spend on Bobwhite's crocks.

In years past, Bobwhite had climbed to the temple when he needed some luck—especially on nights when there was public music. But the bashrefi had discontinued public music while the temple wall was being constructed, and for some reason the tradition had not been reinstated after the wall's completion.

Bobwhite was not certain of his feelings about the wall. Many in Darcliff disapproved. Others disapproved, but were reluctant to disapprove openly. Bobwhite believed that Lashrefi could read his thoughts, so he assiduously worked to keep any disapproval out of them.

To supplement his income, Bobwhite made a few mugs, bowls, and vases, but these brought in even less coin than his crocks. Frankly, his light earthenware was not as elegant as that made by the other potters in Darcliff. Bobwhite was good at crocks. If no one was buying crocks, then his family would have to be more mindful of what they purchased.

But some people *were* buying crocks. They were buying them from the crockmaker in Clifford. As the months wore on and the savings box emptied, Bobwhite realized that it was this rival crockmaker who was the problem. The man sold his crocks too cheaply.

Of course, the Clifford crockmaker's crocks were not as good as Bobwhite's. The rims were not as circular. The ornamental lines were rough. But no one else seemed to care. The Clifford crockmaker sold his crocks cheaply, which meant that Bobwhite had to sell his crocks more cheaply still.

And so one frosty afternoon, Bobwhite climbed the switchbacks of the cliff and entered the temple.

It was smoky. That was first thing he noticed. But he had to admit that it was also warm.

A kind taishrefi welcomed him and suggested he open himself to the smoke of the Goddess. She accompanied the offer with a gesture toward a statue.

Bobwhite was startled. She was almost implying that the statue *was* the Goddess. But it was not. It was just a statue.

The thing was made of red granite. It had arrived in Darcliff by wagon and had been the talk of the town for days after it had been moved into the temple. It depicted a woman holding out her hands as though offering something to the torchlit worship hall. These hands held dancing flames burning some sort of fuel that Bobwhite could not see. The head apparently had a fuel source as well, for gray smoke wafted from the statue's mouth and nostrils. The taishrefis had told people to call it Our Lady of the Flame.

None of this imagery matched the wind-and-song motifs with which Bobwhite was familiar. The new bashrefi had new ways, but this statue was the most radical change he had witnessed.

Bobwhite approached the statue. The face had been carved with a steady hand. The visage was not particularly comforting, but one could only do so much with granite. Bobwhite approved of the care the sculptor had taken to minimize the blotchiness caused by large feldspar crystals.

A taishrefi stood beside the statue, her head only as high as the flame in the hands. She asked, "How is your fortune?"

"Good," said Bobwhite, out of habit. "Although it could be better."

The taishrefi smiled knowingly and said, "Close your eyes and think of how it could be better. Think of what stands in your way. Ask Our Lady for a boon and it may be granted—or not, as she wills."

All this was new to Bobwhite, but the taishrefi's smile gave him confidence. He closed his eyes and thought, *I wish the crockmaker from Clifford would stop undercutting me.*

Later, he would tell himself that was all he had wished for. He certainly had not wished for his rival to slip and plunge his hand into the coals while cleaning his kiln.

But then, it was certainly not his place to judge how the Goddess chose to answer his prayers. Perhaps the Clifford crockmaker was a truly immoral person.

Regardless, the outcome was lucky for Bobwhite. He was quite impressed by the effectiveness of the temple's new ways.

The 29th of Bluemonth,
Evening

THE MOON WAS HIGH when they left the brewhouse. Vinnagon's first reaction was to look up at the temple. He could see only the triangular pediment, which meant that he and the women were not visible from the temple steps.

"If we stay on the cliff side of the street," he said, "we shall be more difficult to see from above."

"Good thinking," said Taishrefi Crystal.

"I just hope vultures can't see in the dark," Gwenshi murmured.

They set out single file, with the taishrefi in the lead. No one was in the street. Here and there, they heard gentle music—the plinking of a lute, voices singing softly—but many of the houses were already dark and silent. Darcliff was not a town that burned much tallow.

Vinnagon could move more easily now. His wife had put linen gussets in his buckskin tunic and trousers. She said the weight of the leather would soon wear out the linen, but Vinnagon did not intend to wear the stolen clothing forever. He would find a way to get clothes of his own. Already he had acquired a belt and a knife, thanks to the generosity of Cicada the brewer. Vinnagon hoped to repay the man somehow—perhaps by helping Taishrefi Crystal confront the temple.

But first, he would need the taishrefi to lift his curse. And it was a curse—of that Vinnagon was certain.

They reached the edge of town without meeting anyone. The taishrefi continued on, even though the street ended. She led them onto a path through the trees.

"This trail is well worn," Vinnagon observed. "Where does it go?"

"Just to here," the taishrefi said as they emerged from the trees.

Before them was an extensive boulder field—not at all the sort of place that Vinnagon would expect people to visit.

"Oh," said Gwenshi. "This is where town kids go when they need some privacy."

"It is," the taishrefi admitted with a smile in her voice. "And Beetle hasn't outgrown it."

"We used to kiss in the cornfields," Gwenshi said.

Vinnagon looked at her sharply.

"A girl has to practice somewhere, Vingo."

Perhaps so, but she did not need to admit it to her husband.

"Just so long as you stay out of the cornfields now," he said.

"I only lie in cornfields with you, husband dear."

"Hmf!"

Gwenshi giggled.

The taishrefi said, "I will have a better chance of receiving Lashrefi's blessing if we perform the ritual in the wind—or at least a steady breeze. Let us move up the slope to where the breeze is stronger."

This reminder of their goal did not make Gwenshi any more solemn, but at least she fell silent. The three of them picked their way through the boulder field until they were some distance from the trees on either side.

The boulders were of various sizes. Some were small enough to lift. Some were as large as rain barrels. Vinnagon concentrated on his steps and his balance, avoiding the gaps between rocks where he could lose a limb if a boulder shifted.

The taishrefi stopped at the base of the largest boulder. It was a giant flat-topped rock, taller than Vinnagon, much larger than the others on the slope.

"Let us get you up in the air more," she suggested.

She placed one foot on a knee-high protrusion and lifted herself up to reach the rock's top edge. She struggled to lift her body onto the rock's flat top. Gwenshi stepped forward, put a hand under the taishrefi's buttocks, and pushed. Taishrefi Crystal glanced down at them, eyes wide and startled.

"I thought you could use a boost," Gwenshi said.

"Ah ... thank you," the taishrefi decided.

Vinnagon braced his hand against the rock to give her a final foothold, and she gained the top.

Now it was Vinnagon's turn. His moccasins were weak-soled, providing no stepping platform, but he could feel the footholds in the rock with his toes. He was just a little shorter than the taishrefi, so only his fingertips grasped the lip of rock above.

Vinnagon hoisted himself, and suddenly his wife was underneath him with her hands on his buttocks.

"Woman, I can climb by myself," he said—but not so gruffly that she would actually stop helping him. He *could* climb the rock by himself, but there was no need to keep the taishrefi waiting.

"The breeze is somewhat stronger up here," the taishrefi observed. "I hope it will be strong enough. I need you to sit down facing the wind."

Vinnagon did so.

"Can I join you?" asked Gwenshi.

Vinnagon turned. His wife was clambering onto the rock. How had *she* gotten up so easily? She was a foot shorter than either of them.

"Are you woman or squirrel?" he asked.

"A bit of both," she said with a grin. "It's all right if I watch, isn't it?" she asked the taishrefi.

"Of course. Help him take off his tunic."

"I'm glad I came already!"

With Gwenshi's unnecessary assistance, Vinnagon took off his tunic. He wondered why she had to make so much of these things. It was not seemly—especially not in front of the taishrefi. Perhaps Gwenshi thought the taishrefi was just another woman, when in fact she was …

Vinnagon did not know what Crystal was to him, now. He knew a bladesman's relationship to the taishrefis of the temple, but now they were both fugitives. Did that mean Crystal was just a woman like Gwenshi?

No. Vinnagon was no longer a bladesman, but Crystal was still a taishrefi. She could still communicate with her goddess. With luck, she and her goddess would free Vinnagon from the temple's curse. And then he would be able to aid her cause and perhaps regain his honor.

"Vinnagon," she said, "I need you to become aware of the wind on your skin. Feel the wind enter your body as you inhale. Feel the way it curls about your shoulders. Let the wind blow through your soul."

The hem of her tunic brushed against his shoulders. Her fingers slid through his hair, and her hands came to rest atop his head.

"Relax," she said. "And let yourself breathe deeply."

Relaxation was not among Vinnagon's strengths. He was a guard. At this time of night, he was accustomed to being alert. And now he was a fugitive, sitting shirtless in the moonlight in an exposed position.

Crystal began to sing:

Lashrefi, be with us. Come blow through this soul.
Cleanse it of evil so it can be whole.

Vinnagon could feel his breaths slowing to match the deliberate tempo of Crystal's song. As she sang the lines over and over, his mind did relax. The song blended into the sound of the wind in the trees. His vision unfocused, and he felt his awareness reach down into the rock underneath him.

Just as he sometimes did when standing guard in the caverns, he allowed his senses to extend through the rock. He could feel the size of the monolith. He could feel its connection to the smaller boulders underneath. Edges met crevices. Flat faces pressed against one another. The structure of the boulder field was so complex. The slightest shift of one stone underneath could cause the entire slope to rearrange itself completely.

A single boulder drew his attention. It supported the crushing weight of the rock on which Vinnagon sat—had supported that weight for who knew how long? And now, as it cooled in the night air, the extra weight of Vinnagon and the two women was causing a hair-thin crack to expand through its heart.

Vinnagon opened his eyes and jumped to his feet. "Get off," he said.

Their rock shifted with a crunching sound. Vinnagon braced his feet and bent his knees to absorb the motion of the shift. Crystal swayed, but Gwenshi seized Crystal's arm and steadied her.

For a moment, the three of them stood stone-still, waiting to see if the boulder field would shift more.

Crystal said, "Well, that was—"

Something underneath them crunched. A boulder tipped and scraped against a boulder below. Their rock began a grinding slide.

"Don't jump for it!" Gwenshi yelled. "Stay on top!"

Below them, all the boulders were sliding and bouncing in limb-crushing chaos. Their own rock seemed to be picking up speed as it tilted with the slope.

The surface lurched. Crystal fell to one knee. Gwenshi stepped lightly to the edge ... which continued rising into the air.

Vinnagon scrambled up the slope of what had once been the rock's flat top. Crystal had one arm over the rising edge. Gwenshi straddled it, one foot on the old top, one foot on the face that was rising.

Vinnagon's moccasin slipped. He reached out a hand and caught the hem of a tunic—the tunic that Gwenshi had helped him remove; she held the other end.

Crystal's flailing leg made contact with his head. Her moccasined toes pushed against his forehead, and she clambered up beside Gwenshi.

As the rock continued its slow roll, Vinnagon's weight pressed against the rock's surface less and less. Tension increased in the muscles that held the tunic. His bare chest scraped against the stone as he dropped another thumbwidth.

And then the rock seemed to swing away from him, and Vinnagon was suspended over the boulder field with the gigantic rock about to tip over and crush him.

"Vingo, don't move." Gwenshi's voice was very quiet.

The rocks were still. They had settled into a new configuration.

A stitch on the tunic popped.

"Vingo, stick out your right foot."

Vinnagon did so. A second stitch popped.

"A little farther," Gwenshi said.

Vinnagon's moccasin brushed stone.

"We need to ease you down," Gwenshi said. "Nothing sudden."

"Where's Crystal?" Vinnagon asked.

"She's on the other side," Gwenshi said.

And Crystal said, "I'm praying to keep the rock balanced."

"Let me give you a little more slack," Gwenshi said.

The tunic dropped and the seams of Gwenshi's handiwork started ripping apart. Vinnagon's foot found the boulder below and he shifted his weight onto it, pushing off with his free hand.

The rock lurched and Crystal cried out. Then everything was still except the wind in the trees.

Vinnagon perched on a boulder, panting.

"Crystal?" Gwenshi asked.

"I am well," she called from behind the rock. "I landed cleanly, thank the Goddess."

"Get clear," Gwenshi said. "I'm coming down and I don't want this thing to shift onto you."

Crystal emerged from behind the boulder.

Gwenshi said, "You, too, Vingo. We don't want to test *your* luck."

She was right. Vinnagon and Crystal moved carefully to the edge of the boulder field.

Gwenshi jumped, somehow managing to land lightly on a tilted boulder seven feet below. She bounded from boulder to boulder, putting distance between herself and the site of the rockslide, but nothing behind her moved.

By the time she reached the edge of the boulder field, she was showing more caution in her steps.

"I reckon your attempt to improve Vinnagon's luck didn't work," she said.

"I am sorry," Crystal said. "I felt the attention of Lashrefi on me, but it was as though Vinnagon did not exist for her." She put a hand on Vinnagon's arm. "I fear I have failed you."

Vinnagon said, "It is not your fault, Crystal."

She blinked.

"What is it?" he asked.

"You called me by my name."

"Aha! I'm sorry, I—"

"No. Do not apologize. I was unable to relieve you of your curse. Perhaps I am no taishrefi."

"You saved his life," Gwenshi said. "Your weight stopped the roll that would have crushed him. I think he was just being friendly."

Crystal gave them a sad smile. " 'Friendly.' Very well. I need friends right now."

Gwenshi reached up and patted her on the shoulder. "Let's go visit Beetle. I'm sure he'll cheer you up."

Crystal acquiesced. They followed her back into the trees. And Vinnagon himself wondered why he had suddenly started thinking of the taishrefi by name.

* * *

I shouldn't be doing this, Crys thought as they turned onto the street where Beetle lived. *I shouldn't get him involved.*

But I've already involved his parents. So he is involved whether I want him to be or not.

That doesn't mean I have to come trotting into his house in the middle of the night.

And when was I planning to come trotting in? In broad daylight when everyone in the street could see me?

She stopped in front of Beetle's door and raised her hand to knock.

Just being here puts him in danger.

"… So this is it?" Gwenshi asked.

Crys nodded.

He's asleep. I should let him sleep.

"… And will you knock?"

Crys nodded.

I have to knock. Just not so loud that it wakes Beetle's neighbors. But loud enough to wake Beetle, of course—

"… When will you knock?" Gwenshi asked.

Crys struck her knuckles against the wooden door. She gave Gwenshi a reproving scowl. Then, because her first knock had been rather weak, she rapped twice more.

That wasn't enough to wake him. Maybe I shouldn't wake him. Maybe I should leave it up to Lashrefi: If he doesn't wake, then it's a sign that we should—

Footsteps shuffled toward the door.

"Who is it?" Beetle's voice was heavy, but not groggy.

"Crys?" She meant to give her name, but it came out sounding like a question. That would never do. "It is Crystal. May … we come in?"

The bolt slid back. The door opened a foot. Beetle stood in the gap, blocking entry, a candle on a wooden candlestick in his hand.

" 'We'?" His face was tired, but he hadn't slept. His gaze was hard.

He was angry. Crys was not certain why. He should be

angry with her for endangering his parents, but she doubted they had told him yet. He might be angry with her for endangering *him*, but his eyes held no fear, just hardness.

"This is Gwenshi," Crys said. "And this is Vinnagon. He—"

"I know who he is," Beetle said. "Why did you bring him here?"

"Because—" Beetle's biceps were tense. His chest seemed expanded. "Oh. You've seen the posters."

"Yes I've seen the posters! The whole town has seen the posters!"

Gwenshi laid a hand on his arm. "Beg pardon, Beetle, but we're fugitives, aye? Can you let us in and shout at us more quietly?"

"Who are you?"

Crys sighed and pushed past him. "She is a wise woman, and you should follow her advice." Over her shoulder she added, "Come in, Vinnagon. He won't hurt you."

Vinnagon snorted like an indignant stallion, but he and Gwenshi followed her in. Beetle stood there gaping like a large-mouthed bass.

Gwenshi shut the door for him and slid the bolt home. "Close your mouth, sweetie. You'll catch flies."

"How could you?" Crys asked.

"How could *I*?" Beetle retorted. "How could *you*?"

"You don't even know what I've done," she said. "Do you really think I would leave the temple to run off with *him*?"

"Hey!" said Gwenshi.

Beetle's face melted into confusion. "Well ... no," he said. "But now that you've brought him here in the flesh ... well, what am I supposed to think?"

Crys poked a finger into his chest. "You're supposed to think that I'm an intelligent woman, and that if I've brought a fugitive to your house, I probably have a good reason."

"Three fugitives," Gwenshi said, holding up her fingers. "I'm wanted for horse thievery," she explained with some pride.

"So you didn't leave the temple because of him?"

"Of course I didn't! Or ... well, perhaps in a way. But not in *that* way. Do you hear?"

"I hear," he said. "But ... do you think you could add a few more details?"

"I can see this will take you two a while to get sorted out," Gwenshi said. "Do you mind if I lie down on your workbench?"

"Ah ... no."

"Thanks."

Gwenshi climbed up onto Beetle's lute-making bench, arranged her skirt, lay down with her head on one arm, and curled herself into a napping position.

She was right. This would take a while. Crys had a lot to explain.

* * *

Vinnagon wasn't sleepy. Besides, he wanted to hear more of Crystal's story—that is, the taishrefi's story.

It was becoming more difficult to think of her as a taishrefi as he became more accustomed to the idea that the temple was his enemy. Taishrefis and bladesmen were now people he had to fight, even though he was still not certain how to go about doing so.

He had agreed to work with Crystal under the assumption that she had some sort of plan, but truly, she had thus far revealed nothing. Nor did she reveal any plan as she explained herself to Beetle—who was certainly her slyman, no matter what she thought of the situation.

"The door was thick," she said. "But I distinctly heard Rathi ask, 'How will people know they are Flamebringer clothings?'"

"She mentioned your grandmother's tribe?"

"Yes," Crystal said. "I'm worried the temple plans to harm them somehow."

Beetle frowned. "I think the Flamebringers can take care of

themselves. People who trade with them say they are fierce warriors."

"My grandmother's band spends their time hunting and singing," Crystal said. "They are not the monsters that townspeople make them out to be."

"I didn't say 'monsters'. I said 'warriors'."

"But you were thinking 'monsters'."

Beetle sighed and put a hand on her cheek. "Don't tell me what I was thinking."

She looked down. "I apologize. I am almost as tired as you are."

"I'll sleep better now, knowing that—" He looked at Vinnagon. "Actually, Crys, you still haven't explained what the Kashramites are doing here."

Crystal's mouth twisted with a wry smile. "Vinnagon is the guard who caught me spying."

"What?"

"He captured me and turned me over to the Holy Council."

"And then what happened?"

Crystal's eyes grew hard. "That glowing-eyed interloper knocked me unconscious."

"The Woshite?"

"She used mind magic. I— I had no warning."

"So how did you escape?"

"When I awoke, I was in a box down by the river. Two men were arguing over whether they should throw me in. Vinnagon won the argument."

"You let her out?" Beetle asked.

"I did," Vinnagon said.

"So I ran away into the forest," Crystal said. "Vinnagon went to report to his captain, and then he had to run away, too, of course. That is why they invented that story: They wanted to explain why a guard and a taishrefi had left the temple on the same night, and they wanted to discredit either of us if we chose to go to a mayor."

"Have you visited any mayors?"

"Not yet," Crystal said. "And Vinnagon and Gwenshi stole horses from the mayor of Clifford while escaping from Camptown, so that complicates matters."

"You should try, though, Crys. You could talk to the mayor of Darcliff. Farmers were complaining about the temple's wheat tax this year, even though the threat of curses makes them afraid to complain too loudly. The complaints will get worse once the wagons come to collect the corn tax. The mayors don't like it when the taishrefis exercise so much influence."

"They don't," said Crystal. "But they always give in."

That was the problem with Lashrefites, Vinnagon thought. The men did not know how to be true men, and the women took advantage.

"It is still worth trying," Beetle said. "I could talk to the mayor, if you want."

"It would be better if we had evidence of wrong-doing," Crystal said.

"They tried to drown you in the river," Beetle said. "Isn't that evidence enough?"

Crystal sighed. "Just a crazy lie from a girl so mixed up that she ran away with a Kashramite, I'm afraid. If *you* believed those posters, I'm certain everyone else did."

"Oh, Crys. I'm sorry."

"I'm sorry, too."

Vinnagon shifted uncomfortably.

"But if you didn't escape together," Beetle asked, "how did you find each other?"

"Lashrefi brought us together."

As Crystal explained the part of the story that Vinnagon knew, he returned to thinking of something he could do to escape the temple's curse. Crystal's invocation had failed. But Vinnagon should have expected that. Shakredo was powerful enough to gain control of Lashrefi's temple, so it was not surprising that Lashrefi was too weak to overcome Shakredo's curse.

But Vinnagon was not a servant of Lashrefi. True, he had been in service to her temple and he had taken an oath to her—or to an entity he had mistaken for her—but his soul belonged to Kashram. And Kashram had helped him. Kashram had given him the quickness to escape his pursuers. Kashram had given Gwenshi strength to save him from being drowned. Kashram had helped him defeat Malk and Shangrel with only a rake.

If he wanted to lift this curse, he should seek the aid of Kashram.

One Year Earlier:
Mayor Duskraven

DUSKRAVEN WAS MAYOR OF DARCLIFF. His daughter was an initiate in the Darcliff Temple.

Duskraven's dream was that he and his daughter would one day share leadership of Darcliff Province—he as mayor and she as bashrefi. The reality was that Duskraven would probably be retired or dead long before his daughter was old enough to be bashrefi. Also, Darcliff Province had only one leader.

The temple had sole authority over the collection and storage of food. It was not a mayor's place to interfere. Yet the mayors of the villages complained to him, as though he had influence with the temple. But Wintersmoke was not some village taishrefi. She was *the* bashrefi—the only person whose authority extended to every edge of the province.

Even so, Duskraven agreed that the time had come to ask. He carefully penned a letter asking if he might be allowed to visit the temple and discuss the provincial tax burden. He showed it to a few trusted advisors, who all agreed that it was well-written and diplomatic.

He put it inside his writing box and resolved to send it the next morning.

That night, he was awakened by a pounding on the door. Upon opening, he saw the Holy Seneschal flanked by four Kashramite guards.

"I apologize for waking you," she said. "I was passing by your residence and remembered that I have a letter for you from your daughter."

She handed him a rolled scrap of vellum. He thanked her.

She and her guards took their leave.

The letter was indeed written in his daughter's hand. It read:

Dear Father,

I am well. The Holy Seneschal is personally overseeing my studies, and I may be too busy to see you if you visit the temple. I am well.

Near her signature was a drop of blood, still sticky.

Mayor Duskraven chose not to seek an invitation to the temple.

The 30th of Bluemonth,
Morning

GWENSHI AWOKE IN PAIN. She had rolled onto her back. With a groan, she flopped onto her side and waited for the soreness to ease.

The scrape on her spine was from that tree in the river, she remembered. And the soreness in her arms was from hauling Vingo out of the water. Saving Vingo on the rock last night had left her with abrasions on her arms and one bruised knee. Oh well, adventures were supposed to be rough.

She couldn't help noticing, though, that the parts she enjoyed—running, jumping, hiding, riding, climbing—had taken little toll on her body. Her scrapes and bruises were all from trying to keep her husband alive.

Vinnagon was snoring on the floor below, wrapped in a linen blanket. He looked so cute asleep—and Kashram knew that Vinnagon deserved his sleep.

The other two were nowhere to be seen. Gwenshi hoped they were doing something interesting in the adjacent room, but probably they were just sleeping. It didn't have a door or a curtain or anything.

She sat up and stretched, arching her back into the pain. When she eased up, it felt a bit better than it had before. Aye, she was ready for another day of adventures.

Maybe they would attack the temple today! She wondered what Crystal's plan was. Did Crystal intend to fight beside them, or would she stay back? She did not move like a woman who knew how to fight.

Gwenshi knew, and she had the scars on her forearms to

prove it. Of course, she had never *killed* anyone, but she had sent a few girls staggering to the healer.

She fingered her dueling knife. She was confident she could defeat any woman in the temple, but she needed Vinnagon to handle the men. She was sure he could, as long as he did not have to fight more than two at a time—maybe in a hallway or something. Hadn't Vinnagon said there were caves? That might work. If they could get rid of that curse.

She got up to see where Beetle kept his food. As soon as her foot hit the floor, Vinnagon was in a crouch, hands raised to a guard position.

Get rid of the curse, and get Vingo a sword—two things they had to do before they could fight everyone in the temple.

"Good morning, Vingo. Sleep well?"

"Well enough," he said.

"Glad to hear it." She studied his appearance. "Say, take off that tunic so I can mend it while those other two are still asleep."

Vinnagon pulled his tunic off and handed it over. He did not re-cover himself with the linen blanket. The house was warm enough for Vingo.

Gwenshi sat down and started sewing. Breakfast could wait.

"I need to see Harl," Vinnagon said.

She looked up from her work. "Back across the river?"

"Yes. He's the only one who can help me."

Gwenshi thought *she* was doing a pretty good job so far. Then: "Oh, you mean help with the curse."

"Yes."

"I don't like the idea of crossing that river again," she said. "The curse might win next time."

"Sooner or later I will succumb to it," Vinnagon said. "That is why I need Harl. But I have a plan for avoiding the dangers of the river."

"Aye?"

"I shall take the ferry."

"The ferry? And what if one of the temple guards decides

to take the ferry?" Gwenshi often met Vinnagon's comrades when she crossed the river. A guard got only one day off in ten, but every day was some guard's day off.

"Obviously, if I see someone who might recognize me, I shall wait and take a different ferry."

"If you can see them, they can see you."

"Not necessarily," said Vinnagon.

Crystal came to the doorway. "If I may make a suggestion?" They waited.

"It may be possible to disguise you so that no bladesman can recognize you. Then you would not need to avoid them. You could walk right past them."

Vinnagon frowned. "How?"

"Well," said Crystal, "I noticed yesterday that you and I are about the same size—not across the shoulders, perhaps, but we are close."

"And?"

"And I happen to have a robe here that could be made to resemble a Kashramite woman's dress."

"And?"

"You have to admit: they won't recognize you if they think you are a woman."

"No," said Vinnagon. "That's ridiculous."

Crystal looked to Gwenshi for support.

"He's right," Gwenshi said. "That's ridiculous."

"It is not ridiculous," said Crystal. "Have you never heard the story of 'How Fel Wooed the Bear'?"

"How what?" asked Gwenshi.

"We can stuff the dress with grass," said Crystal, "to give him a bit of a bosom."

"No," said Vinnagon.

"Bosom or no bosom," Gwenshi said, "there is no way you can make Vingo look like a woman. What about his legs? What about his arms?"

"But Gwenshi, your legs and arms are hairy and muscular. No one will know the difference."

Gwenshi looked at her knife-scarred arms. They weren't *that* hairy. And, well, they weren't very muscular, either, although she was pleased that Crystal thought so.

"Look," Gwenshi said, "our men and women look nothing alike. We aren't like you."

"Like me?" Crystal was surprised.

"Like Stripedfolk," Gwenshi said.

"But *our* men and women don't look alike."

"Well ..." said Gwenshi, "except for their figures, your men look somewhat girly."

"What?" said Crystal.

Gwenshi added, "No offense, Beetle," because he was awake now and had come to stand in the doorway behind Crystal.

"It is so," said Vinnagon. "Your men are as weak as women."

Crystal's eyes flashed. "As *strong* as women, you mean."

Gwenshi thought some of them might be as strong as *some* women, but she could probably pin Beetle in a wrestling match.

"As you wish," said Vinnagon. "All we are saying is that this disguise may be easy for Fall—"

"Fel."

"For Fel, but it is quite impossible among our people. Our men and women are very different."

"I truly think that if we tried it, you would be surprised at how—"

"No," said Vinnagon.

Gwenshi said, "Even if it *would* work, it would just be hunting for trouble. With Vinnagon's luck, the stuffing would come loose just as a bladesman was ogling his bosom."

"What?" said Vinnagon.

"I hear what you say," said Crystal. "But any means of crossing the river will involve some risk."

"Who would ogle ...?"

"That's why I don't want him crossing the river," Gwenshi said.

"Do any bladesmen ogle *your* bosom?"

"But getting help from a Kashramite holyman *is* a good idea," Crystal said.

"Aye," said Gwenshi. "And that's why I'm going to go get him."

* * *

She convinced him. But only because there was no other sensible plan. Crystal could not go outside because her face was on all those posters. And Vingo could not go outside because, even though the man on the poster looked nothing like him, he might run into someone who knew him by name. If an unlucky thing could happen, it probably would.

So Gwenshi took the ferry. And no one on the ferry ogled her bosom, but that was no surprise because they were all Stripedmen. She wasn't much interested in *them*, either.

She'd used Beetle's money for the ferry, and that got her to thinking she should stop by her shack and see if she could pick up a few things. She actually had a good bit of money. As soon as she'd stopped buying herbs, she'd started saving money for a cradle.

The cradle money. She was planning to give it to Vinnagon. She hadn't realized the significance until just now, standing in the street outside her shack.

It made sense, though: Fugitives don't need cradles.

"Are you daft, woman? Get inside!"

Plesi was hissing at her from the window.

"What are you doing in my shack?" Gwenshi asked.

Plesi pushed the door open, grabbed Gwenshi by the wrist, and dragged her inside.

"They're looking for Vinnagon," Plesi said.

"I know that," said Gwenshi. "But why are you in my shack?"

"My kid wanted cheese."

"I'm out of cheese," said Gwenshi.

"I know," said Plesi. "But I thought I'd look."

"Did your kids want my cook pot, too?"

"Gwenshi, you stole a horse and rode away with your husband. I didn't think you'd be coming back."

"Well, I forgot a few things." So the womenfolk knew she had stolen a horse! Gwenshi felt the warm glow of pride. But then she realized: "Hey, you aren't going to tell the militia I was here, are you?"

"I won't admit I saw you," Plesi said. "But Gwenshi, if you love me, I beg you not to tell me anything of Vinnagon."

"What? Why?"

"Captain Brekko said that if any woman helps Vinnagon, he will put her husband to death."

"What? He can't do that."

"He can if he gets the other captains to agree. You know how bladesmen are. If he ordered them to cut off their own heads, they'd probably do it. And they'd probably thank him afterwards."

Well not if they didn't have heads, Gwenshi thought. But Plesi was basically right: A bladesman loved his captain.

"You should go back to your own house, then," Gwenshi said. "So you can say you didn't help me."

"Gwenshi, you could stay with us," Plesi said. "My husband wouldn't let the stripeys take you away."

"Your husband won't be back until winter," Gwenshi said.

"Perhaps," said Plesi. "But he might be able to get leave if I ask him to come and marry you."

Live with Plesi and her three kids? No. Just neighboring those kids was all Gwenshi could handle. But still, it softened her heart to think that Plesi might want her as second wife. She kissed her friend on the cheek.

"Thank you, Plesi, but I shall be leaving shortly after you do."

"Very well. Goodbye, then. It has been—"

"Plesi, this isn't over. Vinnagon is innocent, and we're going to straighten some things out around here."

She looked around her shack. She didn't have much, but it was *hers*, damn it! "And you can borrow anything you need, but

don't let anyone take anything. You tell them Gwenshi will be
coming back."

* * *

Gwenshi had grown up among the Clanfolk, half-sized people
who had been created by Yolim, the god of wealth. They said
that wealth was not about money; it was about land and
livestock. That was all right for farmer-people to say, but
Gwenshi's people were warriors. She reckoned that wealth also
had something to do with blades.

Harl the blacksmith was wealthy. A sword hung over the
door to his house. Two more hung on pegs on either side of
the lithward window. He wore another sword on his belt, as
well as two knives and a hammer. On the wall beside the
hearth, a rack held fifteen knives, two cleavers, and a bonesaw.
His wives were fortunate to belong to such a rich man.

All these were blades he had made himself, and that was the
point: He could make things that everyone needed. That skill
was surely a form of wealth.

Ironworking was Kashram's most sacred gift. Every smith
had to be something of a holyman.

Harl was never pompous about his piety. Gwenshi liked
him because he spoke to women as though they were people.
He did not treat women as equals, of course, but he never
assumed women were stupid just because they were weak.

Gwenshi explained the situation, omitting nothing. Unlike
the other men from Camptown, Harl was not under the
authority of any of the temple's captains. He had nothing to
fear from helping Vingo.

And yet, as she finished her story, Harl did not stand ready
to dash out of the house and go to Vinnagon's rescue. Instead,
he slouched against the wall, arms folded, frowning.

"Can you help him?" Gwenshi asked.

Harl looked away in disgust.

His older wife took the younger by the hand and led her
toward an adjacent room. Was Gwenshi discussing men's

business? Is that what they meant? The younger wife carefully avoided looking at Harl. The older one cast him a single glance. Was it pity?

Gwenshi was left alone with the smith. Their privacy was only symbolic, of course. The wives could hear everything. But now Harl could say whatever it was without demeaning himself in front of them. For that was the way he looked, with his shaggy iron-gray hair hanging in front of his eyes and his liver-red lips twisted in disgust and contempt. He looked like a man resigning himself to a most unpleasant task.

"Vinnagon cannot be helped," he said. "None of those men can."

"But the holywoman said—"

"She knows only the ways of Lashrefi. Kashram does not forgive."

"But Vinnagon has done nothing wrong."

"Yes he has," said Harl. "Every man in that temple has done wrong. Though some are too stupid to realize it."

Could be that speaking directly to Harl had been a mistake. Could be she should have sought his help through one of his wives.

Harl asked, "Do you know what an oath means to Kashram?"

"Ah ..."

"Nothing. An oath is just words. Kashram cares only about our actions."

"But then—"

"Do you know why the bladesmen swear oaths to their employers?"

"Ah ... because ..."

"Because men grew soft during our time among the Clanfolk."

Oh dear.

Harl was nodding to himself. "That is when it started. These oaths. This tradition of *service*." He spat the word.

"We were free men, once. Lords of the plains. And now—"

he gestured at the walls of the room, "—we live in prison cells."

Gwenshi had heard this sort of rhetoric in Camptown before. In her grandfather's time, the Arvethidrel had been the military force of the Clanfolk kingdom of Yarvethi. They had defended the Clanfolk from the attacks of nomadic Stripedfolk and Redfolk. Strong men protecting weaker men—it seemed pious enough to Gwenshi.

The arrangement had worked for generations—until the Arvethidrel lost a war. Then the Clanfolk had turned on them and expelled them from Clanfolk territory.

At least, that was the way the story was told in Camptown. Everyone's parents remembered promises broken, homes abandoned. Harl was old enough that he might have actually fought in that war—or maybe not, but he was certainly old enough to remember the day when the Arvethidrel became a wandering people once more, traveling the Yarl in search of someone who would value their loyalty.

But not all Arvethidrel had been dispersed. The Clanfolk were so named because they organized themselves into clans. A few clans realized how ungrateful it was to expel the Arvethidrel. They had defied the other clans and opened up their lands for Redfolk farmers. Gwenshi's parents were legally part of Clan Underwood.

So, aye, Gwenshi understood why Harl would say that their history among the Clanfolk was the source of all troubles, but she did not really believe it.

"Kashram did not create us to serve these others," Harl said. "We were created to serve Kashram." He hung his head. "And we have failed him."

"Well, then, this is our chance," said Gwenshi. "Vinnagon can—"

"Vinnagon can do nothing! He has sworn an oath!"

"But you said oaths don't mean anything."

"To Kashram, they don't. But what does this oath mean to Vinnagon?"

Quite a bit, Gwenshi realized. "Oh. I see."

"Exactly," said the smith.

"But what about Vinnagon's actions?" Gwenshi asked. "He has taken a great risk by leaving the temple. He is prepared to fight in Kashram's name."

"Is he?" Harl demanded.

"I— I think so."

"Then let him do so! If he holds Kashram in his heart, perhaps Kashram will lift this curse you speak of. But as long as Vinnagon is half a man—believing one thing while doing another—Kashram will have nothing to do with him!"

"Vinnagon not half a man!" Gwenshi said. "He's all man! And he's not going to give up just because you ..."

"Yes? Because I what?" He dared her to complete the sentence.

Because you are afraid is what she had been about to say. But that was wrong. Fear was not the thing holding Harl back.

"If he did this," she said, "if he stopped worrying about his oath and took up a sword for Kashram, would you be able free his soul of the curse?"

"That is up to Kashram."

"Aye. That's clear to me. But would you be willing to help? Would you be able to, I don't know, plead his case a bit?"

Harl looked away. "Kashram cares nothing for my pleas."

"But you're the holyman," Gwenshi said. "Talking to Kashram is what you do."

"No it isn't," Harl said. "Not anymore." All the heat had gone from his voice.

"What are you saying? You performed a funeral just a few days ago."

"That's all it was—just a performance."

"I don't understand."

"Granny Gafi's soul would have gone to Heaven without me. She was in Heaven even before we started the funeral—I hope."

"You don't know?"

He shook his head.

"But I thought …"

"You thought holymen knew those sorts of things."

"Aye."

"I did," he said. "Once."

"Oh."

"When the men swore their oaths to the temple, I knew they were doing wrong. I told Brekko. But then I realized that his soul had already been claimed. All the captains had been claimed."

Gwenshi stared at him. "So what did you do?"

"I tried to talk men out of it. Individually." He waved his hand at the village out the window. "I've never been much of a leader around here."

"And what happened?"

"You know what happened. They ignored me. Or they listened to me, but then their captains convinced them that listening to me was disloyal. I'm sure some thought I was just jealous—of Lashrefi … or perhaps of the captains' authority."

"I see," said Gwenshi. "You tried to stop them with words, but when that didn't work …"

"I did nothing."

"And Kashram abandoned you."

"Yes. Because words mean nothing to Kashram. He cares only about our actions."

Gwenshi studied the respected smith who had just humbled himself before a puny woman.

"Then take an action," she said.

He shook his head. "Kashram will not listen to me. I cannot help you."

"Yes you can," Gwenshi said. "You can give us swords."

* * *

The instrument maker's house stayed cool all morning, for it was built of stone, and stone does not change temperature easily. Vinnagon had nothing to do, so he found his host's whetstone and sharpened the knife he had been given.

Beetle had gone to speak with the mayor of Darcliff. Gwenshi was fetching Harl.

The house was quiet except for the fussing noises Taishrefi Crystal made as she tried to tidy up. There was little work for her. The workshop was small and clean. In the end, she was forced to attack the soot-blackened hearthstones, which yielded only slowly to her efforts.

Finally, Vinnagon gave in to her presence and spoke to her: "Perhaps while they are gone, we should discuss the plan."

Crystal looked up from her work. Her striped cheeks were smudged with soot. Had she not been a taishrefi, it would have been amusing.

"Plan?" she asked.

"I said I would help you against the temple. What is our plan?"

Crystal wiped the back of her hand against her cheek, with no noticeable effect on the smudge. "I was hoping to find a safe place in town, so we would be able to keep watch on the temple's activities."

"Just watch?"

"We need more information before we can act," she said. "Even if Beetle is able to get the mayor's support."

"You do not think he will."

"I do not know," Crystal said. "The mayor's daughter is an initiate. Perhaps he will decide she needs to be rescued. Or perhaps he already knew what was happening when he allowed his daughter to join."

Vinnagon considered the point of his knife. "Let us suppose that we are on our own," he said. "What would you have me do?"

"First I would have you free of that curse," said Crystal. "But after that … Vinnagon, what we need is proof. Everyone knows that the temple is seizing power over the countryside, but we need to show them why. We need proof that the Holy Council serves Shakredo."

"That may be difficult to show," Vinnagon said. "Lashref-ites believe whatever their taishrefis tell them."

"Just as bladesmen believe whatever their captains tell them."

"My uncle was a good man before he came to this temple."

"I am certain he was," said Crystal.

"He is not evil," Vinnagon said.

"Are you certain?"

"He has been led to evil by the seneschal."

"He has," Crystal agreed. "Whether this has put evil in his heart, I do not know, for as I told you, Shakredo's evil is hidden from me. But Vinnagon, I can tell you that Brekko lacks the blessing of Kashram."

"How do you know?"

"I do not sense it in him."

"But you serve Lashrefi. You cannot be certain."

"Vinnagon, I can sense the blessing of Kashram, and Brekko does not have it. Or if he does, it is much weaker than the blessing I can sense on you and Gwenshi."

"Gwenshi?"

"Yes. Is she not as pious as you?"

"Gwenshi is a woman," said Vinnagon.

"As you insist upon reminding her every time you address her," said Crystal. "But perhaps Kashram is not as troubled by her womanhood as you are."

"Troubled? Gwenshi's womanhood does not trouble me."

"But you do not see her as an equal."

"In the eyes of Kashram, she is not."

"Isn't she?" Crystal asked, and she let the words sit there quietly in the shadows.

They spoke no more. No need. She had no plan. Why had Vinnagon expected more of her? Crystal scrubbed at the hearthstones, and Vinnagon assiduously ignored the thoughts she had tried to conjure in his head.

* * *

Gwenshi stopped outside the door to the workshop and said, "It's me—Gwenshi."

The Stripedwoman opened for her, and Gwenshi slipped inside Beetle's shop. Blinking the daylight from her eyes, she crossed the room to the workbench and set down her bundle of garden tools.

Vinnagon demanded, "Why did you bring those, woman?"

Crystal gave him a meaningful look. Vinnagon ignored it, so Gwenshi did, too.

"If you don't want them," Gwenshi said, "I'll keep them all for myself." She could scarcely keep the smile out of her voice.

"Not only do I not want them," said Vinnagon, "I want you to have not brought them. But it is too late for that. Now everyone in town has seen you, and they will be wondering why a Redwoman is carrying garden tools to the instrument maker's shop."

"Oh, that is easy enough to explain," said Gwenshi, unrolling the cloth that held the bundle together. "I'm smuggling a sword to my husband."

"A ... sword? Harl let you borrow a sword?"

Gwenshi grinned. "Two swords." She lifted the second from the pile of tools. "This one is for me."

"For you? You don't know how to use a sword."

She shrugged. "I reckon you can teach me."

"A sword is not just a long knife. It takes years to master the weapon."

"Well, I'm not expecting to *master* it. I just want to defend myself."

"You'd be wiser to practice running," Vinnagon said. "At least you had enough sense to get your boots."

"Aye," she said. "I reckoned I might need them."

Vinnagon grunted, satisfied that he had been proven right.

Actually, Gwenshi had grabbed her boots from her shack so she could wear the boot knife tucked against her calf. Her brother had told her to always keep a knife in her boot because "they never check there." Gwenshi was not certain who "they" were, but she reckoned the extra knife might come in handy when Vingo decided to attack the temple.

She didn't explain any of this, however. It didn't hurt to let him think she was being obedient and dutiful—as long as he didn't get too smug about it.

"But what about the holyman?" Crystal asked.

"The holyman is ..." A fraud? Did she really want to tell them that? They were pessimistic enough. "The holyman is not coming."

"Why not?" asked Vinnagon.

"He said he can't help you. But, Vingo, he also said you have the power to help yourself. If you fight for Kashram, Kashram will fight for you."

Harl *had* said that, more or less. Vinnagon didn't need to know about Harl's doubts.

Gwenshi had no doubts. She had faith. Vinnagon was a good man, and Gwenshi wouldn't let a demon keep him down.

* * *

Beetle had never visited Mayor Duskraven before. The Mayor's Residence was not much larger than his own workshop, but it had two floors. The mayor invited him to the second-floor balcony, from which they had a good view of the temple sitting high on the cliff above the town.

Beetle did not wish to waste the mayor's time, so he spoke directly, saying, "I believe something in the temple has gone very wrong."

"Wrong?" Duskraven seemed surprised. "What do you mean?"

"Have you seen the posters of the runaway taishrefi?"

"I have," said Duskraven.

Beetle swallowed. Here, he was taking a chance. He said, "I know that woman."

"You do?" The mayor was curious now.

"Yes," said Beetle. "She and I are ... well, let us just say that she would not run off with a Kashramite."

"Ah," said the mayor. "I see."

The mayor shook his head sadly. "I would like to help you, young man, but the transgressions of taishrefis are under the authority of the temple. I am not seeking the young lady's apprehension, but neither have I the authority to prevent it."

"There is more," said Beetle.

"More of what?"

"Have you not noticed that the temple now gives curses instead of blessings?"

"That is simply the bashrefi's way," Duskraven said.

"But it is not *Lashrefi's* way," Beetle said.

"That is not for us to judge."

Beetle realized he was now whistling near the bear, but this was the man with the power to give Crys the help she needed. He said, "Mayor Duskraven, I believe the things we are beginning to hear down here are only echoes of troubles that have been happening up there for some time."

The mayor's eyes rose to the temple, and Beetle thought he saw a hint of fear.

"Several initiates and taishrefis have disappeared over the past two years," Beetle said. "Parents are told that their daughter will be serving in a distant village, but she leaves without saying goodbye. And when the family goes to visit—"

"Now stop right there," Duskraven warned him. "Think about what you really want to say."

Beetle knew what he wanted to say—what he *had* to say. "I say those women were murdered. As were those who met unfortunate accidents. Think about that: a *taishrefi* dying from *misfortune*. That is not Lashrefi's way."

"Now you are getting close to blasphemy."

"Just the opposite," said Beetle. "I refuse to associate Lashrefi with the deeds of that evil temple."

"That temple blesses us with the guidance of the Goddess," Duskraven said. He looked afraid now. "How dare you call it evil."

"I speak the truth," Beetle said. "Crystal did not run away

to be with a Kashramite. She ran away because the bashrefi ordered her execution. I am told you have a daughter in the temple. Will she be next?"

Duskraven's voice was cold and shivery. "Who told you about my daughter?"

"Crystal did."

"You know where she is."

Beetle opened his mouth to speak. But he couldn't deny it. Truthfully, it did not matter what he said, as the mayor's next words made clear:

"By my authority as mayor of Darcliff, I am placing you under arrest."

* * *

As the day wore on, the trio hiding in the instrument shop began to suspect what had happened. Gwenshi tried to make up reasons for Beetle's lateness—he had stopped to buy food; he had decided to seek help from the mayor of Clifford; he had gone to visit his parents—but after a while she had to admit that the more dreadful possibilities were more likely.

"I should not have let him go," Crystal said.

"Men go where they want," Gwenshi said.

"I could have talked him out of it," Crystal said.

"Could be," said Gwenshi. "Or could be that would have made him more stubborn."

"No," said Crystal. "He's not like that."

Gwenshi caught the way her eyes flicked unconsciously to Vingo, who was brooding in a corner.

"I should have known how the mayor would react," Crystal said. "I'm a taishrefi. Understanding people is my job."

"I thought your job is to talk to Lashrefi," Gwenshi said.

Crystal shook her head. "That's only part of it. Taishrefis are supposed to lead—not by giving orders, the way men lead, but by understanding people."

"Oh. Manipulating people," said Gwenshi. "Aye, our women try that, too. But I've never been able to make

Vinnagon do anything." That wasn't true, but he was easier to deal with if he believed she couldn't manipulate him.

Crystal said, "I was supposed to understand Mayor Dusk-raven. I was hoping that once he learned more about the temple, he would realize that his daughter was in danger. But he must have known already. Perhaps everyone knows already."

"I didn't know," Gwenshi said. "I thought everything was fine until Vingo showed up and told me it wasn't."

"You were quick to believe me," Vinnagon said.

Gwenshi shrugged. "You're my husband."

That really was the whole of it. It hadn't mattered *why* Vingo wanted to run away. He had been running, and she had wanted to run with him. Could be she loved him. Could be she was just tired of shelling peas. She didn't rightly know.

Crystal put her head in her hands. "If anything happens to him, I'll not forgive myself."

"Now that's no way to talk," Gwenshi said. "Look, would it make you feel better if I went to look for him?"

"That's risky," Vinnagon said.

"I've already been out once today and no one noticed me. To them I'm just another Redwoman."

"But Kashramite women are not very common in Darcliff," Crystal pointed out. "You tend to stay on the other side of the river."

"So?"

"So Vinnagon is correct. It is risky."

Gwenshi studied the Stripedwoman. "But you want me to go," she guessed.

Crystal looked beseechingly at Vinnagon. "If I knew what happened to him …"

Gwenshi joined her plea: "Let me look for him, Vingo. If he's all right, Crystal needs to know. And if he's in the town jail, we might be able to bust him out."

Vinnagon glowered at her. "I did not say you should not go. I said it is risky."

"Aye," said Gwenshi. "All right, then. I'll risk it."

Crystal reached out to touch Gwenshi's forehead. "May the blessing of Lashrefi be upon you."

"Thanks," said Gwenshi. She almost added, *But Kashram is all I need,* but that would have been rude. And foolish.

* * *

There were a lot of Stripedmen in the streets. Gwenshi tried to remember what Beetle had been wearing, but nothing much came to mind. Beetle wore brown. All the Stripedmen wore brown.

But there *was* something identifiable about the way he carried himself. His posture was straight. His movements were deliberate. His hands were always precisely where he wanted them to be. That was the sort of thing she might be able to pick out of a crowd.

And if he *was* out on the streets, she could rely on him to see her. Crystal was right: Gwenshi was the only Redwoman in town.

Which made it difficult for her to scout the mayor's house. A Redwoman wandering around the building peeking in the windows would be noticed. Nor could she make up some excuse to visit. Redwomen lived in Camptown. They had no business with Darcliff's mayor.

So Gwenshi scouted the mayor's house only in passing on her way to the town jail. Despite her attempts at optimism, she reckoned that was the most likely place to find Beetle. And she had thought of an excuse to get in.

The stone jail was not far from the docks. Attached was a small wooden annex that held the jailor's office. Gwenshi knocked.

"Good afternoon," said the jailor. "Can I help you?"

Gwenshi scowled and spat on the paving stones. "I come to see my husband."

"Your husband? I'm afraid he's not here."

"You sure? Big, tall fellow. Red skin." She spoke through

her nose, trying to sound as obnoxious as possible.

"I assure you, we are presently detaining no Kashramites."

"Oh. Well, do you mind if I ask around? Maybe one of *them* has seen him."

"One of ... our prisoners?"

"Aye."

"I'm afraid I cannot let you in."

"What do I got to do? Pick your pocket?"

To Gwenshi's surprise, the jailor remained quite amiable. Could be she was amusing him.

"I'm afraid that would be counterproductive," he said. "Female miscreants are held in the cellar of the inn across the street."

Gwenshi pretended to consider this. "You mean they're locked in with the beer?"

"In those rare circumstances when a woman chances to overstep the bounds of the law, yes."

"Aren't you worried they'll drink it all?"

The soldier was actually smirking now. "I assure you, they are usually too chastened to misbehave further."

"Huh."

"Indeed."

"Well, what about the window?"

The soldier tilted his head in puzzlement. "I do not know. What about the window?"

"Can I talk to someone through the window?"

"Of course," he said. "I am certain they would be delighted to speak with you."

Gwenshi nodded, considered spitting on the paving stones again, decided that would be a bit too much, and swaggered around the corner.

That had gone well. Now she had an excuse to look inside the jail. The only problem was that the window was two feet above her head.

Gwenshi looked around for a barrel or a crate to stand on. Nothing.

She contemplated swiping a crate from the docks. But no, she didn't want to get in trouble here. The cellar of the inn across the street was probably still damp and moldy, even during this late-summer drought.

Well, the jailor had said she could talk through the window. Jumping wasn't illegal, was it?

Gwenshi found a plausible foothold at hip-height. She backed off to get a run at it. Three swift strides, a leap, a push off the foothold, and ... ha! The iron bars of the window were in her grasp. Gwenshi chinned herself up and peered inside.

It was dark.

"Hey," she said, in a low voice.

"Hello?"

"I'm looking for Beetle."

"Huh?"

"Beetle. The fellow who makes drums and flutes and those things with strings."

"Lutes."

"Right. Have you seen him?"

"... Why?"

"Ah ... just curious."

That didn't sound credible even to Gwenshi. Women don't usually jump at seven-foot-high windows and hang there out of curiosity.

"How curious?" the inmate asked.

"Um ... Oh!" He wanted payment. "How curious do I need to be?"

"Let us say ... curious enough to buy me a beer."

"Well," said Gwenshi, "I can probably give you money for a beer. But I can't untie my pouch while I'm hanging from the—"

"No, no. I don't want the money. I want the beer. Money does me no good in here."

"Huh? How can I get you beer? You want me to throw it through the window?"

"No. You can sneak it in through the food slot."

"The food slot? Where's that?"

"In the door."

"Isn't the door inside the annex?"

"Yes."

"The annex is guarded."

"Ah. Yes. Well … use your feminine charms."

Gwenshi thought about this. The guard kind of liked her, but she had a feeling that, if she tried to smuggle in beer, the bloom of cordiality might rapidly fade.

"I don't like that deal," she said. "Pick something else."

"Are you a friend of Beetle's?"

"Aye."

"What?"

"Yes," she said. "Sure."

"Ask him if I can borrow a flute."

"A flute?"

"I promise to give it back when I get out."

Gwenshi tried to make sense of this. "I can *ask* him," she said. "But where do you think I'll find him?"

"Oh. I forgot about that."

"About what?"

"The Holy Seneschal came for him. I think he's charged with aiding fugitives."

"Oh."

That *was* about the worst possibility they had considered. Breaking Beetle out of the temple would be tricky.

"I suppose that means no flute," said the prisoner, glumly.

"Aye," said Gwenshi. "I reckon so."

Feet shuffled disconsolately in the darkness.

"Are you locked up for public drunkenness?" Gwenshi asked.

"Yes."

"You should try to sleep it off," she suggested. "You aren't ready to be let out yet."

* * *

Vinnagon knew he should have forbidden her to leave. Anything could have happened to her by now. The streets of Darcliff were usually safe for a woman, but Gwenshi was now a horse thief, and Vinnagon feared his bad luck might carry over to her.

For Crystal's sake, he pretended to be stoic. Crystal was anxious enough on her own.

How long had it been? Gwenshi should not have stayed out more than half a lithic.

Knuckles rapped on the door.

Crystal jumped.

Vinnagon slid the bolt and yanked the door open. "Where have you been?" he demanded.

"Excuse me?"

The man at the door was not Gwenshi. He was a Lashrefite about Vinnagon's height, perhaps ten years older.

Vinnagon asked, "Who are you?"

"My name is Bobwhite," the man said. "Is Beetle in? I came to pick up my lute."

The Lashrefite peered over Vinnagon's shoulder. He frowned. Then his eyes grew wide.

"I— ah—" The Lashrefite backed away nervously. His gaze flicked to the sword hanging at Vinnagon's side, back to Vinnagon's face. Then he turned and ran.

Vinnagon shut the door and slid the bolt home. "We've been recognized."

Crystal nodded. She looked nearly as frightened as their unexpected visitor.

Vinnagon crossed to the workbench and picked up the second sword. He slid it onto his belt and adjusted the scabbards so he could wear one sword on each hip.

Crystal asked, "Are you preparing to fight or to run?"

Her voice was calm, but Vinnagon could hear the effort behind that calmness.

"To run," he admitted. He was always running. This was no life for a Kashram-created man. A true warrior would take a stand and die fighting … but something told him that this was not yet the time.

"We should part ways," Crystal said. "The townspeople will not recognize you alone."

Vinnagon hesitated. "Is that what your goddess tells you?"

"No. I just thought—"

"They will recognize *you*," Vinnagon said.

"Getting out of Darcliff will take some luck, but—"

"It is time to stop relying on luck," he said. "We need to use our wits. We need the quickest route out of town that leads past the fewest people."

"That would be back to the boulder field, then."

"Very good," said Vinnagon. "And now we need some way to tell the others where we've gone."

"I could write Beetle a message."

"He can read?"

"His parents taught him letters," Crystal said. "It's part of their religious tradition."

Vinnagon wondered how a man from a deviant religion had managed to entangle himself with a taishrefi. Beetle and Crystal were just looking for trouble. But that was the consequence of the haphazard Lashrefite courting customs. Arranged marriages were so much simpler.

"I'll leave a message for Gwenshi," he said.

He opened the front door just enough to collect a few stones from the street outside. These he carefully arranged on the workbench where Gwenshi expected "her" sword to be.

She would realize that meant she should look for him at the boulder field. Probably. The woman wasn't stupid; she was just crazy sometimes.

Crystal had a small bundle of food slung over one shoulder. "I am ready. May Lashrefi smile upon our path."

And may Kashram give us strength, Vinnagon prayed as they went out the door.

A glance up and down the street told him that Beetle's customer was long gone. Would he keep mum? Not likely.

Vinnagon checked Crystal over his shoulder and said, "Stay close behind me."

"Behind you? That will draw attention. Women walk beside men in Darcliff."

Lashrefite women never walked with Kashramites in Darcliff—except for taishrefis escorted by bladesmen. He and Crystal would draw attention no matter what. But it was pointless to argue. They needed to move.

"Stay on my left, then."

Crystal wordlessly acquiesced.

The streets were not empty. But nor were they so crowded that Vinnagon and Crystal could avoid notice.

Vinnagon turned up an alley.

Crystal said, "People will wonder why a Kashramite and a Lashrefite are cutting through alleys. We need to stay inconspicuous."

"Someone will recognize us sooner or later," he said. "Our best hope is to get out of town before the temple can react."

Crystal considered this. "Very well."

They emerged from the alley onto the next street.

"Can I rely upon your eyes?" Vinnagon asked.

"What do you mean?"

"You watch your half of the street, and I shall watch mine."

"Yes. You can rely on me. But if you keep looking over your shoulder, you will look suspicious."

"I *am* suspicious," said Vinnagon. "If they come from behind, I want to know."

From the roof of a house ahead of them, a great bird took flight.

Vinnagon asked, "That's a vulture, isn't it?"

Crystal followed its laborious flapping with her eyes. "It is. And it is flying up to the temple."

"They say the bashrefi can see through the eyes of vultures," Vinnagon said. "Is that true?"

"It is preposterous," said Crystal, though the word was spoken without conviction. "My grandmother never taught me anything like that."

"So it is preposterous for Lashrefi's holywomen," said Vinnagon, "but perhaps possible for Shakredo's?"

Crystal was still gazing skyward. The bird had landed on the peak of the temple's roof.

"Perhaps," she admitted.

A man pushing a wheelbarrow came around the corner. Vinnagon met his gaze, daring him to question why an Arvethidrel warrior was in this part of town.

The man's eyes flashed to Crystal's face and widened with recognition. "Fugitives!" he cried. "Fugitives from temple justice!"

Crystal turned and ran. Vinnagon ran after her.

* * *

Gwenshi halted on the street below the temple. It was time to admit that she was not going to catch up to Beetle and his captors. Or rather, his *captor*. She could see Beetle and a lone bladesman climbing the switchback road.

Gwenshi reckoned the temple underestimated Beetle. Only a single guard? If Gwenshi had gone to look for him just a bit sooner ...

But wait. Her friend in the Darcliff Jail had said that the *seneschal* had come to fetch Beetle. Neither of those men on the road was the seneschal.

The sound of boots on gravel alerted Gwenshi to the fact that the Holy Seneschal and five bladesmen were trotting down the street.

Six enemies. Gwenshi had only four knives. She turned and ran.

She cut hard at the next corner and dashed for an alley. There she waited, listening intently. She *thought* she heard the temple guards jogging along the street, but then the sound faded into the background noise of the town.

Gwenshi came out of hiding. The seneschal and her escort were nowhere to be seen, but above the downstream end of town circled a large, black bird.

Gwenshi knew why the seneschal had left Beetle in the custody of just one guard. Vingo had gotten himself in trouble again.

* * *

Running with two swords was awkward, but Vinnagon was still able to catch up to Crystal. She was carrying that bundle of food.

The street was wide enough for two wagons, so it was easy for them to run side by side. Lashrefites stared as they ran past.

From an open door ahead, a bucket of mop water flew onto the graveled street. Vinnagon's foot hit the puddle and slipped on the mud. He fell.

Crystal stopped to help him up.

"Truly, you are well cursed," she said.

He nodded and rose to his feet, wondering what would get in their way next. Behind him, Lashrefites called, "Fugitives! Fugitives!"

"Those trees," said Crystal, resuming her flight.

Vinnagon kept pace. If they could just get to the edge of town, they could disappear into the forest. The terrain was rugged—that was why the town ended there—but the ruggedness would be to their advantage. Especially if their pursuers had horses.

From behind, a man cried, "I see them! Captain, they've gone this way!"

Vinnagon glanced over his shoulder. For some reason, a mounted militia squad just happened to be at the downstream end of Darcliff. Two more riders came around the corner. And another.

Crystal shouted, "Watch out!"

Vinnagon tripped over a stool someone had left in the street. He sprawled across the gravel.

As he regained his feet, a two-horse wagon appeared at the intersection ahead and slowly rolled around the corner. A hue and cry was coming down a side street: "Fugitives! Fugitives!"

"Come this way!" Crystal said. She cut back into the alley.

Vinnagon dashed after her. Crystal knew what she was doing. With any luck, the wagon would pass by and block off the entrance just as the riders arrived.

But Vinnagon was unlikely to have any luck.

He ran through the alley to the first garden gate. He opened it and left it open. He opened two others as well, hoping to present a visual fence that would make the horses balk.

But it was the hue and cry that reached the alley first. The leaders dodged around the gate. One man took the time to shut it. More came flooding in behind.

Crystal was waiting for him at the other end of the alley.

"I'll catch up!" he called. He turned to face their pursuers.

It was only eleven men. One had a hoe; the rest were unarmed. Vinnagon had two swords, years of training, and the favor of Kashram.

He drew both swords. In truth, he only knew how to use one, but the Lashrefites did not know that. They slowed.

He still had one open gate between him and them. He kicked it closed.

"You have me!" he said. "Now what will you do with me?"

They stopped.

He eased down into an attack stance and glided forward, smoothly swinging the shining blades in controlled arcs.

The hue and cry turned and ran.

Vinnagon turned, too, and saw that Crystal had disobeyed him. Instead of taking advantage of his tactic, she had remained in the alley. She motioned urgently for him to follow her into a garden.

He sheathed his swords and did as she bade, for he heard riders approaching. He closed the gate and ducked down, imitating Crystal who was lying low, pressed against the fence.

Hoofbeats sounded in the alley—a single horse only. They struck close by, then diminished.

Vinnagon opened the gate. Crystal slipped out ahead of him

and scurried to the corner where the alley met the street. Crouching low, she looked both ways. Then she motioned for Vinnagon to follow.

Riders were heading away from them. Crystal and Vinnagon turned up the street and ducked into the next alley.

They had inspired quite a ruckus in the quietest part of town. Now they were heading toward the busier streets. Houses were dense here with no gardens to duck into.

When they were ten strides from the next street, Crystal put up a warning hand. "Riders coming."

Vinnagon flattened himself against the wall. Crystal did likewise.

Two horses passed the alley at a trot, then stopped. One of the horses snorted.

Hooves shuffled. They were coming back for a second look.

Crystal's muscles tensed. She glanced at Vinnagon, and in that glance, he saw what she planned to do.

He nodded.

She leapt out of the alley and shouted, "Hya!"

Vinnagon was right behind her. The riders were Lashref-ites—soldiers in the Darcliff Militia. One was dancing his horse in circles, trying to regain control.

The other drew his sword and shouted, "Halt!" at Crystal, but she was already racing up the street.

The soldier took a swipe at Vinnagon, and Vinnagon had to dive to the ground to avoid the singing blade.

He rolled to his feet and drew his own sword—only one this time, for he knew his opponent would not be bluffed.

The Lashrefite leapt from the saddle and landed in the street to face him.

Slash, slash, thrust! His foe's strokes came viper-quick. But Vinnagon met each stroke and did not allow his blade to be drawn off line.

Vinnagon yielded a step, and the Lashrefite attacked again. The foe was quicker, but he knew only one trick. The third time, Vinnagon was ready.

He blocked the slashes and glided past the thrust, gently pushing his opponent's blade aside. With a left-handed uppercut, he struck the Lashrefite in the jaw, lifting him off his feet. The blade fell from limp fingers and clattered against the paving stones. The Lashrefite landed on his back and did not rise.

By this time, the other soldier had regained control of his horse, but he did not engage Vinnagon, preferring instead to call, "To me! To me!"

Vinnagon chose not to wait for the soldier's reinforcements.

Crystal had not gone far. He found her at the edge of Eggsandfish Square. Only three merchants were selling—one fish basket and two egg baskets—but all were drawing good business.

"Perhaps now is the time to join the crowd," she said.

"And then what?" he asked.

"Wait for them to get tired of looking for us," she said. "Should we walk toward the docks?"

He followed her toward the more crowded Market Square, but he said, "I am not certain we can evade notice so easily."

"It's them!"

A tiny man, only three feet tall, was staring at them and pointing. Beside him, a Lashrefite woman of about five-and-a-half feet was gaping wide eyed.

Vinnagon tensed to run, but Crystal halted, returning their stares with puzzlement.

The unknown woman glanced furtively about, seized the tiny man's hand—he was Clanfolk, probably a visiting merchant—and scampered over.

She said, "You're Taishrefi Crystal, aren't you?"

"Ah ... yes."

Vinnagon had expected Crystal to deny it, but something in the woman's voice expressed just how deeply she *wanted* Crystal to be Taishrefi Crystal.

"And you're Vinnagon," said the little man, looking up at him in admiration.

The woman was almost breathless. "I thought it was a sin to love a man of another people. But when I heard that you—" Her voice caught. "And now that I've met you—"

"You're an inspiration," the little man told Vinnagon earnestly.

"It's a sign from Lashrefi!" the woman squeaked.

Crystal looked at Vinnagon in dismay.

"We need to go," said Vinnagon. And it was true, for across Market Square he saw the Holy Seneschal.

* * *

Gwenshi dashed into Market Square. The seneschal was shouting to clear out the crowd. A vulture perched on the roof of the tailor shop told Gwenshi that Vinnagon was probably here, too.

Gwenshi needed a weapon—something longer than a knife.

Between her and the seneschal, she saw an ironmonger's stand. She veered toward it, shouting, "I need to borrow a hoe!"

Before the confused vendor could react, she snatched a hoe from his display and charged after the seneschal. It was time for a duel!

* * *

"Seize them!" the seneschal cried.

Vinnagon turned back towards Eggsandfish Square, but the way was blocked by riders from the Darcliff Militia.

"Should we chance the river?" Crystal asked.

"Too late," said Vinnagon. The riders had seen them, and two were moving to cut off that avenue of escape.

"The forest," said Crystal.

Vinnagon looked up the street. They could make a dash for it, but they would be ridden down from behind.

"Too far," he said.

"So what then?"

Vinnagon drew his blade. "I fight."

Bystanders were abandoning the center of the square, leaving only bewildered vendors between Vinnagon and his opponents. The bladesmen had already crossed half the distance. They formed a line with the seneschal in the middle. She was fair with a blade, but weak of arm. Vinnagon thought he could overpower her.

But he did not truly wish to fight her.

"Stay close," he said, looking for a weak point in the line of bladesmen. "When I charge, you have to be right behind me."

Crystal put her hand on his shoulder.

Behind him, another militia rider entered the square and started shouting orders.

The seneschal called, "Dead or alive, Crystal? The choice is yours."

Even making a death threat, she spoke in a woman's voice—high and sweet. It was eerie. Someone with a voice like that should not be allowed to have weapons.

Behind the seneschal, a hoe was bobbing above the heads of the marketplace, coming closer.

"Yyyyyaaaaaaaah!"

Gwenshi's scream was high, but definitely *not* sweet. The seneschal turned in surprise.

Vinnagon was surprised to see Gwenshi, too, but his legs were already charging, reacting faster than his mind.

Hilligram, the bladesman on the far right, had turned at the sound of Gwenshi's scream, weakening that flank. Vinnagon thrust at his comrade's shoulder, driving his sword point into the muscle, pinning Hilligram so that he could not turn back and fight.

Crystal—obeying orders for once—followed his charge and passed him while he held Hilligram. Vinnagon spun away to free his blade. By then, Gwenshi was in over her head.

* * *

Gwenshi had three feet of hoe between herself and the seneschal, but the Stripedwoman seemed determined to close the distance. In a knife fight, Gwenshi would have tried to seize the wrist and counterthrust, but now she realized that swords and hoes were not knives.

The seneschal was pushing Gwenshi back. Gwenshi couldn't wind up for a good swing without exposing her belly. And she could not jab at the woman's striped face without stepping toward that flashing blade.

So she fought a defensive retreat and hoped that Vinnagon would step in to save her.

Her back foot bumped into an apple basket and the Stripedwoman lunged. Gwenshi spun away, planted a foot, dropped to a crouch, and struck at the seneschal's leg.

Contact!

But her blow was weak, and her foe's stance was firm.

The seneschal drew her blade through the air in a slicing arc that glanced off the hoe handle and shaved off a wooden curl. Before Gwenshi could rise from her crouch, a booted leg snapped up and caught her under the jaw.

Gwenshi rolled with it, releasing the hoe and somersaulting backwards to land on her feet.

The seneschal pressed her advantage, gliding forward.

Gwenshi leapt away from the thrust and reached for her dueling knife.

"Gwenshi, run!"

Oh. Aye. She didn't have to defeat the temple's best woman fighter in single combat. Could be a quick diversion was good enough.

Gwenshi left her dueling knife in its sheath and bolted toward Vinnagon.

Crystal was with him. Good. Gwenshi was glad they were all together again. She hoped that Crystal wouldn't slow them down.

The consensus seemed to be that they should run for the river. She checked over her shoulder. They were actually building a lead. Once the crowd thinned, the horsemen would be able to catch up, but for now—

"This way!"

Vinnagon dashed toward a dock. Gwenshi and Crystal followed.

Vinnagon was so strong! He could sprint this fast and still have breath to shout at them.

A riverboat was gliding by. Vinnagon leapt off the end of the dock. Gwenshi planted her foot and soared through the air behind him.

He landed with a grunt and she crashed into his back, knocking them both to the deck of the boat.

Gwenshi looked up to see Crystal flying through the air, arms and legs flailing wildly, a cloth bundle trailing behind her. The Stripedwoman splashed into the river three feet short.

"Crystal!" Gwenshi called. She leaned over the side of the boat. White hair floated just below the surface of the river.

Gwenshi reached in, grabbed a fistful of hair, and lifted, pulling herself off balance.

Crystal's head bobbed up, mouth gasping.

"Vingo, grab my legs!" Gwenshi called, for it seemed a current was pulling Crystal away, pulling Gwenshi into the water.

Firm hands seized her calves. People were talking excitedly in words she couldn't understand. As the current eased, blue arms reached out beside hers and caught Crystal's striped hand. In moments, other blue arms joined in, and Crystal was hoisted into the boat.

An arm wrapped about Gwenshi's middle and hauled her back so that she could sit on the deck. Gwenshi looked up into a sky of bald, blue Riverfolk wearing linen sheets and puzzled faces.

* * *

Beetle had not visited the temple often, not even after getting to know Crys. He respected her dedication to Lashrefi, but his parents had taught him that life's spiritual journey was personal, that he should not allow institutions like the Darcliff Temple to overshadow the authority of the deities above.

This was his first time in the caverns, and he was in a prison cell. It was square, wide enough for him to lie down in, tall enough that he did not bump his head, although he could touch the ceiling.

The door had no window. It bolted from the outside.

The mattress was stuffed with corn husks—from last year, or possibly the year before. Musty, but softer than the limestone floor.

He had expected darkness, but they had given him a torch—a flaming bundle of tallow-soaked rushes ensconced high on one wall. As a woodworker, he would never have allowed such a thing in his shop. It seemed dangerous rather than comforting.

It was also smoky. The torch would have been clean enough on the street, but Beetle's cell had no ventilation.

How long would he be held here? He was charged with aiding fugitives—which he had done.

Somehow, the vultures knew where Crys was. One vulture had come swooping up toward the temple, catching the seneschal's attention. A second vulture had circled over his neighborhood. These signs had convinced the seneschal to leave Beetle in the custody of a single guard while she and the others ran off.

Beetle hoped Crys and the Kashramites could escape somehow, but if the seneschal saw them fleeing his shop, that would prove his guilt. And then what would the Holy Council do to him? Probably whatever they wanted to do to Crys. Last time, they had tried to drown her.

Drowning. Now that was a grim fate. To go to Lashrefi, a corpse had to be placed in the open air for the crows to eat. To go to Yolim, a body had to join the soil. Beetle knew there were some deities who would fetch a person's soul from water, but none of them were likely to fetch *him*.

Not for the first time, Beetle wondered how Crys had let herself be caught up in the Darcliff Temple. If only he could have found her before she became an initiate.

But she had already joined the temple when she walked into his instrument shop—so tall, so beautiful, so certain of herself.

His parents had never warned him against falling in love with a woman of traditional faith. The opposite, in fact. "Good women are hard to catch," his father had said. "If you catch one, keep her, even if she's not a Bargainkeeper."

His father had not been thinking of taishrefis.

The bolt outside his door slid back. The door opened. Two hulking, stern-faced Kashramites walked in.

They seized his arms and pushed his face to the wall. They were bigger men, stronger men. Beetle did not resist.

One untied the rope that bound his wrists. Beetle flexed his fingers, careful not to make any moves that might seem threatening.

Were they taking him somewhere? Were they letting him go?

No. The rope wrapped around his wrists again. They were just resecuring his bonds.

"And don't try burning through this rope," one of them warned. "Your flesh is thin, and the rope is thick."

Burning through the rope had not even occurred to Beetle. The torch was at eye level. With his hands tied behind his back, how would he even reach it?

"Turn around and be respectful," one said.

Beetle turned around. Standing in the doorway were two women. Another temple guard waited behind them.

The Lashrefite woman was Bashrefi Wintersmoke. Beetle had never met her—she rarely left the temple—but he recognized the symbols embroidered on her sky-blue tunic. She was old, though still young enough to be "middle-aged" if one were feeling charitable. Her cheeks were plump, but they held no dimples.

Beside her stood a grey-skinned woman of less than half the bashrefi's girth. Beetle couldn't guess her age. Her hair was silver, but her face could have been anywhere between twenty and two hundred. Her eyes glowed green when they met his, and he felt as if she were staring into his soul.

Remembering Crys's account of the Woshite's magical powers, Beetle realized that she *was* staring into his soul.

No one spoke. No one moved. The slender Woshite held his gaze for ten breaths before breaking the silence with the words, "We may begin."

The bashrefi spoke to one of the guards: "Take that thing off him." When the guard did not react, she said, "That brooch! Remove it."

A red hand seized Beetle's dragon brooch and yanked it from his tunic. Beetle tried not to flinch. It was just a chunk of metal. His faith was in his heart.

"I could have you executed just for wearing that," the bashrefi said.

It was not true. Or at least, the implication that he had committed a capital sin was not true. But that didn't matter. This bashrefi could have anyone executed for any reason.

"Where is she?" the bashrefi asked.

Beetle did not know what to say. He assumed the seneschal was already searching his shop. She would give a full report as soon as she returned to the temple. Beetle could think of no way to lead these people astray.

The Woshite frowned. "Ask it again," she said.

"Where is she?" the bashrefi repeated.

"Wood place," said the Woshite woman.

"The forest?"

"No. A house. With wood inside."

The bashrefi relaxed. "Ah. His workshop. Well, that was simple." She cocked her head at Beetle. "Do you have anything to add? Anything you would like to say before we fetch your ... whatever she is to you."

"Why should I speak, when you can steal my thoughts from my mind?" Beetle demanded.

"If he speaks, it should be politer," said the tiny woman in her strange Woshite accent. "Make the mens punish him."

The bashrefi ignored her. "You should speak," she told Beetle, "because your words may save Crystal."

"You already attempted to drown her," Beetle said.

The bashrefi smiled. "Your words may save her … from torture."

Beetle hoped Crys could save herself by escaping from the seneschal. If Lashrefi was not with her, then she would be just as doomed as he was.

"She knows things," the bashrefi said. "Things she mustn't know. And we must find out whom she has told before we kill her."

"You don't need to torture her," Beetle said. He nodded at the Woshite. "You can read her mind."

"True," said the bashrefi. "But sometimes I prefer traditional ways."

She smiled. "We can have this conversation again once Crystal is in custody. I might even let you see her … or at least, pieces of her. Let me know which piece is your favorite."

They left him to think on these things with his hands tied behind his back and the torch still smoking.

* * *

Vinnagon thanked the Riverman for the bandage and began wrapping it around Gwenshi's arm. "You're lucky it's just a flesh wound," he said. "You almost lost a tendon."

"I thought I got away clean," Gwenshi said. "I don't remember getting cut."

The wound was bleeding more than Vinnagon liked. "Keep this arm above your head."

"Sure, Vingo. This isn't my first cut, you know."

It was true. Her arms were scarred from knife fights— mostly playing, she had explained the day they first met.

But Vinnagon had never seen her wounded before, and it affected him strangely.

"Be more careful," he said. "You could have been killed."

Gwenshi's eyes brightened. "I know! It was wonderful!"

"Wonderful?"

"Aye! I could have been killed … and I wasn't! Vingo, I want to fight her again."

"Woman, you have lost your mind."

"Could be," she said. She tossed her head back and laughed.

The Riverfolk looked at her with worried smiles.

The boat was some way downstream from Darcliff by now. Crystal was negotiating with the boat's captain. From their faces, Vinnagon gathered that their conversation was more serious than his. Well, of course it was more serious: Neither Crystal nor the captain was talking to a madwoman.

"Thanks for telling me to run, though," Gwenshi said. "I had forgotten about that part of the plan."

"You had a plan?"

"Not really." She giggled. "But it worked!"

Vinnagon shook his head. "Gwenshi, you are …" But he let the words trail off. Insufferable? She wasn't truly insufferable. She had given him the opportunity he needed. And in truth, he was grateful.

He brushed a stray lock of hair away from her cheek. It flopped back. Stubborn. Just like his wife.

The boat drew near the riverbank, in the shadow of the forested bluffs.

Crystal said, "Vinnagon. Gwenshi. We must go."

Her face was a stern mask. Vinnagon wondered what she thought he had done wrong. He did not appreciate her tone.

But the captain of the boat was staring at him with hard eyes, and this did not seem to be a good moment to make a fuss.

The boat drew up against the bank. The water was so low that the bank was a foot higher than the boat. Vinnagon stepped off. There was a game trail here, a narrow ledge of flatness at the bottom of a nearly vertical bluff.

Gwenshi followed, and Crystal came last. The taishrefi raised three fingers and blew a blessing toward the boat as it drifted gently away.

"Nice folks," Gwenshi said. "A bit hard to talk to. But nice."

"They speak our language quite well," Crystal said. "They are just shy."

"What did you and the captain discuss?" Vinnagon wanted to know.

Crystal shook her head and her shoulders relaxed a little. "Oh, I had to convince him that I would take you to justice."

"To justice?" Vinnagon asked.

"Yes," said Crystal. "We were running, Gwenshi was wounded, and you had blood on your sword. I told him the situation was complicated and out of his jurisdiction. In the end, I convinced him, so he let us go."

So that explained the stern look. She had felt a need to feign displeasure. Lashrefites did not equate dishonesty with impiety. Perhaps Lashrefi did not, either.

"So we're free," Gwenshi said. "That's good."

Crystal looked at the steep bluff. "I fear the walk back to Darcliff will not be easy."

"Did you bring food?" Gwenshi nodded hopefully at the bundle over Crystal's shoulder.

"I did," she said. "But the bread is soggy."

"I'm hungry, not choosy."

"There's a draw with trees around the bend," Crystal said. "We should get out of sight of the river."

* * *

Crys sat down with the Kashramites for a meal among the pines, though Gwenshi was the only one with an appetite. Between mouthfuls, Gwenshi told them that Beetle had been captured by the temple, that she had seen him climbing the cliff-side road.

Crys wondered if Gwenshi would be the last person to see Beetle alive. Then she realized that, no, it would be someone inside the temple. Someone like Rathi. The last person to see Beetle's face, the last person close enough to touch his hand.

Crys had to do something.

Gwenshi said, "I reckon we should break him out tonight. No telling what might happen if we wait."

Yes. Crys couldn't do it alone, but with Vinnagon ...

No. She had to be a taishrefi. No matter how much her heart wanted to rush after Beetle, she had to think with her head.

"The temple is well guarded," she said. "Vinnagon can't fight them all."

"I don't know," said Gwenshi. "He's done pretty well so far."

Vinnagon made a derisive sound by expelling air through his nostrils.

"Fighting in the temple would not be like fighting in the street," Crys said. "Shakredo's power is greater inside."

She spoke as though she were certain of this. In truth, however, Shakredo's power was something she had to infer. She could not sense Shakredo through her connection to Lashrefi. After three years in the temple, she still could not discern the difference between Lashrefi's bond and Shakredo's. Perhaps that ability to remain hidden was itself evidence of Shakredo's power.

Perhaps the deity and the demon were too similar. Lashrefi liked ravens and wind. The bashrefi had brought vultures and smoke. Two sides of the same coin. It was easy to twist good luck into bad, to offer blessings while dispensing curses.

"Well, we just need to break the curse," Gwenshi said. "Then Shakredo won't be able to affect him."

"Woman, if we knew how to break the curse, we would have done so."

"Harl said the power is inside you, Vingo. You just have to use it."

The Kashramite made that sound with his nostrils again.

Crys had failed him. She was the one who deserved his scorn, not his loving, little wife. Against Shakredo, Crys was powerless.

Was it because the powers of fortune and misfortune were too similar?

She had not been feigning wisdom when she had told Vinnagon that she sensed the power of Kashram inside him and Gwenshi. Kashram's power was not exactly stronger than Lashrefi's, but it was different. It was harder and ... more passionate, perhaps—less about thoughts and more about actions.

And so when Vinnagon was in action, when he turned to confront his foes as the god of battle wished him to, Shakredo's power could not cause him misfortune. Because he was not relying on fortune. He was relying on his muscles and his instincts.

Crys asked, "What does Harl do when he wants to invoke Kashram?"

"I don't know," Gwenshi said. "I'm not a holyman."

"But you have been to weddings," Crys said. "And funerals."

"Oh, aye," Gwenshi said.

"So what do your people do?"

"We do a lot of yelling and dancing," Gwenshi said.

"And at funerals?"

"The same."

"Ah," said Crys. Kashramites were an odd people.

"Sometimes men spar," Vinnagon said.

"Aye," said Gwenshi. "My brothers crossed blades at our wedding, didn't they, Vingo?"

Vinnagon had a distant look in his eye. "Harl and Uncle Brekko dueled above my father's grave."

"Oh," said Gwenshi. "You never told me that."

Crys studied the two swords Vinnagon wore on his belt. Gwenshi claimed that one of those was hers. The holyman had given her two.

Combat was as important for Kashram as singing was for Lashrefi.

Crys arose and brushed the pine needles from her leggings.

"Vinnagon," she said, "I believe I know how to break your curse."

"Good," said Gwenshi. "And once we've done that, we can go rescue Beetle."

* * *

The bolt scraped and the door opened. Beetle retreated to the rear wall of his cell.

A Kashramite entered carrying a chamber pot. He set it in the corner, then took up a position by the door, arms folded.

The bashrefi was in the passageway, and she remained there. The Woshite and the seneschal entered.

"If you want to go free, tell us what you know," the seneschal demanded.

"About what?" Beetle asked.

"Anything Crystal told you," the seneschal said. "We want to know everything she knows, and we want to know who else knows it."

Why were they asking him instead of Crys? Had she eluded them once again?

"I have not seen her," Beetle said.

"You are lying." The seneschal put her hand on the hilt of her sword. "If you want to live, you *will* cooperate."

Beetle *did* want to live. He said, "She told me she feared there was evil within the temple."

The seneschal took a step toward him. Beetle flinched, but the flinch was not enough. Her fist struck his jaw, spinning his head. Light exploded in his mind, and his knees buckled.

He sat with his back against the wall, blinking. The seneschal towered over him, her boots uncomfortably near his face.

"We know there is evil within the temple," the seneschal said. "What did she plan to do about it?"

"I— I told her I would tell the mayor."

The seneschal drew back her boot. Beetle flinched. The foot hung there a moment, then stamped the ground in frustration.

"Is he an idiot, or can he answer our questions?" The seneschal was addressing the Woshite, who stood quietly against the wall, hands folded.

"He is confused," the slender gray-skinned woman replied. "The striking in the head is not help."

"I suspect we could smoke the truth out of him," the seneschal growled.

"The truth ritual will not work," the bashrefi said from the hallway. "He is protected by Yolim."

Beetle believed he was protected by Yolim and Lashrefi. It was comforting to think this might thwart the bashrefi somehow.

"We could try it anyway," said the seneschal. "To be certain."

"The Goddess dislikes having her powers tested," the bashrefi warned. "I suggest you let Rathi ask the questions."

The seneschal snorted. Apparently, she didn't like the little Woshite. But she stepped back to one wall to give Beetle and Rathi an unobstructed view of each other.

"You will not sit," the Woshite told him. "You will stand on the knees."

With two soldiers in the room, I imagine I will do almost anything, Beetle thought. *But that doesn't mean I'll like it.*

He shifted onto his knees.

"And you will think respect at me," the Woshite said.

Perhaps I will. Perhaps I will not.

You will, she said inside his head.

Something like talons seized his mind and pulled his consciousness upwards. His vision swam. He felt stretched between consciousness and oblivion.

She released the tension before he passed out. Her glowing green eyes danced back into focus.

"You will give respect. Or I will take respect and fear. See you?"

"What? Ah ... yes. I hear you."

"Good. I am not their kind." She gestured over her shoulder

at the other two members of the Holy Council. "I am not thinking mens are persons. Mens are animals. See you?"

"I ... am not certain I understand."

"No," she said. "Man mind is small mind. It not understand. But it obey. Now: think with your small man mind. Tell us persons Crystal saw. Today. Yesterday. Yesteryesterday."

"Crystal has been hiding," Beetle said. "She has not seen anyone."

Yolim and Lashrefi help me! Don't let me think of my parents.

"You think what? Think it again."

No.

"You think ... mother. Crystal saw her mother? No. Your mother."

"No, please!" He turned to the bashrefi. "She told my parents nothing, I assure you."

"Ask him where they live," the bashrefi said.

"No ..." said the seneschal in a deeply suspicious voice. "Ask him if they run a brewhouse."

* * *

The plateau above the river was a wild place of old trees, fallen logs, and saplings shooting up into any patch of sunlight they could find. Vinnagon enjoyed the peace of the forest. He could have enjoyed it more if the women had been able to keep quiet for any length of time.

"The lith is rising," Crystal said. "That is a good sign."

It was no "sign". The lith circled the lithward sky nine times a day. That was why time was measured in "lithics". But taishrefis saw everything in terms of fortune, as though a man could never take charge of his fate himself.

"Vinnagon," Crystal said, "let us know if we come to a place that feels right."

"Right?" he asked. "In what way?"

"It should feel like ... like Kashram. You should feel it in your soul."

Vinnagon had no idea what she was talking about, and

perhaps neither did she. Kashram did not have temples or shrines or sacred places. Kashram's power was not something a man went to visit. It was something he carried with him, like the sword at his hip.

Vinnagon patted his own sword—Harl's sword—the sword Harl had given Gwenshi to give to him.

Gwenshi now wore the other. It seemed long in comparison to her short legs. It looked out of place on her curvy hip. And yet she moved as though she had always worn a blade. He liked watching her walk.

"We must be nearly back to Darcliff by now," Gwenshi said.

Vinnagon had not seen anything he recognized, but he had never been up here before. From the slope, they might be able to see some fields or villages that would tell them where they were, but then they could also be seen. It was better to stay on the plateau, hidden by the trees.

"Are you sure we need a special place?" Gwenshi asked. "Our people don't really have temples and places like that. Kashram is more like ... I don't know ... like something you carry with you."

Vinnagon stared at her. She had echoed his thoughts!

"What?" Gwenshi asked.

"Nothing," he said, for he was not certain what to make of it.

"Anyway," said Gwenshi, "instead of wandering through the forest looking for someplace special, could be we should just pick a place and try it ... whatever 'it' is."

Crystal gave a little smile. She had not yet told them how she thought they could break the curse. Taishrefis liked their secrets.

"Perhaps we should have a little faith that the deities will guide us," Crystal said.

"Oh, aye," said Gwenshi. "But they can't help us if we aren't doing anything. How about that rock over there?"

A short distance away was a twenty-foot-high outcrop of limestone, jagged like a giant tooth. Vinnagon could feel a strength emanating from it, resonating with his bones.

He walked over to it and pressed his sword hand to the stone, sensing its depth.

"Its roots are deep inside the mountain," he said.

"It's a rock," Gwenshi said. "Rocks don't have roots."

Vinnagon ignored her, focusing instead on the feeling that rose in his heart as he opened himself to the solidity of the stone. "I think, Taishrefi, that this is perhaps the place."

Gwenshi and Crystal gave each other smug looks, as though each were saying to the other, *See? I told you.*

Vinnagon wondered how any man could handle two wives.

"So we're here," said Gwenshi. "Now what?"

"Now you need to clear your minds, open your souls to Kashram, and then …"

Gwenshi frowned. "And then *what?*"

Crystal's mask of certainty slipped. "I think you need to fight."

Gwenshi's face broke into a grin. "Oh! So that's why you wanted me to carry a sword."

"That will not work," Vinnagon said. "Gwenshi is a woman."

"It *might* work," said Gwenshi. "And I don't see any men that you can spar with."

"But neither can I spar with you," Vinnagon said. "You do not know how to use a sword."

"So teach me. I need to learn anyway, so I can help you rescue Beetle."

"The sword is not a weapon you can learn in one afternoon. You must *train.*"

"Well, this could be my first lesson."

"Vinnagon," said Crystal, "I believe this can work. What matters is that Gwenshi has the blessing of Kashram. She does not need to fight well."

"Hey!" said Gwenshi. "I fight well! I held my ground against that seneschal, and all I had was a hoe."

Vinnagon recalled the queasy feeling in his stomach when the seneschal had swung her steel blade at his tiny wife. How much worse would it be to have Gwenshi dead or maimed by his own hand?

"This is not a good idea," he said.

"You won't hurt me," Gwenshi said. "We can go slow."

Of course they would go slow. He wasn't going to spar against a novice at full speed. But he had seen things go very wrong on the training grounds even when men thought they were going slow.

"Vinnagon," said Crystal, "when we perform sacred acts, the power of the deities blows through our souls, cleansing us of any impurity. To break the curse of a demon, you will need as much of that power as your soul can hold. If we sought Lashrefi's help, I would ask you to sing. But songs are not sacred to Kashram. Combat is. Do you understand why this must be done?"

"Taishrefi Crystal, I do not think …"

Vinnagon paused. Why was he so reluctant?

Well, it was because he did not want to harm his wife. But he was truly skilled with his blade. He knew how to pull his blows. Recent events had left him feeling like he had no control, but he was still in control of his body. He could control his sword. And although sparring was always risky, it was no greater than the risks Gwenshi had already taken.

Actually, that last thought was not comforting.

"Yes, Vinnagon?"

Vinnagon sighed. "Very well. We shall try it."

Gwenshi beamed. And Vinnagon realized that, if he didn't teach her now, she would just find an excuse to draw the sword later. Perhaps a solid introduction to the fundamentals would help her realize her deficiencies. Perhaps this would make her think twice before putting herself in danger.

No. She was Gwenshi. Gwenshi didn't even think once.

Regardless, if he was allowing her to carry a sword, he should at least teach her something about its use.

"Here is the first lesson …"

He began with the draw, the most vulnerable moment in

combat. He showed her how to keep her guard up and what to do if an opponent was close enough to strike before she could free her blade.

Crystal found a mossy spot at the base of the limestone outcrop and watched with an unreadable expression on her face.

Vinnagon checked Gwenshi's footwork next. She had the nimble feet of a knife fighter. He was impressed at how well she moved, but:

"Your stance is too open," he said. "My blade is as long as your reach. You won't be able to catch my wrist with your free hand, so keep your hand out of the way."

He showed her how to put her entire, curvy body behind the narrow width of the blade. "You want to move in and out," he told her. "Not side to side."

It was a lie, but she was a beginner. It was best to keep things simple.

"Are you ready?" he asked.

"I am," she said.

"Block my blade."

He stepped in with a gentle overhand swing. She caught the blow, and his arm flowed automatically into the reverse strike. She caught that, too.

"Good," he said.

"You gave me an opening," she said.

"Right now, you are practicing blocks."

"I know." She grinned. "Otherwise I would have struck."

Vinnagon rolled his eyes. "Just stay in control, woman. If you want a second lesson, we must survive the first."

"Fair enough. Again?"

Vinnagon stepped in with the same two strikes. Then, recalling the style of the striped soldier he had fought earlier that day, he added a thrust.

"Eep!" Gwenshi sprang back.

"Ah, forgive me. I must show you how to block a thrust."

He ran through all the basic attacks and gave Gwenshi a

chance to learn the proper blocks. They paused once or twice to rest their arms, but in truth, Gwenshi did not need much rest.

"Hoeing, pulling weeds, picking peas, lifting cookpots," she said. "I'm using my wrists all day long."

He had never noticed what full forearms she had. The scars had always been endearing, of course, but now he saw the strength of the muscles underneath. Her biceps were woman-smooth, but still firm. Her red face was bathed in a cheerful glow. Beads of sweat left mud stains on her cheeks and descended along jawline, throat, and collarbone to disappear within her dress.

Had the taishrefi not been present, Vinnagon would have begun talking Gwenshi out of that dress.

"We are losing our daylight," Crystal observed. "And the lith is nearing its height. I have a feeling that your best chance of success is to complete the ritual before the lith begins its descent."

Gwenshi grinned and wiped the sweat from her eyes. "I'm ready."

"What do we need to do?" Vinnagon asked.

He addressed his question to Crystal, but Gwenshi answered. "Fight to first blood, as men do at a funeral."

"I don't want to cut a woman."

"I'm already cut," Gwenshi said. She flapped her bandaged arm. "Let's spar."

Vinnagon shook his head. With great misgivings, he raised his blade into a guard position. "Stay at quarter speed," he warned. "Don't do anything foolish."

Gwenshi raised her blade and grinned. "Come at me."

Vinnagon glided in and drew his blade toward her shoulder. Gwenshi blocked, backstepped to disengage, then lunged at his thigh.

She was obediently moving at quarter speed, so Vinnagon was able to withdraw his leg from her reach in time. But she had caught him by surprise. That counterattack was sophisticated.

He withdrew a step and reset. Gwenshi closed the distance by half a step, but did not attack.

He shifted sideways. She shifted to match.

He raised his blade, she lifted her guard, and he drew an arc down toward her shin. Gwenshi swept her blade down to meet his just in time.

"Good one," she said.

Then she lifted her point and thrust at him.

Vinnagon pulled back and Gwenshi stopped her thrust short of overextension. They reset.

The next exchange was more fluid. Vinnagon stopped thinking about testing Gwenshi's defenses and simply allowed his body to move naturally. Gwenshi also loosened up, flowing smoothly from block to riposte to block. She became more aggressive, forcing him back one step, two steps, three. And Vinnagon decided she should not mislead herself into believing she could push him around, so he stepped into her next attack, caught her blade on his guard, and shoved her firmly with his free hand.

Gwenshi fell sprawling among the thin shrubs of the forest floor and rolled to her feet laughing.

Vinnagon waited until she raised her sword in readiness, then they crossed blades again.

It was very much like a dance, especially at one-quarter speed. They moved back and forth beneath the trees, intensely aware of the movements of each other's body.

Vinnagon saw many openings in her defense, but the slow tempo allowed her to react in time. She moved well, and her ripostes were as good as those of an experienced swordsman. She was a beginner, but she sparred like a beginner inspired by Kashram, and Vinnagon remembered that Crystal had said Kashram's power was in both of them.

By wordless agreement, the tempo gradually increased to half speed. Vinnagon was aware of his mind and body separating. His body moved under an instinct of its own. It did not need direction from him. Was this the presence of Kashram?

No, but it was a path—a path to a power that lay within. Kashram was with him and had always been with him from the moment he had let Crystal out of her box. Vinnagon could feel the power of Kashram, and he began to have a sense of what was holding that power back.

* * *

As Gwenshi demonstrated her ability to handle the sword, Vinnagon allowed her to increase the tempo. She reckoned they were at three-quarter speed now—fast enough that she had no time to think about what she was doing and just slow enough that she still had some control.

She could learn this. She was good at this. The sword was an easy weapon to wield.

It was not a stick to swing; it was an extension of her hand. In motion, its weight augmented her strength. She guided the blade, flowed with its momentum.

When she met Vinnagon's blade perfectly, the shock passed through her body, through the soles of her feet, and into the earth. She had the strength of the entire world underneath her.

As the tempo increased, her opportunities to attack grew fewer. She concentrated instead on holding her ground, yielding only half steps. She was breathing heavily now, and an ache was growing in her shoulder. It felt wonderful, and she never wanted to stop, but she knew that soon she must. Soon, Vinnagon would call a halt, if only to let them catch their breath.

But he did not. He only increased the tempo again. And Gwenshi realized she was now past her limit. She no longer had control of what the blade was doing. She had to let it fight for itself. And this frightened her, for she knew it was a sharp and dangerous thing, and she knew it could kill him if any of her now-infrequent ripostes should find a way through his guard.

She marveled at his skill. How could he be so swift, so confident? But surely he would not lose control. Surely her husband would protect her from harm. That warrior, that killer inside him, would never be allowed to harm his wife.

Then she met his eyes, and she saw that he was in a trance. Vinnagon would not halt, and the ache in her arm was creeping through her elbow.

Her muscles were tired, and this time she raised her guard too slowly. Her block was not perfect and the force of his blow sent a shiver through her arm.

His sword deflected cleanly, flashed in the last ray of sunlight, then whipped back at her head.

* * *

Vinnagon froze, his blade a hairsbreadth from his wife's cheek. Gwenshi's eyes were wide, staring at the sword that could have sliced her head in half.

He and she stood perfectly still. Even the slightest breath—

Gwenshi grinned and twitched her head, slicing her cheek on his blade. "First blood! You win."

Panting, Vinnagon lowered his sword.

The fool woman! She could have—

No. *He* could have—

She closed the distance and laid her head against his heaving chest. "That was wonderful," she murmured. "Just wonderful."

He wrapped his free arm around her. She didn't even know. Didn't even know.

She was breathing hard. Her dress was soaked with sweat. She could have been soaked with blood and not breathing at all. He had come so close to killing her.

But he hadn't. He had given control to Kashram, and Kashram would not make him do the wrong thing.

A drop of his wife's blood fell from the point of his steel blade and struck the earth. The lith was at its height and he could feel a force that joined the heavenly body to the limestone outcrop overlooking the site of their combat. Kashram was watching. And in Vinnagon's heart, nothing felt different, because Kashram had always been watching. Kashram had always been there, ready to guide him, ready to show him how to fight.

Vinnagon had been reluctant to fight. He had known the temple was evil, but he had followed orders. He had not challenged his uncle even though his uncle served a demon. Brekko was not evil in his heart, but he served evil women anyway. Such weakness was a sin for a Kashram-created man.

Vinnagon had to confront him. Perhaps he would even have to kill him—slay his own uncle. But now he understood—now he *knew*—that Kashram would not let him do the wrong thing.

Crystal approached.

Gwenshi lifted her head. She left a bloodstain on his tunic.

"I felt it," Crystal said. "I felt the whirlwind of Kashram around you two. Has the curse been lifted?"

Vinnagon took a breath and felt a faint tightness in his chest. He had broken his oath to serve the temple, but until he turned against his uncle, part of that oath still bound him.

"Shakredo is still in my heart," he said. "But Kashram is mightier. He will give me the power to control the curse, and I will do what Kashram wills."

Half a Year Earlier:
Sunlark

SINCE BEING THE FIRST WOMAN ELIMINATED in the game that made Wintersmoke the bashrefi, young Sunlark had grown and matured. She had not dwelt on her humiliation. Instead, she had embraced the new ways and ingratiated herself to the new bashrefi.

Sunlark was somewhat more clever than the other women in the temple. She had realized immediately that Wintersmoke's rituals invoked power from the demon Shakredo. Most of the women had remained unaware until the arrival of the granite statue.

Some had embraced the Lady of the Flame as Sunlark had. Others had pretended to believe they were still serving Lashrefi. A few had spoken out, but Sunlark had been happy to silence them. The bashrefi had taught her a trick:

Mix a select variety of herbs in a certain proportion. Boil for ten lithics, starting and ending at the moon's nadir. The vapors of the resulting concoction could stun a person's mind into oblivion.

The forget-all brew was difficult to administer. Sunlark had found that the most reliable technique was to dampen a hand-kerchief and hold it over her victim's nose. When it worked, it worked on anyone, even those who served Shakredo. This fact was relevant because Sunlark needed to eliminate Rathi, the little gray-skinned Woshite.

Wintersmoke had brought Rathi home from the annual conclave, the meeting of the bashrefis from every province of

Yardwen. The Woshite had been in the temple less than a month, but already she had attached herself to Wintersmoke like a leech.

What had Rathi done to earn such high status? Sunlark was the one who had questioned Marshwind's roll and enabled Wintersmoke to take control of the dice game. Sunlark was the one Wintersmoke relied on to silence dissenters. And now this tiny, gray-skinned thing was at the bashrefi's side, in Sunlark's rightful place.

Rathi's arrival had been a stroke of bad luck. But Sunlark knew how to take care of her own luck. She did not fear the Woshite's strangeness. Rathi was eerie, but small. Sunlark could overpower her easily once she had administered the forget-all brew. She could make the little gray woman disappear as mysteriously as she had arrived.

Rathi often took walks in the dark caverns. Sunlark volunteered to supervise the cavern-lighters in the hope that she could find a way to catch Rathi alone.

For five days, Rathi eluded her, but on the sixth, Sunlark had Shakredo's favor. Rathi emerged from the darkness at the back of the store room as Sunlark was opening a crate of candles.

Sunlark slipped her hand inside the sleeve where she carried the poisonous handkerchief. The crate was between her and her victim, so she could not yet strike. She kept her face calm and waited for Rathi to come closer.

"Good morning, Holy Advisor," she said, using the ridiculous title that Wintersmoke had invented for Rathi.

Rathi just stared at her with glowing green eyes.

"Am I in your way?" Sunlark asked.

"You think I be in your way," said Rathi. "But I am not the log in path. You are the log in your own path."

"I'm sorry," said Sunlark. "I didn't understand what you said."

"There is much that you do not understand," said Rathi. Then Sunlark's vision blackened and she stopped thinking.

She awoke lying in an undignified position atop the crate of candles. The poison-soaked handkerchief was tied to her wrist.

Her first reaction was anger. Her second was fear. Rathi had left her alive, but how did Wintersmoke feel about women who seized the initiative? For the first time, Sunlark thought about fleeing the temple.

But it was already too late to flee. Rathi had certainly told the bashrefi, and now Sunlark would discover if Wintersmoke had any mercy.

For three days, Sunlark expected to be called to explain herself to the bashrefi, but no call came. The three women of the Holy Council behaved as though nothing had happened.

On the fourth day, the Holy Council convened a gathering in the grand worship hall. Bashrefi Wintersmoke announced the formation of the First Choir, a group of women whose devout service entitled them to privileges above the other taishrefis in the temple. Sunlark was the third woman named.

All her fears were washed away by the satisfaction of seeing the lesser taishrefis' jealous faces. Under Lashrefi, they had pretended all taishrefis were equal. Now Wintersmoke had shown them who was equal and who was better.

Do not think Wintersmoke rewards you for your crime. The thought entered Sunlark's mind, but it was not her own. Rathi was staring into her eyes.

I did not tell, Rathi thought at her.

Sunlark tried to shut the other woman out, but she did not know how.

You use vapors when we say. Not when we not say.

Or what? Sunlark thought. *You'll tell Wintersmoke?*

Worse, said Rathi's voice in her head. *I will send you to Hell and make you tell Shakredo.*

The 30th of Bluemonth,
Evening

BATS CAME OUT IN THE TWILIGHT and flitted among the trees.

Lashrefi had sacred crows. This Shakredo-thing had vultures. Gwenshi wondered if anyone had sacred bats. Maybe a nature spirit or something.

She was cold. When had she last felt cold? That night in Greenmonth, when she had worried her vegetables would freeze.

It was nowhere close to freezing now, but the sun had gone down and her dress was still damp from the sweat of sparring. She shivered a little whenever a breeze came up.

Vinnagon and Crystal were planning. They were going to rescue Beetle.

That sounded like fun. Running away was all right, but sneaking into the temple at night and breaking a man out of jail was a real challenge. They'd surely be heroes if they could manage that. Well, heroes among themselves, anyway. Bamboozling the bashrefi wasn't the sort of thing you could brag about around town.

Gwenshi reckoned her arm would be sore for a while, but that was a small price to pay. She'd learned a lot. And Vingo hadn't taken the sword back! At least, not yet.

They had fought with live steel, and his bad-luck curse hadn't killed her. Somehow, that meant his soul was going to be all right.

Gwenshi's soul was all right. She was having the best time of her life.

"I should go alone," said Vinnagon.

"No," said Crystal. "You shouldn't."

"The curse is under control now."

"That is not the point. The point is—"

"Taishrefi, I understand that he means much to you. And that is why—"

"I know those caverns just as well as you. I know them—"

"Taishrefi—"

"I know them *better* than you. And if you think—"

"Taishrefi—"

"If you think divine rapture is all it takes to defeat a temple full of guards—"

"Taish—"

"—then you will get yourself killed! You need a plan. A *good* plan. And you'll need help. Tell him, Gwenshi."

Gwenshi glanced sideways at Crystal. The Stripedwoman's face showed up well in the twilight. "I reckon you've already told him, Crystal."

"I am not intending to walk in and challenge every blades-man in the temple to a duel," Vinnagon said. "I intend to move in and out as quietly as I can. Which is why I do not need a woman shuffling along behind me."

"I move quietly."

"But not as quietly as you think," said Vinnagon, "or I would not have caught you spying on the Holy Council."

Darkness edged Crystal's voice: "Much would be different had you not caught me."

"But I did," said Vinnagon, "and so here we are."

"But that's a good thing," Gwenshi put in. "Don't you see? We were all brought together. Whether by Lashrefi or Kashram, it doesn't matter. Because now, here we are. Together. We've got Vinnagon's swordsmanship, Crystal's holiness, and my … fierce determination. Frankly, I think the temple should fear us."

"Your fierce determination?" Vinnagon asked.

"I was going to say 'skill with a hoe,' but that didn't sound so good."

Vinnagon laughed, surprising her. When had she last heard him laugh?

"I'm not just 'holy'," Crystal was muttering. "I'm *stealthy*. And quick."

"Of course you are," Gwenshi assured her. "The point is that we're together. So we might as well do this jail break together."

Vinnagon gave in. Gwenshi reckoned he was a bit tired, too.

* * *

"That's it," Crystal said, pointing. Her striped hand shone in the moonlight.

Gwenshi stared at the shoulder-wide crack in the stone. Would there even be room to turn around in there? How would she breathe?

"You are certain this leads to the storage chamber?" Vinnagon asked.

"I scouted it last month," Crystal said. "Gwenshi, you and I will climb down until we reach a cavern big enough to allow us free movement of our arms. From there, we will stay close to the cave wall. We'll know we're close when we start seeing torchlight."

"Understood," said Gwenshi. *What have I gotten myself into?*

"Do either of you have any questions?"

"I question the wisdom of this plan," Vinnagon said. "I don't like sending you two down on your own."

"We shall not be on our own," Crystal said. "We shall have each other. And we shall have your help as well, should we need it."

"Aye, Vingo, we'll be fine," Gwenshi said, patting her sword. She was terrified of that hole, but damn it, she had earned the right to join the jail break. She couldn't back out now.

"That sword is your last resort," Vinnagon told her. "If you have to draw it, you've already done something wrong."

"I know," she said. And she patted it again. It was small comfort against the darkness.

"I suppose I should go first," Crystal said. "I know the way."

"Aye," said Gwenshi. At least she wouldn't be alone in there.

Crystal sat down and dropped her legs into the hole. Then the darkness seemed to swallow the Stripedwoman and she was atop the plateau no more.

Gwenshi could hear no noise from the opening. Crystal had warned her that any sound in the "chimney" might carry down to the passages of the temple, but Gwenshi wished she had some assurance that all was well inside. What if there were bats?

"Go if you are going, woman."

Vinnagon—always so comforting.

Gwenshi sat down and dropped her legs in. Nothing bit her.

She looked down between her knees, hoping to see Crystal's striped face, but the hole held nothing except eye-watering blackness. Gwenshi took a deep breath and lowered herself.

When she was chest-deep, her foot found a hold. It seemed to support her weight. She bent her knee and reached down with the other foot, searching.

Now her hands were on the rim of the hole. She could hear Vinnagon's footsteps heading away. Oh, she should have gone with him!

But no. Vinnagon didn't want her underfoot. And Crystal might need her help. Crystal was just a weak Stripedwoman, after all. Not a brave, strong, heroic Arvethidrel like Gwenshi.

Gwenshi reached down for the next foothold and tried not to whimper.

* * *

Vinnagon moved swiftly through the dark forest, trying to get into position before the women reached the main caverns of the temple.

The women could probably handle their part of the mission. Crystal knew secret ways through the caverns, and Gwenshi would be able to help if it turned out that they needed to carry Beetle. But breaking into the temple was dangerous. What kind of man allowed women to expose themselves to danger?

Women protect children. Men protect women. That's what his father had taught him.

Of course, if Beetle was unconscious, they would need to carry him out the back way. And for that, they would need Vinnagon to handle the back sentry—which would probably be Kennadarl unless Brekko had removed him from the post. Well, no matter who it was, any commotion inside would distract the sentry and allow Vinnagon to creep up from behind. It was clever to have Vinnagon on the outside.

It was clever, but he wished he were with Gwenshi.

The leaves under his moccasins grew thicker. The ground started sloping downward. He was getting close.

Vinnagon was not exactly certain where he was in relation to the back exit. He lowered his stance and glided forward on the balls of his feet, pausing every three steps to listen.

The ground was full of the chirps of crickets. The trees still buzzed with cicadas, even though the autumnal equinox was one night away. Vinnagon could not hear a bored sentry shuffling his feet. Out here, sound didn't carry as much as it did underground.

Vinnagon decided that was to his advantage.

The slope grew steeper, and he wondered if he had missed the mouth of the caverns. Silver moonlight shone among the branches overhead, but it illuminated little of the ground on this side of the bluff.

Vinnagon looked for a way down and caught sight of a twisted pine that he remembered from the night he and Kennadarl had carried Crystal down to the river.

That had been ... three nights ago? Yes, this was his fourth night as a man-who-was-not-a-bladesman. He wasn't certain what he *was*—perhaps he was nothing, yet—but the presence of Kashram in his heart gave him the rock-solid conviction that he was becoming *something*.

The position of the twisted pine told him he had misjudged the location of the back entrance. He found a deer trail through a patch of snowberry and glided along the contour. The slope was quite steep here.

"You don't have to pace."

Vinnagon froze. That was Kennadarl's voice. But it wasn't a challenge. Kennadarl sounded annoyed and bored. Perhaps he was not speaking to Vinnagon.

"I was just checking the trail."

That was Lubol. He was one of the men who had joined Brekko's bladesmen after last year's recruiting effort. It seemed that the captain had doubled the guard this evening.

"I can see the trail well enough from here," Kennadarl said. "Just stand calm and stay alert. You can't hear anything if you're pacing."

Vinnagon judged he was about twenty strides away now. The guard post was past the edge of the bushes, around the curve of the bluff.

Lubol asked, "Will he come, do you think?"

"Vinnagon? I wish he would. I'd knock *him* unconscious this time."

Kennadarl had not been knocked unconscious, but Vinnagon was not surprised that this was the story he had decided to tell.

"It doesn't make sense, you know," Lubol said. "If he ran away with the taishrefi like they say, then he wouldn't come back to rescue her slyman."

"He didn't run away with the taishrefi," Kennadarl said.

"Hilligram saw her with him this afternoon."

"Hilligram was likely confused," said Kennadarl. "The two of them went their separate ways."

Lubol grew suspicious. "How do you know that? You said you were unconscious."

"When I woke up, I tracked 'em," Kennadarl said. He lied easily.

"But what about—"

"Look: if you want to be on cavern duty, you should learn to think less. Bladesmen don't ask questions. Not unless they want to end up like Vinnagon."

"Vinnagon got away."

"No he didn't," Kennadarl said. "None of us are ever getting away."

Step by silent step, Vinnagon crept closer. He was grateful that Lubol was here to distract Kennadarl, but he hoped that this was the only post where the guard had been doubled.

* * *

Just one more step. Just one more step. Just one more step.

Gwenshi's breaths were shallow pants. The rock was all around her, closing in, squeezing the air out of her.

Just one more step.

Where was Crystal? Had Crystal even gone into this hole? What if Gwenshi had misseen? What if she was in the wrong hole? What if it had no bottom?

Gwenshi climbed down and down for ever and ever.

Just one more step. Just one more step.

* * *

Crys eased herself around the bend of the chimney. It branched here. One branch led to the hole in the ceiling of the main passage; the other led down to the storage space near the council chamber.

She had best wait for Gwenshi. It would be unfortunate if the Kashramite should get lost.

She could hear Gwenshi panting above her—short quick breaths, like a rabbit in the heat of Yellowmonth. Her boots made soft scuffing sounds, coming closer.

Crys waited until Gwenshi was one step away from her head. Then she reached up and lightly patted Gwenshi's toe.

Gwenshi emitted a tiny squeak.

Crys squeezed her toe firmly, then descended one step.

Gwenshi did likewise. Crys grabbed Gwenshi's ankle, showing her the proper branch with a gentle tug. She hoped Gwenshi would calm down once they were clear of the chimney.

* * *

Gwenshi backed down the steeply sloped tunnel. Her weight was on her knees and elbows now. That was good, wasn't it? That meant they were almost done, didn't it?

Crystal was here with her. She had felt the Stripedwoman's hand on her foot. That had to be a good sign.

Just one more step.

The slope grew flatter as Gwenshi slithered backwards. She would make it. She would make it.

Just one more step.

Her foot hit Crys's. Not Crys's hand, Crys's foot.

Gwenshi lifted her head, gently. It did not hit rock.

She pushed herself up on all fours. Then, hands scrabbling along the jagged wall of the tunnel, she stood up.

Not much room to move here. She couldn't turn around without bumping a hip into the rock wall. But she could stand up.

Her hand was grasped by another—warm and dry. Gwenshi's own palms and armpits were wet with sweat. And her smell! It was the bitter sweat of fear.

She had to calm herself. She couldn't let the Stripedwoman see her like this.

Of course, neither of them could see anything. Why did caves have to be so *dark*?

Crystal's hand was trying to lead her somewhere. Gwenshi followed, feeling along the wall with her free hand to make sure she didn't smash her head on any protrusions.

Crystal halted, and Gwenshi bumped into the Striped-woman's soft backside. She listened. She could hear no sound above her own breathing. Her breaths did not echo back to her the way they had in the chimney. She was in a larger room.

This was better. It was still a dark cave, but it was better. Gwenshi could handle this. After climbing down that chimney, she could handle anything.

Crystal led her through the darkness, moccasins gently shuffling along the stone. One part of the darkness seemed somehow different from the rest. An illusion created by Gwenshi's desire to see something?

No, it was no illusion. She could see the outline of Crystal's head. At least, she could *imagine* she saw the outline of Crystal's head.

A glowing thing swam at her and Gwenshi raised her free hand to ward it off. The thing disappeared.

Gwenshi lowered her hand cautiously and discovered that the patch of light floating in air was actually an opening in the chamber. It grew larger as they drew nearer, and now Gwenshi could see again. She was no longer an eyeball floating in a well of blackness. She was standing in a faintly lit natural cavern, holding hands with a Stripedwoman.

Gwenshi let go. She was a Redwoman, not some little girl.

Crystal glanced back at her, then advanced toward the illuminated opening at the other end of the cavern. Vinnagon was right: The Stripedwoman's shuffles were not silent. Gwenshi followed, gliding on the balls of her feet in an attempt to do better.

They slid past a stack of crates. Crystal stepped over a bundle of something, and a scabbard clacked.

Gwenshi stopped, one foot on each side of the bundle. Her hand went reflexively to her own scabbard, but the sound had come from the lit place beyond.

Crystal turned around and made hasty pushing motions.

Gwenshi retreated to the blackness in the rear of the chamber, but not in haste. She moved deliberately, careful to make no sound. Crystal retreated part way, then crouched behind the stack of crates.

Somewhere out there, a door opened. Or perhaps it shut. There was no squeak of hinges, just a percussive thump, like the beat of Gwenshi's heart in her chest.

Moments later, she heard a woman's voice from just beyond the illuminated entrance: "Watch you?"

Crystal's silhouette tensed.

The woman had a strange accent. "Speak, mans! Watch you?"

"Y— yes. Yes, we're watching, Holy Advisor." A man's voice. A big man, but mysteriously afraid of the woman.

"Good. I go to speak with prisoner now. You mans stay here."

"Yes, Holy Advisor." He spoke in the bladesmen's accent. And he had referred to "we". That meant at least two bladesmen nearby. Vinnagon had said there should be only one.

Crystal slipped to the back of the cavern. She took Gwenshi's hand and led her not into the light, but into a tunnel that was dark, tight, and twisted. Crystal knew a way around the guards, and Gwenshi was not going to like it.

But at least they could stand upright and hold hands.

* * *

"Leave."

The word was muffled by the thick wooden door of Beetle's cell, but he heard it clearly enough, for he was still awake. Was it late at night or already morning? His only means of telling time inside this stone cell was by the length of the torch.

Hm. The torch was longer. Someone must have replaced it. He must have slept.

"I fetch you when I am done talking to man. Go stand with other guards."

The guard outside Beetle's cell murmured reluctant acquiescence. Booted footsteps diminished down the passageway.

The iron bolt of his cell door scraped against the wood, and the door opened. The Woshite stood there alone, eyes glowing green.

She entered with one delicate step, leaving the door partially ajar. The passageway behind her was lit, and Beetle could see no one else there. The bonds around his wrists had been removed after the Woshite's previous visit. Still, he knew it would be foolish to run. The tiny woman had such confidence in his compliance that he feared to test her ability to stop him.

The Woshite sniffed. She glanced at the contents of the chamber pot in the corner. "Good," she said. "The man is trained."

"What do you want?"

"I reward the man."

She tossed something at him. Beetle started. He had thought her hands were empty.

A small, round, brown object thumped onto his cornhusk mattress. It was a sunflower-seed cake.

"Thank you," he said, automatically, before he realized it could be poisoned.

"It is good," she said. "You spoke truth. You get reward."

His stomach rumbled. He ignored it.

"Truth about what?"

"Your mother and her mate. They know nothing. As you say."

"What did you do to them?"

"I ask. They answer. They answer quick. No problem." She looked out toward the hallway. "They not far. If problem, you hear screams. No screams, no problem."

"Can— can I see them?"

"No," she said. "You are prisoner."

Poisoned or not, that cake looked good. He was hungry.

"What lithic is it?"

The Woshite shrugged. "Your time is not my time."

Beetle had no idea what that meant.

She cocked her head as though listening for something. Beetle couldn't hear it, and he had good ears.

"I need to know something," she said. "Be good again. Speak truth."

"About what?"

"About the equinox."

The equinox? "It is on the first of Purplemonth," he said. "Which is today."

"Not today," she said. "Tomorrow. Knows Crystal that thing which we plan tomorrow?"

"Ah ... what thing?"

"I forget. Mans are simple. Evil thing. Knows Crystal that evil thing we do at moonrise?"

"Forgive me," he said. "I do not know what you are speaking of."

"I speak of—"

She paused to listen, then stepped out into the passage.

* * *

Crys froze in the main passageway, not twenty feet from Rathi and the open door. The Woshite had heard them coming? Crys thought she and Gwenshi had been quiet, but ...

Ah. Thoughts. Rathi did not need to hear. She could sense minds.

Rathi's glowing eyes were fixed on Crys.

"Strike swiftly!" Crys told Gwenshi. "Before—"

A fist slammed against her mind. Crys staggered into the limestone wall. Her eyes blurred.

Beside her, a sword slid free of its scabbard.

"Die, fiend!" Gwenshi's cry reverberated throughout the caverns, loud enough to alert the entire night watch.

So much for our numerical advantage, Crys thought.

She steadied herself, and the passage came back into focus. Gwenshi was pursuing Rathi around the corner.

"It's a trap!" she called. "Gwenshi, come back!"

But she did not wait to see if her words had been heeded. She caught sight of Beetle standing in the doorway.

"Beetle! Are you all right?"

"Crys! Crys, they have my parents."

"Oh Hell. Where?"

* * *

From deep within the caverns came an echoing cry. Vinnagon could not make out the words, but he recognized his wife's voice.

Kennadarl and Lubol looked at each other. Then they turned to peer into the darkness of the cave.

Vinnagon glided up behind them and drew his blade.

"Hands on your helmets," he said.

Kennadarl jumped and spun around.

"I'll pierce the first one who reaches for his blade," Vinnagon said.

Kennadarl leapt away into the cave. Vinnagon glided forward in pursuit, exposing his flank to Lubol.

Vinnagon spun, expecting to catch Lubol in mid-draw, but Lubol's hand was not on the hilt of his sword, and he was edging away.

Kennadarl drew and lunged. Vinnagon beat the predictable attack aside and stopped his own riposte a thumbwidth from Kennadarl's throat.

"Drop the blade," Vinnagon growled.

Kennadarl's gaze flicked to Lubol, somewhere behind Vinnagon's shoulder. Vinnagon could not afford to delay so much as a heartbeat.

Kennadarl sprang back, and Vinnagon, instead of completing the thrust that would have ended Kennadarl's life, spun to block the blow … that was not there.

"Damn it, Lubol! Draw!" Kennadarl's shout was certain to resound through the caverns, bringing more comrades that Vinnagon would have to fight.

Fighting was easy, but killing was hard. Perhaps that was why Lubol did not draw.

Vinnagon charged into the cave. He swung high, allowed their swords to cross, ducked under Kennadarl's guard, and drove his shoulder up into Kennadarl's midsection.

Their feet tangled, and Vinnagon stumbled. Kennadarl bounced off the wall and went sprawling across the stone floor.

Vinnagon dashed past him and through the heavy curtains that hid the torchlit passage to the temple.

Kennadarl cried out—a sound sharp and sudden. What did that mean?

Vinnagon slipped around the corner and waited, back pressed to the wall, as footsteps drew closer. A nearby torch provided plenty of light for combat.

The approaching man came around the corner blade first. The blade was bloody.

"Vinnagon? It's me—Lubol."

Vinnagon chose not to leap upon him. Lubol rounded the corner and positioned himself out of reach. His bloody sword was not in a guard position.

"You stabbed Kennadarl," Vinnagon realized.

"Aye," Lubol said. "Killed him."

"But why?" Vinnagon still did not lower his guard.

"I want to help you, Vinnagon. I want to help you liberate the temple."

Liberate the temple?

"Lubol, I'm just here on a rescue mission. I can't single-handedly fight the entire watch. Not even with you on my side."

The torch on the wall sconce flickered, wafting smoke toward Lubol's corner. Lubol rubbed his eyes.

"We aren't alone," Lubol said. "There are others." He coughed and stepped out of the smoke.

With a tiny *crack*, a stalactite broke loose from the ceiling. Lubol looked up, and a club of stone smashed into his forehead.

The crash of shattering stone was followed by ringing silence. Vinnagon stared in horror at the body at his feet. Lubol's misshapen face and crushed helmet left no doubt that he was suddenly dead.

"Kashram guard us," Vinnagon breathed.

He knelt over his comrade's body, stared at Kennadarl's blood on Lubol's sword. He looked up, as though expecting to find an assassin in the ceiling, but all he could see were stalactites and shadows.

Vinnagon couldn't see into that darkness, but he could sense the stalactite's stump, newly broken, a wound in the rock. The base had been slender compared with the girth of the deadly mass of stone. It could have broken at any time. That it should break precisely when Lubol was about to name potential allies was not just bad luck—it was evil luck.

Please, Kashram, Vinnagon prayed, placing his shaking hand on Lubol's shoulder. *Shakredo claimed his life. Don't let it have his soul.*

A power filled the rocks around him. A cry of gratitude rushed through his arm into his heart. And then the power was gone, leaving only the lingering certainty that Kashram had answered his prayer.

* * *

Gwenshi was not certain what the creature was. It was about her height, but much skinnier, with loose, silver hair.

It ran away from her with scurrying steps. She could catch it easily ... and then what? Slice off its head from behind? Stab it in the back?

It was just some helpless woman-thing. True, it had glowing green eyes and unnatural skin, but it wasn't exactly a threat, now, was it?

Gwenshi slowed and let the creature escape up the stairs. She had chased it away from Beetle. She had done her duty.

Gwenshi turned and jogged back to the cell where she had left Crystal. The doorway was now occupied by a puzzled bladesman. He caught sight of her and became a surprised bladesman.

Gwenshi sheathed her sword and said, "Hello. I'm Vinnagon's wife. He didn't come home last night. Have you seen him?"

"Wh— what? What are you doing here?"

He let her walk right up to him.

There was this trick her brothers had taught her for knocking someone on his butt when you wanted to start a fight. Gwenshi hook-stepped behind his heel and shoved hard on his hip. To her delight, the trick still worked perfectly! The big fellow fell into the cell and Gwenshi jumped back and slammed the door.

Now just— Oof! The fellow hit the door, opening a gap.

Gwenshi put her weight against the door and seized the bolt, but a muscular red arm reached out through the gap and grabbed her hair.

Her hair! The indignity riled her. In one smooth motion, she whipped her dueling knife from her belt and drove it between the bones of his forearm.

The hand released her hair. She slammed the door on it— once, twice—and it withdrew from the door jamb. Gwenshi slid the bolt home.

Ha! That accounted for the guard. Now, where was Crystal? She'd said something about a trap.

"The caverns! The caverns!"

Shouts came from the passage down which the silver-haired, glowing-eyed creature had disappeared. Gwenshi heard the sound of running boots, coming closer.

* * *

Beetle's parents had been locked in separate cells—an unnecessary cruelty that Crys attributed to the Woshite. Beetle's father had one eye swollen shut. Well, she was leading them through the unlit caverns. He didn't need his eyes here.

Beetle's mother was limping with one bad knee, and that *was* a problem. Not that Crys had imagined either of them would be able to climb out through the chimney, but now the possibility of running out the back way was reduced to limping out the back way. She hoped Vinnagon had dealt with the guard at the exit.

Dealt with. She meant *killed*, didn't she? She hoped one man had killed another—*hoped* for that.

Oh, how Shakredo has twisted us all!

"Crystal?" Gwenshi's voice sounded small as it echoed through the caverns.

Crys seized Beetle's shoulder and murmured, "Wait here."

She hurried toward Gwenshi's voice, hoping that Beetle and his parents would stay quiet enough to not be heard above the stomping boots of the Kashramite guards. Those boots were fast approaching.

Crys caught a glimpse of Gwenshi running past.

"Gwenshi!" Her cry emerged as a squeak. She dared not draw the guards to her hiding place.

Gwenshi, of course, did not hear.

* * *

The passage echoed with the distant sounds of running boots. Vinnagon did not know where the women were, but it seemed they had been unable to accomplish their task quietly.

From the commotion, he judged they had not been caught yet. Reluctantly, he took a gamble:

"The way is clear!" he called. If the women were between him and the bladesmen, they would know they could run to him for safety. And if the bladesmen were between him and the women—

"No, Vinnagon. The way is not clear."

Two men, Ruthav and Tharn, eased their way around the corner ahead, blades drawn.

"What happened to Kennadarl and Lubol?" Tharn demanded.

Vinnagon wondered if he could talk to these men, persuade them to join his side. Probably not. They were advancing on him.

"He caught them by surprise," Ruthav sneered. "Probably stabbed Lubol in the back."

That was a reasonable guess. Vinnagon was unlikely to kill Lubol in a fair fight.

"I suppose he thinks he's a big hero," Tharn said. "Run away, then sneak back to kill us one at a time."

"Not this time," said Ruthav. And the two rushed forward together.

Vinnagon feinted at Ruthav and blocked Tharn's lunge. He retreated one step, and the two comrades closed the distance cautiously.

Tharn raised up for an overhand strike, trusting Ruthav's blade to guard him. Vinnagon leapt back and Ruthav pursued, darting forward with a quick thrust that Vinnagon parried.

He caught a piece of Ruthav's leg with his riposte, opening a tear in Ruthav's trousers. The man winced, and a moment later, Vinnagon saw he had drawn blood.

Tharn's brows wrinkled as though he were attempting to count sums. Vinnagon could almost see his thoughts, for they mirrored his own. Ruthav and Tharn needed to agree upon a strategy. But Vinnagon knew all the two-on-one strategies that they knew. Once they agreed, he would be able to predict their attacks.

He feinted at Tharn, blocked Ruthav's counterstrike, slid his blade up toward Ruthav's face, and disengaged before Tharn could stab him in the foot.

Ruthav had retreated easily. The leg wound was little more than a scratch.

Vinnagon rocked back into a defensive stance. Footsteps behind Ruthav and Tharn were getting louder. No doubt, they would be content to wait until they had reinforcements behind them. Vinnagon was content to wait until he could be certain that the women were not coming this way.

Gwenshi came around the curve of the passage. Her eyes widened as she took in the situation, then narrowed as she focused on Tharn's back. The sound of running boots echoed behind her. This was about to get messy, and Vinnagon did not want Gwenshi in the middle.

He thrust at Tharn's knee, blocked Ruthav's counterattack, blocked Tharn's riposte, blocked, blocked, blocked, and then

Tharn went down with the point of Gwenshi's blade in his calf.

Ruthav checked to see what had hit Tharn, and Vinnagon thrust at Ruthav's throat. His blade pierced cartilage with a gristly crunch, and Ruthav died a bloody death.

* * *

Gwenshi thought she had the bladesman down, with the point of her sword triumphantly stabbed into the back of his leg, but somehow he spun on his good leg and thrust straight at her face. She raised her blade in a feeble block and flinched away.

Hot pain seared her breast.

The man snarled at her and drew back his blade for a final, skull-splitting backhand.

But Gwenshi did not want her skull split.

She stepped into him, leading with her shoulder. They both went down, Gwenshi on top. She released her sword and reached for her dueling knife.

Damn! She had left it in that other fellow's arm.

Her foe's bear-sized hand seized her throat. She reached for her throwing knife, but his other arm wrapped around her back and squeezed her close, pinning her knife hand between them.

She would have to defeat him off-handed, then, unless she wanted her windpipe crushed.

She tried to punch him in the gap below his cuirass and her hand hit hard iron—his knife hilt!

Gwenshi seized the weapon and slid it from its sheath. She gritted her teeth and jabbed the point into her enemy's side. He gasped, and his eyes went wide.

She drew the blade through his guts. His hot body convulsed beneath her, but his grip on her throat only tightened.

Spots swam before her eyes. They could both die here, lying on the floor. Was that funny? She wondered if it was funny.

A moccasin flashed in front of her nose and the grip on her throat released.

Gwenshi gasped for breath. The moccasin stomped squarely on her foe's face, producing no reaction.

"He's dying," Gwenshi said. The pressure of the arm on her back was weakening.

She rolled off the man's hot body. She tugged at the knife handle, but the resistance was stronger than expected, as though his guts were reluctant to let the blade go. She left it inside him.

She tried to stand and discovered his fingers still clutched her dress. Beastly tenacity! She pried them loose.

Vinnagon stared at her with a sickly expression on his face, blood dripping from the point of his sword.

Gwenshi picked up her own sword, wondering how this was done. Did she clean her blade on the dead man's clothing? She couldn't just ram the sword back into its scabbard. How would she clean the scabbard later? It didn't come apart, did it?

Vinnagon seized her by the elbow and started tugging.

Oh. Aye. A lot of men were coming.

She turned and ran.

* * *

His wife vomited as they ran down the corridor, but she kept running. Vinnagon didn't vomit until he was out of the caverns.

"The river," he said, not wanting to lead their pursuers to Crystal and the narrow chimney. He knew the trail, so he went first.

In truth, he did not know it well enough. At the first twisting, his foot slipped from under him and he fell. If the fall had been caused by the curse, he would have broken something, or at least sprained his knee. But he didn't. Kashram was still protecting him.

Gwenshi was immediately upon him. She gasped but did not falter. Instead she leapt, and the billowing black shadow of her dress passed over him. She landed with hardly a sound and continued down the trail, disappearing into the darkness.

Vinnagon rose and ran after her, descending with a little more caution this time. He reached the foot of the trail and turned toward the river, but Gwenshi called to him from the bushes on the other side of the road.

"Vingo! This way!"

He crawled in beside her. She smelled of death and fear. He put his arm around her shoulder and discovered she was shivering—hot and shivering. He wanted to say something—to chastise her or console her—but the bladesmen were still descending. If Gwenshi could run no longer, their only hope was to hide and be silent.

They heard voices.

"What do you think? Up the road?"

"We should have brought a torch."

"Watch yourselves. He could be lying in wait."

"I bet he swam the river."

"I hope the coward drowns."

Voices of men he knew, all jumbled together. They were looking for *him*. They'd seen four men dead, and they probably believed he had killed them all—though how they would interpret Lubol's death, he did not know.

Lubol had said there were others who wanted to over-throw the temple. Vinnagon wondered if any of them were here now.

"Report?" That was his uncle's voice.

"We've lost him, Captain."

"Rathi could find him." The seneschal's voice. Of course she *would* be close to his uncle this time of night. "Shall I send someone to fetch her?"

"No." His uncle's voice was heavy. "He's gone now."

"We need this trail guarded," the seneschal said. "And apparently, we need guards in teams of three, at least."

"Vinnagon's good with a blade," his uncle said. "But to defeat two men at once, he would have to be lucky."

"It seems he got lucky twice," the seneschal said.

"I know," said his uncle. "You told me that enemies of the temple cannot be so lucky."

"I do not know what happened," she admitted.

"I know."

"Tell me, then," the seneschal said, annoyed.

"Vinnagon must have had help. Kennadarl was stabbed in the back. Vinnagon would never have done that. Lubol was clubbed in the head, somehow."

"Very well. He had help. What does that mean?"

"It means," his uncle said, "that we might still have a killer up there in the temple. Forget guarding this trail. We need to do a full cavern search."

Everyone fell silent, waiting for the seneschal's response.

"A full cavern search is too dangerous and too time-consuming," she decided. "If there is anyone still in the caverns, we must smoke them out."

* * *

Crys had thought the bladesmen would not come this deep into the caverns. But now, torchlight illuminated the wall opposite the alcove in which she hid. Beetle pressed against her more tightly, and she could feel his heartbeat thudding against her back. His father, Cicada, was breathing rapidly and not at all quietly. Flicker, Beetle's mother, was there, too, but at least she had stopped whimpering. Crys doubted that her leg had stopped hurting her, though. Flicker was the smallest, so they had made her squeeze into the very back.

Crys was wishing they could all squeeze in a little more.

Torchlight crept across the stripes of Cicada's face. A dancing flame reflected in each terrified eye.

Below, the footfalls of the bladesmen were quiet, but purposeful. Crys asked Lashrefi for protection, but she knew they were deep in Shakredo's domain.

The light swung. A glimpse of fire blinded her. She shut her eyes—too late to shut out the brightness. The bright flame stayed with her, inside her head. She tried to blink it away, but the afterimage floated in her vision. She wondered why this false image terrified her so, when she had learned to navigate these caverns in total darkness.

Beetle let out a long, slow sigh, and Crys realized the footsteps were receding. Flicker whimpered.

The wise thing to do would be to wait a while to be certain the searchers were truly gone. But Crys was not cold-hearted enough to force an old woman with an injured leg to keep herself crammed in an alcove until the situation was more certain. She climbed out, trusting the men to help Flicker get down safely.

After some shuffling, scraping, and panting, Beetle and his parents were quiet once more. Crys judged they were all standing on the cavern's uneven floor.

"Now what?" Beetle asked.

Crys didn't know. She had hoped to take Beetle out the chimney, but they couldn't leave his mother behind. Vinnagon had assured her that the back exit and the door to the main temple would both be guarded. But with a little luck, Gwenshi had confused the guards so much that Crys would find one of those paths open.

"Now you let me scout ahead," she said, using the confident voice of a taishrefi. "If the way is clear, I shall come back for you."

"And if it isn't?" Beetle asked.

"I shall come back, and we shall wait until the way *is* clear."

Perhaps Beetle nodded then. Or perhaps he made a face of extreme displeasure. Either way, Crys was putting her plan into action. She asked Lashrefi to help things turn out right, but the Goddess seemed very far away.

Crys followed the route she knew, climbing upward from cavern to cavern, until she was once again in the storage room near the Holy Council's meeting chamber.

She recognized these bundles on the floor. They held the clothing she had inspected two nights earlier.

How will people know they are Flamebringer clothings? Rathi had asked. That meant it was important that people *did* recognize the clothing as Flamebringers'. But why? Was it some sort of disguise?

Footsteps sounded in the corridor. Crys ducked behind a stack of crates.

The steps sounded like more than one person. They were grunting, as though carrying something heavy.

Crys moved her head to peer around the crates.

Two bladesmen passed by. Their burden was a limp body.

Crys saw only enough to tell that the body was that of a bladesman. She knew not whether he was alive or dead.

Either way, it meant that Vinnagon and Gwenshi had engaged in serious violence to earn Beetle's escape. Crys did not want the deed to be wasted.

Perhaps the main passage was now clear. She crept out into the light. Moving as swiftly as she dared, she followed the passage toward the back exit.

Dark stains on the floor told of a mortal struggle. She hoped Vinnagon and Gwenshi were all right. Thinking back on it, how could she be certain that the limp body had not been Vinnagon's?

Her attempt to recall the details was interrupted by voices. Someone *was* at the exit. Bad luck. Or perhaps it was good luck that she had chosen to check before bringing the others. Crys retreated back the way she had come.

"Passage all clear!"

The shout was loud, but distant. It came from the doorway to the main temple—and then it echoed again and again from caverns deep within the cliff.

A reply sounded from the back exit: "Lighting fire!"

Moments later, the same from the temple doorway: "Lighting fire!" This was not an echo. Fires were being lit at both ends of the main passage.

Crys gave up trying to be quiet. She ran down the passage and veered off into the dark caverns. She had just enough light to jump over the bundles of clothing. Then she was in darkness, trusting to memory.

Her toe struck a rough outcropping and she stumbled, scraping her elbow against a stalagmite. Her memory was good, but not good enough for sprinting through the dark. Crys was forced to slow her pace, to scuttle through the caverns with hands outstretched so she could avoid running into walls.

"Beetle?" she called when she was close.

"We're still here, Crys."

"They've lit fires," she said.

"... What do you need us to do?"

She didn't know what to do. Or rather, she knew what had to be done, but she couldn't bring herself to say that they needed to get out as fast as they could and leave his parents to the mercy of Lashrefi.

"Flicker," she asked, "do you think you can climb?"

"I am not certain, dear. I think not."

"Now, just calm down," Cicada said. "We must be at least two hundred paces from anything that will burn. We don't have anything to fear from fire."

"Not the fire," Crys said. "The smoke. They can do ... things with smoke."

"What sort of things?" Beetle asked. Suspicious? Afraid? She wished she could see his face.

"Wintersmoke knows demonic rituals," Crys said. "She uses her power to change ordinary smoke into something else. She can use it to addle your mind, choke your lungs, poison your blood, whatever she wants." Probably the power had limitations, but Crys did not know what they were.

"Well, smoke rises," Cicada said. "We should be safe enough down here."

"The bashrefi's smoke goes where she wills it," Crys said.

"They have to get out," Flicker said. "Beetle, take her to safety."

"What?" said Beetle. "No, Mother. We're not leaving you behind."

"We four are the only ones who know the temple plans to do something harmful tomorrow night. You and Crys must go warn the mayor."

"Mother, the mayor is the person who got me imprisoned."

"Then tell Crys's Kashramite friends. Warn someone. But go!"

"It's no use," said Cicada. "Smoke rises. If the only way out is through the chimney, then Crys is better off staying with us. We're deep under ground. I like our chances here."

Crys didn't like their chances. They were deep inside a temple claimed by Shakredo, the demon of misfortune. She knew who ruled here.

There was only one sensible course of action, and Crys did not have the will to take it. She couldn't abandon Beetle. And she couldn't ask him to abandon his parents.

Crys prayed that Lashrefi would show her another way out.

* * *

Gwenshi and Vinnagon climbed through the forest on the back side of the hill. Gwenshi wondered how they would find Crystal. The plan had been for her and Crystal to fetch Beetle and wait at the top of the chimney for Vinnagon, but things had gone wrong when they met that silver-skinned woman in Beetle's cell.

What *was* she? Well, apparently she was a Silverwoman, but she was the first Gwenshi had ever seen. Her skin had looked like ugly moth wings.

"You did well," Vinnagon said.

"What?"

"You heard me."

"I'm sorry, Vingo. You took me by surprise."

They puffed up the hill a few steps, then Vinnagon said, "You are the one who has surprised me, Gwenshi. I did not know I had married such a woman."

"Well …" He had her off balance. "I always wanted to see where you work."

"Is it still a game to you?"

Gwenshi shook her head. "No," she said. "No, Vingo. I liked fighting that seneschal in the market today. That was a good game. But killing that man—" She could still smell his guts, maybe on her dress, maybe just in her memory. "Well, I can't say I enjoyed it, not at the time, nor now."

Vinnagon grunted.

Gwenshi curved her palm against the hilt of the sword she wore. "Even so, a part of me wants to keep playing. I don't want to kill again, but I love fighting when my life is at stake."

Vinnagon said nothing.

"Is that crazy?" she asked.

"Yes," he said. No hesitation.

"Is that the way you feel?" she asked.

"No."

"… Oh."

The slope was leveling off. Gwenshi followed Vinnagon's lead. He acted as though finding a narrow rock fissure in the forest at night would be no problem.

"Vingo?"

"Yes?"

"Is it like this every time?" she asked. "Or do you get used to killing?"

They stepped over a fallen log. Her husband's silence stretched. Gwenshi wondered if she had violated some blades-men's etiquette by daring to ask such a question.

"I do not know," he said. "I believe it would be a terrible thing to get used to."

He had vomited, too, Gwenshi remembered.

Vinnagon said, "His name was Ruthav, and I stabbed him through the throat."

"Your first one?" she asked. "Or the man you killed tonight?"

"He *was* my first one."

"Oh."

She wanted to reach out to him then, to hold his hand. She wanted to let him know he was not alone.

Vinnagon said, "He would tell stories about his childhood. He could make herding geese sound hilarious."

Gwenshi didn't know what to say to that. She waited, but Vinnagon did not go on.

198 JASON A. HOLT

She had to ask: "Was the other one a friend of yours, too? The— the one I killed?"

"No," Vinnagon said. "He was a bad man who always bullied the newcomers."

His voice was flat. Gwenshi wasn't sure she believed him.

"They were all your friends, weren't they?"

Vinnagon shook his head. "We were *comrades*, Gwenshi. Not really friends. More like brothers."

"Could be it was a mistake to talk you into staying," she said. "Could be I should have let you run away."

"I make my own decisions."

"I know."

"I killed Ruthav. Lubol killed Kennadarl. The temple killed Lubol." He stopped, seized her wrist, forced her to meet his gaze. "Gwenshi, the temple is evil. We have to fight it. Running away would be a sin."

His words were determined, but his face was pleading with her.

She said, "You're right, Vingo. We have to fight it."

Her husband relaxed. She slid her wrist from his grasp and offered her hand instead.

He took it. They resumed walking.

Gwenshi's heart was filled with gladness. He had said *we*.

* * *

Crys heard a voice—distant, yet strong enough to carry through the twists of the caverns: "We know you're still in here. The door to the temple is barred against you. If you seek the Goddess's mercy, answer now, while your soul may yet be saved."

Cicada asked, "Is that the bashrefi?"

"It is," Crys said.

He said, "The exit must still be clear of smoke if she has come in to speak to us."

"No," Crys said. "Shakredo protects her from her own smoke."

"Perhaps Lashrefi will choose to protect us," said Flicker.

Crys said, "She would if she could."

"Perhaps Yolim can help us," said Cicada.

Crys said, "Perhaps."

A faint wisp of smoke tickled her nostrils.

"We'll ask Yolim to help you, too," Beetle's mother offered.

Crys had no reply for that. Other deities *could* help her, if they so chose, but she doubted the deities would be influenced by the prayers of heretics.

Heretics? Was that truly what she thought of Beetle's parents? What that truly what she thought of Beetle?

No. She thought of him as a true servant of Lashrefi—but one with a misguided religious upbringing. There, deep inside the caverns of the cliff, with smoke thickening in the air, Crys admitted to herself that her acceptance of his religion was temporary. She believed he was a good man, but she would not pledge her life to him until he had pledged his soul to Lashrefi. That was what she waited for. She didn't want to marry him until he had rejected his parents' religion.

Flicker coughed.

"Get low, Mother," Beetle said. "Try not to breathe the smoke."

"She is low," said Cicada. "I think the smoke is filling the air from the bottom up." He coughed, too.

"Don't talk," said Flicker. "Trust in the deities."

They were all coughing now.

Crys wondered if she should pray for rescue, or if the time had come to pray that they all got a swift trip to Heaven. She wasn't certain Bargainkeepers *could* go to Heaven.

"Over there!" said Beetle's father. "A light."

Hallucination smoke, Crys thought. *To make it easier for Rathi to control us with mind magic.*

Crys tried to filter the smoke by breathing through her sleeve, but she saw the light, too.

Perhaps it was real.

She grabbed Beetle's arm. "Follow me," she croaked. "Hold hands and follow me."

Every gasping breath set her lungs aflame, yet she was forced to draw in the smoke, if only to feed her convulsive coughs. The tiny light floated seemingly within reach, yet as she groped her way through the cavern, she could not cause it to come closer.

She squeezed Beetle's hand in encouragement. From the coughs, she could tell his parents were still following.

Perhaps the air was clearing somewhat. Every breath punished her throat, but the haze in her thoughts was relenting. As they descended, she became convinced that the light was real.

But then it vanished utterly.

Crys stopped.

Beetle bumped into her. "Keep going," he gasped. "The air is getting ... better."

Crys took a step toward where the light had been, and her outstretched hand bumped a stony surface. The cavern floor curved up to become a wall here. But there had to be an opening of some sort.

Ah! There it was—about thigh high.

"Crawl," she said. "Beetle, get in back. Help your mother."

Crys climbed into the narrow tunnel. Cicada's leathery hand grasped her exposed ankle. Crys kept moving. She could go on all fours, although if she hunched her back too much, it brushed stone.

This fissure Crys had not explored before. As they went deeper, she had the feeling she could see some sort of opening ahead. The faint outline grew larger as she approached, and then suddenly she saw the light again, up and to her right. It was a dancing candle flame.

The breeze that blew past the candle was faint, but it was clean. Eagerly, Crys began climbing, forgetting about Flicker until she heard the old woman's whimpers and Beetle's reassuring murmurs: "Just keep going, Mother. The air is getting better. We're almost out."

Crys picked up the candle and took it with her. Beetle was proven correct. The passage took a sharp twist, and suddenly

Crys *was* out, sitting in the dry duff of a mixed forest.

Beetle's parents followed. Then Beetle.

For a few moments, they all just sat on the ground catching their breath, too dazed to speak. The moon glowed silver among the treetops. Crys blew out the candle.

Who had lit the flame? Who had come to find them in the deepest caverns and lead them out through a passage even Crys had not known?

Of their savior, the warm tallow candle was the only sign.

Three Years Earlier:
Malk

FOR SEVEN YEARS, Malk had served as the personal bodyguard of Shom Blackfield. Shom was a very old man who did not have nearly as many enemies as he thought he did, and so Malk's time in service was uneventful.

When Shom died, Malk had to look for a new job. He found himself in an inn talking to a confident man named Brekko.

"Are there bandits in Darcliff Province?" Malk asked.

"Some bandits," Brekko agreed.

"Ever fight any?" Malk asked.

"Not yet," Brekko said. "Most of my bladesmen stay at the temple. But I do sometimes need an extra man to guard the Holy Seneschal."

"What's that?"

"She's a woman," Brekko said.

"What kind of woman?" Malk asked.

"Striped," said Brekko.

"Oh," said Malk. Of course. That made sense. It was a Stripedfolk temple.

"Lot of women in this temple?" Malk asked.

"It's full of women," Brekko said. "You can look at women all day long."

Stripedwomen of course. But he would just be looking, so what did it matter?

"All right," said Malk. "I'm your man."

Even if it was just standing around in the temple all day, it couldn't be worse than being a bodyguard for a man who treated him like a personal attendant. Aye, meeting Brekko was a stroke of real luck.

The 1st of Purplemonth,
Morning

CRYS THOUGHT SHE RECOGNIZED THESE TREES, but she had already thought that twice this morning, so she held her tongue. Behind her, Cicada and Flicker asked for yet another break. Crys offered to let them rest while she scouted ahead.

She had not taken three steps before a voice rang out through the forest:

"Ha! I knew you'd come back here!"

Crys froze, but it was only Gwenshi. Crys hoped Beetle and his parents were too startled to notice her reaction. She was supposed to be the taishrefi, the one who had everything under control.

Vinnagon, too, had been startled by Gwenshi's cry. He was on the balls of his feet, sword in hand.

Gwenshi said, "Sorry, Vingo. Didn't mean to wake you."

Vinnagon gave Gwenshi a disgusted look as he straightened up. He slid his sword back into its sheath with a forceful *clunk!*

"Where were you?" Vinnagon asked Crys. "And why have you brought *them* here?"

Crys would have preferred a more respectful tone, but—

"Don't mind him," Gwenshi said, sidling up close to Vinnagon and patting his chest. "He was just worried about you."

Vinnagon gestured to the opening in the ground and said, "When I smelled the smoke coming out, I thought you were dead." His tone was accusatory—he didn't like admitting he had been worried.

"How did you get out?" Gwenshi asked. Blood stained her

skirt. A rip in her bodice revealed a nasty chest wound. But she seemed as cheerful as always.

"Our escape is a long story that we should perhaps discuss away from any entrances to the temple," Crys said. "Especially those which we hope to keep secret."

They heeded her words, and she led them away through the forest.

They were all following her now. Vinnagon walked with Gwenshi's arm about his waist, his hand on her shoulder. Cicada supported Flicker so she could favor her bad knee. Beetle walked alone.

Crys would have liked to hold his hand, but they needed her to be the taishrefi.

They stopped at an outcropping of limestone that was catching morning sunlight. There, Crys allowed them to rest while they recounted everything that had happened the night before.

Crys was intrigued by what Vinnagon had to say about the bladesman Lubol. If one bladesman was willing to join their cause, perhaps there were others. True, it was disheartening that Shakredo had so easily disposed of their ally, but perhaps there was a way to ask for Kashram's protection. Vinnagon's curse had not impeded him last night.

Thinking on her own escape, Crys knew there was at least one more person in the temple who was on their side. Their rescuer could have been one of the bladesmen, although the fact that the person had chosen to remain unseen made Crys suspect it was one of the taishrefis. Which one, she could not even guess. Whoever it was would have to be very good at hiding her true allegiance.

So they had allies in the temple. But to make good use of those allies, Crys felt she first needed answers to some questions: What was the Holy Council planning? And how was the Flamebringer clothing involved?

Her companions' conversation brought her no closer to the answers until Flicker said, "Well, everyone knows that the greatest threat to villages along the Dothedarl is the Flame-bringer tribe."

"What?" Crys exclaimed. "The Flamebringers *defend* the Dothedarl by keeping the Kashramites from expanding their territory."

Flicker glanced uneasily at Vinnagon.

"Not these Kashramites," Crys said. "The nomadic Kashramites."

"If you grow up in a town," Flicker said, "nomadic Lashref-ites look just as wild as nomadic Kashramites. Many people fear the Flamebringers."

"But there are also a lot of people like Crys," Beetle said.

" 'Like me' how?" Crys asked. "You mean people with Flamebringer relatives?"

Beetle nodded.

Crys considered this. "Perhaps Wintersmoke is trying to turn us against each other," she said. "Not us personally, but town people against farmers, the sunward villages against those that have ties to the Flamebringers."

"Perhaps," said Flicker. "In Darcliff, we know nothing about Flamebringers except that they ride horses and carry weapons."

"They carry *hunting* spears," Crys said.

Flicker raised her hand defensively. "I'm just telling you what people think."

Vinnagon looked down at his Flamebringer clothing. "So if a band of riders dressed in buckskin clothing attacked a village on this side of the river ..."

"... then people would assume it was truly a Flamebringer attack," Flicker said.

"Even though the nearest band of Flamebringers is three or four days' ride away?" Crys asked.

Flicker said, "I'm afraid no one knows that but you, dear."

"A war against the Flamebringers would certainly distract the people who've been complaining about the taxes," Beetle said.

"And Rathi said they were planning something for to-night?" Crys asked.

"Yes," said Beetle. "She said they were planning an 'evil thing'."

"That's an odd way of putting it," said Vinnagon.

"She has an odd way of speaking," said Beetle.

"True," said Vinnagon.

Even so, Crys had never known Rathi to be so direct. And Beetle getting the information moments before his rescue was a stroke of great luck. As a taishrefi, Crys expected great luck, but anything connected with Rathi made her suspicious. The Woshite would not have given the information to Beetle unless she had gotten something more valuable in return.

"She was trying to find out if I knew about their plan?" Crys asked.

"Yes," Beetle said.

"Well, we know about it now," said Gwenshi.

"Not everything," Crys said.

Gwenshi waved a hand dismissively. "Oh, we don't need to know everything right now. We know when it is, and we know it's evil. Let's go stop it."

* * *

It took some time for them to get off the bluff. Beetle had been afraid his mother would have to be carried, but with help from him and his father, she was able to negotiate the rough terrain and get near enough to the road. They knew a carter in Darcliff who would be able to smuggle them back into town and hide them until they knew whether Crys had succeeded or failed.

"Be careful," she told him as he was about to set out to fetch the carter.

He shook his head. "You are the one who must be careful."

"We'll just be hiding in the bushes," Crys said.

"Yes, but then what?"

She couldn't answer.

"Crys," he said, "when this is all over ..."

She looked at him expectantly.

"Well, Mother has said she would sell you my workshop ... if you didn't mind me living in your house."

Crys smiled and shook her head. "She has made me that offer many times."

"Oh," said Beetle.

She took his hand. "I am sorry I got your family involved in this. When this is over ... if ..."

He waited for her to complete the thought, but she just gave his hand a parting squeeze and said, "We'll have to talk about it later."

Crys was always putting that talk off until later. This time, Beetle didn't mind. Talk or no talk, he just hoped there would be a "later".

* * *

The women fidgeted too much. They knew they were not supposed to talk, and when they couldn't flap their jaws, the motion had to go into their limbs or else their souls would explode. At least, that was Vinnagon's thought when he was feeling uncharitable. In truth, the women were just bad at waiting.

Vinnagon was good at waiting. Hiding in the forest was a lot like standing guard. The difference was that, in this situation, Vinnagon could reasonably expect something to happen. Those bundles of clothing were likely to come out the same way they had gone in, on the trail from the caverns' back exit. That was the only way down, and Vinnagon had it under surveillance. They were in perfect position to learn the bashrefi's plan. If the women didn't like waiting for it, they should try standing guard against nonexistent enemies.

Vinnagon had stayed alert every night for four years. And his alertness had eventually paid off—in an unexpected way. He thanked Kashram that he had been the one to catch Crystal spying.

The sun was sinking low, and the day's heat was beginning to fade. The trees were giving off their evening scents, but not strongly enough to overcome the dusty dryness of the duff on the forest floor. When had it last rained?

"Horses," Crys whispered.

"Another cart?" Gwenshi asked.

Several carts had rolled past today, including one that carried Beetle and his parents safely back to Darcliff.

"I am not certain," Crys said. "I just heard a horse snuffle."

She had good ears.

Vinnagon said, "If we stay quiet, perhaps we shall hear more."

Vinnagon had a nice vantage point. Through gaps in the brush, he could see portions of the road. Turning his head slightly, he could see the steep path through gaps between the trees. The sun was sinking directly behind him, meaning that anyone on the path would have trouble seeing him or the women.

But Vinnagon hadn't seen anyone yet.

Gwenshi poked him in the back.

This was not a good time for distraction. Vinnagon could count on only brief glimpses of a traveler on the road. He needed to focus on his task.

Gwenshi poked him again. Repeatedly this time, as though she were attempting to tenderize his back muscles.

With a scowl, Vinnagon turned. Gwenshi pointed. Vinnagon saw the horsemen, and his sweaty back prickled with a sudden chill.

Horsemen were approaching through the forest, along the same trail Vinnagon had taken to get into his current position. They were Kashramites—bladesmen from Captain Gil's patrol company—and each was afoot, leading a saddled horse. Vinnagon and the women would certainly be seen if they remained in place. But discovery was also likely if they moved.

Crystal looked to him as though asking what they should do. Vinnagon gave her a pushing gesture, and she obediently moved upslope. He took Gwenshi's hand and pointed into a willow thicket.

She nodded and crawled in. Vinnagon was proud of her for keeping calm and moving slowly so she would not be seen. He was also frustrated that she did not move a little faster, but he couldn't have it both ways, could he? Though he followed on her heels, he was only partially inside the thicket when the first bladesman passed.

Vinnagon lay flat and prayed to Kashram. It was foolish to ask the god of battle to keep an enemy from seeing his legs so he could avoid a fight. Instead, he asked for protection against Shakredo's curse so that he would be given a fair chance—if there was such a thing in this world.

Apparently there was, for the first bladesman passed without altering his stealthy pace. So did the next. And the next.

The fourth bladesman stopped, and Vinnagon wondered if he had been discovered.

* * *

Crys had thought it was sweet the way Gwenshi had stayed so close to Vinnagon. Not wishing to intrude on their closeness, she had chosen a waiting place a short distance away. But now she wished she had been closer. With the bladesmen arriving unexpectedly through the forest, she found herself compelled to flee upslope, away from Gwenshi and Vinnagon, whose moccasins were still sticking out of the thicket that he and Gwenshi had chosen to hide in.

Crys considered what to do should Vinnagon's feet be seen. A distraction of some sort seemed in order. She could call out and try to lead the soldiers upslope. As she considered the merits of such a plan, she realized that revealing herself to save Vinnagon and Gwenshi was unwise. It would be better to let the bladesmen think they had chased away—or even captured—all the spies. Her purpose here was to learn the bashrefi's plan and find a way to undo it. If that meant sacrificing Vinnagon and Gwenshi, she had to be willing to do so.

Crys was not certain she was willing.

Truth told, she had obligations to her companions. Vinnagon had given up his career to spare her life. And had Gwenshi not been with her the night before, Rathi would certainly have knocked her stone-senseless again. She owed her life to the Kashramite couple.

But that was a personal debt. She had a higher duty to Lashrefi. Bargainkeepers could focus on personal, worldly obligations, but a true Lashrefite had to be aware of the higher calling.

The column of men and horses stopped. Had Vinnagon been seen. Had *she* been seen?

She heard a tiny *skip, skip, ponk* sound behind her. A pebble bounced past her face and fell into the brush below. Someone was coming down the trail from the temple.

The bladesmen below did not react. At least, Crys didn't hear anyone reacting. Her limited range of vision did not include any man's face. She could, however, see one horse, who looked bored.

From above came the scuffing sound of leather slipping on dirt and the puffs of a man carrying something bulky. Crys wanted to see what was being carried, to confirm that it truly was bundles of Flamebringer clothing, but the fact that she could not see the trail meant that she could not be seen, so she stayed where she was and thanked Lashrefi for helping her choose a good hiding place.

The descending man drew closer, and Crys discerned that he was not alone. Footsteps followed behind him—more puffing men.

The last person in line was sure-footed and deliberate. Crys suspected that was the seneschal, and her suspicion was confirmed when everyone's footsteps finally reached the bottom of the trail.

"Good evening, Captain," said the seneschal.

"Good evening," the leader of the Kashramites replied. The voice was not Captain Brekko's. Crys surmised it was Captain Gil of the temple's patrol company.

The seneschal said, "You have chosen to slice the cheese thin."

Captain Gil hesitated before replying, and the gritting of teeth was suggested by the tone of his voice: "We endeavored to comply with our orders as closely as was practical."

"And comply you have," the seneschal said. Her tone was amused, not placating at all. "Do your men understand what they are to do?"

"They do."

"Captain? Your tone suggests you are displeased."

That had been Crys's impression, too.

"My men and I will follow our orders," he said.

"But …?" inquired the seneschal.

"I am not certain this course of action is wise."

"Ah," said the seneschal. "Fortunately, you have sworn an oath to the Darcliff Temple. This guarantees your obedience even in the face of uncertainty, does it not?"

"I have already said as much."

"Good. Then keep your doubts to yourself. There is much of this plan that you do not see. We must all be guided by the bashrefi's wisdom, not yours."

"Of course, Holy Seneschal."

"I am glad we understand each other." The seneschal had certainly enjoyed putting Captain Gil in his place. Crys wondered if she was easier on Captain Brekko or harder on him because he was her lover.

"Your punishment for your lack of faith shall be at your own discretion," the seneschal concluded. "I trust it will be severe enough to impress upon your men the importance of showing faith in the bashrefi."

"Yes, Holy Seneschal." He sounded neither humbled nor humiliated, but Crys had no doubt that the stalwart bladesman would discipline himself as sternly as the seneschal expected.

There was something admirable about the way the temple had put itself in control of these proud, female-despising men. If Crys had stayed, she could have learned much from the seneschal. She resolved to go take a walk if she ever caught herself acting that way toward Beetle.

The salutations complete, Captain Gil began relaying the seneschal's orders to his men. The clothing was passed out, and the men disrobed. They dressed themselves as Flamebringers, handing their armor to one of the seneschal's guards and complaining, as Vinnagon had done, about the tight fit of the clothing.

Crys caught a glimpse of small pots being distributed. She had to crane her neck a while to discover the significance, but in the end she had a good view of a Kashramite dipping his fingers into a pot and smearing white paint on his comrade's face.

Crys's first reaction was that this could not possibly fool anyone. A red-skinned Kashramite could not be painted to look like a black-and-white Lashrefite. But in the shadows of sunset, the white paint yet seemed bright, and the streaks of red were dark enough to be mistaken for black.

The bladesmen's sword-callused fingers lacked the fine dexterity to define the sharp points, curves, and edges of true Lashrefite stripes, but in this light, Crys's eyes told her that all the sharp details were there, even when her mind knew they could not be.

She still could not mistake them for *Flamebringers*. Flamebringers were lean; these men were muscled like beef cattle. Flamebringers moved like wary coyotes; these men moved with the straightforward assurance of bears.

But people near Darcliff knew only that Flamebringers were exotic. And these illusions of buckskin and paint certainly matched what the locals would expect.

They kept their Kashramite swords, which looked out of place to Crys's eye. A temple guard handed out sticks which Crys at first mistook for spears until she recognized them as long-handled torches.

Up until that moment, this was a plot she had hoped to thwart, one more round in the complex game she had been playing against the Holy Council. But when she realized that the riders would be carrying *torches*, she suddenly felt the horror of the situation.

From the head of the column came the seneschal's voice: "Don't open the ember pot until you are in position to strike. And for the Goddess's sake, don't *drop* it—not unless you want to be at the center of the biggest forest fire Darcliff has seen in a hundred years."

"You know," said Captain Gil, "this forest might catch fire anyway if the wind picks up."

"If the fires spread to the forests, that is the will of the Goddess," the seneschal replied. "Your job is to be certain they first take a large bite out of the corn crop."

"I understand my orders," Gil replied, in a tone that made Crys reevaluate her impression that he had earlier been put in his place. "But I also understand the consequences. I truly hope the temple is prepared for war."

"You are afraid to fight Flamebringers?" She was mocking him.

"My men and I fear nothing," he replied. "But we are Arvethidrel. Our grandfathers died fighting an unwinnable war. And those who survived received poor thanks for their loyal service."

"We have the Goddess on our side," the seneschal replied. "And once people learn of your Flamebringer attack, we shall have the support of every town and village within three days' ride. I assure you, Captain, your men shall not be outnumbered."

* * *

Vinnagon lay still for what seemed a very long time.

Hiding was not at all like guarding. As a guard, he had an obligation to sound the alarm and confront his enemy. As a fugitive, with two women depending on him, he had to lie motionless and hope no one saw his legs.

When Gil gave the order to step out, Vinnagon did not heave a sigh of relief. Rather, he held his breath until the sounds of the patrol company were far enough away that he was certain he could no longer be seen.

He pushed himself up to a kneeling position and met Gwenshi's eyes.

She said, "Vingo, we've got to do something."

"Be still," he said. "They aren't even out of earshot yet."

"We have to do something now," Gwenshi insisted, "before they get too far ahead."

Vinnagon tried to reason with her. "Gwenshi, you and I can't kill them all."

Her face softened with some feminine emotion like affection or gratitude. Why, Vinnagon could not say.

"We've got to do *something*," Gwenshi repeated gently. "If they know they've been seen, could be they'll abandon their plan."

Vinnagon shook his head. "Unlikely. Captain Gil will follow his orders to the letter."

The patrol captain had already made it clear that he thought this was a foolish idea. After his exchange with the Holy Seneschal, the only way to save face was to do exactly as told and let the seneschal take the blame for the consequences.

The consequences would be war against the Flamebringers—Vinnagon was certain of that—and not even a war that *meant* something. Just a pointless external conflict to distract the Lashrefites while the Holy Council solidified their control of the province.

Something rustled in the brush behind him.

Vinnagon started, but it was only Crystal.

"I need a horse," she said. "I have to warn the villages."

Vinnagon considered this. "Do you think villagers will dare to draw blades against bladesmen?"

"Fight bladesmen, fight fires. Farmers will do what it takes to save their crops. But I need a horse."

"Very well," he said. "If the horsemen wish to remain hidden, they will walk their horses through the forest until they reach the place where the Shankito road meets the trees. Can you run?"

Both women nodded.

"Then we can get there before they do and take a horse from them."

Gwenshi looked excited.

"We won't be attacking the entire company," Vinnagon warned. "Gwenshi and I will try to isolate and unhorse one man. Only one. Is that clear?"

Gwenshi beamed. "Yes, Vingo."

"What are you smiling about?"

Gwenshi put her head on his shoulder and her hand on his chest. "Vingo," she said, "you *included* me."

A Few Months Earlier:
Malk

MALK HAD NIGHT DUTY IN THE INITIATES' HALL. It was a position of trust.

The initiates were the youngest women in the temple—so young that the taishrefis called them girls, but they were curvy enough to be women. That was the problem, really. A few years ago, a bladesman had pinched one of those curvy butts and the Holy Seneschal had lopped his head off. Poor fellow hadn't known that "don't abuse the women" meant no butt-pinching. Brekko and the seneschal had made the rule clear.

The rule was "don't abuse the women," and yet here was Malk latching their cell doors every night. Could be that wasn't so bad. Could be he was doing them a favor. They were safe in the cells. Outside ... well, the rule didn't apply to taishrefis.

The cell doors were thick, but they didn't seal tight. Malk could hear the women when they cried. After a while, he knew each one—the sobber, the snuffler, the one who got those awful choking coughs.

The one at the end never cried. She never made a sound except when she used the piss bucket. Malk never had to shut her in because she was never allowed to leave. He'd heard she was the mayor's daughter.

She was quiet like that until one night in Orangemonth when, in the heart of midnight, she screamed.

It was a crazy, terrified scream. Malk ran to the end of the hall and nearly put his hand on the latch. But his job was to close the latches; the seneschal opened them.

"What's wrong?" His voice came out as a hoarse cry.

"N— nothing's wrong," said the girl on the other side of the door. "It was just a nightmare."

This guard post was a nightmare.

She asked, "Wh— what's your name?"

Malk thought about it. The only way this could end was with him putting his hand on that latch and helping her escape. That wasn't what he had told Brekko he would do.

"None of your business," he said.

At the end of that watch, he requested a post on the temple steps.

The 1st of Purplemonth,
Evening

CRYS HAD TOLD THEM SHE COULD RUN. But she hadn't realized just how *far* Vinnagon wanted to run.

Gwenshi and Vinnagon were panting, too, but for them the pace seemed to be an easy lope. For Crys it was a struggle— too much time in a smoky temple, not enough time in La-shrefi's clean wind.

When Vinnagon finally called a halt, Crys stopped in her tracks. She stood gasping in the middle of the road, leaning forward, supporting her weight with her hands on her knees— exhibiting very un-taishrefi-like posture.

Vinnagon impatiently motioned for them to get off the road. Crys nodded and staggered into the stand of pines.

"I need you to remain here," Vinnagon said. "When we get the horse, Gwenshi will bring it to you. But I don't want to be worrying about you while Gwenshi and I are in combat."

Crys nodded.

"Good," he said. "Gwenshi: you are with me."

Crys gasped, "Wait."

"What?" Vinnagon's wary eyes flicked up and down the road. He begrudged her even one moment more.

"Don't strike until they light the first fire," she said.

"We need to *keep* them from lighting the fire," Gwenshi said. "That's what this is all about."

Crys shook her head. "No, it's not. It's about trapping Bashrefi Wintersmoke."

"It's about getting you to the nearest village ahead of any pursuers Gil sends after you," Vinnagon said. "We will strike when we have the best chance of taking a horse. Any other plan invites failure."

Crys could see his point. "Very well."

"Aye," Gwenshi said. "We'll trust your judgment, Vingo."

* * *

The silver glow in the moonward sky told Gwenshi that the moon was rising, yet it remained hidden by the forested hills. The sunward sky held dusky purple clouds. The stars had come out overhead.

Her dress was still damp from running. Now that she was standing still, a cloak would have been nice. This was the equinox, the end of summer. The evening did not have the bite of autumn, but the dusty day's lingering heat was too thin to warm her.

She pressed against Vinnagon, felt his scabbard against her thigh. He wrapped his arm around her waist, letting his hand rest on her hip.

They stood like that, alongside the road in the shadowy darkness of the pines, and listened to the sound of approaching horses.

After a time, Vinnagon murmured, "They are walking farther than I thought they would. It takes strong discipline to keep a horseman off his horse."

"Do we need to move?" she asked.

"Yes, let us do so. Stay close."

On the balls of his feet, Vinnagon glided out of the stand of trees and onto the packed-gravel road. He was not soundless, but he was quiet and swift.

Gwenshi attempted to imitate his glide, keeping her steps smooth, her seat low. After twenty strides, muscles started to burn from the uncustomary gait, but the burning felt good, and she kept going.

Now that she understood what it was like to kill a man, it seemed wrong to be excited by combat. Better to be somber, grim, and professional, like Vinnagon. But as they advanced to intercept the enemy, Gwenshi realized she could only be Gwenshi.

Woman, if you knew what combat was like, you would not seek it so eagerly, she told herself, imagining Vinnagon speaking in a stern-and-wise voice. But she did know, now. She surely did. And still she was eager. Vinnagon was right: She was crazy. And being crazy felt good.

After about a hundred paces, the burning in her muscles had turned to a dull ache, spreading through her legs. The pain ceased to be something to push against. It was now incorporated as part of her being.

Without warning, Vinnagon sidestepped.

Gwenshi hastily tried to adjust, scuffing her boot on the gravel as she shortened her stride.

A shadowy figure appeared on the road ahead.

Move naturally, Gwenshi, she told herself. She relaxed her stance and followed Vinnagon into the forest. They stopped behind the nearest tree.

Gwenshi listened. She could hear the scrape of hooves on gravel, but no sounds that indicated she had been seen.

"We need to get closer," Vinnagon whispered, so softly that she was not certain she had heard.

She put a hand on his back. "Right behind you," she said.

He took her hand.

"This signal means, 'Wait for me to circle around,'" he said, giving her hand two quick squeezes. "I'll give the signal when I've picked our target."

She squeezed his hand once. "Sounds good."

Walking through the forest holding hands with her husband—it was romantic! They moved with the grace of buck and doe, and Gwenshi felt she finally understood why Kashram had made her.

The forest was less brushy here—not rugged and wild as it was on the bluff, more like open woodland where villagers might graze livestock. On the other side of the road were rail-fenced fields of corn, dry and rustling in the twilight.

Vinnagon halted in the shadows, not really close to any tree or bush that might hide them, but he was so still that Gwenshi herself could have believed him a tree, had he not been holding her hand.

Ahead she could see dark horses munching dry grass in a clearing. The men spoke to them in low, easy tones, checking saddle cinches, untying long-handled torches from saddle straps, guiding horses to tree stumps where climbing astride would be simpler. In the twilight, their disguises were complete. Their white-painted faces were the only aspect of the scene that could be discerned with clarity. Their stripes seemed to shift strangely in the shadows.

Gwenshi remained as still as Vinnagon and tried to be as confident that they would not be seen. She narrowed her eyes so the whites would not show.

On the road, an orange flame burst into being.

"To me!" came the order. "Come light your torches!"

Mounted men encouraged their horses out of the clearing, onto the road. Those still afoot hastened their preparations as torches lit with flame.

"Do you need help, Lazall?" Only two men were left in the clearing now.

"I can't find my cursed hobbles," said the other. "I had them tied to the saddle on the same strap as the cursed torch, and now they're gone."

"Were they still there when we stopped?" The speaker led his horse over to the other.

"Yes ... I don't know ... I think so. This grass is so damned tall I'll never find them in the dark."

A voice from the road asked, "Is there a problem?" And it was clear that there had better not be.

After a brief murmured exchange, the helpful one called, "No, Captain," and he mounted up.

The other one knelt, cursing and searching through the grass.

This was their chance!

But Vinnagon didn't move. And Gwenshi realized that the horse had him spooked.

Vingo wasn't comfortable around horses, and the gelding was between them and the bladesman. Vinnagon couldn't get a clear line of attack.

But Gwenshi didn't need Vinnagon to attack the bladesman. The man was already off the horse and paying hardly any attention at all. Gwenshi gave Vinnagon's hand two quick squeezes and launched herself into a sprint.

The horse shied, dancing awkwardly, not certain where to jump because his rider was someplace in the grass near his rear legs. The gelding's round rump turned toward Gwenshi.

She was now in a good position to get kicked in the face, but every plan had its risks.

Gwenshi closed the distance and leapt. The heels of her hands hit the horse's rump, and she vaulted herself into the saddle.

The gelding's head twisted sideways and he bucked, sending Gwenshi into the air.

She landed astride—more or less—and this time, she grabbed the saddle. The gelding bucked again, jarring her body from tailbone to teeth, but she hung on.

On the third buck, she realized from the twist of the gelding's neck that Lazall the bladesman still held one rein.

After the fourth buck, she tried to draw her sword to cut the gelding loose. Then she heard a crack of bone, and the gelding broke free. They bolted into the forest.

Gwenshi gathered the reins, though she knew the horse would need a bit of a run before he was willing to heed her. Her father had taught her to always approach horses calmly. Her adventures with Vingo were teaching her why.

* * *

Lazall lay sprawled in the grass at Vinnagon's feet, unmoving. Well, Vinnagon had hit him hard enough to break his jaw. No surprise, then, that he should be somewhat stunned.

And thank Kashram!

Vinnagon crouched low and scuttled into the forest.

Fool woman! She should have obeyed orders and waited for his signal. Instead, she had charged into combat while the entire company was still close by, and she had raised enough ruckus to get the horsemen's attention even had they been a hundred paces away.

Captain Gil had already ordered two men to snuff their torches and chase after Gwenshi. The only good news was that, in the darkness, Gil did not realize it was Gwenshi and not Lazall.

"I was afraid Lazall would do something like this," he said.

"Perhaps something startled his horse," someone suggested.

"Badger?" Captain Gil was incredulous. "Badger's as level-headed as they come. I know. I'm the one who broke him to ride. But Lazall, now ... Well we can ask him when they catch him."

"Yes, Captain."

"Unless they have to bring him back dead. But that will be an answer, too, won't it?"

"Yes, Captain."

"We have a job to do, men. Let's get it done."

With flaming torches, Gil's patrol company rode away.

* * *

Gwenshi leaned low against the gelding's mane—not because she wanted him to go faster, but rather because he was not paying any attention to low branches.

At least he allowed for fallen logs: Muscles bunched underneath her and for a moment, they were silently flying. Then hooves struck turf and they were again galloping among the trees.

Aside from the fact that a wrong turn or false step would break both their necks, things were working out well. There was still the matter of turning him around and pointing him back toward Crystal, but for now, Gwenshi was glad to be going this direction. She could hear horses in pursuit, and she did not wish to lead them back to the Stripedwoman.

She tried some experimental tugs on the reins, but the gelding was not yet willing to listen. She knew a couple techniques for regaining control of a runaway horse, but they involved twisting its head and making it go where it did not want to go. And right now, making the gelding go where he didn't want to go would probably run him into a tree.

She heard a distant shout behind her. It was answered by a shout from the road.

The gelding's gallop eased into a lope.

Oh, now you slow down. Now that we're being chased.

A shout from the road again. Gwenshi could hear galloping hoofbeats on the gravel.

From somewhere behind her in the forest, a man called, "Lazall?"

The gelding pranced to a halt and lifted his head.

Oh wonderful, Gwenshi thought. *Now he's going to whinny.*

He did, of course. He gave a ridiculously dramatic cry that strained to reach a high note, then gave up and fell into the registers of a chuckling sort of growl.

"*That's* your whinny?" she asked. "You sound like you're trying to speak donkey."

A more respectable whinny answered from the road.

The gelding shook his head to loosen Gwenshi's grip on the reins and turned toward the sound.

Gwenshi allowed him to slacken the one rein, but she tugged on the other, keeping him turning until he was once again pointed away from the pursuers.

"Lazall?" called the one in the forest. He was getting closer.

Gwenshi rocked slightly forward and said in a low voice, "Ho-hey!"

The gelding took three steps before he realized he was obeying. Then he turned his head back to look at Gwenshi.

"That's right," she said. "I'm the one holding the reins. Now let's go." She brushed his ribs with her heels.

The formerly-runaway gelding ambled ahead. Plainly, he hadn't expected to be ridden by a woman who wanted him to go deeper into the forest, but if that was the way things were ... well, a horse had to accept a little mystery.

Gwenshi gave him an encouraging pat on the shoulder.

Snuffling sounds from the woods suggested that the horse behind them was coming at a trot. Gwenshi knew another was on the road. Those seemed to be her only pursuers.

The trick now was to take her gelding to a place that the other riders would naturally avoid. She convinced the gelding to push between two young pines growing so close together that their needles brushed the gelding on both sides. Next, she found a fallen log and convinced him to step over it.

He was a good sport—not overly sensitive to her reining, but certainly willing to do what she asked once he was quite certain it was what she wanted.

They worked themselves into a place where the trees were thicker. Occasional limestone outcroppings protruded from the earth. The gelding was surefooted, but Gwenshi tried to keep him away from stones, lest the sound of a hoofstrike should reveal their position.

There was no twilight left now. They were seeing by starlight. And in the thicker parts of the forest, they advanced mostly by intuition.

Gwenshi reined the gelding to a halt so she could listen better.

As she had thought, the other horse was passing quite close now. It was probably at the place where Gwenshi had turned aside. The bladesman had no way to track her at night. She just had to stay quiet, let him continue, then slip behind him and make her way back to Crystal.

Donkey-gelding lifted his head and let loose his whinny-bray.

The other horse loosed an answering whinny.

The rider called out, "Lazall?" He sounded hopeful.

"Nice work," Gwenshi muttered. Horses could be taught so many things. Why had no one ever taught this one to shut up when its rider was trying to hide?

Oh well. Gwenshi had another idea. And when she had a good idea, she didn't need to think twice.

Gwenshi slid off the gelding and secured his reins to the branch of the nearest tree. The gelding didn't think much of this. He shook his reins and whinnied again. So far, so good.

Gwenshi had to move swiftly now. Keeping herself on a line between the protesting gelding and the nearby rider, she worked back the way she had come, pushing through brush, stepping over fallen logs, and trying not to get her dress caught on anything.

She didn't have to be silent—just quieter than the horses. But even this proved quite the challenge. Gwenshi realized how much she had taken the gelding's night vision and sure-footedness for granted.

The nearby rider had stopped calling for Lazall and was now calling, "Badger?"

She had to admit that was a nicer name than "Donkey-gelding", but her name matched the whinny better.

The bladesman drew close enough that Gwenshi could guess his path. She found a tree he was likely to pass under and climbed up into it.

She fingered the hilt of her knife. She had left her dueling knife in the forearm of that guard in the caverns, but in this situation, her meat-cutting knife would be just as good. She could just drop onto the saddle behind the rider and threaten to slit his throat.

Would that work? What if he didn't take her threat seriously? Then she would have to slit his throat. Could she do it? Could she kill again? Just the thought was making her sick—the memory of slicing Tharn's knife through his guts.

The rider's horse snuffled.

"Easy, Winddrinker. Easy."

The bladesman pushed his way between the two pine trees that she and Badger had ridden through. He was afoot. He had left his horse behind.

"Badger?" he called. "Don't be silly now, old boy."

Badger answered with another bray. Gwenshi could translate the horse's protest: "She tied me up! She rode me into this godsforsaken maze of a forest, then tied me up!"

"There, there," the bladesman said. "Easy, now."

His voice receded as he moved toward the indignant gelding. Winddrinker was Gwenshi's for the taking.

Gwenshi dropped to the ground and passed between the two pines. Her eyes picked out the horse's silhouette in the gloom.

The horse snuffled.

"Easy, Winddrinker," Gwenshi said. "You're a fine filly. Yes you are."

Her hands found the reins and undid the hitch binding them to the tree branch. The horse sniffed at her shoulder.

The bladesman called, "Lazall?" A note of worry had entered his voice.

Gwenshi patted Winddrinker, put her hands on the saddle, and vaulted onto the horse's back. The filly took a step for balance, then let Gwenshi adjust herself in the saddle.

"There," said Gwenshi. "That's a proper introduction, isn't it, girl?"

"Who's there?" the bladesman called.

"Ho-hey, Winddrinker!"

Astride the fresh-legged filly, Gwenshi set out to find Crystal.

* * *

Orange flame lit the countryside. Two cornfields were on fire, and Crys could see the beginnings of a new blaze in the distance.

"Where is Gwenshi?" she asked.

"I wish I knew," Vinnagon said.

They stood on the road, for with the riders gone, there was no longer any reason to hide. Gwenshi should have no trouble finding them. But Vinnagon said he had last seen her riding in the wrong direction.

"I shall have to go afoot," Crys said.

"You need a horse," said Vinnagon. "If you ride hard, you can outflank them and warn villages they have not yet reached."

"I know I need a horse, but I shall have to go afoot."

"I am sorry we failed you, Taishrefi."

She looked into his dark face. "The night is not yet lost, Bladesman. While we live, there is hope."

"Shall I go with you, then?"

"You should wait for your wife."

"Perhaps," he said. "But she can take care of herself."

Two days ago, such an admission would have required great effort. Crys studied him, though there was little she could discern from his dark face.

"I am glad you trust her competence," she said.

"Bah! Were she competent, she would be here now!"

Crys heard the *clip clop* of a horse trotting on the road.

"Perhaps she is," she said. "Do you see a lone rider?"

Vinnagon's gaze followed hers. "Perhaps."

"Crystal!" Gwenshi called.

"Woman, where have you been?"

Crys put a hand on Vinnagon's arm. "Easy," she said. "At least she is here now."

When Gwenshi reached them, Crys said, "You could not have come at a better time. Vinnagon and I were about to set out on foot."

Unabashed, Gwenshi dismounted. "Well, I would have been here sooner, but I had to change mounts." There was a grin in her voice. "In the long run, it will save time, I think. This filly's name is Winddrinker." She handed the reins to Crys.

"How do you know the horse's name?" Vinnagon demanded.

"Oh, I overheard."

"I can't believe that, at a time like this, you decided to dally and play games!"

Crys chose to intervene: "What he means is, he was worried about you and he is glad you are safely back."

Gwenshi's grin flashed in the starlight. "I'm married to him. I know what he means."

Crys mounted and scanned the countryside. Though this part of the road was still in the shadow of the mountains, the road along the river was lit by the rising moon. Silver moonlight glinted off something in the distance—helmets?

She asked, "Do you see them? Are those bladesmen?"

Vinnagon followed her gaze. "Perhaps. They seem to be coming from Darcliff."

"Oh," said Crys. "Of course. If my people are playing the villains in her story, then her people must be the heroes."

"Beg pardon?" Gwenshi asked.

"The temple guards are going out to fight the fires and warn the villages. That way, the temple gets credit for any corn that is saved."

Vinnagon said, "If my uncle leads them, then I must confront him."

"I am not certain that is wise," Crys said. "It would be better to wait until you know how many bladesmen might be sympathetic with our side."

"Kashram tells me I must confront him now," Vinnagon said, with a certainty that Crys envied. Lashrefi always communicated in probabilities.

"But Vinnagon ..." She felt the odds were against him now, and she would need him later. And yet, if Kashram was truly guiding him, then she must accept the decision.

"Very well," she said. "Do what you must."

"Do not fear for us," Vinnagon said. "I shall have Gwenshi with me."

"We'll meet again," Gwenshi said.

Crys was not certain of that. But all she said was, "Fare well, then. I must ride."

"Ride swiftly," said Vinnagon. "Spread the truth, Taishrefi. While the truth lives, there is hope—even if we do not survive the night."

* * *

In the village of Fallowmarsh, people climbed on rooftops to see the approaching fires.

"There's one starting at Willow's Mill now. I'm telling you, it's not lightning."

"Stray ember," someone suggested.

"I see torches," another insisted.

"Does it matter?" the village taishrefi asked. "We need to plow a firebreak."

There was silence a moment, while they all pondered the wisdom of that.

"Unless the wind shifts," someone on the ground said.

"Pray that it does," said a rooftop watcher.

"Lashrefi helps those who help themselves."

The rider came while they were hitching up their plow teams. She told them the fires were set on orders from the Darcliff Temple. Many were incredulous. But the village taishrefi admitted she was not surprised.

The rider rode moonaway. The villagers began plowing their firebreak. And none of them noticed the vulture watching from the shadows.

It spread its wings and flew off toward Darcliff.

* * *

Standing in the shadows of the trees, Vinnagon could hear the bladesmen approach. They came at an easy walk, with no sign of haste.

Brekko was in front. Vinnagon could feel the oath that bound him to his uncle ... and to Shakredo.

That oath had to be broken. Vinnagon had to defy his captain. Or perhaps— perhaps there was still a chance to reconcile. Brekko was an honorable man.

Vinnagon stepped out of the shadows onto the moonlit road. The bladesmen halted. Some reached for their swords, but no one drew. Vinnagon folded his arms across his chest to keep his own hands from straying toward his hilt. He had no wish to provoke a fight and squander his chance to speak.

"Captain Brekko," he said.

"Vinnagon." His uncle's face was in shadow, unreadable.

"You know what evil the temple does here tonight," Vinnagon said. "Why do you allow your men to participate?"

Brekko hesitated before replying, "You should not have come back, Vinnagon. You know traitors are not welcome here."

"I have betrayed my oath to a demon cult. You have betrayed your oath to Kashram."

The hesitation was briefer this time. "If you have come to provoke a duel, you have miscalculated. I shall not give you such honor. Your oath was to me. You swore to obey my orders. Once you ran away, you should not have come back."

A few days earlier, Vinnagon would have agreed. But now he knew there were more powerful obligations than those which bound men to other men. Now he must speak out where all the bladesmen could hear. Lubol had wanted Vinnagon to lead the bladesmen against the temple. Perhaps there were others who felt the same.

"Have you told these men what they do here tonight?" Vinnagon asked. "Have you told them they act in service to a demon? Have you—"

"Seize him!" Brekko ordered.

"Have you told them the fires were set by their comrades in Gil's patrol company?"

Bladesmen surrounded him now. Malk had hold of his arm. Their eyes met, and Malk looked uncertain.

Then Vinnagon's arms were yanked behind his back. He rose involuntarily on his toes to ease the sudden pain.

"Have you told them these fires are a ploy to gain support for a corrupt-hearted bashrefi?"

"Enough!" Brekko shouted. With three quick strides, he closed the distance and struck Vinnagon on the cheek.

Vinnagon's knees buckled. He shook his head to regain his senses. The pain in his shoulders flooded back into his awareness, and he rose on tiptoes again.

"You are right, Uncle." Vinnagon spoke quietly now, but every man was listening. "We did swear our oaths to you. Lead us, Uncle. Lead us back to Kashram. It is not too late. He will give us the strength and courage we need."

"You do not understand," Brekko said coldly. "The world is not as simple as you think."

Then Brekko shouted, "Take him to the bashrefi! It is time for this traitor to face justice."

* * *

The filly could cover the ground. They were already nearing the village of Hackberry, close enough now to see people gathering with hoes and spades. The fires were yet distant, but already, work was beginning on firebreaks to protect outlying haystacks.

Crys chose the largest group of people and guided Winddrinker toward them. Their reaction was ... not quite what Crys had expected. She caught their attention, yes. But instead of curiosity, they displayed attitudes of hostility. The gardening implements were raised like weapons, and the people bunched shoulder to shoulder, as though to form a wall between her and their haystack.

Crys drew rein well out of their reach.

"People of Hackberry, do you know why the fields burn tonight?"

From somewhere in the second rank came the reply, "Because you set them on fire, Flamebringer!"

What? "No," she said. "I am no Flamebringer. I am a taishrefi."

"You are dressed like no taishrefi we know."

Crys dismounted. The horse was confusing them. She hitched the reins to a fence rail and approached the people on foot.

"I am a taishrefi who studied among the Flamebringers," Crys said. "And then I studied at the Darcliff Temple. I understand them both."

She kept her voice quiet so that the crowd would have to remain quiet, too. They were scared, but she could show them she was no threat.

"These fires," Crys said, "have been set by men dressed to *look* like Flamebringers. But they are not Flamebringers at all. They are not even Lashrefites. They are Kashramite bladesmen with painted faces."

"How do you know all this?" The challenger spoke from the anonymity of the crowd.

"Because I saw them don their Flamebringer garb," Crys said. "I saw them paint their faces. I saw them ride off and light the fires. So I have come to warn you."

Another group of people was approaching from the village. Heads turned. Some people relaxed—or at least lowered their tools to a less threatening position. Crys had not yet convinced them she was speaking the truth, but she had convinced them that she was not here to singlehandedly set the village aflame. They began murmuring among themselves. Crys decided to wait so that the new arrivals could also hear what she had to say.

The newcomers advanced purposefully; the crowd at the haystack gave way deferentially. Clearly someone important was in the center of the approaching group.

Moonlight flashed off a helmet, and Crys felt a sick feeling creep into her middle.

"Taishrefi Crystal! So this is where you have been hiding!"

The crowd parted, and out stepped the Holy Seneschal.

Crys's feet could not move. Her tongue could not speak.

Hand on sword, the Holy Seneschal approached.

"She's the one!" Crys blurted out. "She's the one who gave the order to burn your fields."

The seneschal's lip curled, and she drew her sword.

"Lying, filthy Flamebringer. I knew you were a runaway, but I did not know you to be a blasphemer."

"The truth will come out," Crys said, knowing that each word could be her last. "Slay me here, and all will see the depths of your evil."

The fist holding the sword drew back.

Crys closed her eyes and waited for the deathblow.

* * *

When Crys regained consciousness, she was bound hand and foot, riding belly-down across a leather saddle. Her cheekbone ached, and her face was so swollen that she could see only out of one eye.

* * *

Sword at her hip, Gwenshi moved like a shadow, following the temple guards. She glided among the cottonwoods, along trails that paralleled the River Road.

The enemy had her husband. She would get him back.

Vinnagon's hands were tied behind his back, and he was guarded by four bladesmen. He surely was in a bad spot.

Gwenshi reckoned she could take one bladesman by surprise, but that would leave Vingo to fight three—using only his feet.

Even taking one by surprise was not a sure bet. Last time Gwenshi had done that, the man had nearly killed her. The stink again came to her nostrils, despite the effort she had put into washing her dress that morning.

No, she reckoned she would have to be patient. Thing was, she wasn't always good at being patient.

Trees grew sparser along Gwenshi's trail as the road entered the village of Soval. She lurked behind a cottonwood at the edge of the riverside grazing commons. At the river was a livestock watering hole and a rickety dock with no boats. Soval was not a very fancy place to stage her husband's execution.

The men disappeared behind some houses—all the activity seemed to be at the other edge of the village. Gwenshi waited a moment to be sure that no one else was about, then she dared to leave her hiding place and run across the main square.

She cast a long shadow. At least she would have warning if someone tried to sneak up behind her.

Gwenshi crept around the side of a house, listening for voices or footsteps on the other side. She heard nothing. The house had a garden behind it. The garden appeared empty.

From the garden fence, she surveyed the next row of houses. One had candlelight in the window, so she chose to avoid that one. The others seemed quiet.

Gwenshi advanced.

A figure came around the corner. Gwenshi froze, halfway between rows of houses. A white, striped face glanced her way, hesitated a moment.

Gwenshi put her hand on her sword hilt.

The Stripedwoman shook herself and hastened down the street.

Gwenshi relaxed. She had been mistaken for a bladesman! Wait till she told Vingo! But first, she had to rescue him.

Gwenshi eyed a rain barrel at the corner of a nearby house. It put the eaves within easy reach. Well, why spurn such an opportunity? With a run and a jump, Gwenshi grabbed the eaves and clambered onto the bark-shingled roof.

On hands and knees so that she would not show up against the skyline—at least not much—Gwenshi crawled up the roof. She tried to be quiet, but she doubted anyone inside would mistake her for an owl. Oh well. Too late now. Gwenshi crawled to the top and peeked over at the final row of houses.

Vinnagon's uncle was talking to a pudgy woman who Gwenshi guessed was the bashrefi. A bevy of fancy women stood nearby—a respectful distance away, but probably close enough to overhear whatever they wanted. Vinnagon was off to the side, down to only three guards now, but there were enough people between Gwenshi and him that she reckoned she would have to be patient some more, even though most of those people were just ordinary Stripedfolk villagers.

The meeting broke up, and Brekko began visiting knots of villagers and giving them orders. Vinnagon was sent to sit with his back against a house, and Brekko paid him no mind. In fact, the captain pointedly avoided looking at his nephew.

Villagers were sent scurrying back to their houses for supplies. Gwenshi realized that, well-hidden as she was from those on the other side, sooner or later someone would look at her side of the roof and see her lying flat in the moonlight. Her dress did not match the shingles well.

Gwenshi climbed back down, dropped from the eaves, and scuttled around the side. She found a garden gate and let herself in. Her dress rustled among the dry leaves. Bean harvest was done for the year. The pumpkins were doing well, but they would not get much bigger—not unless the sky remembered how to rain. Gwenshi's own garden seemed very far away.

At the edge of the garden, she peered out through a gap in the willowstick fence. Villagers were clearing a wheat field, sweeping straw and stubble away from the village to make a bare-earth firebreak. Torches had been lit, but not for light. The village was preparing a backfire.

Gwenshi reckoned that was risky. And she reckoned the bashrefi didn't care. It wasn't *her* house that would catch fire if an ember jumped the firebreak.

Vingo was still where she had seen him last. Only difference was that the bladesmen were tying him to a long pine pole.

This was not good.

Gwenshi couldn't see anyone between her and Vingo. She couldn't hear anyone close by. She reckoned the time for patience was over. She wasn't exactly sure what the pole meant, but she was pretty sure it was for an execution. She didn't have time to inquire about the details.

She jumped the garden fence.

It was only a twenty-yard sprint. One of Vinnagon's guards had his back to her. It was a cowardly way to kill a man, but she needed the advantage, didn't she? She was outnumbered and only a woman.

In one smooth motion, Gwenshi drew her sword and thrust at the place where his cuirass left his back exposed.

A blade met hers and pushed it off line. A broken-nosed bladesman—not the one she had been aiming for—had seen her coming.

He stepped around their locked swords and shoved her to the ground.

Gwenshi tucked, tumbled, and sprang to her feet. So much for surprise. It was one against three.

Gwenshi feinted right, deflected the center man's strike, and rushed at the one on the left. He stepped back, and Vinnagon, only partially tied to the pole, rolled over the bladesman's calf. That bladesman went down. For a moment, Gwenshi needed to fight only two.

But those two pressed her hard. The broad-shouldered one attacked high, the broken-nosed one attacked low. Gwenshi blocked, blocked, blocked, blocked, matching their rhythm even as they accelerated. She backed away, step by step, until her heel bumped against the wall of another house.

One more high block, one more low. Now her back was to the wall. One more high—but this time the foe's sword was not there to block, and her rising blade left her stomach open for the bladesman who punched her just below the ribcage.

Gwenshi doubled over and fell to her knees. She couldn't breathe.

The broad-shouldered one said, "Nice fighting, woman."

He stepped on her sword, pinning it to the ground. She let go.

The other grabbed her by the hair and dragged her away. Gasping for breath, Gwenshi did not resist.

* * *

Vinnagon watched Malk and Shangrel tie Gwenshi to a pole. They dropped her to lie in the dirt with her face one foot away from his own. She kept repeating, "I'm sorry, Vingo. I'm sorry I let you down." And Vinnagon could say nothing because of the gag in his mouth.

He had a pole of his own, to which his hands and feet were bound so that he could not even reach out and touch her. All he could do was look at her tear-streaked face and wish for some means to offer comfort.

This was his fault. He had told her not to confront Brekko with him. He had told her to be his rescuer in case his plan failed.

But that had just been an excuse to keep her out of trouble, so he could focus on facing his uncle. Until he did, until he had somehow reckoned with or wrestled with that oath, Shakredo would still have a hold on him.

He knew this somehow—just as he had known how to send Lubol's soul to Heaven. Kashram was granting him powers he had never dreamed of asking for. And yet he lacked the power to console his wife, to tell her she had fought well, to tell her he was proud of her even though they were both about to die.

"Oh, Vingo. I'm so sorry."

Then the gag was in her mouth, and Vinnagon knew those were the last words he would ever hear from her. He could give her nothing but a tear.

* * *

Think, Crys told herself. *You're still alive. You still have the grace of Lashrefi. Find a way out of this.*

The horse bounced to a halt and snorted. Face down across the saddle, Crys could see only fetlocks, hooves, and moonlit pebbles in the road.

"Where shall I find the bashrefi?" the seneschal asked.

"She and Captain Brekko are over there," answered a man—a Kashramite, if Crys was any judge of accents.

The bouncing resumed.

So she was being taken to the bashrefi. Apparently, the temple needed to make an example of her. Otherwise, the seneschal could have disposed of her in the river along the way.

Crys was still alive. And that meant there was hope.

Moreover, Brekko was nearby, and that meant Crys was right where Vinnagon and Gwenshi were likely to appear. She thanked Lashrefi for her allies and prayed that they might arrive in a timely manner.

This trot was short. "Bashrefi," the seneschal announced, "I have found Crystal, the runaway."

"Well done," Wintersmoke answered. "Bring her before me."

Someone grabbed Crys's bound legs. The seneschal grasped her by an arm and heaved. Crys's ribs grated across the saddle, a hand pressed against her buttocks, and then she was standing at the edge of a village with a temple guard on either side of her.

Behind her, the seneschal said, "Don't be bashful, boys. She's not a taishrefi anymore. She's just a runaway blasphemer."

Somewhat reluctantly, the men dragged her to Winter-smoke. There was no dignity in the situation, but Crys saw nothing to be gained by struggling. They set her on her feet and held her upright. Her legs were bound so tightly she could not stand on her own.

A little temple formality had been added to the village commons. The bashrefi was flanked by four women of the First Choir holding smoking torches. Crys met their eyes, but none was a woman she could call friend. These were hand-picked women—those taishrefis most loyal to Wintersmoke's warped reforms.

Wintersmoke looked up at Crys and said, "She may kneel."

Obediently, the guards lowered Crys to a kneeling position.

She looked about her. Some bladesmen stood nearby, as did many worried villagers. Everyone knew of the temple's cruelty in the abstract. It was another thing to confront it in the village meadow in the moonlight.

Wintersmoke sighed, as though faced with a most unpleasant task. "Crystal, you ran away from your calling to engage in an illicit intimate relationship with a Kashramite. If you have any words of repentance, speak them, for the Goddess is merciful."

"You false-tongued viper." Her words came thickly as she tried to talk around the swelling in her face. "Your lies will not—"

At a gesture from Wintersmoke, a gag was put in her mouth and cinched painfully tight against her aching cheek.

Wintersmoke shook her head. "You disappoint me, child. You had so much promise. But you threw it all away for lust. Your lover is already in custody, and he has confessed to everything."

Smoke from the attendants' torches filled her eyes. Crys coughed, fighting the smoke and her confusion. Her lover? Beetle? Confessed? No, perhaps her lover was Vinnagon?

As the smoke cleared, Crys realized that the tears rolling down her face would be taken as an admission of guilt. The smoke held the power of Shakredo, muddling minds and making Wintersmoke's words seem true. No lover had confessed anything. This was just a performance for the watching villagers.

"Your Fortuitousness!" Captain Brekko approached.

Wintersmoke looked up. "Yes, Captain, what is it?"

"Forgive my interruption, but we have discovered the identity of the unknown prisoner. She is the fugitive's wife."

"His wife?"

"Yes. You know how our women are. Apparently she was trying to murder her husband as revenge for—" he looked at Crys, returned his gaze to the bashrefi, "—for his indiscretions."

What were they talking about? What sort of game was this?

"Ah, that is indeed a sad state of affairs," said Wintersmoke. "Bring them before me and let us settle this."

It was all a performance. Crys could tell. But whom had they coerced into playing along? And what would Wintersmoke say when the *real* Vinnagon and Gwenshi arrived?

Please, Lashrefi. Please let them arrive soon.

Captain Brekko returned with two pairs of guards. Each pair carried a pole. Each pole had a burden of some sort, a figure ... a person.

The Holy Council truly *had* captured Gwenshi and Vinnagon. *Oh, Lashrefi, where is your mercy?*

Wintersmoke stepped forward and approached Gwenshi. "This is the wife?" she asked, looking at the captain.

"Yes, Your Fortuitousness."

"Did she harm your men?"

"No, of course not."

Tied up, Gwenshi seemed small and helpless. Flickering torchlight illuminated tears on her face. Tears. On Gwenshi!

What had they done to her? Crys suddenly realized how much she had admired the little woman's courage. Seeing those tears made her heart ache.

This was all Crys's fault. Had she not solicited their help, Gwenshi and Vinnagon could be well away from Darcliff by now. They could have made a new life somewhere, among Kashramites. But instead, Crys had talked them into staying here and handling her problems for her. In that respect, she was no better than Wintersmoke.

The evil bashrefi took the sleeve of her robe and gently wiped away Gwenshi's tears.

"The Goddess is merciful," Wintersmoke said, making it sound like a decision. She turned to Brekko and declared, "Release her! Send two of your men to escort her back to Camptown. She has suffered enough. We shall not force her to witness her husband's execution."

Crys understood. Gwenshi was a problem for the story the Holy Council wanted to tell. The poster had shown two fugitives, so executing three would be problematic. Gwenshi had to be disposed of more quietly.

* * *

Uncle Brekko did not have the courage to say goodbye. He did not even have the courage to look Vinnagon in the eye. Instead, he ordered others to carry Vinnagon and Crystal out into the middle of the cornfield.

The tactical part of Vinnagon's mind realized that this

would have been a good time for Gwenshi to come and cut them loose. But Malk and Shangrel were "escorting her back to Camptown." She might already be dead.

The bladesmen dug two holes in the soft earth of the cornfield. As they were lifting Vinnagon's pole, he grunted at them until one removed his gag.

"What?"

"I want you to do the same for the taishrefi," he said. "Remove her gag."

"Why?"

"So she can breathe in more smoke and perhaps die before the flames come."

They did so. Then they planted the poles and left.

The pole held Vinnagon's body high enough off the ground that he could see the village over the waving tassels of rustling corn. As soon as the four bladesmen entered the cleared firebreak, villagers began lighting the backfire. Vinnagon twisted his neck to see how close the fires behind him were. They were much closer than he expected, coming under a steady wind.

The backfire was the closer threat, but it was burning against the wind. If the wind shifted, he and Crystal would be cooked in moments. If the wind stayed steady, they would have a little more time.

"Thank you," Crystal said, "for convincing them to take off my gag."

Her speech was slurred, but understandable. Vinnagon could not see her face well, but it seemed she had been hit quite hard. His own face was sore as well, of course, but it was of no consequence—especially not now.

"I hoped that it would make it easier for you to pray, Taishrefi."

"I pray in my thoughts," she said. "But thank you."

She did not sound as though she was about to produce any miracles.

"At least they let Gwenshi go," she said.

Vinnagon considered the idea, then answered, "You do not truly believe that."

"No," she said. "But if *you* did, I did not want to disillusion you."

"I suppose I should be grateful that I will be seeing her in Heaven soon."

"As a taishrefi, I should be pleased to be going to Heaven myself," Crystal said. "But in truth, I would not have minded going later."

Vinnagon could not argue with that.

"I am sorry I involved you in this," she said.

"I involved myself, Taishrefi."

"Perhaps," she agreed. "But if you see Gwenshi, give my apologies to her as well."

Vinnagon smiled. "Very well."

"You were lucky to have her, you know."

"I know," Vinnagon said. "I wish I had told her so."

* * *

Gwenshi stood at the front door of an isolated farmhouse just outside of Soval. Her legs were free, and her wrists were now bound in front instead of behind, but the seneschal had ordered her captors to leave the gag on so that she would not be able to refute the temple's ridiculous tale.

Standing outside with her was the broad-shouldered guard who had taken her weapons. She didn't know where he had put her knives, but his broken-nosed companion had her sword. He was inside, muttering curses.

"How am I supposed to find a spade in the dark?"

Gwenshi's companion looked uneasily up and down the road. "Just find something to dig with—and quick, before the stripeys come home."

Gwenshi hoped the farmers would catch her escorts in the act of looting the farmhouse, but that was unlikely. The backfire was being lit. Everyone likes to watch a big fire. And this fire had the added excitement of a double execution.

The broken-nosed guard emerged from the farmhouse holding a wooden spoon. "This is all I could find," he said. "Unless you want to dig a grave with a spoon, we'll have to throw her in the Dothedarl."

"The captain said to bury her."

"The captain isn't here."

"Look, this is Vinnagon's wife. We have to give her a proper burial."

How sentimental. But at least they were arguing. This might be her one last chance.

Her brother had been right about that trick: The bladesmen had neglected to search her boots. Gwenshi eased herself to the ground, as though she were weary from standing so long.

"A 'proper burial'? Why?"

"I like Vinnagon. I want him to have his wife when he gets to Heaven."

"None of us are going to Heaven," the broken-nosed guard said as Gwenshi's fingers found the hilt of her boot knife. "We're all going to Hell, and the bashrefi is sending Vinnagon's slywoman to keep him company."

She had it! She raised the knife and slipped it inside the cord that held the gag in place. With a quick twist of her head, the cord snapped and fell loose.

"She's got a knife!" the broken-nosed one said, drawing his sword.

Gwenshi spat out the gag and said, "Crystal is not Vinnagon's slywoman! Do you really believe that witch's lies?"

"She's got a knife and she uses it to cut off her gag," said the broad-shouldered one. "Just like a woman."

Gwenshi ignored him.

"Vinnagon left the temple because they ordered him to drown Crystal in the river," Gwenshi said. "And he decided that a Kashram-created man doesn't kill helpless women just because some other women told him to."

She waited for the implication to sink in, but the broad-shouldered one only said, "*You* aren't helpless. You have a knife."

"Aye, and if you'll give me a moment to cut loose these wrist bonds, I'll fight you in single combat. Or we could work together."

"To do what?"

"To save Vinnagon!"

"Gwenshi," the broad-shouldered one said, his voice gentle, "I like Vinnagon, but he broke his oath."

"His oath to a *demon*!"

"His oath to the captain."

"The captain who serves a *demon*! Are you so blind?"

"My father said no man ever went to Hell for following orders."

"Are you sure about that?" Gwenshi asked. "Because you have bet your soul on it."

They were quiet a moment, almost as though they were capable of thinking.

"What's your plan for saving Vinnagon?" asked the broad-shouldered one.

"I don't know," Gwenshi said. "I'll just rush in there and save him."

"Through the flames?"

Gwenshi glanced at the backfire. Though burning against the wind, it was going good now.

"Well, I reckon I'll have to go around the flames," she said.

"And what do you need from us?"

"Malk, you're not really going to—"

The broad-shouldered one raised a hand to silence his companion. Again he asked, "What do you need from us?"

Gwenshi offered him her knife. "Just cut me loose," she said. "Oh, and give me my sword back. Once Vinnagon gets out of the fire, he might need it."

* * *

Malk and Shangrel watched the little woman run away into the cornfield.

Shangrel stared as if in shock. "Now you've done it," he said. "I can't believe you disobeyed Brekko's order."

"Brekko and the bashrefi want her dead," Malk said. "We just let her run off into a fire. Of her own free will. Dying this way fits their story better."

"But what if she doesn't die?" Shangrel asked. "What if by some miracle she saves him?"

Malk put a hand on Shangrel's shoulder. "Friend, if Kashram has a miracle like that for Vinnagon, then perhaps he will have one for us."

* * *

Gwenshi ran through the cornfield with her sheathed sword tucked under her arm. When one arm grew tired, she switched the sword to the other and kept running. Soon both arms were sore. She wished swords weren't so heavy.

The corn was taller than Gwenshi. She saw Vinnagon and Crystal only in occasional glimpses.

The flames of the backfire were rising high. The fire set by the disguised bladesmen was advancing from the other direction. The deeper she got into the cornfield, the closer came the flames on either side.

She had one last glimpse of Vinnagon still two hundred strides away, and then a cloud of smoke enveloped him.

She told herself that it was only smoke. Vinnagon was not in the flames, yet. She still had time to reach him.

Of course, that did not mean they would have time to escape.

Gwenshi ran into the haze. Smoke stung her eyes and burned her throat. Her head grew dizzy. Damn the Flamebringers for starting this fire!

She staggered forward and fell to the ground, bruising her chest on the hard scabbard. Coughing, she pushed herself to her hands and knees.

"Gwenshi!" Vinnagon called. "This way!"

The air was still breathable down here. She drew a breath and rose to her feet. Blinded by smoke and tears, she shut her eyes and ran toward the sound of Vinnagon's voice.

Her legs began to wobble. She exhaled and stumbled to the ground for another breath.

Spots swam in front of her. She blinked until she could see the base of a moonlit corn stalk.

From somewhere above—not too far now—Vinnagon called her name again. How could he breathe? How could he find voice?

Vinnagon never gave up. Gwenshi would not give up either.

She rose. A gasp of smoke reminded her to hold her breath. She staggered forward sixteen steps and hit her head on a pole.

Vingo!

Drawing the sword from its sheath, she sliced the ropes that bound his feet. Vinnagon groaned in pain. With a leap, she sliced the ropes at the top of the pole.

Vinnagon fell to the ground in a heap.

"Crystal," he said. "Save Crystal."

Save Crystal? But wasn't she the enemy? Wasn't she a Flamebringer? And hadn't she and Vinnagon … ?

No. No, it was something in the smoke that made Gwenshi think those thoughts. Some twisted trick of the bashrefi's. Some ensorcellment by the demon Shakredo.

Gwenshi approached Crystal's pole. Vomit stained the tai-shrefi's tunic and her head lolled limply to one side. The Stripedwoman gave no response when Gwenshi sliced the ropes binding her feet.

Gwenshi leapt for the top of the pole, missed, and fell to the ground again.

She tried to clear her lungs. Her legs were wobbly. She didn't feel strong.

One clean breath. That's all I need.

The air was clearer around Vinnagon. She knelt beside him.

He put a hand on her shoulder and said, "Kashram, give us strength."

Gwenshi took a breath. Her head cleared. She rose to her feet.

As she jumped, the smoke seemed to part around her. The ropes atop the pole focused into sharp moonlit clarity. Her strike was true, and Taishrefi Crystal fell from the pole.

Gwenshi landed in a knife-fighting stance, legs springy, ready to dodge in any direction. But no direction was open to her. She and Vinnagon and Crystal were encircled by flames.

The smoke had lifted away from the heat, and the evil lies no longer poisoned her mind. Yet still the air did not taste clear. The heat parched her throat. In a short time, they would all begin to roast.

But Gwenshi was a Kashram-created woman. She had a sword in her hand. She would not surrender. She was a fighter.

And she was a gardener.

With swift whirling strokes, she laid the corn flat, clearing a circle around Vinnagon and Crystal. The fires crackled with cruel heat. Her sword flashed orange with flame and silver with moonlight.

Her husband dragged Crystal to the center of the circle. Then he began pushing the fallen cornstalks outward. Around and around danced Gwenshi with her blade, and the fire's fuel fell back.

A sword-callused hand gripped her shoulder.

"Come!" Vinnagon told her. "Lie low!"

Gwenshi followed him to lie beside Crystal as flames rose overhead to make a dome against the sky.

At the center was Gwenshi, legs shaking, skin blistered, heart strong with the strength of her creator.

* * *

Crys awoke with an aching head and the taste of ashes in her throat. Blearily, she lifted her gaze to the smoking landscape.

She was lying in a patch of low corn stubble, a circle of cool earth in a plain of smoldering ashes. Here and there, embers glowed red in the darkness.

On either side of her lay Gwenshi and Vinnagon, their hair and clothing singed, dark Kashramite faces now black with soot. Each had an arm around her. Gwenshi smiled and her teeth gleamed in the moonlight.

"She's awake, Vingo. Let's go get 'em!"

"Bide a moment," Vinnagon said gently. "Give her a chance to remember herself."

Remember. Remember. What did she remember?

Oh no.

Thousands of bushels burned. And now thousands of people would go hungry. All because of some Flamebringer madness.

Her grandmother's people had done this. Without provocation, without cause. Was it some imagined slight? Had it amused them to see farmers' fields burn? Flamebringers were nomads and could never understand the labor required to bring forth food from the land.

"Did they take any food?" she asked. "Did they take any livestock? Or did they just burn the fields and ride away laughing?"

"Crystal," Gwenshi said, "you were the one who went riding across the countryside. You saw more than we did."

Riding? Yes, she had ridden a horse. "Winddrinker."

"I reckon the temple confiscated her, aye?"

"I don't remember," Crys said. "I hitched her to a fence ... so perhaps she is still there. But then ... Gwenshi, why was I riding Winddrinker?"

"To warn the villages," Gwenshi said.

"About what?"

"About the fires," Gwenshi said patiently.

"Oh ... yes." Why had she been doing that?

"The bashrefi's ritual has addled your mind," Vinnagon said.

"Yes," said Crys. "She does that. I remember."

"Do you remember us?" Gwenshi asked.

"Of course. You are dear Gwenshi." She turned her head to the Kashramite on her other side. "And you are noble Vinnagon, who ..."

Was he her lover? No. No, her heart belonged to Beetle.

Vinnagon was not even attractive. But why, then … ?

"Will Lashrefi take offense if I ask Kashram to clear your head?" Vinnagon asked.

"I … don't know."

"Your thoughts are addled by Shakredo," Vinnagon reminded her. "And Kashram is strong against Shakredo."

"Yes, I remember." And she *did*, somewhat. "Very well, then."

She was still lying on the ground. Vinnagon straddled her back, shoved a fistful of dirt into each of her ears, and shouted, "Demon, be gone!"

Crys shook her head. Vinnagon got off her, and she sat up, furious at the indignity.

"Why did you do that?"

Vinnagon looked apologetic. "To scare the demon, Taishrefi."

"You can't scare demons, fool! They're big enough to devour the world!"

"But did it clear your head?" Gwenshi asked.

Crys picked dirt out of her ears. "Clear my head? Are you insane? My head aches from a blow the seneschal gave me when …" Her anger died down. She had ridden Winddrinker to tell people of the bashrefi's fires.

Flamebringer attack? How could she have believed such nonsense?

"Very well. I suppose it did clear my head. But was it necessary to be so rough?"

"I am not certain," Vinnagon admitted. "I have not been a holyman for very long."

"When did you become a holyman?" Crys asked.

"I am not certain," Vinnagon said again. "Perhaps when I realized it was the only way to keep the smoke from killing us before Gwenshi arrived to cut us down. Or perhaps when I sent Lubol's soul to Heaven in the caverns last night. Or perhaps when I barely stopped myself from decapitating Gwenshi."

Crys put a hand on his shoulder. "If holyman is truly your calling, Vinnagon, then your path shall not be an easy one."

Gwenshi snorted. "Do tell."

Crys nodded. "It has ceased to be fun, hasn't it, Gwenshi?"

"Oh," said Gwenshi, "I reckon a woman has to take the good with the bad. Some parts have been plenty fun. Like this." She nodded toward the nearby village. "This is going to be fun."

"What is?" Crys asked.

"It is time for us to confront the temple again," Vinnagon said.

Crys considered this. The previous confrontation had not gone well, but now, when they came walking into the village after their own executions ... well, she had to admit it was the sort of thing that impresses people.

Vinnagon added, "If you feel you are ready, Taishrefi."

Crys nodded. "I am ready, Holyman."

They stood up.

Gwenshi held out a scabbarded sword. "Here, Vingo, let me buckle this onto your belt."

Vinnagon took the scabbard from her. "No, Gwenshi. Let me buckle it onto *your* belt. The only thing better than a good blade at a man's side is a stout-hearted comrade to wield it."

Crys could not believe she had heard those words. Vinnagon knelt to buckle on the sword. Gwenshi lifted her chin. She looked so proud.

Gwenshi said, "Don't look at me like that, Crystal. If I cry, it will ruin the whole thing."

* * *

Three figures strode across the smoldering ashes of the cornfield, two of them tall and imposing, like commanders come to deliver punishment, one low and wary as a fox—or perhaps a vixen.

Malk and Shangrel watched from the shadow of a cotton-wood on the edge of town.

"I'll be damned," said Shangrel. "I suppose that means I owe you a day's wages."

"The bet was two days' wages," Malk said. "But if we both survive this, I'll call it square. Let's go help Vinnagon, and could be we won't be damned after all."

* * *

Vinnagon strode toward the houses and gardens of Soval calling, "Bladesmen! Sons of the Arvethidrel! All true men of Kashram, to me!"

A cluster of Lashrefites at the edge of the village were already looking his way. One of them turned and ran off, while the others continued to stare.

Walking beside him, Crystal called, "People of Soval, tell your mayor that it is time to stop cowering before the Temple of Darcliff. Tell your taishrefi it is time for her to decide whether she serves Lashrefi or Shakredo!"

Vinnagon admired her poise. Though her face was bruised and swollen, though her skin was marred by blisters and her hair was singed to curls, she walked with her head held high. She had the bearing of a taishrefi in command.

On Vinnagon's other side, Gwenshi moved like a knife-fighter, as though, at any moment, she expected someone to rush forward and attack.

The Lashrefites did not rush forward, of course. They waited for Brekko to arrive on the scene, as Vinnagon had hoped. Behind Brekko were the seneschal and the bashrefi. Several bladesmen were on Brekko's flanks, and more emerged from various corners of the village to fall in beside their captain.

Vinnagon halted while he was still behind the smoldering piles of straw that had been used to ignite the backfire. Brekko gave no orders, and they waited for the bladesmen to form a line.

"Why do you hesitate?" the bashrefi asked. "Kill these blasphemers!"

"Fire could not kill us!" Crystal said. "What makes you think that blades can?"

"This is trickery!" the bashrefi said. "Someone helped them escape."

"We helped," said a voice. "But it was no trick."

Malk and Shangrel stepped out of the line and walked into the ashes.

"We let his wife go," Malk said, pausing to address the crowd while Shangrel scurried toward Vinnagon. "She ran into the flames to save him. I thought she had no hope, but they have survived. This is the work of Kashram!"

Shangrel turned to call nervously over his shoulder, "It's true!"

Shangrel handed Vinnagon a sword—no, it was *Vinnagon's* sword, the one that Gwenshi had fetched from Harl. "Malk said you'd need this," he mumbled, "and I knew where to find it."

Vinnagon smiled. "Thank you, Shangrel."

He buckled the sword onto his belt.

"Thank you, Malk," he said, as Malk and Shangrel took a place beside Gwenshi.

Shangrel handed Gwenshi a small bundle. She unwrapped it and grinned—it held her meat-cutting knife and her throwing knife.

While Gwenshi slipped the knives back onto her belt, Vinnagon addressed the opposing bladesmen: "Is anyone else tired of being ordered to murder women? Who else will come and stand for Kashram?"

For a moment, there was silence. Then, a man cried, "I will!"

His voice encouraged another. And another.

"Brekko," the bashrefi commanded, "slay these deserters!"

But Brekko knew his men, and he understood the situation. It would be most unwise to test their loyalty right now by ordering them to kill their comrades.

"Return to the temple," he told the seneschal. "Quickly."

The seneschal's eyes widened, but she gave him a curt nod. She, too, could tell that this was not a time to ask the men to prove their loyalty to the bashrefi—they were unsure even of their loyalty to Brekko. She put her hand on the bashrefi's arm, and the two women withdrew.

It was the only time in four years that Vinnagon had seen Brekko give an order to the seneschal.

More villagers were gathering to watch, but it was plain that they would not be participating. Brekko gave some quick orders, and a few men left the line to join the bashrefi. Others turned their backs on Brekko and came to join Vinnagon.

When the lines were done reshuffling, Vinnagon had about fifteen bladesmen on his side. Brekko still had twenty.

"So now we fight?" Gwenshi asked.

"Not yet," Vinnagon said. The bladesmen were standing with him, but that did not mean they were ready to kill their comrades on the opposite side.

Vinnagon studied his uncle. Brekko had not chastised any man for deserting him. Nor had he exhorted his men to stand their ground and be firm in their resolve. He *wanted* them free to make their choice. Perhaps ... perhaps he even wanted them to choose Vinnagon.

"Hold this ground," Vinnagon murmured, and the order was passed to the ends of the line.

He stepped forward, leaving his men—and women— behind him.

"Uncle," he said, "cross over to my side. Bring me all your men, and Kashram will protect your souls from the temple's curse, just as he protected us from the fire."

"Hold this ground," Brekko said gruffly, and his men obeyed, remaining behind as he stepped toward Vinnagon. One step, two steps, three steps ... a fourth, but no more.

Brekko drew his sword. He gestured to the men behind him and said, "These men obey me because they are true Arvethidrel. Their hearts are loyal. Their oath is a bond that cannot be broken. They uphold the honor of their fathers, their grandfathers, and all Arvethidrel who have come before them. They did not swear to obey if the orders were convenient. They did not swear to follow as long as I led them where they felt comfortable. They swore to obey without question, to follow wherever I led. This is the loyalty of true Arvethidrel, and may their honor never die."

Brekko looked along Vinnagon's line, then fixed his gaze on Vinnagon and said, "You … I do not know what you are. But you are not Arvethidrel."

He lifted his sword, turned back to his line, and said, "Men: hold that ground!"

Their eyes went wide, for plainly they had been expecting the order to attack. Instead, they were forced to stand at the edge of the village grass while their captain stomped through the ashes.

Brekko shouted, "Defend yourself, Nephew!"

Vinnagon swallowed to clear his throat. He looked over his shoulder at Gwenshi and said, "Hold that ground."

He waited for Gwenshi's nod. Then he drew his sword and stepped out to fight his uncle.

Brekko had already crossed most of the intervening distance. Vinnagon took five steps and they were close enough to engage. Brekko circled, and Vinnagon matched him, waiting to see if there were more to his uncle's plan or if this truly was to be a duel to the death.

They circled again, this time the other way. Vinnagon's feet told him the ground was uneven and soft. One could not expect to react sharply.

Brekko's face grew disgusted, and he raised his blade into a wild swing. Vinnagon deflected it and ignored the opening to his uncle's throat.

"Yrah!" Brekko shouted, accompanying the cry with another blow. This one Vinnagon had to catch on his handguard, for he could not sidestep it in time.

Brekko drew back, just outside engagement distance. "Miserable footing," he said. "Why did you pick this place?"

Brekko charged. This time Vinnagon *did* sidestep, because the only alternative was to run his uncle through. Brekko shoved him in passing and Vinnagon went down, but he rolled to his feet and came up with his blade in a guard position.

"You can't win by defending," his uncle said. "Sooner or later, you will have to attack."

And he came again, an awkward three-step charge with his blade high above his head, and Vinnagon—to avoid a blow that would certainly have split his skull—stepped into the charge and drove his shoulder into his uncle's stomach.

Both men fell. They struggled a moment among the ashes. Vinnagon got a knee on the other man's chest.

"Now draw your knife and end it," his uncle said.

"But, Uncle," said Vinnagon, "I have no knife. It was taken when you captured me."

With a roar, Brekko tried to push himself to his feet. Vinnagon sprang back and let the old man get up.

Brekko closed the distance, and this time his blade left no openings. It was wings of steel flashing in the moonlight, and Vinnagon fell back blocking strike after strike.

"I give you every opportunity," his uncle snarled, not relenting in his attack. "And you refuse to employ your training. No man should ever give a bladesman openings like that and live. Did you come here to win or to die?"

Vinnagon could not answer, the attacks were coming so swiftly. But his uncle was weakening, and when Vinnagon felt that weakness, his body reacted unthinking. He pushed the strike off line, caught the blade on his guard, guided it out of the way, and punched Brekko with a left cross to the face.

His uncle staggered back, nose bleeding.

Vinnagon said, "I came to free you from the demon, old man! Why do you fight me?"

"Because I am loyal!"

"You are a fool!"

"But I am loyal!"

Brekko lunged. This time there was no easy opening.

Vinnagon deflected the thrust, but his sidestep was slow. A stinging cut opened on his arm.

"I don't want to kill you!" Vinnagon said.

"If you love me, you will!" Brekko said. "My oath cannot be broken. I am Arvethidrel. Nothing can free me except an honorable death!"

It was so. Now Vinnagon understood. Brekko's soul could not be saved by forsaking his oath to the temple. Brekko's oath and Brekko's soul were one.

Vinnagon said, "You are true Arvethidrel, and I am honored to know you."

Brekko raised his blade and charged. Vinnagon pointed his blade and lunged, striking squarely in the middle of Brekko's hard leather cuirass.

The armor was designed to shed such thrusts, but Vinnagon's sword point did not slip off its mark—perhaps because his hand was guided by Kashram, perhaps because Shakredo had caught the point on a flaw in the armor. Whether by god's blessing or demon's curse, Vinnagon's thrust pierced the layers of thick hide and passed through his uncle's body.

His uncle blinked, as though trying to clear a bit of ash from his eye. He lowered his sword and opened his mouth to speak. But no words came, only a breathy croak.

Brekko's sword fell from limp fingers. Then his knees buckled, and Vinnagon had to rise from his lunge and drive his uncle backwards so that the collapsing body would not pull his sword from his grasp.

Brekko fell onto his back. Panting, Vinnagon placed a foot on Brekko's chest and drew his blade free. A second blow would not be necessary. His uncle's soul was leaving the body.

With his uncle's death, Vinnagon was no longer bound by his oath. His soul was no longer bound to Shakredo. Inside his heart, the power of Kashram slammed a stone door, finally shutting out the curse.

* * *

As a taishrefi, Crys had visited deathbeds. She had seen people die. But this was the first time she had seen someone killed.

The horror was gut-wrenching, as though the sword had been driven into her own body. She thought she might vomit, but her stomach was empty, and she could not pull her eyes away from the lifeless corpse and Vinnagon standing above it, blood dripping from his sword.

Vinnagon's shoulders shook. Even at this distance, Crys could hear his panting breaths. Then he knelt in the ashes, placed his hand on Brekko's shoulder, and lowered his head.

"Lashrefi be with us," she whispered.

The grace of Lashrefi blew a breeze through Crys's mind, and for an instant, she saw the scene with purest clarity. Brekko's soul was like a leaf twirling in the wind. Vinnagon was beseeching Kashram to lift it to Heaven. Shakredo was dragging it down toward Hell. Vinnagon had released Brekko from his oath to the temple, but Shakredo still had a claim on Brekko's soul.

Crys looked to the faces of the bladesmen in the opposite line. They were unreadable in the darkness, but bladesmen were always either impassive or one breath away from rage. And now that Brekko was dead, they were no longer bound by his order to remain standing at the edge of the firebreak. Any man in that line could now seize the initiative and lead a charge.

Crys stepped from her own line and ran toward them shouting, "Stay, stay! Vinnagon fights for your captain's soul!"

Brekko's soul continued to dance in the whirlwind, but Vinnagon remained motionless. And vulnerable.

A voice from the end of the line challenged, "Why do *you* not fight for our captain's soul?"

Because I am powerless against Shakredo, she thought. She did not say this, however, because she needed these men to heed her words, and bladesmen would not be ruled by weakness.

Her hesitation was weakness in itself. A convincing bluff would hold them long enough for Vinnagon to complete his work, but she did not want to bluff. It would be just another lie, and these men had been lied to enough.

"I will do what I can," Crys said. "But your captain's soul is claimed by Shakredo, the demon of misfortune. He is cursed, as are all of you who have served the Darcliff Temple. My goddess is weak against this demon's curses. But there is a deity who is strong. If you would save Captain Brekko, pray to Kashram."

* * *

Gwenshi wasn't the praying sort. She reckoned Kashram had enough to do without her nagging him every time something didn't go her way. She fingered the hilt of her sword, unsure of what would happen next.

She understood the fight between Vinnagon and Brekko. That made sense. Combat was a personal thing.

But now she was standing in a line of men with a line of men opposing them, and she wasn't entirely sure what she was supposed to do. When would the fighting start? Or had Vingo already won the battle?

She reckoned it depended on those men on the other side—on whether Vingo's victory had persuaded them or just made them angry.

If any of them made a move toward her husband, Gwenshi would lead the countercharge, orders be damned!

But those men didn't move. Crystal had them thinking. Could be they were even praying. And why not? True, they hadn't come over to Vinnagon's side, but that didn't mean they were demon worshippers. Even Vinnagon had been loyal to Brekko up until four days ago. And he wasn't a demon worshipper. He was becoming a holyman!

Gwenshi didn't know what to make of that, but she reckoned that if her husband was going to be a holyman, she should probably learn to pray, at least a little.

Good evening, Kashram. I hope the harvest is going well in Heaven.

That seemed like a pretty good start.

You know I don't usually do this, but my husband wants to keep his uncle's soul from going to Hell, and Crys thinks praying might help.

No answer. That was fine by Gwenshi. She wasn't sure what she would do if Kashram started talking back.

So if there's anything you can …

And then she felt it, some sort of vibration in her bones. The man beside her—Shangrel—gasped, and Gwenshi knew they were all feeling it, this strange otherworldly force, a deep bass rumble as though mountains were singing.

A sudden *crack!*—like stone breaking.

Gwenshi sagged, as though she had been carrying a sack of flour on her shoulders and could now put it down.

Vinnagon rose to his feet and said, "I have … not succeeded."

"No," said Crystal. She held up her hands and shook her head. "No, that is not true. Kashram snapped the connection that bound Brekko to Shakredo. Brekko is now free."

"Yes," said Vinnagon sadly. "Kashram did free him. But Kashram chose not to accept him into Heaven. Brekko must remain here, as a ghost."

He turned to the onlooking villagers—Gwenshi had forgotten they were still there—and said, "I am sorry. This will be his place for now. Please do what you can for him. Perhaps he will someday atone and rise to join Kashram in Heaven."

Vinnagon turned to face the men who had remained standing with Brekko. "My fellow bladesmen, men whom my uncle named true Arvethidrel, your lives are not yet done; your fates are not yet sealed. Kashram has granted me the power to cut your bonds to the demon of Darcliff, to free you from the temple's curse, if you will join me. We must stand against the evil that we have served so long. I ask you to pledge your souls to Kashram. And for this night, pledge your blades to me."

No one moved. Gwenshi glanced sideways.

"Hold the line," Malk murmured. "Give one of them a chance to be the first."

A young man coughed, stepped away from the opposing

262 J A S O N   A.   H O L T

line and into the freshly spaded firebreak. "I'll pledge you my sword, Vinnagon." He looked nervously over his shoulder, then hurried across the firebreak into the ashes.

Another man did likewise.

"Now we can go," Malk said, stepping out toward Vinnagon.

Others followed him. Gwenshi went with them, a small woman among tall, sweaty men, walking through the soot toward Vinnagon and a corpse.

"We spit on you, Vinnagon!"

All heads turned. Seven men remained standing in Brekko's line. The speaker, a gnarled man older even than Brekko, said, "Your father would not have done this, Vinnagon! He would not have divided the bladesmen. You and your sycophants are not true Arvethidrel."

For a moment, it seemed Vinnagon would reply, but then he shook his head and held out his hands to receive another blade.

Shangrel said, "I pledge this blade to your service, Vinnagon."

Vinnagon took the blade and said, "I accept you as my bladesman, Shangrel."

The seven who would not pledge turned to walk away.

Malk called after them, "We'll see you at the temple!"

He received no reply.

Gwenshi stepped forward, held out her sword, and said, "I pledge this blade to your service, Vinnagon."

Vinnagon smiled. "It has already served me well this night." He took it and said, "I accept you as my bladesman, Gwenshi."

Gwenshi took her blade back and slammed it home into her scabbard. She swaggered out of the cluster of tall, sweaty men, daring them to make something of it.

* * *

The bashrefi had used the entire countryside as fuel for her ritual fire. Vinnagon had seen the ritual's effect on Crystal. If *she* had been convinced that the devastation was wrought by

Flamebringers, then certainly others had been deluded by Shakredo's mind-poison.

Vinnagon believed Shakredo's power flowed through the bashrefi. If she could be sent to Hell, then Shakredo's hold on Darcliff would be broken.

Malk was right: Vinnagon had to lead his bladesmen to the temple.

As they entered Darcliff, Vinnagon saw figures descending the temple road. They moved hesitantly, with fearful glances upward.

He asked Crystal, "Are those the initiates?"

"No," she said. "Taishrefis."

They did not move with the confidence of taishrefis. They moved like barefoot women in night dresses.

"Let us meet them," Crystal suggested. "Perhaps they can tell us what is happening inside the temple."

Vinnagon agreed. He led his men to the road, reaching it while the taishrefis were still descending.

When the taishrefis turned the final switchback, they saw Vinnagon and his company of well-armed bladesmen. They halted, turned, and ran back up the road.

Crystal stepped out in front and called, "Wait! Sister taishrefis, wait!"

At the sound of her voice, the women stopped. Vinnagon held his ground, waiting to see what Crystal could learn from these skittish women.

One of them called, "Crystal?"

"Yes. It is I."

"Why are you with these men?"

"I fear I do not have time for the entire tale. Will it suffice to say that we are here to free the temple?"

"The seneschal says the bladesmen have gone mad, that some have turned on Brekko."

Vinnagon's men shifted uneasily at these words.

"Brekko is dead," said Crystal, "but his death is from the madness that we all have endured under the rule of Wintersmoke."

Brekko's death was by Vinnagon's hand and no one else's, but he let Crystal tell her story. He did not want these frightened women to run back to the temple. That would complicate his assault.

"The seneschal said we had to leave before the bladesmen killed us all."

"And what of the First Choir?" Crystal asked.

"They were to stay and help the Holy Council protect the temple."

"They were building a bonfire," another taishrefi volunteered.

Flames and poisonous smoke—these were the weapons of the bashrefi. But Vinnagon had defenses now. He would not let his men waver.

"And what of the initiates?" Crystal asked.

The women murmured among themselves but did not answer.

"Did none of you think to fetch the initiates?"

Their guilt tumbled out of them in an avalanche of excuses:

"They were guarded."

"The seneschal told us—"

"Rathi was watching."

"*I* said we should—"

"Crystal, we couldn't."

Gwenshi murmured, "Vingo, what's going on?"

"The initiates are shut in their cells at night," he explained. "The latches cannot be worked from the inside. If no one lets them out, they will be helpless against whatever the bashrefi plans to do with her bonfire."

"And none of these cowards thought to let them out?"

"Gwenshi, except for Crystal, all the brave ones are dead."

"Oh."

Kashram, forgive me, Vinnagon prayed. *Forgive me for waiting so long.*

He raised his voice and spoke to the group of women on the road above: "Taishrefis of Darcliff Temple, my men and I must free the young women whom the bashrefi holds hostage. Please step aside so that we may advance. We will not harm you."

There was no sense in giving them time to debate it. Vinnagon set out at once and his men followed.

"What do you think?" he asked Taishrefi Crystal as she fell in beside him. "Did the Holy Council keep the initiates just to lure us inside?"

"That seems likely," she agreed.

Vinnagon had to lead his men inside anyway. He doubted his bladesmen could be taken by surprise. They knew that temple. They knew the alcoves and blind corners that could conceal an ambush. And he had already given them the blessing of Kashram to shield them from its curses. There was little more he could do, other than draw his sword when the time came.

The taishrefis gave way and allowed his men to pass. Vinnagon remained alert for signs of trouble above, but no rocks tumbled down on them as they climbed the road. They reached the final switchback safely.

No men were visible on the temple steps, but three vultures perched on the roof, looking down at him with malevolence. He had no doubt that the bashrefi was somehow watching him through their eyes.

A puff of smoke billowed from the vent in the roof of the temple.

"I pray we are not too late," said Crystal.

Gwenshi said, "That's not normal smoke."

Indeed it was not. Instead of climbing into the air, the smoke oozed out of the vent and tumbled down the slope of the roof, accumulating in the crease where the roof met the rough limestone.

"Let us move swiftly," Vinnagon said.

By the time they reached the temple steps, the smoke was oozing out of the entrance.

Vinnagon turned to address his men. "The blessing of

Kashram will be upon you. His courage will protect you. Draw your swords."

Blades slid from scabbards. Gwenshi drew her blade with a grin.

Vinnagon turned to Taishrefi Crystal, who had no sword to draw. "The blessing of Kashram is upon you as well," he said. "Your courage has certainly been proven."

She placed three fingers on his forehead and blew through his hair.

"Lashrefi thanks you for coming to her aid," she said with a smile.

Gwenshi looked thoughtful.

Smoke oozed down the steps, and Vinnagon strode into it. Malk quickened his step so he could climb at Vinnagon's side. This entrance was the first likely ambush point.

Vinnagon had expected a transition from moonlight to darkness, but the bonfire had the interior of the temple well lit. A scaffolding had been built from available lumber—including the taishrefis' beds—and from this scaffolding hung what looked to be most of the temple's supply of candles and torches. The blaze was impressive.

The brightness of the flames made it that much more difficult to discern what lurked among the pillars around the semicircular hall.

"Look for shadows, not flames!" Vinnagon said.

His bladesmen followed him inside, fanning out on both flanks. No enemy leapt from the shadows.

Heavy smoke, orange with firelight, billowed from the bonfire and rolled along the floor in a thick layer just below knee level. Although it seemed to be a dense liquid, they could move through it unimpeded, as though it were not there at all. Even so, Vinnagon feared to breathe it—or even touch it with his hands.

The Holy Council and the First Choir had to be nearby, feeding this unnatural abomination. They would be defended by bladesmen that Vinnagon would have to convert or kill if he were to succeed in cleansing this temple.

On Vinnagon's command, the line of bladesmen shifted, gliding toward the initiates' cells. They kept their backs to the nearest wall, staying alert for any signs of opposition.

A man on the right flank slipped on something unseen. With a cry, he dropped to one knee. The men on either side of him parted, staring in horror as smoke billowed up and flowed into his mouth, like a malevolent spirit trying to smother him.

"Help him up!" cried Vinnagon.

They did so. He rose coughing gobs of green phlegm.

"Get him outside!" said Vinnagon. "Get him to fresh air!"

Shangrel took the coughing man's arm and put it around his shoulder, helping him stumble out into the night.

The others were looking at Vinnagon with apprehension. They were willing to die in a fair fight, but they needed his protection against these mysteries that their blades could not defeat. Even Gwenshi looked scared.

Vinnagon said, "If the smoke is strong enough to poison true servants of Kashram, it is strong enough to poison our enemies as well."

"But what of the curse?" said Malk. "It was the curse that caused him to slip."

"When you fight with the resolve of Kashram, you also fight the curse," Vinnagon said. "If you stay with me and drive the curse from this building, you will also drive it from your souls."

Taishrefi Crystal spoke up quietly: "The smoke is rising. The initiates lying in their beds may already be underneath the poison. We must move swiftly."

"Heed her," Vinnagon said. "Come, bladesmen."

Despite the need for haste, Vinnagon led the advance at a cautious pace. Normally torchlit, the passage to the initiates' cells was now dark.

On a hunch, Vinnagon shouted down the hallway, "Bladesmen of Darcliff, turn your swords to the service of Kashram! Help me lift our curse and drive the evil from this place!"

"Deserter!" came the reply from the end of the hall. "We will not follow you. We are true to *our* oaths."

Blades glinted in the darkness, and Vinnagon wondered why he did not see the reflection of the bonfire on the guards' helmets. Perhaps they had removed them, so as to blend better into the shadows.

An unknown number of men were in there, and the hallway was wide enough that no more than three could fight shoulder to shoulder. The wise course of action would be to draw them out. But the initiates locked in their cells might not have time to wait.

"Wife, I would have you on my right. Malk, I would have you on my left. Form ranks of three. Advance!"

Vinnagon stepped into the hall, his chosen companions beside him. Malk's stalwart presence was reassuring. Gwenshi was panting with excitement.

"Advance with me," Vinnagon murmured. "Protect my flank. Do not rush ahead."

Gwenshi was his shortest bladesman. If the smoke continued to rise, she would be the first to fall.

The hallway echoed with a sudden yell. Dimly seen figures were charging out of the darkness.

Vinnagon dropped onto his back foot, preparing a lunge to meet the charge. But the enemy halted well out of sword's reach.

"Did you come to quiver in fear, or did you come for battle?" The speaker was Baz, oldest of the bladesmen. His brother had once been Brekko's captain.

"We came to ask you to join us," Vinnagon replied.

"Then join us in battle!" Baz shouted. "Cowards! Women!"

"Hey!" said Gwenshi. "Who are you calling women?"

"If you are so eager for battle," Vinnagon asked, "why did you halt your charge?"

Gwenshi took a step forward and crouched into a leg sweep. There was a scrape of metal on stone. She kicked a shiny helmet out of the smoke and into the layer of breathable air. It gleamed with the reflected light of the bonfire. Gwenshi caught it with her free hand at the apex of its arc.

"This is where they put their helmets," she said. "And who knows what else. I reckon we were supposed to trip over this junk as we came charging down the hall."

"Your wife is clever," Baz said. "Is she ready to die?"

Vinnagon shrugged. "We are bladesmen. We are *all* ready to kill or be killed. Men, watch your step! Advance!"

In addition to the helmets, Vinnagon's feet discovered a heavy marble vase and two chamber pots that had been placed in his path. He advanced cautiously.

Baz and his men held their ground.

Vinnagon closed within lunging distance of Baz. He crouched into a low stance, feeling ahead with his front foot. This time, he encountered no obstacle.

Baz lunged. Vinnagon deflected the thrust to the gap between him and Malk.

Gwenshi threw the helmet and it smacked into Baz's face. Vinnagon pulled his sword through an overhead arc and cracked open Baz's skull. The veteran bladesman collapsed into the smoke.

Malk drove his opponent back. Vinnagon shifted forward and shoved the man lunging at Gwenshi into the wall. Her tiny fist flashed in the firelight and popped the man in the nose. Vinnagon stepped up to engage the second rank and hoped that Gwenshi and the bladesman behind him could handle Gwenshi's opponent.

Vinnagon's thrust was met by a blade he could barely see in the darkness. He drew back into a guard position to fend off the riposte.

Something flew over his right shoulder, distracting his opponent enough that his blade found a clear path to the other man's throat.

The flying thing turned out to be Gwenshi. She struck her target in the chest with both feet. He fell over backward and she landed on top of him, springing away as his head disappeared under the smoke. The hallway filled with the sound of his gagging gasps.

Malk grunted in pain. He stepped over a crumpling body and staggered forward.

Two opponents remained. They slidestepped back, but they had no means of escape. This hallway had no exit.

Vinnagon said, "If you die like this, you will be Shakredo's forever. Yield your blades, and you may yet live as men of Kashram."

Two blades clattered to the floor.

Vinnagon assigned two men to escort their defeated opponents outside. He wiped his sword off on his trouser leg and returned it to its sheath.

"Let us get these doors open," he said.

He reached for the bolt on the door of the last cell, but Malk's hand was there first.

"Vinnagon," Malk said, "let me take this one."

"Very well."

Malk opened the door and stepped into the darkness. He staggered out a moment later with a woman over his shoulder.

"This isn't her," Malk said. "She smells too clean."

"I don't understand," Vinnagon said.

"The one in this cell was never allowed out."

Malk's face looked ghastly. Vinnagon suspected he was wounded.

"Give her to me," Vinnagon said. "Perhaps the one you seek is in some other cell."

Malk complied, and Vinnagon took the woman's weight on his shoulder. The other cells were all open by this time. Blades-men were assisting women in various states of consciousness. Two initiates were awake enough to ask questions. Some were walking. Most were coughing. The woman over Vinnagon's shoulder was breathing evenly. Vinnagon was not certain if this meant she was better or worse off than the others.

As Malk started pushing his way into the crowd, searching for his initiate, Vinnagon murmured to Gwenshi, "Stay with him. He's wounded."

Gwenshi nodded and hurried to catch up.

The bladesmen filed out of the initiates' wing with Vinnagon near the rear. When he reached the heat of the grand worship hall, his burden shifted. The woman stirred.

One of her hands flailed about and pushed a handkerchief toward his face. It smelt of lilacs and parsnips and something else that Vinnagon could not quite remember.

Vinnagon could not remember anything.

"Put me down," the woman suggested.

Vinnagon set her down. In the firelight, he recognized her as Taishrefi Sunlark of the First Choir. Why had he been carrying a taishrefi?

She pushed the handkerchief to his nose again. "Sniff," she commanded.

Vinnagon sniffed. It smelt of lilacs and parsnips and something else that—

"Follow me," she said, and Vinnagon followed because he was a bladesman, and bladesmen always follow orders.

* * *

Crys thanked Lashrefi that the battle had been fought so quickly. The smoke in the grand hall was waist high and still rising. Fortunately, most of the initiates looked as though they would recover once they had a chance to breathe Lashrefi's clean wind. Bladesmen escorted them out.

Crys spied Malk hobbling to the exit, leaning on Gwenshi. He was the only wounded man she had seen.

She looked about for Vinnagon. Perhaps he had already gone out. It would have been easy to miss him in the rising smoke.

Out of the corner of her eye, she caught a glimpse of something moving at the back of the grand hall. Fearing a surprise attack by the bashrefi, or perhaps by a remaining squad of temple guards, Crys peered through the flames of the bonfire, trying to get a better view of whatever it was.

It was a small figure scurrying along the curve of the wall, behind the statue known as Our Lady of the Flame. A pair of green eyes flashed through the smoke. Rathi!

The eyes blinked once and disappeared through an open doorway.

Did Rathi know she had been seen? Crys needed to be cautious. Stepping softly, she crossed the grand hall and followed Rathi into the day wing.

No torches were lit. She had only the flames of the bonfire to see by. Whereas Rathi, the little viper, could see in the dark.

A voice echoed faintly in the darkness: "That's the last of them. Quickly now."

That was the seneschal.

A door opened. Booted feet ran into the grand worship hall.

Crys stepped back to the hall and peered at the scene.

Seven bladesmen with long poles charged at the bonfire in the center. They planted their poles at the base of the scaffolding and the entire structure shuddered into motion. Across the floor polished by centuries of worshippers, the fiery scaffolding slid smoothly.

Crys heard a shout from outside. She caught a glimpse of a surprised bladesman's face. Then the scaffolding slammed into the entrance, cutting off her escape.

* * *

Gwenshi stared at the wall of flaming wood that now blocked the entrance. "Vinnagon's still in there!"

The bladesmen looked at one another. No one knew what to do without their leader.

Gwenshi ran up the steps, trying to see beyond the hot flames.

"Don't even think about it," a bladesman told her. "There's no way you can go through until the flames die down."

Gwenshi scowled at him. She wasn't daft enough to run into a flaming wall.

There was a gap between the tips of the flames and the triangular pediment that supported the roof. But it was of no use. Even if she could miraculously jump high enough to clear the flames, she couldn't clear the heat.

She took a few steps back to study the problem. The way had been blocked not as an afterthought. It had been blocked *because* Vinnagon was still inside.

Gwenshi just needed to find a different way.

She turned to Shangrel.

"How big is the vent?" she asked.

"Beg pardon?"

"The vent that lets the smoke out of the roof," Gwenshi said. "How big is it? Could I fit through?"

Shangrel looked up at the roof. "The temple is three stories high."

"Aye," said Gwenshi. "But I can fit through the vent, can't I?"

"Most likely," said Shangrel. "But I am not certain that is a good idea."

"It's a bad idea," Malk said, wincing with pain.

"How would you even get up there?" Shangrel asked.

"I'll climb," Gwenshi said, striding to the natural cliff face at the edge of the temple steps.

"We don't even have rope," said Shangrel.

"I don't need rope," she said.

"Gwenshi …"

"Let her go," said Malk. "It's a bad idea, but it's the best one we have."

Gwenshi didn't need Malk's permission. She was already climbing.

Her boots were so stiff that she could not feel the rock with her toes, but whenever she wedged a toe tip into a crack, the leather sole made a stout platform. She could climb this cliff.

"Don't you be looking up my dress!" she told them—but only for the sake of decorum. She knew they *would* look up her dress. Boys always do.

The sword banging against the limestone cliff was distracting, but she reckoned she would need it. As long as it didn't get hung up on anything, she'd be fine. The trick was to focus on one handhold at a time, never look down, never look up. Just stay calm and keep her eyes on the part of the moonlit cliff face just above her head.

She knew she was getting close when the smoke started stinging her eyes. But this was just normal smoke now, not that vile ooze she had encountered earlier.

"Gwenshi!" Shangrel called. "The vultures!"

Malevolent eyes emerged from the smoke. A sharp beak grabbed her nose and tried to rip it off. Gwenshi shifted her weight, freeing up a hand.

She found her meat-cutting knife, drew it, and stabbed upward. Iron met flesh.

With a squawk, the vulture holding her nose let go. But another swooped past and bit a piece from her wrist. Blood trickled down her arm.

The wounded vulture was not discouraged. It flapped its wings and jumped up onto her head, sinking its talons into her scalp.

She shut her eyes just in time to save them from a hungry beak.

Talons dug into the hand that grasped the cliff face. The pain made her angry. She gripped the rock more tightly.

As though in answer, the one on her head dug more tightly into her scalp.

Fine. The harder it held on, the less it could move.

She pressed the blade against the bird's leg. With a quick yank of her wrist, the knife snapped through skin and bone. The vulture screamed.

The other vultures squawked in sympathy. Wings flapped at her bleeding knife hand. Gwenshi opened one eye and stabbed upward.

The knife went in hilt deep. For a moment, she feared she had struck only feathers. Then the vulture tried to pull away and ripped its own guts out.

The one that had seized her hand lifted away from her then. As it let go, her hand slipped.

Gwenshi scrabbled to catch herself with her knife hand. The deer-antler hilt skidded on the stone. She released the knife. Her fingers found purchase. Her meat-cutting knife slipped free and fell toward the steps below.

She hoped it didn't hit anyone looking up her dress.

Gwenshi clambered onto the roof. The disemboweled vulture was lying on its back making piteous squawking sounds. The one-footed vulture was … gone, she hoped. She reached up and brushed its severed foot off her head.

For the moment, her only foe was the one who had punctured her hand. It stood with outstretched wings, blocking her path to the vent.

She took a step to the side, and the vulture shifted to compensate.

"So this is the game?" She fingered the hilt of her sword. "You know you can't stop me so you've decided to slow me down."

She sidled up the slope. The vulture hopped to the apex of the roof.

Gwenshi shook her bloody knife hand. The vulture's eyes eagerly followed the flying drops.

Gwenshi squeezed her fists. Both hands were in pain, but they were still strong. She feared her knife hand was too slick, so she drew her sword with her off hand. Did the vulture know that was her off hand? How intelligent was that thing, anyway?

Pressing her bleeding wrist against her dress, Gwenshi rushed at the vulture, sword waving.

It rose with speed she had not expected from such a large bird. Wind from its wings blew through her hair.

Its exposed belly was an inviting target, but Gwenshi knew she was too short to reach the bird. Sword raised to fend it off, she passed underneath and glided toward the vent.

No smoke was coming out now. She wondered whether that was good or bad.

A shadow passed. The one-footed vulture was not gone.

Gwenshi turned, drew her throwing knife, and threw it into the vulture's heart. It fell without a cry.

One vulture yet survived. As Gwenshi approached the vent, it dove, trying to force a fatal misstep. Gwenshi met its descent with an off-hand sword thrust.

Three down, and only Gwenshi left standing.

She sheathed her sword and retrieved her throwing knife. "Thought you could outsmart Gwenshi?"

It didn't answer—for which she was grateful.

She peered over the edge of the vent. Below her was a large granite statue of a woman. Her hands held actual flames from which blue-robed taishrefis were lighting torches.

Two iron candelabra stood a short distance from the pile of ashes where the bonfire had been. Vinnagon stood between the candelabra, one arm and one leg tied to each.

* * *

Vinnagon stood before the dais of the grand worship hall. He could not remember why he was here instead of standing guard in the caverns.

His hands and feet were tied to iron candelabra set into the limestone floor. Perhaps that was part of the puzzle.

The Lady of the Flame loomed before him, dancing flames in her hands, smoke pouring from her mouth and nostrils. Below the statue stood Bashrefi Wintersmoke, explaining something to the attendant taishrefis known as the First Choir.

Taishrefi Sunlark met his gaze and detached herself from the flock. She withdrew a handkerchief from her sleeve.

That handkerchief disturbed Vinnagon. He couldn't remember why, but it was bad.

Vinnagon held his breath. Taishrefi Sunlark waved the handkerchief under his nose.

"Vinnagon, smell this."

Vinnagon met her eyes. He did not inhale.

"Don't be obstinate," she said.

She held the handkerchief over his mouth and nose. With

the heel of her hand, she pressed his lips into his teeth until he tasted blood.

"Lose your mind or lose consciousness," she said calmly. "The choice is yours."

Vinnagon remembered now. The handkerchief was bad because it made him forget. And it made him pliant. That was why he had allowed himself to be tied here, spread-eagled and unable to move.

"Sunlark? What are you doing?"

"He is refusing his dose, Bashrefi."

"Return to your place," Wintersmoke said. "We want him lucid now."

Fear and shame flickered in Sunlark's eyes. "Of course, Bashrefi. Forgive me."

Sunlark withdrew.

Bashrefi Wintersmoke turned to the Holy Advisor. "Rathi?"

"His memory returns," the Woshite said. "In him the vapors do not persist."

"It is Kashram who gives me the strength to fight your foul poisons," Vinnagon said. "He defeats your demon once again."

The bashrefi studied him, with the air of a woman contemplating a new arrangement of the furniture.

"I like him better this way," she decided. "Defiant, yet helpless. Yes, this will suit the ritual much better."

She called to someone behind Vinnagon: "Are the coals ready?"

"They are, Your Fortuitousness." It was the seneschal who answered.

"Bring them."

The bashrefi returned her attention to Vinnagon and gave him a dry, wrinkled smile. She said, "You think you are protected from me, but it is not so. Your protection is only supernatural. You remain vulnerable to the mundane."

Something scraped along the floor behind Vinnagon, drawing closer.

"You Kashramites have a high tolerance for pain," the bashrefi said. "But my experimentation has proven that it is not limitless."

The scraping stopped, directly behind him. Vinnagon kept his gaze on the bashrefi. He would not show fear of that which he could not see.

The bashrefi nodded. Iron scraped against iron. Something spilled onto the floor between Vinnagon's feet. Heat warmed his trousers.

"Enough," said the bashrefi. "For the moment."

She smiled. "Let me explain how this game is played: I will order coals added at regular intervals. Should they grow cool, my attendants will add fresh fuel and fan the flames with a bellows. Your bottom half will be roasted, while your head remains able to make rational decisions ... and able to scream."

She pursed her lips distastefully. "I am a merciful woman. I regret that you have forced me to such extremes."

Vinnagon gave no reply, and the bashrefi continued, "The goal is for you to admit that I am stronger than Kashram. You may simply say so. You may ask for death. Or you may scream in pain. Any of these three actions is an admission of defeat, at which point the Holy Seneschal will grant you a swift and immediate death."

The seneschal stepped forward into Vinnagon's field of view and bowed her head to the bashrefi.

"Is there anything you would like to say before more coals are added?" the bashrefi asked.

Vinnagon remained silent.

One scream of pain? That was sufficient to end this ritual? Vinnagon knew it was not as simple as that.

He could smell the taint of Shakredo with every breath. He could feel it in the stones, not just in the statue, but even in the limestone bedrock. Wintersmoke's corruption had infused this building.

Kashram sought to drive that corruption out. Vinnagon was the point of impact—the fist meeting the jaw, the sword point piercing the artery. If the bashrefi could break him, then she might yet retain her power over Darcliff.

If one cry was all it took, she could have dropped a hot coal down the back of his tunic. Taken by surprise, he certainly would have cried out in pain. So it was not the cry itself that was important.

Vinnagon had to *know* he was admitting defeat. The coals had to be added gradually so that ending the ritual would be a conscious decision.

Vinnagon wondered where his bladesmen were. If he could withstand this discomfort for a little while, perhaps someone would be able to help him.

Kashram give me strength, he prayed.

More coals were shoveled onto the floor below him. The heat penetrated his trousers and began cooking his skin.

* * *

Crys crouched low in the open doorway, watching the coals slide across the tiles between Vinnagon's feet.

She was certain that Wintersmoke would keep Vinnagon alive until he acknowledged Kashram's defeat. To regain control, Wintersmoke needed to get rid of Vinnagon *and* the blessing he had given his bladesmen. This ritual would coerce him into revoking it.

Crys did not doubt Vinnagon's ability to endure pain. But she knew that Wintersmoke, the seneschal, and Rathi would not be performing this elaborate ritual unless they were convinced they had much to gain from it.

A woman like Gwenshi would have been able to charge in, cut Vinnagon loose, and fight off not only the seneschal but also the seven bladesmen who were tending the fire at the entrance. But Crys was just Crys. She couldn't fight the seneschal. And Rathi would simply knock her senseless again.

There might be something she could do, if she could get close enough without being seen. But Rathi's glowing green eyes saw everything.

280 JASON A. HOLT

Please, Lashrefi. Make Rathi leave. Please make Rathi leave.

The prayer was useless, of course. It had been a long while since Lashrefi had graced this temple.

* * *

The heat was decidedly uncomfortable. And the bashrefi was correct in her assessment of Kashram's powers. Vinnagon could draw on his creator's strength and courage, but this did not lessen the heat's intensity. If the pain grew strong enough, perhaps he could pass out and thus deny Wintersmoke the victory. But to reach such overwhelming pain, his body would first have to pass through the pain that makes men shriek with madness. Vinnagon would discover if he had the strength to endure that.

"Is his mind weakening?" the bashrefi asked.

"All man minds are weak," the Woshite said.

"Yes," said Wintersmoke. "But is he becoming weaker?"

"Wait more time," the Woshite answered. "Now excuse me please."

She stepped off the dais.

"Where are you going?" Wintersmoke asked. Clearly this was not part of the ritual.

For a moment, Vinnagon feared she was coming toward him—that she had an idea for expediting his surrender—but she said, "I think one initiate was left behind. I seek her."

Wintersmoke frowned. "Very well. Leave if you must. But report back immediately."

"Yes," the Woshite agreed. "Immediately."

* * *

Crys held her breath. For an instant, it seemed her heart had stopped beating.

But Rathi did not even look in her direction. Instead, the little gray woman set off toward the initiates' cells.

With no eyes on her, Crys crept into the grand hall. She circled through the shadows toward the dais.

* * *

Gwenshi peered down through the vent. The strange-looking, silver-haired thing was walking away. She wished the seneschal would follow. Instead, the seneschal remained close by Vingo. Even if Gwenshi could somehow drop in without breaking her ankle—or her neck!—even if Gwenshi somehow landed ready to fight, the seneschal could draw her sword and stab Vinnagon through the ribs before Gwenshi was close enough to do anything about it.

She flexed her sword hand. At least her wrist had stopped bleeding.

Below her, the bashrefi said, "And now it is time for more coals, unless there is something you would like to say?"

Gwenshi had a few things she wanted to say.

"It is no shame to admit defeat," the bashrefi said. "I do not ask you to revoke your vows to Kashram. I merely ask you to admit that I have won."

Not yet, you haven't. Gwenshi slipped her legs into the opening. She leaned forward to grasp the opposite edge firmly.

"The battle was well fought," the bashrefi said. "And now that you have lost, there is no shame in asking for a swift death. Just ask, Vinnagon, and the seneschal will send you to Heaven."

"I have a better offer!" Gwenshi shouted.

She leaned forward and swung down through the hole in the ceiling. Releasing the edge, she tucked into a somersault. Her singed hair flew out behind her as she spun through two quick rotations. Then she extended and reached for the giant granite statue.

Her hands caught the statue on the shoulder and she twisted around behind it. Her bone-breaking fall became a much safer tumble into the soft stomach of an attending taishrefi.

The woman fell with a heavy grunt.

Gwenshi sprang to her feet and drew her throwing knife. "How about I send *you* to *Hell*?"

Gwenshi threw. The distance was only five paces. Her aim was true.

The bashrefi flinched and the knife bounced off her neck, falling with a clatter to the dais underneath the statue.

"Seize her!"

Taishrefis on either side grabbed Gwenshi's arms. Gwenshi was too astonished to escape.

The seneschal was already moving to the bashrefi's side. "Are you injured?"

The bashrefi scowled and rubbed her neck. "No," she said. "Fortunately, I was struck with the hilt. Praise be to the Goddess."

"Praise be," murmured the taishrefis holding Gwenshi's arms.

The bashrefi's eyes softened. "You must love your husband very much, to take such a risk for him."

Gwenshi did not like her tone.

"And I am certain he loves you just as much. Yes, it is fortunate that you came. Fortunate for Vinnagon, too. Now that I have you in my power, I am certain his capitulation will come much more swiftly."

Gwenshi bit her lip. She should have thought this one through.

"You miscalculate," Vinnagon said. His voice was strong; Gwenshi could hardly tell he was in pain.

"You do not love her?" the bashrefi asked. She seemed to find the situation amusing.

"You miscalculate your fortune," Vinnagon said. "You say she is in your power, but none of your First Choir has ever trained in combat."

Damn! I'm an idiot!

Gwenshi jerked her right arm free and drove her elbow into that taishrefi's gut.

And now I'll never hear the end of it.

She ducked into the one holding her left arm, grabbed the

taishrefi behind the knee, and heaved her at the seneschal.

Maybe I'll ask how this gaggle of goosegirls captured him. That might shut him up.

Gwenshi drew her sword and flashed it about. All the taishrefis backed away.

"And now," she said—and that was all she had time to say, for the seneschal had drawn her own blade and leapt into battle.

* * *

Wintersmoke screamed, "Guards, kill her!" and Crys thought, *She truly does not understand Kashramites.*

Vinnagon's voice was strident, resounding off the walls of the grand hall: "Men of Kashram, stay your hands. You know well that this is a women's quarrel."

It was more than a "quarrel". The two swords were clashing so swiftly that they sounded like an entire company battling. The seneschal was driving Gwenshi away from the dais with fierce attacks. Gwenshi blocked just as fiercely, but she yielded step after step, making no attacks of her own.

Crys thanked Lashrefi for the diversion and prayed that Gwenshi might be able to survive at least a short while longer.

With everyone's attention on the fight, Crys left the cover of her pillar and scurried toward the statue.

* * *

Damn it, Vingo, I really wish we'd practiced this more.

A sword was not just a long knife. Gwenshi knew she needed to attack, but her attacking hand was busy blocking.

* * *

"It is you who has miscalculated, Vinnagon." Bashrefi Winter-smoke advanced toward him, vying for his attention. "Everything inside this temple is within my power."

The coals beneath his loins flared with new intensity. "I control the heat of the fires."

She looked over at the battling women. "I control the air."

The torch on the wall behind Gwenshi began spewing black smoke. Gwenshi coughed, weakening her block. The seneschal's blade sliced a cut into Gwenshi's cheek.

Wintersmoke said, "I control everything."

From the corner of his eye, Vinnagon caught a glimpse of a woman in Flamebringer trousers darting behind the Lady of the Flame.

"She cannot win this fight," Wintersmoke said. "But say the word, and I will spare her life."

Vinnagon remained silent and prayed that Kashram would give Gwenshi strength.

* * *

Smoke stung Gwenshi's eyes and choked her throat. *I should be used to this by now,* she thought. But she wasn't.

"Don't you want to say you beat me fair?" she asked.

The seneschal struck a blow Gwenshi barely saw. Gwenshi's own weak block bounced back into her face, slicing a vertical cut through her eyebrow.

Gwenshi shut her eye so the dripping blood would not distract her.

Damn, she thought. *I'm losing.*

* * *

Crys peeked around the statue, checking to be certain that Wintersmoke stood directly in front of it. Satisfied, she placed both hands on the back of the statue and heaved.

* * *

Vinnagon could no longer see Gwenshi's face through the smoke. The seneschal forced her back one more step and Gwenshi's heels were against the wall.

The seneschal stepped into the smoke and a blade clattered to the floor.

Then the two women emerged. The seneschal held Gwenshi in an armlock.

* * *

The statue was just too heavy. Crys couldn't move it.

From the other side, Wintersmoke said, "So you see, Vinnagon, this temple remains my domain. Devout service has its rewards."

Devout service? Crys would show her devout service!

She braced her legs and shoved against the stone, but nothing moved.

* * *

The bashrefi leaned over and picked up Gwenshi's throwing knife. She held it up for Vinnagon's inspection.

"She dropped her knife, Vinnagon. Shouldn't I be so kind as to return it? Bring her here, Seneschal. Bring her here so that I can return her knife while Vinnagon looks into her eyes."

Vinnagon had seen Crys peek around the statue. He had thought he understood her intention. Why didn't she push it over?

The seneschal marched Gwenshi toward the dais. Gwenshi walked on tiptoes, trying to ease the pressure on her arm twisted behind her back. Blood seeped from cuts on her face.

The bashrefi nodded at one of the torch-bearers of the First Choir. The woman lowered the torch until it was quite close to the bashrefi's face. Placidly, the bashrefi extended Gwenshi's throwing knife into the flame, never taking her eyes from Vinnagon.

"This temple is an extension of the Goddess's realm," the bashrefi said. She slowly shook her head, as though admonishing a child. "You cannot defeat me here."

She withdrew her hand from the flame, admiring the knife's red-hot glow. "I am invulnerable."

The seneschal presented Gwenshi to the bashrefi. "The prisoner, Your Fortuitousness."

Kashram, Vinnagon prayed, *give us strength.*

* * *

Crys placed her forehead against the stone, trying to focus her thoughts. She had no more ideas, except prayer. And she realized to whom she needed to pray.

Kashram, give me strength.

Power flowed from the stone into her body. With sudden understanding, she placed her legs and arms so that this power could flow into the granite statue. She pushed, not with her legs, but with her heart—with her heart and with the power of the deity who had the strength to help her.

The statue rocked forward …

* * *

… and leaned on one edge for a moment. Then it tipped back. And Vinnagon held the bashrefi's gaze because he knew that if he could hold her in place for one moment more …

* * *

Crys caught the statue's weight, let it compress her, and then, as it began rocking the other way, she pushed forward and up, sending it teetering toward the bashrefi of Darcliff.

* * *

"Watch out!" cried the seneschal.

But the bashrefi only smiled, returning Vinnagon's gaze.

"Invulnerable," she said.

Bashrefi Wintersmoke turned toward Gwenshi and stepped out of the statue's path.

* * *

Gwenshi reckoned this was as good a time as any. She dropped to a crouch, putting all her weight on the seneschal's armlock.

The seneschal held firm, and something in Gwenshi's arm snapped.

But Gwenshi was moving faster than the pain. She drew her knife from her boot, burst from her crouch, and drove the knife up through the soft spot in the middle of the seneschal's lower jaw. Bone crunched as the point penetrated the woman's skull.

Gwenshi's leg rose in the same motion. She thrust her heel straight into the bashrefi's middle, shoving her backwards. Finally, the old woman looked surprised.

The falling granite statue crushed the bashrefi to the temple floor.

* * *

Crys covered her ears against the crash of stone on stone, the crack of breaking granite, the rumble of reverberating limestone.

The First Choir scattered away from the spray of splintered rock.

Air rushed from the statue's line of impact, billowing dust and ash that curled in the eddies of the statue's wake.

And then, for an instant, the temple fell silent. The First Choir cowered in shock. The guards behind Vinnagon uncertainly reached for their swords, but did not draw. The seneschal lay unmoving, staring up at the ceiling with a knife handle protruding below her chin. Of Wintersmoke, Crys could see only two legs and one hand. The rest of her body was buried under granite.

Gwenshi, hair singed, face bleeding, stared down at the bashrefi's legs. She took a deep breath and emitted a piercing wail. Cradling her useless arm, she collapsed to the floor and curled around herself. Crys knew nothing she could do for her.

A breeze blew in through the vent in the roof. It swirled around the hall, picking up the ashes of the bonfire. It ruffled Crys's hair, flapped Gwenshi's skirt, then shot across the floor and scattered the coals that had been under Vinnagon.

The force of the wind hit the flaming barricade at the temple's entrance. Flames flashed, and then were forcefully extinguished as pieces of charred wood blew out the doorway and onto the steps, where Vinnagon's bladesmen jumped back in alarm.

Crys found herself standing on the bashrefi's dais as the breath of Lashrefi returned to the Darcliff Temple.

"Shakredo is defeated!" she said.

She glared at the First Choir and said, "Repent! For Lashrefi has returned!"

Crys didn't actually care if they repented or not. Truly, she hoped they would all burn in Hell. But she needed them to hesitate. She needed them to be intimidated. For she was surrounded by Wintersmoke's favorites, and armed men stood between her and Vinnagon's bladesmen on the steps. In the midst of Crys's enemies, Gwenshi lay crippled with pain and Vinnagon was yet tied up. And somewhere in this temple, there still lurked Rathi, whose evil council had wrought such devastation.

So Crys would not let the First Choir know that they still had a chance to take hostages and negotiate. She would not let them know they had time for desperate acts of revenge on behalf of their demon. One more time, she would play the all-knowing taishrefi and hope that these women were too shaken to call her bluff.

Crys strode forward and plucked Gwenshi's throwing knife from the hand that stretched out from beneath the granite statue. The handle was still warm. Crys hid her shudder of revulsion with a sneer of contempt.

Coming to stand before Vinnagon, she declared, "In the name of Lashrefi, I release you!"

Quick strokes, now. Make it look decisive. Oh no. I didn't quite slice all the way through. Ah, thank you, Vinnagon! Yes, that's it. Snap your hand free. Show everyone how strong you are. Don't let the guards behind you realize that you have no weapons.

As she cut the final ankle bond, she found that she was kneeling at his feet—not quite the attitude of authority she had hoped to project right now.

But Vinnagon calmly waited for her to rise. Then he bowed to her and said, "Thank you, Taishrefi."

No, she thought. *It is I who must thank you, for I know who gave me the strength to topple that statue.*

But this was not the time to say so. Instead, she murmured, "You have seven men behind you, at twenty paces. The nearest available sword is the seneschal's."

To her surprise, Vinnagon placed a hand on her shoulder and gazed on her with affection. "Thank you, friend."

Vinnagon turned and addressed the men behind him: "This temple has been cleansed of the evil that has enslaved us. The bargain between Brekko and Wintersmoke has come to an end. You are now free men of Kashram. Leave this place!"

The guards stared at him in a daze. Then, one by one, they turned and walked toward their comrades on the temple steps.

As soon as the last back was turned, Vinnagon immediately turned his back on them. Forgetting that he was still surrounded by the women of the First Choir, he hurried to Gwenshi's side, gave a grunt of pain, and knelt beside her.

"Gwenshi, Gwenshi, my darling. You fought bravely. Don't cry."

But all Gwenshi could do was rock on the floor and say, "Dammit, dammit, dammit."

And then—while Vinnagon was still well away from a sword, while Gwenshi was incapacitated, while the loyal bladesmen yet stood on the steps watching the approach of those whom Vinnagon had dismissed from the temple—then Rathi stepped out of the shadows and strode into the torchlight.

Rathi's face was impassive, inscrutable—as though her rival on the council did not lie dead with a knife in her brain, as though the woman whose power she had manipulated did not lie crushed under her own statue. Crys wondered what it would take to shake Rathi's confidence, to disturb her poise.

And Crys, still holding Gwenshi's throwing knife, realized that a knife in the chest just might suffice.

290 JASON A. HOLT

She had to be swift, before Rathi could strike with her mind-stunning magic. Crys knew nothing of knife-throwing, but she knew it required a lot of luck, and she knew that Lashrefi had returned to the temple.

"Do you not wonder?" Rathi asked as Crys drew the knife up by her ear.

Vinnagon turned at the voice, but he did not rise to a combat stance.

"Vinnagon!" said Crys. "She is not helpless! She is dangerous! Do not let her fool you."

But Crys herself had not yet thrown the knife. Because …

"Wonder what?" Vinnagon asked.

Rathi ignored him and spoke to Crys as though Crys had asked the question. "Do you not wonder who brought light?"

Light? Oh, she was playing some sort of game. If she took one step toward Vinnagon, Crys would have to throw.

But Rathi remained standing in place, like a granite statue. So Crys asked, "What light?"

"Light for you. And man. And man-mother, man-father." Rathi nodded toward the back wall. "In caverns."

"That was one of my sister taishrefis," Crys said.

"I see," said Rathi. Her face remained calm, but Crys knew the little Woshite was mocking her.

"Knowing about our escape does not prove you helped with it," Crys said. "You stole the memory. You can read minds."

"Do you not wonder why I go there—" she pointed down toward the initiates' cells "—instead of there?" She pointed to where Crys had been hiding.

"You made a mistake," Crys said. "And now you cover it by lying. When *I* was at *your* mercy, you ordered that I be drowned."

Crys tried to imply that now *she* was the one in position to grant or withhold mercy, though she feared her hold over Rathi was tenuous and waning fast.

"Did you drown?" Rathi asked.

"No. Because Vinnagon rescued me. That had nothing to do with you. *You* knocked me unconscious."

"And then you wake up," Rathi said. "Just in time for rescue. Such luck."

"Crystal," said Vinnagon, "the lid of the crate was nailed only lightly. You would have had a chance to escape before it sank into the river."

Had Rathi truly arranged Crys's escape? The Woshite had shown no qualms about tormenting Beetle—but she had also revealed that the bashrefi's plan had to be stopped tonight. And she had moved guards out of Crys and Gwenshi's way as they had crept toward Beetle's cell.

Ensuring that Beetle's information reached Crys, guiding them out of the caverns to escape the poisonous smoke, moving away from the dais just when Crys needed her to ...

"Vinnagon," Crys asked, "do you truly believe that Rathi has been helping us all along?"

"I do not know," Vinnagon admitted. "If she were truly on our side, I would have expected more help."

"Man ways are not woman ways," Rathi said. "I did not help you. You helped *me*."

Rathi spread her hands in an enigmatic gesture. "You do wise to fear me, Taishrefi Crystal. Lashrefites are simple to manipulate. And Woshites are not all nice as Rathi. You do wise to fear me, but wiser to fear the demon you name Shakredo. She haunts your people. Darcliff is not the only one."

She looked around her at the broken statue, the ashes of the bonfire. "But it was the worst one."

She walked over to the body of the seneschal. "The demons are now all over the land. Sister peoples need the Woshites, need the magics we can do, the things we know."

She bent down and drew the seneschal's sword. Holding it by the blade, she carried it to Vinnagon.

"Take, please."

Warily, Vinnagon took the sword from Rathi.

"Bashrefi and seneschal had all those mens," Rathi said gesturing at the entrance. "You had only one man, but yours was the best."

Vinnagon stared at her, unblinking. Gwenshi lifted her tear-streaked face but made no comment.

"You wonder," Rathi said. "You wonder if I lie. You can be certain. Tell your man to kill me. Then you will see my soul rise to the moon. Then you will know. Or you can let me leave. I think you will let me do this. Even though it means you must wonder."

Rathi turned her back on them and walked toward the door to the caverns.

Crys let her go.

Gwenshi said, "I can see why you hate her."

* * *

Crystal reminded Vinnagon that the taishrefis of the First Choir could not be trusted, so Vinnagon ordered his bladesmen to confine them to the initiates' cells. He was not certain they were all guilty, nor did he believe that all the initiates his men had rescued were innocent, but these were questions that could wait until morning.

It did not take long for his men to realize that his mind was truly on Gwenshi. Malk promised that he would assign trustworthy men to the remainder of the night's watch. Vinnagon and Gwenshi were sent to the privacy of Brekko's chamber while they waited for the arrival of the healer.

Vinnagon helped Gwenshi lie down on Brekko's bed.

"You're the one who should be lying here," she said. "You're the one who can't sit down."

Vinnagon smiled at her. "You are the hero who crippled her own arm so she could kill two enemies at once. You have earned the bed."

"If it weren't for your burns," Gwenshi said, "it would be fun share it."

Vinnagon grunted. It was good to hear her jesting.

"Vingo, seriously now ..." She ran her eyes over his trousers. "How bad is it?"

It was bad enough that he wanted to take off his trousers and jump in the Dothedarl, but he said, "My skin will heal. Not soon. But it will heal. We have not lost our chance to have children."

Gwenshi tried to sit up without moving her injured arm. Wincing, Vinnagon knelt to help her. They ended up with their faces at the same level, his arm supporting her back.

"Vingo," she said, "what if I want to start taking herbs again?"

"Why?" he asked.

"Because I don't want to be a mother right now," she said. "I want to be a bladesman."

* * *

After locking the First Choir in the initiates' cells, the bladesmen searched the remainder of the main temple. Malk could not find the one he sought, so he led the search party into the caverns.

They found her in the first prison cell. Her hair was stringy, and her skin was filthy. In the torchlight, Malk could hardly tell the dirt from her stripes. The woman's gaze was lifeless, but she was alive.

"My name is Malk," he said. "And the nightmare is over."

* * *

The bladesman who had fallen under the smoke died shortly after the healer arrived. Crys hoped he was the last victim of the temple's evil, but fires yet burned across the countryside. Then there were those who would suffer through the winter with no corn crop.

The temple held corn in reserve—corn that Wintersmoke had planned to use to control the impoverished farmers. Crys believed that would be enough to prevent a famine, but the farmers also needed corn to pay for goods. At the very least, they would need timber to replace their fences. Crys prayed that none of them had lost livestock.

"Lungs are tricky," the healer said of those who had inhaled the poisonous smoke. She could do little for them.

The healer offered to soothe Crys's burns. Crys had hardly noticed she *had* burns—so much had happened since Gwenshi had saved her and Vinnagon from the cornfield fire. She requested instead that the healer direct her attention to Vinnagon and Gwenshi.

Gwenshi offered to let Crys come into Brekko's quarters and see how bad Vinnagon's burns were. It seemed that Gwenshi, at least, would be all right.

Crys entered *after* the healer had left and after Vinnagon had put on a loose-fitting robe that he seemed terribly embarrassed by. Crys tactfully ignored his clothing. Gwenshi said nothing, but ... well she *ogled* him. Yes, Gwenshi was definitely feeling better.

Crys nodded toward Gwenshi's sling and asked, "Was she able to start your arm toward healing?"

"No," said Vinnagon. "Gwenshi will have to visit the surgeon in Clifford."

"Aye," said Gwenshi, grinning. "The healer said my elbow needs to be sewn back together."

"But it will heal?" Crys asked.

"We shall see," said Vinnagon.

"In the meantime," Gwenshi said, "I can practice sword-fighting left-handed."

"You do need the practice," Vinnagon said.

"And I'll have a good teacher," Gwenshi said. "Look how well I did after only one lesson!"

"You lost," Vinnagon said. "You let your opponents back you into a wall and take your blade. Twice!"

"Aye, but my blocks were solid. Except for the one that bounced back into my face."

"Well," said Crys, "I am glad to find you in good spirits. Do try to get some sleep. I shall see to it that you are not disturbed

... and I suppose I shall have to put together a kitchen crew soon. Breakfast should begin cooking within the lithic. I know your men are hungry."

"Thank you," said Vinnagon.

"So when my arm heals up," Gwenshi asked, "can I be the new seneschal?"

Vinnagon laughed. "It is a holy office, woman. It is only for taishrefis."

"All right, but I did kill the old seneschal. I reckon that if you get to be captain and Crys gets to be bashrefi, I should get *some* special title."

"I will not be the bashrefi," Crys said.

"Why not?" Gwenshi asked. "You killed the old one."

"That is not the way it works," Vinnagon said. "And for that matter, I will not be captain."

"But Vingo ... we pledged our blades to you!"

"For one night," Vinnagon said. "But now all my bladesmen must be free to choose whom they will follow."

"I choose you."

"And I have chosen Kashram," Vinnagon said. "And Kashram tells me that Darcliff Temple should not need armed guards."

Crys sighed with relief. "Thank you, Vinnagon. Leading the bladesmen away from the temple is the best thing you could do for it right now."

"And the best thing *you* could do for it," Vinnagon said, "is to lead the temple as the new bashrefi."

Crys studied him. He was her friend, now, but that did not mean he knew her yet.

"That is what you truly believe, isn't it?"

"It is, Taishrefi."

"Call me 'Crys'. Both of you. Especially because I do not intend to be a taishrefi for much longer."

"What?" Gwenshi exclaimed. "Why not?"

"Vinnagon should know," Crys said. But his face was as bewildered as Gwenshi's.

"I did not kill Wintersmoke," Crys said. "I tried to push the statue over, but I could not. Not by myself. I had to call upon aid from Kashram, as Vinnagon can tell you."

"I did pray for you," Vinnagon admitted. "And I am glad Kashram came to your aid. Yet I do not see why you would cease to be a taishrefi. Is that even possible?"

"I do not know," Crys said. She would need to consult Lashrefi on this—perhaps even speak to her grandmother when the Flamebringers returned to their winter villages. "But I know I cannot stay at Darcliff Temple."

Gwenshi asked, "Because you got help from someone else's god?"

"Yes," Crys said.

"Crystal," said Vinnagon. "Crys. There is no shame in needing help. I think perhaps this is why the gods are so many—so that the weaknesses of one can be covered by another's strength."

"Vinnagon," Crys said, "I believe that is so. But it has long been my people's tradition to serve only our creator. The traditions of the taishrefis are not receptive to interference from other deities. And that is why I fear that I am no longer a taishrefi."

"Because you needed help from Kashram?" Gwenshi asked.

"Because I was willing to ask," Crys said. "No taishrefi I know would ever have done so. I am not certain what this means. I am not certain what this makes of me. I have only questions, no answers."

No answers except one. Her unwillingness to open her life to other religions had prevented her from marrying the man she loved. That was a mistake she was now prepared to correct.

Two Months Later:
The Wedding

VINNAGON SAT BESIDE HIS WIFE, listening to the Lashrefites sing their wedding songs.

"How many songs do they know?" Gwenshi asked.

"A good number," Vinnagon said.

"Well, then, how many more will they sing, do you reckon?"

"I do not know."

"Do you think Crys and Beetle would mind if we went home now?"

"I doubt they would notice."

"Then let's go. I'm tired."

They walked through the streets of Darcliff amid gently falling flakes of snow. Gwenshi shivered in her fur cloak and pressed close to him. Vinnagon put his arm around her. Her arm was still in the sling, but his touch would not pain her. The arm was healing well.

"Orangemonth is not a good time for a wedding," Gwenshi said. "At least, not if you plan to celebrate outside."

"True," said Vinnagon. "But Crys and Beetle have waited long enough."

They turned down a street that led toward the river.

"Well," said Gwenshi, "marrying for love is certainly romantic."

"Yes," agreed Vinnagon.

"But I like our way better," Gwenshi said.

"Wife! Do you mean to say you did not marry me for love?"

"On our wedding day, did you even know my name?"

"Of course!" And then he admitted, "I had practiced saying it so I would not shame myself during the ceremony."

"Oh, Vingo, I'm glad my father gave me to you."

"As am I, Gwenshi. I have no regrets."

"I have one regret," Gwenshi said.

"What?"

"Well, it's not really a regret. I'm glad everything has turned out this way, of course, and I'm sure it's all for the best …"

"… but?"

"Nothing. Just that with Crys married to Beetle, I won't get to see any striped red babies."

The Following Summer:
Traz

TRAZ HADN'T BEEN WITH GIL'S RAIDERS when they had first dressed as Flamebringers and set the countryside on fire. He'd been part a river patrol garrison. But he knew Gil's story.

When the temple's scheme to burn the corn crop had been exposed, the taishrefis had turned against Gil, sending militias to hunt him down. Traz's captain reckoned that if the stripeys punished honest men for following their orders, then it was better to join forces with Gil and be bandits.

So now Traz was a bandit. They were working the Shalbroon Trail.

Traz had Captain Gil's left flank as they rode toward a pair of merchant wagons. Easy target—two drivers and no guards.

They rode in a wedge formation. Against such pitiful resistance, strict adherence to formation was unnecessary, but Captain Gil wanted them to stay sharp.

Traz reckoned that discipline was a good thing. It reminded them of a time when they had been bladesmen.

Gil raised a hand in salute. The wagons halted. The merchants returned the salute uncertainly. At this distance, with their faces painted, Gil's Raiders appeared to be a band of Flamebringers.

As their easy trot drew them nearer, the wings spread out to discourage escape. Escape was impossible at any rate, but it was simpler if the merchants did not try.

Now Traz was close enough to see their faces, which meant that he was close enough that they could see what he was—not a black-and-white stripey, but a Redman wearing white paint.

The Clanfolk merchants did not look surprised, but they certainly were scared. And they had every reason to be scared. They were unarmed, unguarded, and only half the size of Kashram-created men.

The men on the wings drew their swords. Captain Gil reined to a halt beside the first wagon, horse snorting at the smell of the oxen.

Gil said, "This is a toll road today, Mister Ironmonger. Hand over your brinnacs."

The merchant removed his pouch from his belt and held it up with a shaking hand.

"Don't make me reach," Gil warned, with the threat of steel in his voice. Traz liked the way Gil handled these situations. Merchants usually did what he wanted. "Toss the pouch here."

Reluctantly, the merchant did as Gil bade.

"Thank you kindly," Gil said. "Do not hesitate to use our road in the future."

They turned their horses and rode back to the second wagon.

The second merchant did not wait for the ritual request. He tossed his pouch as they were still approaching. The pouch fell well short, landing heavily in the grass.

Gil halted. His horse sniffed at the pouch.

Gil drew his sword and pointed it at the second merchant. "Pick it up," he ordered.

"Pick it up? Yes. Yes, I'll just climb down from my wagon and pick it up. I can see you want to stay on your horses. I'm so glad you have decided not to dismount and inspect our wagons."

He said these last words quite distinctly. And Traz realized that, although this robbery was going smoothly, something here was quite odd. The merchants were nervous, but not surprised. Their reactions seemed a little off. And the lumps under the wagon's canvas seemed a bit too round.

"Now!" shouted a Redman, throwing off the canvas and

leaping from the wagon bed. It was Vinnagon, captain of the fiercest company of bandit hunters. Bladesmen arose from the beds of both wagons.

Traz's horse jumped into Gil's, striking Gil's leg with its shoulder. Traz kept his seat and tried to regain control of the animal.

Gil shouted, "To arms! To arms!"—which meant that Traz could not allow his horse to flee.

Tugging one rein, he turned his mount toward the nearest wagon. Something flew at his head. He raised his arm to block it.

The thing flying at his head turned out to be a short, muscular woman leaping from the wagon. Traz was knocked from his horse to the tall grass below. He rolled to his feet and drew his sword.

The woman jumped to her feet and drew two.

For an instant, Traz was frozen with disbelief. Then she beat his blade aside with her left-hand sword, and he was forced to jump back from her swift right-hand strike.

Traz recovered, feinted to draw her blades off line and swung for her knee.

She withdrew her knee. Her right-hand sword swept his blade away.

Traz pivoted into her and slammed his elbow into her face.

She staggered back. He turned to drive his blade through her chest, but she was now out of reach ... and grinning.

She charged. He lunged. But the charge had been a feint.

She sidestepped his thrust, caught his wrist with her blade, spun into him, and drove her other sword into his calf.

Traz screamed and collapsed in pain.

A round knee shoved into the small of his back, pinning his pelvis to the turf. A hand seized his wrist, twisted, and he found himself immobilized by an armlock.

"Hello, Traz," said the woman on his back. "Glad to see you again."

Traz made no reply, although he dimly recognized that voice.

"It's me, Gwenshi, your next-door neighbor. Good thing I didn't kill you, aye?"

When he didn't respond, she tugged his arm and asked, "Aye?"

"Ow! Aye!"

"Aye," she agreed, easing up on the armlock a bit. "Anyway, I'm glad I caught up with you. Your little kids are getting bigger every day. Plesi says it's time you came home."

Acknowledgments

I'D LIKE TO THANK SCOTT THATCHER for his help with an earlier draft of this novel.

Bryon Quertermous helped me find places where I could make the manuscript even better. I did my own copy editing, so any mistakes that remain are mine and mine alone.

Finally, I'd like to thank my wife, Sierra, for reading an earlier draft, for her helpful and encouraging comments, and for owning many swords.

About the Author

JASON A. HOLT has a Ph.D. in mathematics. He is fluent in Czech, and he lives on a remote Montana cattle ranch. In other words, he is well qualified to write fantasy novels.

To learn more about Jason, visit `JasonAHolt.com`.

To learn more about the world of Edgewhen®, visit `edgewhen.com`. Or look for *The Dragonslayer of Edgewhen* at your favorite retailer.

CHRONOLOGY OF EDGEWHEN® ADVENTURES